Mr. Lucky

Mr. Lucky

A Novel

James Swain

LARGE PRINT

This large print edition published in 2005 by
RB Large Print
A division of Recorded Books
A Haights Cross Communications Company
270 Skipjack Road
Prince Frederick, MD 20678

Published by arrangement with Random House, Inc.

Publisher's Cataloging In Publication Data
(Prepared by Donohue Group, Inc.)

Swain, James.
    Mr. Lucky : a novel / James Swain.

    p. (large print) ; cm.

    ISBN: 1-4193-2877-8

1. Valentine, Tony (Fictitious character)—Fiction.   2. Private investigators—New
Jersey—Atlantic City—Fiction.   3. Gamblers—Fiction.   4. Large type books.   5. Las
Vegas (Nev.)—Fiction.   6. North Carolina—Fiction.   7. Mystery fiction.   8. Suspense
fiction.   I. Title.   II. Title: Mister Lucky.

PS3569.W225 M72 2005c
813/.6

Printed in the United States of America

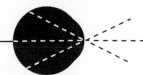

**This Large Print Book carries the
Seal of Approval of N.A.V.H.**

For Deborah & Shawn Redmond

ACKNOWLEDGMENTS

The author wishes to thank the following people for their help in writing and researching this novel: Peter Ballas, Chris Calhoun, Michael Connelly, Steve Forte, Joni Hatch, Jerry Hooten, Dana Isaacson, Linda Marrow, Deborah Redmond, Robert Knuts, Charles & Margaret Swain, and my wife, Laura.

"Everybody's honest, when they can afford to be."

—Benny Binion
Famous casino owner

CHAPTER 1

The moon looked funny that night, so bright it seemed to sport a face with droopy eyes and a sly little grin, and for the rest of his life Ricky Smith would think of that face whenever he paused to reflect upon the series of events that had turned his life upside down.

"So how did you win all that money?" the beautiful girl in his room wanted to know. Her name was Rita, and somehow he'd talked her into coming up to his room high above the Las Vegas Strip, her statuesque body parked beside him on the lumpy double bed. *God, is she gorgeous,* Ricky thought. Her eyes demanded an explanation, and he shrugged like winning twenty grand at blackjack was no big deal.

"Come on," she pleaded, giving his knee a squeeze. *"Tell me."*

The little man in Ricky's crotch snapped to attention. Divorced six months and eleven days, he found himself getting aroused walking in a stiff wind. Time stood still as he struggled for something clever to say. "I got lucky," he mumbled.

1

Rita's eyes narrowed. "I don't believe that for one minute."

He looked at her face, seeing double. "Believe it."

Rita's tongue did butterfly kisses on his earlobe while her hand crawled up his thigh. The little man was six degrees from exploding, and Ricky squeezed his legs together.

"You were cheating, weren't you?"

His head snapped. "No."

"Card counting?"

Ricky shook his head. He played a system developed by a legendary counter named Stanford Wong, but tonight it hadn't been necessary to memorize a single card. As every gambler knew, for all the calculations and odds and multiplying strategies of working the percentages, there were days when things just went your way.

"You're holding back on me," she cooed.

The little man was ready to pounce. Battle stations were ready, all men on deck. He swallowed hard as Rita's hand climbed farther up his leg, her pink fingernail tickling the crotch of his pants. "I'll make you tell me."

Ricky didn't think that was going to be very difficult. Rita coyly pulled her hand away, waiting for him to say something. He coughed awkwardly. "You want a drink or something?"

She crossed her arms. Not pissed off, but getting there. "Or something? What have you got in mind?"

Ricky's cheeks burned. Talking to women always tied him in knots. Maybe that was why he'd married the first girl he'd ever slept with. Trying to get up, she grabbed his hand.

"Tell me your secret," she demanded.

His tongue felt as thick as a potato. "If I did that, I'd have to kill you."

Rita fell backward onto the bed and started laughing. Ricky would have been hurt, only she pulled him down for the ride, the two of them rolling around in each other's arms like a couple of kids on a hayride. His lips brushed her mouth, and suddenly they were kissing. Ricky's heart beat out of control. *This is how it was meant to be*, he thought. She did not seem to mind that he wasn't good-looking or well dressed and that he had as much hair on his head as most guys had on their ass, and all Ricky could hope for was that the magic spell he'd cast over her wouldn't wear off before morning.

"I'll take you up on that drink," Rita said when they pulled themselves apart.

"Name your pleasure."

"Gin and tonic, heavy on the gin."

He went to the room's minibar. Once his winnings had started to mount, the casino had plied him with free drinks, and now he could barely walk. Stopping at the boxy TV mounted to the wall, he paused to stare at his disheveled appearance in one of the smoky mirrors that served as wall decorations. His face was smeared

3

with pink lipstick, and his hair stood on end. He looked like shit. In the same reflection he caught Rita firing up a butt. She was a mess, too, but in a sexy way, like she'd just woken up, and it occurred to him that no matter what she did to herself, she was always going to be beautiful, and he would always be a grunt. He staggered into the bathroom, slamming the door behind him.

"*Jesus.*" The bathroom light was bright and harsh. Filling the sink with cold water, he dunked his head, came up for air, then plunged his face in again.

"Are you all right?" she asked through the door.

He pulled his face out of the sink. "Give me a minute, okay?"

"You want a drink?"

"Coke."

"Want some rum with that?"

"No, straight."

Another dunk and he felt a little better. Drying himself, he examined the pocks and crevices of his face in the mirror, his wet hair hanging limply from the circular edge of his freckled head. His pride had been crushed long ago, and he felt the skeptic in him rear itself. What did Rita really see in him, besides the twenty grand? No immediate answers came to mind. Then he had a brilliant thought; he'd ask her.

He cracked the bathroom door. She was at the minibar, her back to him. In the smoky mirror he watched her fix their drinks. She'd slipped off her shoes and found Kenny G on the radio, her feet dancing as she poured his soda. She was primed, and the little man sent a message to his brain telling him to drop his drawers and march right up to her. "Or something," he'd say wittily, then throw her on the bed. Wild, uncontrollable sex would follow, and life would be perfect for a little while.

"Don't drown in there," she called out.

His pants were hanging around his knees when he saw Rita dig a tiny vial from her purse. *Oh no,* he thought, *a coke head.* Unscrewing the top, she dumped the contents into his bubbling soda and mixed it with her pinky.

"I'm waiting," she called out.

Ricky shut the door and leaned against it, breathing heavily. Not coke, a mickey. *Knock out the dummy, take the money.* He wanted to cry; would have had he been alone.

"Time's up," she called out.

A strained laugh came out of his mouth. Being a nerd, Ricky carried a miniature screwdriver in his shirt pocket, and he got on his knees and unscrewed the air-conditioning vent, then removed his winnings from his belly pack and stuffed them into the small rectangular hole in the wall.

A strange smell was coming out of the vent. He took a deep whiff, trying to place it. Like badly burnt toast. Rita knocked on the bathroom door.

"Rick-y!"

"I'm coming."

5

"Not without me!"

"Ha-ha," he said.

He screwed the vent back into place. Opening the bathroom door, he saw Rita sitting on the bed with their drinks, her blouse partially unbuttoned.

"Here I am," he said, sitting down beside her.

She passed him his soda. "Bottoms up."

They clicked glasses, and Ricky felt her stare. He put his drink on the floor, then said, "Listen, something's come up. I think it would be best if you left."

"But we're just getting started."

She had a mouth that could make your heart melt. Ricky was a sucker for beautiful girls and had to remind himself that this one wanted to roll him. Staring past her, he said, "I really think you need to go."

She squeezed his leg. This time the little man did not respond. "What's wrong? You got a wife at home you're not telling me about?"

"Something like that," he said.

"Sure you don't want to play around?"

"I'm sure."

The dreamy look vanished from her face. Putting her drink on the floor, Rita picked up her purse. "And I thought you were someone special," she said.

Ricky looked into her eyes, trying to see into the soul of a woman who'd take advantage of a lonely guy and steal his dough. Did she care that he was hypersensitive to sleeping medication and that her mickey might kill him? No, she probably didn't. He stood up and pointed at the door.

"Get out," he said.

Her face turned to granite. She went to the minibar and slipped on her pumps. She didn't seem tipsy anymore, and walked calmly to the door before stopping.

"Maybe some other time," she said.

"I don't think so."

She scowled, the lost money eating a hole in her. In the movies the guy got to say something clever right about now, and Ricky pointed at the door. "See you around, sweetheart."

"Who said that? Bogart, or was it Edward G. Robinson?"

"Jimmy Cagney."

She lingered at the door, smiling coyly. "Sure you don't want me to stay?"

"You don't quit, do you?"

"Quitting is for losers, big boy."

"Get lost, or I'll call security."

"You're so brave."

"Keep it up and I'll toss you myself."

"A slob like you?" She pulled a can of mace from her purse. "I don't think so."

Ricky blinked. A thick black snake about nine feet long had slithered into the room and wrapped itself around Rita's shapely legs. Thinking the booze was messing with his head, he watched the snake begin to squeeze the life out of her, only to melt away in a harmless puff of smoke.

Rita looked at the floor, sensing something was wrong.

"What's that funky smell?" she said.

"Something's burning. You'd better not open that door."

"Why not?"

Because somewhere deep down inside I want to believe you might really care for me, he thought. "I think the hotel's on fire," he said.

Rita put her hand on the knob and twisted it. "Right. And you and I are going to stay in this room until the firemen come. My hero. Well, if I stay, it's going to cost you, toilet-bowl head. Four hundred bucks an hour, a grand for the night."

Ricky winced. All his life people had soiled him with names, but for some reason this dagger hurt more than the others. He hadn't intentionally lost his hair, but women seemed to think something was wrong with his genetic makeup because he had. His lower lip began to tremble, and he had to think hard.

"How about twenty bucks, and you have to shine my shoes in the morning?"

Rita's mouth dropped open: score one for RS. Jerking the door open, she said, "Stick it up your ass, fat boy," and marched into the hallway.

A loud *whoosh!* greeted her as the fire smoldering in the hallway sucked up the bedroom oxygen and caused the hallway to burst into flames. Rita stood in the center of it. She acted confused, like someone trapped in a carnival fun house, and

Ricky watched in morbid fascination as her flowing blond hair and baby-doll red dress sparked, then burst into bright orange flames.

The smell of burning food was unmistakable. He imagined a fire raging out of control in the hotel restaurant, perhaps caused by a punctured gas line or a greasy stove. Once the fire exceeded eighteen hundred degrees, its radiant heat flux would travel up the elevator shafts and air-conditioning ducts and cook the building like a giant soufflé. Rita was getting the full treatment, and she ran back into the room like she'd been shot out of a cannon.

"You bastard!" she screamed.

Ricky sidestepped her mad charge and watched her sail headfirst through the glass slider. Choking black smoke filled the room, and he kicked out the remaining glass and followed her onto the balcony.

Only, Rita wasn't there. He went to the railing and stared down. Her burning body lay in the grass five floors below. She had landed with her arms spread out, like a kid making an angel in the snow. *I could have saved you,* he thought. He lifted his eyes. The moon wore a face that resembled a sly little grin.

Screams carried up from below as other guests opened their sliders and came outside. Suddenly, Ricky remembered his twenty grand in the bath-room. He tried to go back inside and was met by a blinding column of smoke.

He staggered off to the side of the balcony.

9

With his hands he found the wall of the hotel, and put his back to it.

He asked himself how this could be happening. Tonight, his luck had finally changed. He'd made a huge score on his own. But instead of staying downstairs in the casino and continuing to gamble, he'd let the first pretty girl to wink at him talk him into coming upstairs. He'd ruined a beautiful thing and had no one to blame but himself.

The hotel began to shake. He could hear flames roaring through the building and guessed that the fire had gotten so hot that a deadly electromagnetic wave had been created. The soufflé was just about done.

Time to talk to the Big Guy, he thought.

In college he'd written a paper about all the novels Ernest Hemingway had written in which characters had prayed at the point when prayer wasn't going to do them any good. For Hemingway, prayer and tragedy were forever linked, the world a sad, distrustful place. Ricky's opinion was about the same. Life sucked, then you died. But just in case God was listening . . .

"Oh, God, please spare me from dying," he said, his eyes tightly shut. "Please, God . . . I won't ever fuck up again."

Flames jumped onto the balcony, singeing his arm. He let out a cry and opened his eyes. He was thirty-five, no family, a guy with big dreams but nothing to show for it. He looked over his shoulder into his room. The fire had eaten away the ceiling, and conduits and sheets of insulation were dropping onto his bed. Soon the room would be roaring with flames; then the walls would melt; then he'd catch on fire like Rita.

He went to the railing and started to climb over. So far, the fire had confined itself to the main hotel, and he stared down at the glass rooftop of the hotel's plush spa, where a pair of identical Swedish bimbos named Olga and Hilga gave body massages and had a waiting list three months long. Next to it was a swimming pool, and what Ricky remembered about the pool was that at its deep end it was pretty deep, at least twelve feet. If he jumped and hit the deepest part, he'd probably break every bone in his body, but he might also survive, and that was all he cared about right now. The question was, did he feel lucky?

"Well," he said, puffing his chest in his best Clint Eastwood imitation, "do you, punk?"

All his life, he'd been stealing tough guys' lines from the movies, and it had never made him any braver. His ex-wife had asked him to stop a thousand times. Like he'd told her at the divorce trial, he didn't know how. The words just leapt out of his mouth.

The railing was growing warmer; soon it would be too hot to touch. His time was running out. *Well*, he thought, *at least I get a say in the matter.* He put one foot into space, then hesitantly drew it back. Jump, or turn into a cinder. What a choice.

"Your move, Mr. Bond."

His move indeed.

CHAPTER 2

The sharp wind that blew through Tony Valentine's house made the hurricane shutters rattle and the bamboo trees in his yard shake their branches. It dropped the temperature by several degrees, and he felt his skin harden beneath his clothes. A storm sitting out in the Gulf of Mexico was churning up the ocean, and a small-craft advisory had been issued for boaters. A good night to stay indoors, the TV weatherman had cautioned.

Sitting at the desk in his study, Valentine stared through the lone window at his backyard. Although he could not see the ocean from where he lived, he could taste it in the air, and that was all that mattered. Even on a night like tonight, it was a friend, always there to comfort him when his soul was troubled.

The phone on his desk rang. His private line. The caller ID said UNKNOWN, but his gut told him it was Lucy Price, a woman in Las Vegas he had helped out a month ago. At the time, it had seemed like the right thing to do; only, he hadn't counted on her tracking him down in Florida.

"Go away," he said to the phone.

It kept ringing. The sound was like a hammer tapping on his conscience. He had nothing to say to her; nothing that would change the horrible thing she'd done. Another stiff wind blew through his house and infused the air with the ocean's spirits. It made him feel better, but only for a little while.

Finally the phone went silent. On his desk was a clock in the shape of a roulette wheel. It was nearly ten. Normally, he didn't work this late, preferring to read a book until his eyes gave out. Only, he'd let his work pile up, too disturbed about the situation with Lucy to put in a full day's work. He stared at the pile of FedEx envelopes stacked on his desk. Each was addressed to Grift Sense, his consulting company. He'd opened it up as a way to fill his days after his wife had died, never expecting it would lead to a second career.

He pulled the thickest envelope from the stack. Inside was a certified check for three thousand dollars, his usual fee, along with several decks of playing cards and a letter from the manager of the Golden Dragon casino in Macau.

He'd worked for casinos in Macau before. It was a strange place. Gambling was the number one source of revenue, with prostitution a close second. It could be reached by boat from mainland China, and every day, thousands of rich Asian businessmen made the trek and descended upon the island's casinos like hungry locusts.

According to the letter, one of the Golden Dragon's blackjack tables was bleeding money, and the casino's head of security, an Aussie named Crawford, was convinced the cheaters were using "paper," which was cheater's slang for marked cards. The problem was, Crawford couldn't find the marks.

Crawford had never used Valentine for a job before. But according to his letter, he'd heard through the casino grapevine that Valentine was good at reading paper, so he'd taken a chance and overnighted a few decks, along with his money. Crawford was desperate.

Valentine *was* good at reading paper. Twenty years policing Atlantic City's casinos had exposed him to hundreds of marked-card scams. So many ways existed to mark cards that he'd developed a test that was as good as any for finding the work. It required a normal deck of cards, which Crawford had sent him straight from the plant.

The Golden Dragon used cards manufactured by the United States Playing Card Company in Cincinnati, Ohio. They were thicker than regular cards, so that the ink wouldn't rub off after continued use. Opening the normal deck, Valentine removed a single card and held it next to a suspected marked card beneath the light on his desk.

To the naked eye, the two cards looked identical. But that didn't mean anything. He placed the marked card beneath the normal card. Then, he snapped the normal card away and stared intently at the marked card for several seconds.

He did this twenty times. By the twentieth time, his eyes had found the marks. They were in the center of the card, white, and almost microscopic. Cheaters called them block-outs. Usually, cheaters marked cards at the table with a substance called daub, or with lipstick or nicotine. The Golden Dragon's cards were being marked by a professional on the outside, then brought into the casino by an employee. Which meant it was an inside job.

He put the cards down and smothered a tired yawn. Tomorrow was judo practice. He went three times a week to a dojo in Clearwater and always tried to get plenty of sleep the night before. He would call Crawford tomorrow and break the bad news. He started to turn off the light on the desk, then stared down at Crawford's letter. His eyes caught the last line on the page. *Management's given me twenty-four hours to solve this.*

He flipped the FedEx envelope over and stared at the label. It had been sent yesterday morning. Which meant Crawford's hourglass had just about run out. He didn't know the man but couldn't help feeling sorry for him. He found Crawford's phone number on the letter and picked up his office phone.

It was tomorrow in Macau. Crawford was at work, watching his blackjack tables through the monitors in the casino's surveillance control room. Valentine explained what he'd found, and took Crawford through the test with the two cards. Crawford let out a laugh when the marks on the cards became apparent.

"Would you look at that? They're right in front of my nose."

"You've got a rotten employee bringing the cards into the game," Valentine said.

"That would be the dealer at the table," Crawford said. "He's got a real gripe with management. Only one problem, though."

"What's that?"

"These cards won't hold up as evidence."

Valentine had started to file the Golden Dragon's marked cards with the hundreds of similar marked casino decks he kept in a drawer. "Why not?"

"My casino is filled with cigarette smoke. You can hardly read the cards when they're *faceup*. No judge will believe this is anything more than a printer's mistake."

Valentine smiled into the phone. He'd liked how Crawford had reacted to seeing the marks. Like he knew he'd been bested and didn't mind learning something new. Valentine said, "You'll need to take the judge through the snapping test. Then show him how the snapping test is no different than when the cards are dealt from a shoe. The cheater stares at the shoe and frames the cards as they come out. Whenever a marked card is dealt, the eye instantly knows."

16

Crawford let out another laugh. "If I had a hat, I'd take it off to you, mate."

"You're welcome," Valentine said.

"One more request. The gang we suspect is in the casino right now."

Valentine smothered another yawn. "Want me to look at them, see if I can tell who's doing what?"

"I'd be forever in your debt," Crawford said.

Valentine booted up his computer. He subscribed to a high-speed Internet service called Road Runner, and within a minute, he was staring at a live surveillance picture of the Golden Dragon's blackjack pit, courtesy of a feed from Crawford's computer.

"Who's winning all the money?" Valentine asked.

"Mr. Chan, the gentleman at third base," Crawford replied.

Third base was the very last seat at the black-jack table. Mr. Chan, a diminutive man in his forties, was standing behind his chair, drinking and smoking and banging his hand on the table on every round. Crawford was right: The casino's visibility was lousy, and there was no way Mr. Chan was reading the cards. Which meant someone else at the table was reading them and secretly passing the information to Mr. Chan.

Valentine brought his face inches from the computer screen. The table had seven players, and a crowd stood behind the table, clapping and making a lot of noise. One guy stood out. He was thin, wore glasses, and was staring at the dealer. Gambling was part of the Asian culture, and as a group they were passionate about it. Except the thin guy. He was as stiff as a statue.

Valentine relayed his suspicions to Crawford, then said, "See if you can pull the thin guy with glasses off the floor without arousing suspicion."

"Got it," Crawford said.

Soon, an attractive hostess appeared by the thin man's side and spoke to him. The thin man nodded and walked out of the picture with the hostess.

"You were right," Crawford said a few minutes later. "We took the thin man into a back room and frisked him. He's wearing a thumper."

Valentine banged his desk with his fist. He felt just as excited as the men on the screen. He had been catching cheaters for a long time but still got a thrill when he nailed someone. Thumpers were simple electronic transmitters that sent signals to other players at the table. The person on the receiving end—in this case, Mr. Chan— wore a buzzer against his leg, which would vibrate for a second or two each time the thumper was pressed. On the computer screen, Valentine saw Mr. Chan look around, no doubt wondering where the thin man with the thumper had gone. Mr. Chan scooped up his chips, preparing to leave.

"Your suspect is about to run," Valentine said. "Want to have some fun?"

"What do you have in mind?" Crawford asked.

"I have a trick I used to pull on cheaters in Atlantic City I caught wearing thumpers. Who has the thumper right now?"

"One of my men on the floor."

"The thumper has a switch to increase or decrease the power of the charge. Tell your guy on the floor to increase the power and start sending signals to Mr. Chan."

Crawford made the call on another phone. Valentine stared at the screen. So many people were crowded around the blackjack table that Mr. Chan was having a hard time making a hasty getaway. Holding his chips protectively against his chest, he tried to push his way through. No one budged.

"Here goes," Crawford said.

Suddenly Mr. Chan's right knee convulsed into the air and nearly hit him in the jaw. Valentine jerked the phone away from his ear as Crawford exploded with laughter. Mr. Chan's leg flew into the air again. He looked like a marching soldier. A look of panic spread across his face. His leg flew into the air a third time, and he dropped his chips. Sensing something was wrong, the crowd parted, then watched as he convulsed around the floor, his leg flying into the air every few seconds, as if keeping time to a beat that only he could hear. Crawford laughed so hard he sounded like he was crying.

"We call that doing the Funky Chicken," Valentine said.

"You Americans have the best senses of humor," Crawford replied. "Thanks for sharing."

Hanging up, Valentine endorsed Crawford's check, then added it to the stack sitting on his desk awaiting deposit. It had been a good week, yet it didn't change how he felt. Money had never made him feel better.

He pushed himself out of his chair. He'd stayed up too long and no longer felt tired. His office phone rang again. He glanced at the caller ID and saw that it was his neighbor Mabel Struck. Mabel was the most important woman in his life. A retired Southern lady, she ran his consulting business, cooked him a hot meal when he needed it, and kept him from killing his son, Gerry, who'd moved across the street with his wife and newborn daughter two months ago.

"I hope I didn't wake you," Mabel said.

"I was working on a case," he replied. "I figured it was time to start tackling this work that's been piling up."

"Are you feeling better?"

Better was a relative term when your mood was lousy. Mabel knew about the situation with Lucy Price and had been intercepting her phone calls on a daily basis.

"A little," he said.

"Glad to hear it. Do you have your television set on? There's a special report from Las Vegas. Something terrible has happened."

"Let me guess. One of the casinos had a losing night."

"Tony, this isn't funny. There's a bad fire at one of the hotels."

He walked out of his study with the cordless phone cradled in his neck, his bare feet making the hardwood floors creak. He lived on Florida's laid-back west coast in a New England-style clapboard house. The house was sixty years old and had withstood a dozen hurricanes and tidal surges. Everything about its construction was solid.

He switched on the TV in the living room. He was a news junkie, the set always tuned to CNN. A picture of a burning hotel appeared, the flames dancing fifty feet in the air. The caption said it was the Riverboat. He knew lots of people there. As deadly black smoke poured out of the hotel's windows, a feeling of helplessness sunk him into his La-Z-Boy.

"You still there?" his neighbor asked.

He'd forgotten the phone was still pressed against his ear. "Yeah."

"You watching?"

"Uh-huh," he grunted.

"I'd thought you'd want to see it. I remember you saying you had several friends there."

The picture switched to one from a helicopter, and Valentine found himself staring at the side of the hotel. The camera zoomed in on a man standing on a balcony. He was balding and overweight, and was climbing over the railing as flames

21

danced around him. He crossed himself, then stared directly into the camera. The camera did a close-up on his face.

"Don't show it," Valentine said to the screen.

The man on the balcony hesitated. There was a courage in his eyes that you didn't see very often. The look of someone who's accepted his fate. He opened his mouth.

"I only regret that I have but one life to lose for my country," he yelled at the camera.

Then he jumped.

CHAPTER 3

Max Duncan, a twenty-eight-year-old blackjack dealer, watched the first fire trucks pull in front of the Riverboat Casino across the street. More trucks followed, along with dozens of wailing police cruisers. *The joint must be on fire,* he thought.

Max wanted to go to the windows and have a look; only, house rules forbid him from leaving his table. There was a famous story about a dealer who left his post to help a man having a stroke and was fired on the spot.

The pit boss hurried past Max's table. He was a tough nut named Harry. Every day before the shift started, Harry made the dealers assemble in the employee lounge and on an easel wrote a single word in giant letters: WIN.

After a minute Harry returned, his face cast in stone. Max tried to get his attention.

"Harry, what's going on?"

"Deal your game," Harry snapped at him.

Harry made it sound like a threat. He made everything sound like a threat. Max looked at the elderly woman sitting at his table. Her name was

Helen, and she was a retired bookkeeper. Helen had won the first bet she'd made a few hours ago, and allowed the memory to take up permanent residence in her imagination.

"Place your bets," Max said. "You know what they say. You can't win if you don't play."

"You can't *lose*, either," she replied testily. The cards had punished her since her first win, but she'd hung tight and almost pulled even. She placed a green twenty-five-dollar chip in the betting circle.

"Be nice," she said as Max dealt.

Her two cards totaled sixteen. Helen had a stiff, the worst hand possible. She slapped the table hard.

"Now, now," Max said. "Be kind to the furniture."

More fire trucks raced past the casino. Someone opened one of the front doors, and the trucks' wail filled the interior like a chorus of screaming cats. A chip girl walked past the table, and Max caught her eye. "What's going on?" he asked under his breath.

"There's a fire over at the Riverboat."

"Is it bad?"

"People are jumping from the balconies."

"Jesus," he swore under his breath.

"Hit me," Helen said.

Max looked at her. She'd heard everything the chip girl had said.

"Come on, lady," he said testily. "Show some respect. People across the street are dying."

"It's no surprise," she said, talking in a loud voice. "The owners rushed to make their grand opening. A lot of palms got greased to get the building up to code. Now, hit me."

Max dealt her a four, giving her a twenty.

"Was that so hard?" she cackled, her foul mood vanishing.

Helen had started the evening with five hundred dollars, dropped to twenty, and was now slightly ahead. Max wanted to tell her to go home, but the rules prohibited it. He watched her slide all her chips into the betting circle.

"Let it ride," she said.

The table limit was five hundred. Max called the pit boss. As Harry approached the table, Max said, "Lady wants to bet the kaiser roll."

"She counting?" Harry asked.

"Naw."

"Let her."

The other blackjack tables were clearing out, the players going to the windows or walking outside to watch the fire. Helen ignored their departure, her eyes fixed on the plastic shoe as if the next card to be dealt contained the secret to the universe.

Max dealt the round. They both had twenty. A push. It seemed sinful to be gambling while people were dying; only, Helen didn't see it that way, her mouth working a two-hour-old piece of gum like a piece of cud.

Max dealt another round. This time, Helen had

twenty, while he had sixteen. He drew a card and snapped it over: a five. The retired bookkeeper gritted her teeth and swore.

"Always the big ones," she said as Max took away her chips.

"Seems that way, doesn't it?" Max said.

Busted, Helen got up to leave. An overweight man had walked into the casino and stood behind her, holding her chair. Helen thanked him, then made a funny sound. Max followed her gaze. The overweight man was soaking wet, his shoulders and balding head sprinkled with shiny slivers of glass.

"Where are your shoes?" Helen asked.

"Lost them," the man said.

He took Helen's chair and pulled his body close to the table. Helen hung close to his side, waiting to see what he was about to do. Rifling his pockets, the man scowled; no wallet. Removing his watch, he dropped it on the felt table and pushed it toward Max. "How much will you give me for this?"

"I'm sorry, sir," Max said, "but house rules prohibit me from pawning chips."

"Anyone ever tell you that you sound like a robot?" the man asked. Turning to the retired bookkeeper, he said, "How about you? It cost me eight hundred."

Helen appraised the timepiece. Placing it on the table, she said, "It's broken, mister. You just come from across the street?"

The man stared at the shattered face of his Movado. "That's right."

"You jump into the pool or something?"

The man pointed at the watch. The hands were frozen at 12:05. The retired bookkeeper nodded, understanding immediately. The man said, "I jumped through the skylight in the spa's roof and landed on some mattresses lying in the pool. They broke my fall. When I pulled myself out of the water, I discovered my shoes were gone."

Helen took the seat next to him. "What's your name, mister?"

"Ricky Smith."

"This is your lucky day, isn't it, Ricky?"

"It sure is. I won twenty grand earlier."

"Twenty grand! What were you playing?"

"Blackjack."

Helen looked into the young man's eyes. A silent understanding passed between them. Taking her purse from her pocketbook, she extracted a twenty tucked behind a picture of her cat. "When I was growing up, my mother made me carry a hidden twenty whenever I went out. I thought it was stupid until a boy tried to rape me on a date. I ran and ended up calling a cab. Guess what?"

"What?" Ricky said.

"The fare came to exactly twenty dollars." She dropped the grainy bill on the table and slid it toward Max. "Chips, please."

Max took the twenty, called out "Changing twenty," and shoved the money into the drop box in the table with a plunger. Then he took four red five-dollar chips from his rack and slid them toward Ricky.

"Good luck, sir," the dealer said.

Ricky fingered the small stack of chips while looking at Helen. She blinked three times, as if unable to control a nervous tic. Ricky smiled at her, then slid his chips into the betting circle on the table. He fixed his eyes on the dealer.

"Let's dance," he said.

CHAPTER 4

Two days after the tragic fire at the Riverboat, Bill Higgins, the director of the Nevada Gaming Control Board and one of Valentine's closest friends, called from Tampa International Airport. He had just flown in from Las Vegas and needed to talk.

"You here on business?" Valentine asked him.

"Afraid so," Bill replied.

A yellow cab deposited Bill on Valentine's doorstep thirty minutes later. He was dressed in a somber black suit and walking without his cane, the color of good health having returned to his cheeks. Four months before, a gangster had shot him in the leg, and his rehab had been slow but steady. He was a Navajo by birth, and wore his emotions several layers below the surface.

Valentine pumped his hand, then showed him into the living room and got two Diet Cokes from the kitchen. Serving his guest, he said, "So how's life treating you?"

"Crummy," Bill said, loosening his tie. He took a long swallow of soda, then said, "You know, you've gotten me addicted to this stuff. I'm up to three cans a day."

"Sorry."

"Where's Mabel? You know, we talk all the time, but I've never met her."

"She has the day off," Valentine said. "She's been working a lot of weekends, and I figured I'd better give her a vacation before she quit."

Valentine saw Bill's eyes scan the living room. Piles of casino surveillance tapes were on every piece of furniture and every table. Attached to each tape was a note from the casino's head of security, describing the alleged cheating taking place. The notes always came with a check, and Bill whistled through his teeth.

"Business must be good."

"It's picking up. How about you?"

Bill drained his can and wiped his mouth on his sleeve. "Lousy. I've gotten myself in a real jam and need to ask you a favor."

"Sure."

"Don't agree just yet. Hear me out."

Valentine stretched out in his La-Z-Boy. A young kid had tossed him hard at judo class the day before, and he'd woken up that morning feeling like a one-legged man after an ass-kicking contest. "Go ahead."

"I'm sure you've been following the Ricky Smith story in the newspapers."

He nodded. Ricky Smith was an overnight media sensation. After jumping off the balcony of the burning hotel into a swimming pool, he'd waltzed into a casino across the street called the Mint, borrowed twenty bucks from a retired bookkeeper, and proceeded to win more than two hundred thousand dollars playing blackjack. From there, he'd gone and played roulette, won another quarter million bucks, then went to the craps table and won another three hundred thousand. He capped off the evening by playing poker with a legend named Tex "All In" Snyder and beat the pants off him. It was an amazing streak even by Las Vegas standards, and the newspapers had dubbed him the world's luckiest man.

"I got a call from the owner of the Mint that night," Bill said. "He didn't have enough cash in the cage to pay Ricky off. Ricky agreed to come back the next day for his money. The owner decided to put the time to good use and asked me to check him out."

"Just in case he was cheating," Valentine said.

"Exactly."

"Was he?"

"Ricky Smith is a straight arrow; no criminal record of any kind. I got a credit card company to pull up his files. He lives in a little town in North Carolina called Slippery Rock. This was his fourth trip to Las Vegas since January. Each time he was here, he stayed at the Riverboat. That was all I had to go on. Four trips in the past year.

"I got the Mint to give me the surveillance

videotape of him beating them. I watched it for a few hours. Everything appears normal. He sits down, places a bet, and wins. No hanky-panky on anybody's part. It looks like he got lucky, plain and simple.

"For the heck of it, I decided to call around and see if he'd played at any other casino during his other trips. Come to find out, he did. He played blackjack at the Bellagio two months ago. Guess what? They pegged him a card counter."

"Did they ban him?"

Bill shook his head. "He was losing, so they let him continue. But they kept a file on him, just in case he decided to come back."

Valentine tossed his empty soda can into the trash. "Let me guess. You then looked at the tape of him playing at the Mint a little differently."

"I sure did," Bill said, leaning forward in his seat. "And I found a discrepancy. When he played blackjack at the Mint, he didn't card count. Matter of fact, he didn't adhere to Basic Strategy. He played like a moron, yet won every hand he played."

"Every hand? No losses?"

"Not a one."

Basic Strategy had been developed by a mathematician named Edward Thorp and was the optimal way to play blackjack. Card counters knew Basic Strategy like the back of their hand and never deviated from it. For Ricky to have stopped using Basic Strategy was like saying he'd woken up one morning and started brushing his teeth with a different hand.

"I called the owner of the Mint and told him what I'd found," Bill went on. "I told him I thought it was suspicious, but that there could be an explanation."

"The jump from the burning hotel," Valentine said.

"Exactly. Ricky Smith was in shock and therefore deviated from normal behavior." Bill grew silent and stared at the worn spot in the rug beneath his feet. "This is the rug you had in Atlantic City, isn't it?"

Valentine said that it was. Since moving to Palm Harbor, he hadn't bought a single piece of furniture except a wide-screen TV, and that was because the old one had gotten blown out of the wall during a lightning storm. Spending money had been his wife's job, not his.

"I think I wore that hole in it," Bill said, still staring. "Anyway, the owner of the Mint tells his people to delay paying Ricky Smith off. Legally, they're allowed to conduct an investigation if they suspect any impropriety."

"That was dumb," Valentine said.

"Tell me about it. Ricky Smith's lawyers filed papers against the Mint yesterday afternoon. The casinos in town are freaking out. They think the publicity will be horrible. I got called on the carpet last night."

"Why you?"

"The owner of the Mint is saying he based his decision on my recommendation. He left out the part about Ricky maybe being in shock."

"How convenient."

"I need your help. My gut tells me Ricky Smith's winning streak isn't on the square. Ricky told a newspaper that except for blackjack, he'd never played any of the other casino games before, yet he still somehow managed to win."

"Beginner's luck? Come on."

"That's what I said. I need you to tell me what he's doing."

Valentine had known Bill a long time and considered him one of his best friends. He liked to think he'd do just about anything to help Bill out of a jam; only, this was Las Vegas they were talking about, the only city in America where rats wore thousand-dollar silk suits and screwed people because it suited them.

"I'm afraid I can't help you, Bill," he said.

Bill didn't act mad or particularly surprised. He went outside the house to make a call on his cell phone. Palm Harbor didn't have many cell towers, and the reception was rarely good. Besides the great weather, Valentine considered the lack of reception one of the area's greatest attributes. Bill returned to the living room, shaking his head.

"I can't get a line out. Can I use your office phone?"

"Sure," Valentine said.

Bill disappeared into the back of the house. Valentine guessed Bill was calling the casino owners to explain the situation. Las Vegas's casinos routinely alerted other casinos around the country about cheaters and card counters they'd spotted playing in their establishments. Six weeks ago, they'd sent a notice out calling Valentine's son, Gerry, an undesirable. As a result, Gerry had been forced to quit working for him, and was now unemployed.

Valentine had responded by refusing to do any more work for Las Vegas's casinos. Gerry was no choir boy, but did not deserve the leper status. To replace the work he'd lost from Las Vegas, Valentine had started taking jobs from casinos in Europe and the Far East. The time difference was a drag, but like his mother used to say, their money was as green as anyone else's.

Picking up the remote, he got the VCR working, and stared at a surveillance tape of a Japanese gambler playing craps at a posh casino in New Zealand. The Japanese gambler was betting a few hundred dollars a roll. Then, out of the blue, he bet five thousand dollars and won. It looked suspicious as hell.

Valentine found the letter the casino boss had sent him and reread it. According to the boss, the Japanese gambler made a single five-thousand-dollar bet each time he played. He bet this amount only when another player was throwing the dice. And he always won.

Valentine rewound the tape and hit play. This time, he watched how the Japanese gambler placed his bets. Instead of using chips, he was using cold hard cash. As the dice were in the air, he leaned forward over the table to make a Field Bet. This meant if the shooter tossed a 2, 3, 4, 9, 10, 11, or 12, the Japanese gambler won. But the shooter threw the dice too fast and yelled for the Japaese gambler to watch out. The Japanese gambler pulled back, never letting go of his cash. Instead, he looked at the craps dealer running the game. The banker nodded, accepting his bet. Valentine felt a smile cross his face. The scam was as old as the hills. The Japanese gambler had a hidden fold in the bills. The big money was folded in half, giving him two bets. If the shooter won the Field Bet, the Japanese gambler would drop all of his money on the layout. If the shooter lost, the big money was palmed in the Japanese gambler's left hand, while the visible bills were dropped to the table with his right hand. When Bill came out of the study, Valentine killed the tape.

"That your granddaughter in those pictures on your desk?" Bill asked.

"That's her. Her name's Lois."

"She's a real beauty." Bill parked himself on the couch and cleared his throat. "I just had a conference call with the Strip's major owners. They want to offer you a deal."

"I hope you told them to go to hell."

"It's a good deal."

"Not interested."

Bill frowned. It was rare for him to show emotion, and Valentine guessed it hadn't been a pleasant conversation. "Let me guess. They threatened to fire you if I didn't play ball."

Bill nodded solemnly.

"Think they'll do it?"

"Of course they'll do it."

"When you up for retirement?" Valentine asked.

"Next year."

"Getting fired would kind of spoil that, huh?"

"Just a little."

Valentine tossed the remote on the table beside his recliner. He missed, and it hit the floor and shattered, the batteries rolling under the couch. It was a well-known fact that the Mafia had been run out of Las Vegas years ago. What wasn't well known was that the men who'd replaced them were just as ruthless; only, they had MBAs from the Harvard Business School.

"Let's hear their deal," Valentine said.

CHAPTER 5

"**W**atch out!"

Valentine jammed the brake pedal to avoid a barefoot man in ragged jeans picking his way between cars. It was late afternoon, and the single lane of traffic crawling along Key West's famous Duval Street had halted. The tops of cars gleamed with bright, shadowless light as a storm rumbled in the distance. Newsboys danced in the road along with women hawking flowers and an enterprising guy with lottery tickets trailing from a roll like toilet paper.

The barefoot man stopped in front of Valentine's rental. Clenched in his fist was a soda bottle. Valentine tensed, guessing it was about to come through his windshield. Instead the man took a swig and, holding his body erect, ignited his breath with a lighter. An orange balloon of flame burst from his mouth. As he started to do it again, Valentine pulled his wallet out and motioned the man over to his window.

"Here," he exclaimed, stuffing five dollars into the man's hands. "Now, get out of here before you blow us all up!"

The man sauntered away, barely avoiding a motorcycle weaving in and out of traffic. Valentine shifted into drive and the rental rolled forward a few yards, and then traffic stopped again. He'd killed an entire day traveling from Palm Harbor to Key West, and now watched the sun balance on a cluster of palm trees.

A flower seller tapped his window. She was Cuban, and in broken English hawked flowers for any occasion: birthdays, young mistresses, even suspicious wives. He smiled for the first time that day. "I'm looking for the Coral House. It's supposed to be right off Duval."

She pointed to the next block. The street sign had been covered by a banner announcing a festival that started tomorrow. A dented Volkswagen bus cut in front of him, its rear panel removed to help cool the engine. Raising her voice, the flower seller said, "At the end of that street, hidden behind a big hibiscus hedge, is the Coral House."

"*Gracias, señorita.*"

"You want to buy flowers?"

He shook his head.

"Maybe there is a woman you secretly care about," she insisted, trying to get him to take a handful.

Traffic had finally started to move, and Valentine frowned and drove away.

Valentine had given Gerry and his wife a week's stay at the Coral House as a present. They had both taken the ban by the Las Vegas casinos hard.

Until Yolanda could get back to work, they were existing solely on Gerry's income. Losing that had put Gerry in a real bind. He was thirty-six years old and, except for running a bar that had fronted a bookmaking operation, had never held down a legitimate job in his life.

Walking up the path, Valentine was happy to see the place wasn't a dump. The old Victorian two-story had a wraparound porch and rockers that looked like they got plenty of use. The reception area was right inside the front door. A prim little man sat at a desk, drinking herbal tea while balancing his checkbook. Looking up, he said, "Good afternoon."

"Hello," Valentine said.

"Are you . . . Mr. Valentine?"

The guy didn't look like anyone he'd ever busted. "That's right. How did you know?"

"The resemblance to your son is remarkable. They're upstairs, room 7."

Valentine thanked him and climbed up a winding staircase to the second floor, stopping halfway to admire the black-and-whites of old Key West hanging on the walls, Ernest Hemingway's grizzled, sunburned face shining out from several. He'd toured Hemingway's home during an earlier trip and come away impressed. A nice place, but nothing lavish.

Room 7 was at the hallway's end. He tapped lightly and heard his son say, "It's unlocked." He opened the door and went in. Gerry was standing over the bed, attempting to change his two-month-old daughter's diaper. He looked like he was on the verge of a nervous breakdown, his daughter kicking and screaming her displeasure.

"Let me show you how to do that," Valentine said.

It had been Yolanda's idea to name the baby after Valentine's late wife. Gerry liked to say Yolanda was psychic, and in this case, she was. The baby had his late wife's genes: china-delicate features, black hair, and bee-stung lips. Holding her in his arms, Valentine often found himself feeling incredibly happy and immensely sad at the same time. He tickled his granddaughter's toes and got her to stop crying, then changed her diaper. When he was done, Gerry lifted her into the air and said, "Grandpa's a star, isn't he?"

"I changed her diaper, I get to hold her," Valentine said.

"Sure. Just promise you won't bite her."

"Very funny."

Handing the baby to his father, Gerry said, "So what's going on? The way you sounded on the phone earlier, I thought you'd won the lottery until I remembered you don't gamble."

Valentine cradled the baby against his chest. He'd decided that grandkids were the greatest thing ever invented. All the fun, and none of the hassle. "I had a unique opportunity presented to me yesterday. It includes you."

"I'm all ears," his son said.

41

Yolanda came out of the bathroom and kissed her father-in-law on the cheek. She wore white shorts and a man's white cotton shirt and looked stunning. His son had married a wonderful young woman who was a doctor. She also put up with Gerry's nonsense, which qualified her for sainthood in Valentine's book.

"Thank you again for giving us this vacation," she said.

"Yeah, Pop," Gerry said. "Thanks."

Valentine handed the baby to her mother and said, "I need to talk to my son. I hope you don't mind if we disappear for a little while."

Yolanda gave Gerry the eye. The vacation had obviously agreed with them, and a mischievous look crossed his son's face.

"Just don't make it too long," she said.

His son had always liked scenes, so Valentine was not surprised when they ended up on the pier at the end of Duval Street, watching street performers while the sun set. There were jugglers and buskers and a female contortionist covered with biblical tattoos, but the act attracting all the eyeballs was an emaciated guy with four trained house cats. The cats, all marmalade colored, were as skinny as their owner, and jumped through hoops and rang bells in return for tiny scraps of meat. The animals looked a few breaths away from expiring, and Valentine wanted to buy them a good meal but instead threw ten bucks into the guy's hat.

"You're such a soft touch," his son said as they walked away.

"You think so?"

"That guy drives a Mercedes."

"Then why is he so thin?"

"That's his gimmick. People feel sorry for him and the cats. He makes a bundle."

As daylight faded, the crowd dispersed, leaving Valentine and his son standing at the end of the pier, eating chocolate ice cream cones they'd bought from a vendor. Gerry bit off the end of his cone and sucked the ice cream out of the bottom.

"How would you like to come back and work for me?" Valentine asked.

His son's head snapped, and melted ice cream ran down his chin. "You serious?"

"No, I just killed a day traveling here to pull your leg."

Gerry wiped his face with a napkin. "You fix it with the guys out in Las Vegas?"

Valentine nodded. Bill Higgins had offered him a simple deal. Take the Ricky Smith job, and the casino owners would wipe the slate clean with his son, while paying him the biggest fee he'd ever earned. He had a lot of pride, but not enough to turn down a deal like the one Bill had offered him. Gerry tossed his cone into the ocean and threw his arms around him.

"Oh, man, Pop, you're a lifesaver."

★   ★   ★

The dying sun had turned the horizon pink, and long ragged strips of orange clouds were torn across the sky like a poster ripped in half. They left the pier and walked back to the Coral House. Key West had informally seceded from the Union years ago, and colorful Conch Republic banners hung from every tree and storefront.

Streetlights flickered a block from the guest house. Valentine stopped at the corner to watch a bicycle rickshaw with two drunk tourists. When it was gone, he said, "Here's the deal. I need you to go to Gulfport, Mississippi, and talk to a poker player named Tex Snyder."

"Tex 'All In' Snyder?"

"That's right. You know him?"

"Just from the TV. Won the World Series of Poker twice, considered one of the best Texas Hold 'Em players alive. How's he involved in this?"

Valentine took a pack of nicotine gum from his pocket and popped a piece into his mouth. Forty-five days without a cigarette and he still hadn't killed anyone. As the nicotine entered his bloodstream, he felt himself relax. "I'm sure you've heard about the guy who won a million bucks at the Mint last week."

"Ricky Smith, the guy they're calling Mr. Lucky?"

"That's him. Bill Higgins of the Nevada Gaming Control Board thinks he might have cheated."

"You're kidding. How?"

"I don't know."

44

"So you don't think he's cheating."

Valentine shrugged. "I've watched the tape of him playing at the Mint a dozen times. I'm not seeing any cheating. Granted, his play is irregular—he makes some wild bets and seems oblivious to the odds against him—but he jumped out of a burning building, so you can't expect his play to be normal."

"How's Tex Snyder involved in this?"

"Ricky Smith beat Snyder silly. Snyder's had plenty of time to think about it. I want you to feel him out and see if he thinks he was swindled."

"What's Snyder doing in Gulfport? Playing in a poker tournament?"

"You're psychic."

"How am I going to get him to talk to me?"

"Charm him."

A mosquito as big as a bird flew by. Gerry said, "Excuse me for sounding rude, but what are you going to be doing while I'm in Gulfport?"

Valentine popped another piece of the foul-tasting gum into his mouth. *Excuse me for sounding rude.* That was definitely a new addition to Gerry's lexicon. Was Yolanda putting him through finishing school and getting him to clean up his manners? Valentine looked his son over. Gerry had lost the annoying earring, and his shirt was recently pressed. Yeah, she sure was.

"I'll be in a little burg called Slippery Rock, North Carolina," Valentine said. "It's Ricky's hometown. I'm going to do a little digging, see what I turn up."

"I hope you don't find anything."

"No?"

"I'd hate to find out Ricky Smith was a cheater."

Valentine chewed his gum vigorously. He knew exactly what Gerry meant. Ricky Smith had cheated death, and then he'd gone and cheated the odds. It was the kind of story that people never got tired of hearing, and Valentine hoped he didn't go to Slippery Rock and discover that Ricky's halo was really a pair of horns.

CHAPTER 6

As small towns went, Slippery Rock was a pretty nice one. The downtown dated back to the early 1800s and still boasted brick-lined streets and streetlamps, and plenty of businesses owned by people instead of faceless corporations. On Main Street there was an old-fashioned ice cream shop, a farmers' market on weekends, and a movie theater with a Mighty Wurlitzer theater organ. Nine thousand hard-working souls lived here, and everyone knew everyone else's business.

Now that Ricky Smith was a celebrity, he could not run out and buy a newspaper or loaf of bread without getting stopped on the street. It was strange being recognized after so many years of not, and in his neighbors' eyes he saw a rainbow of feelings: happiness, envy, downright jealousy, and, in several guys he'd known in high school, quiet desperation. And everyone had peppered him with the same goddamned questions.

"You going to sue the Mint for your money?"

"Probably," he replied.

"Think you'll win?"

"Sure," he said.

"What are you going to do with the money when you get it?"

"Rule the world," Ricky said.

The truth be known, it was nobody's business what he did with the money, not that he could convince his neighbors of that. Because he was from Slippery Rock, it was their money, too, and they would spend it vicariously through him whenever they got the chance.

Not having the million dollars he'd won at the Mint did not prevent Ricky from going on a shopping spree. His credit was good everywhere. At Moody's car lot, the sales manager had welcomed him with open arms.

Moody's was the only Lexus dealership in the county and did good business. Ricky scoured the lot and quickly settled on a silver Lexus LS430 four-door sedan. It was exactly the statement he wanted to make. The car screamed that he had arrived.

Driving the car off Moody's lot, Ricky gassed it, and the fuel-injected V8 monster beneath the hood emitted a muffled roar. He headed for the open road. Soon, Slippery Rock's hilly farmland and wooded fields were racing by his windshield like an accelerated movie.

He'd paid extra for a carousel CD player, and he jumped back and forth between tracks of a bootleg Stevie Ray Vaughan CD recorded at Red

Rocks Amphitheatre, Vaughan's screaming Fender guitar ripping a hole in Ricky every time he heard it. Ricky hadn't appreciated the blues until after his divorce; now he listened every day. A lone, pathetic figure caught his eye, and he pulled the car onto the highway's shoulder.

It was Roland Pew, the heartthrob of every girl in town ten years ago, pushing a rusty old bicycle with a flat. Ricky had babysat Roland as a teenager and always liked him. He pressed a button, and the window on the passenger's side automatically lowered.

"Hey, Rolls," he yelled, "what happened to your car?"

Roland shook his head wearily, indicating another sad chapter in his sorry life.

"You don't want to know," he replied.

"Don't tell me you totaled it."

"Worse."

"Can't be anything worse."

"I can't find it."

"Come on. I'll give you a lift."

Roland had changed considerably since Ricky had seen him a month ago. Gone were his ponytail and thick yellow mustache and pirate earrings. Along Slippery Rock's grapevine Roland's tale had been a topic of discussion for days. As the story went, Roland had knocked up a local Piggly Wiggly checkout girl named Wanell Bacon, and Wanell had opted to have the kid, inspiring Roland to drink enough Jack Daniel's to render himself comatose. Awakening a few days later in his uncle's house, he had discovered himself shorn and shaven.

The aluminum bike folded easily into the trunk. Roland settled in the passenger seat and immediately began touching the upholstery. When they were a few miles down the road he said, "Mind my asking how much you forked over for this little beauty?"

"Seventy big ones. It's fully loaded."

"Jesus. What did you do, win the lottery?"

Ricky nearly said *Where you been, stupid?* Only, he knew exactly where Roland had been—sleeping it off at his uncle's house. Roland's family was basically illiterate, and news traveled to their part of the world slow, if at all. So Ricky told him what had happened out in Las Vegas. Roland whistled through his teeth.

"It's about time somebody from here hit the big time," Roland said. "I guess you heard my news."

He said it with a trace of irony, and Ricky nodded. Roland's father had dropped dead back in senior year, and Roland's luck had been on a downward spiral ever since. Wiping his mouth on his sleeve, Roland said, "You know what's got me worried?"

"No."

"Not being able to provide for my kid. I haven't had a job in *two years*."

Ricky stared at the road. He nearly said *I'll help you,* but people had been saying that to Roland for years, and nothing anyone had done had helped change Roland's situation. Besides, Roland didn't want help; he wanted a break, something that would restore his faith in humanity. True to form, Roland began to hum his favorite song, Warren Zevon's "Roland the Headless Thompson Gunner," the baneful melody drowning out a signature Stevie Ray six-string rift over a churning rhythm accompaniment. Had it been anyone else, Ricky would have told him to shut up.

A convenience store loomed in the distance, the lot filled with boisterous high school kids. Ricky parked near the front door, letting the engine idle. Inside the store, another high school classmate, Barry Clarkson, stared through the windshield at the car, then at him. Ricky smiled, and Barry turned away to take care of a customer.

The kids in the lot were spraying each other with pop. Watching them, Ricky saw himself and his high school friends twenty years ago, the world yet to drop its thunderous weight upon his shoulders.

He glanced sideways at Roland. His friend was still pawing the upholstery. Everything had gone wrong since Roland's old man had kicked the bucket. He didn't deserve the hand he'd been dealt. Ricky touched his sleeve. Roland lifted his forlorn gaze.

"Last night I had this crazy dream," Ricky said. "In my dream, I'm driving and I pick up a hitch-hiker, guy about your age, nice guy, and as we get near town he says he needs a smoke. I pull into a convenience store, and as he's getting out he says, 'Want anything?' So I think about it and say, 'I've got ten bucks burning a hole in my pocket. Get me ten lottery tickets. If we hit the big one, we'll split the money.'"

"Like you was partners," Roland said.

"Exactly." Taking out his wallet, Ricky removed a stiff ten-dollar bill and snapped it before Roland's world-weary eyes. "Guess what happened then?"

"You . . . won?"

"Yeah."

"How much?"

"Fifty big ones."

A look that almost resembled happiness crossed Roland's face. Ricky stuffed the money into his friend's hand, then watched him slip out of the car and shuffle nonchalantly into the store. Roland had written the book on being cool, his one great talent.

A car pulled into the spot beside Ricky's Lexus, the blue-hair at the wheel flashing him a brutal stare. Miss Axe, his high school math teacher two years running, the woman who'd given him D's and ruined his young life and was still ruining young lives, got out of her car. Seeing him, she came over and rapped on his window. Whatever she had to say wasn't going to be pleasant, and he hit the volume control on his steering wheel, the car's eight speakers blasting Stevie Ray's apocalyptic rendition of Jimi Hendrix's "Voodoo Child (Slight Return)."

"Mr. Lucky, my left foot," she said through the glass.

Ricky stuck his tongue out at her.

Shaking her fist, she stalked away and entered the store, his recent good fortune obviously not to her liking. A few moments later, Roland came out and got into the car, the ten Quick Pick Six tickets fanned out in his hand.

"Split the money," he said by way of reassurance.

"Absolutely," Ricky said. He saw a slight hesitation in Roland's eyes. "Want to shake hands on it?"

"No. I just wanted to be sure."

Ricky smelled beer on his breath, and saw an open can peeking out of his denim jacket. He pointed, and Roland pulled out a Bud tall boy.

"Have some," Roland said.

Ricky took a long pull and felt the ice-cold suds tickle his throat and expand in his empty belly. He hadn't had any beer in a week, one of his first resolutions after coming home from Vegas. He took another pull. It was an easy one to break.

"In your dream, which one of us had the winning ticket?"

Ricky shrugged. "Does it matter?"

"I've never won nothing in my life."

"You want me to pick it?"

"It was your dream."

Ricky pulled one of the lottery tickets out of Roland's fist. It had already stopped being a game for Roland, and Ricky found himself wishing he had written Roland a check and told him to go rent an apartment and have his baby and get out of the rut he was in. Roland pulled a quarter out of his pocket, and dropped it in Ricky's hand.

"You do the scratching," he said.

Every Quick Pick Six ticket had twelve covered boxes on it; the player scratched off the latex, and if six boxes matched, the player won that amount. Ricky took his time, and on his first five scratches, he hit $50,000 circles. He passed the card to Roland and got the tall boy in return. Ricky pointed at the box in the left corner of the ticket.

"That one," Ricky said.

"You think so?"

"Damn straight."

Ricky killed the tall boy, seeing Miss Axe come out of the convenience store and shoot him a dagger. He rolled down his window.

"Miss Axe?"

She was fitting her key into her door and turned. "What, Ricky?"

"I love you. I really do, Miss Axe. I always loved you. It's why I did so poorly in your class. It was you."

Scowling, she climbed into her car and drove away. Ricky slapped the wheel of his new car, the beer lifting his spirits to impossible heights. Roland frowned, no longer being cool, his anxiety paralyzing him. The coin was frozen in his hand.

"What's wrong?"

"It's just . . . I don't know."

"You want me to do it?" Ricky asked him.

"Yeah," Roland whispered.

Taking the ticket and the coin from him, Ricky scratched out the box in the corner. It was for $50,000. He showed it to Roland and watched his friend melt into his seat, and close his eyes.

"That was intense," Roland said.

CHAPTER 7

Mabel Struck had seen some strange things during her life, especially during the past two years, running Tony's business and watching him catch hundreds of casino cheaters. But she'd never seen anything as strange as the item she was now holding, a candy bar worth a hundred thousand dollars.

She was going through the mail while sitting at Tony's desk. Her boss had left a few hours ago for Slippery Rock, and she'd gone onto his computer and dealt with a dozen e-mails, then started sorting through his mail. It was heavy, and she put the priority letters in one pile, the it-can-wait items in another. The very last letter was a padded envelope. When she ripped it open, a giant 3 Musketeers candy bar fell out. With it was a letter from Ron Shepherd, the head of gaming enforcement for the Royal Canadian Mounted Police.

Hey Tony,
    Here's the $100,000 candy bar for your collection. The store owner copped a plea and

will end up doing a year, plus pay back the government for all the taxes he didn't pay on his ill-gotten gains. I thought I'd seen them all, but this scam takes the cake. Thanks for your help in cracking this one.

Ron

Mabel held the candy bar in her hand. There was a price sticker on it. It cost a dollar thirty, Canadian. Their money was worth about 70 percent U.S., which made the candy bar worth about a dollar. So what made it worth a hundred thousand times that?

She put the candy bar on the desk and stared at it. There was an expression Tony liked to use. *In the know.* It was what differentiated the smart from the dumb. And she wasn't in the know about this stupid candy bar. It frustrated her no end, and she picked up the phone and called Yolanda, who was across the street cleaning her house. Ten minutes later, Yolanda was standing in the study, holding little Lois against her chest while reading Ron Shepherd's note.

"I thought you were kidding," Yolanda said, putting the note down. "What do you think the scam is?"

"I have no idea. You know what frustrates me the most?" Mabel said. "Tony never told me he was doing a job for this man."

"He probably did it as a favor. Gerry says he does that a lot."

Mabel heard herself grinding her teeth. Tony had asked her to run his business, and she'd gone about it with the idea that people should be charged for her boss's services. Yet it didn't stop him from dispensing free advice and help whenever it suited him.

"At least he could have told me," she said.

"Maybe he didn't want to bother you. He thinks you work too hard."

"Well, sometimes I do. But this is so . . . interesting."

"So call him. He'll be happy to explain it."

Mabel examined the candy bar again. Ron Shepherd's note said a convenience store manager was going to serve time. Had the manager covered the candy bar with a towel and pretended it was a gun? No, she decided, it was something infinitely clever; that was why Ron Shepherd had asked for Tony's help. She glanced up and saw Yolanda holding the phone.

"You want me to call him?" she asked.

Mabel shook her head. "No, I'll do it."

Tony's cell phone was turned off. Mabel left a message and asked him to call back. Her boss picked up his messages sporadically, which meant it might be a few hours, or even a day, before she got an explanation out of him.

Yolanda had to feed the baby, so Mabel showed her out. Shutting the front door behind Yolanda, Mabel suddenly had an idea. She didn't remember

Tony making any trips to Canada recently, which meant he'd probably solved the candy bar scam from the comfort of his La-Z-Boy. Going into the living room, she looked through the stacks of videotapes that were scattered around the room. Tony's handwriting was hard to decipher—Gerry likened it to the cartoon character Bullwinkle's—and she squinted at the labels.

She looked through every stack, then the tapes stuck in drawers and cabinets. It wasn't anywhere to be found. Now she was getting mad. It had to be here somewhere.

On the La-Z-Boy was a yellow legal pad and the remote, Tony's two main work tools. It occurred to her that the tape might still be in the VCR, and she powered up the TV, then hit play on the VCR. A grainy surveillance of a balding man with bare feet filled the TV screen. It was Ricky Smith at the Mint. She had read about Ricky's exploits in the newspaper, but wasn't prepared for what she now saw.

Ricky played like a man possessed. With one hand he bet; with the other, he rolled the dice or flipped over his cards. No movement was wasted. *Bam bam bam!* What made it so amazing was that he didn't lose. Not once. That wasn't possible, and Mabel slowly lowered her posterior onto the La-Z-Boy, her eyes fixed on the screen.

According to MapQuest, the town of Slippery Rock, North Carolina, was six hundred and sixty miles from where Valentine lived in Florida, and nowhere near a public airport. So he'd gotten the oil changed in his '92 Honda and taken to the highway.

He drove in the right lane most of the way, and caught the drivers of passing cars giving him the eye. The Honda was definitely showing its age, the navy blue paint job fading to a less vibrant color. He kept thinking of trading it in; only, the engine still turned over every time he fired it up. What more did he want in a car?

Crossing into North Carolina, he felt his ears pop, and he grabbed MapQuest's directions off the passenger seat. He'd been a flatlander all his life and hadn't bothered to check the town's elevation when he'd printed the instructions off his computer. Slippery Rock was twenty-nine hundred feet above sea level and in the foothills of the Appalachian Mountains. No wonder it was taking him so long to get there.

He kept his eyes peeled for a gas station. He'd run out of nicotine gum an hour ago, and the craving for a cigarette was killing him. He fiddled with the radio and found local news and Billy Graham saving souls. A Sinatra CD was in the player, but he saved that for special occasions, leaving silence as his traveling companion.

His cell phone rang, jolting him out of a daydream. The caller ID said HOME.

"Sick of driving yet?" his neighbor asked.

"Just about," he admitted.

"Not to say I told you so, but flying to Atlanta would have been much easier."

"If I didn't hate airports so much, I'd agree with you."

"I know, they remind you of medium-security prisons," Mabel said. "Look, I just had a look at this tape of Ricky Smith, and I'd have to agree with your friend Bill Higgins. Something is definitely not on the square, to use your favorite expression."

Valentine sat up in his seat. "You think so?"

"I'd bet my hat on it."

Mabel rarely disagreed with him, especially when it came to his work. This sounded more like a scolding, and before he could answer, she continued.

"I think you need to take a fresh approach to this case, Tony."

"You do?"

"Yes. You're still angry at the casino owners in Las Vegas for what they did to Gerry. You have to forget about that."

He swallowed hard. "Okay."

"You also have to forget that Ricky Smith jumped out of a burning building," Mabel said. "You're letting that cloud what happened inside the casino. The man won eighty separate bets at blackjack, craps, and roulette. He didn't lose once."

"People get lucky," he heard himself say.

Mabel laughed. "Not like this."

He suddenly felt like an idiot. Mabel had obviously spotted something on the tape. He'd watched the tape again late last night after getting home from Key West. He'd been sleepy and dozed off near the end. "What did you see?"

"The surveillance tape in your VCR of Ricky Smith is actually four tapes spliced together," his neighbor said. "There's a time posted on each segment. Did you bother to check them?"

"No."

"The times are continuous. He was running from game to game in his bare feet. Is that the way winners act?"

The sun was starting to set, and Valentine realized he was smiling. "No, they sure don't."

"The whole thing stinks, if you ask me."

His headlights caught a green billboard on the side of the highway. Slippery Rock was another thirty miles, and he punched the accelerator with his foot.

"You're a genius," he told his neighbor.

From the elevated interstate, downtown Slippery Rock looked like something out of a storybook: four blocks square, the red brick streets laid out in a perfect grid, the buildings no more than three stories high, with old-fashioned storefronts and no neon lights. It was a pleasant step back in time, and as Valentine entered town, the bell in the tower of the Old First Presbyterian Church tolled six o'clock. The roads were slick from a rain he hadn't encountered, and he inched the vehicle down Main Street while searching for the Century 21 office.

62

Turning around, he drove through downtown a second time. It reminded him of several bucolic burgs he and his late wife had considered as places to retire to. In the end they'd chosen Florida, but a town like this would have been high on the consideration list. It was so clean it sparkled, and that was always a good sign.

He found the Century 21 office on a side street, the mullioned front window a montage of available homes and condos. Tapping his keys on the front door, he stamped his feet to stay warm. The mountains were always colder. Too bad he hadn't remembered that when he'd packed. A cleaning lady unlocked the front door.

"I'm looking for Dolores Parker," he announced.

The cleaning lady shrugged. "Who you?"

"Her seven o'clock appointment."

The cleaning lady pointed across the street at the Holiday Inn. "Try the bar. Short blond lady. Fast talker."

He thanked her and crossed the street. Dolores Parker was Ricky's ex-wife. Her name had popped up in a newspaper article Valentine had found on the Internet. The article said she sold real estate, so he'd called the chamber of commerce and found out where. Making a phony appointment wasn't entirely kosher, but neither was cheating a casino.

The bar, called the Beef & Brew, was just off the lobby. It was a dark, low-ceilinged room filled with loud people, the loudest of which, a spitfire blonde with inch-long fingernails, stood barefoot on a table while singing the Monkees' "Last Train to Clarksville," the lyrics drowned out by her unappreciative audience. When she was done, Valentine stepped forward and helped her down from the table.

"Thanks, mistah," she slurred.

"Tony Valentine," he said, offering his hand. "Your seven o'clock appointment."

Her hand went up to her mouth, then she giggled, reached out, and pumped his hand hard. "Dolores Parker, nice to meet you. My friends call me Polly or P squared. Let me guess—your flight was delayed. Or was it the roads? They're horrible this time of year. Well, the important part is you made it to Slippery Rock safe and sound. So how do you like our little oasis?"

"I like it," he said.

"Well, good!" Slipping on her pumps, she grew three inches, the top of her perky little head reaching Valentine's chin, and wrapping her arm in his, she let out a loud "See ya later, boys!" and hustled her client out into the cold and rainy night.

He followed Polly Parker to the north side of town. The drive had made him sleepy, and he rolled down his window and let the night air blow in his face. Slippery Rock was a pretty place, but he now remembered why he and Lois had decided against living in the mountains. It was cold six months of the year.

Polly drove her Acura into a cul-de-sac, the modest ranch houses sitting on heavily wooded lots, and he pulled his Honda up a sloping driveway and parked beside her. As he got out, he saw her window come down. She was on her cell phone, and he heard her say, "Hey, Kimberli, it's Polly. I'm doing fine. Look, I'm showing a client from out of town the Muller place on Willard Court. I'll call you when we're done. Bye-bye."

That was smart, Valentine thought. *Tell a friend and warn me at the same time.* She got out, and they walked down a narrow brick path to a double-story shingle house.

"Slippery Rock doesn't have many rentals this time of year," she said, fumbling with the keys. "Not that the house is bad, it's just that for the same money, I can get you much better in the next town over."

"Why don't you just tell me what's wrong with the place and get it out of the way?"

She hesitated, key in the door. "You sure?"

"I'm a big boy. I can take it."

A noise came out of her mouth that sounded like a purr. Her bloodshot eyes betrayed how hammered she was, the tip of her tongue licking her finely shaped little teeth as she spoke. "Well, let's see, the roof leaks and the basement floods when it rains and the carpets have a permanent damp smell you can't get rid of and the street isn't wired for cable so all you get is three channels and two of them are Billy Graham's Evangelistic

65

Association. And then there's your neighbor, Hank Ridley. Ridley's daddy once owned most of this county. Over time, he'd sold off parcels to pay for things he needed, like a new car or a kid's education, and when he died, the last parcel was willed to Hank, who fancies himself an aging Beat Generation poet. Hank sits around all day and smokes pot and never cleans his place up so you can imagine—"

Valentine had a feeling she was going to give him the town's entire history. Holding up his hand like a cop directing traffic, he said, "Why don't you just show me the place?"

"Why, sure!" she said brightly.

Grabbing his arm, she barged inside.

Polly gave him the twenty-five-cent tour. By the time it was over he was almost feeling sorry for her. Seven-thirty on a Friday night and she didn't have anything better to do than work him over. Several times, he'd tried to get her to open up and talk about herself. Only, Polly wasn't going there, and by the end of the tour, he realized that he'd wasted her time, as well as his own. They were in the kitchen, and she filled two glasses with water and handed him one.

"So what did you say you did for a living?"

"I'm a retired cop," he said.

"What brings you here?"

"I'm writing my memoirs. I needed a little peace and quiet."

"From Florida?"

Her third degree was starting to wear on his nerves. He took out his wallet and let her see the snapshots he proudly carried around. "From my granddaughter and my son and his wife."

She stared at the picture of little Lois, and he saw something in her face melt.

"You must be very proud," she said.

Valentine said that he was.

"Not to change the subject, but the house goes for six hundred a month, plus a security deposit. What do you say?"

He started to tell her he wanted to think about it. But a noise from outside got his attention. Over the sink was a window with peeling paint that looked onto the wooded backyard. He opened it with both his hands and stuck his head out.

The screeching sound that can only be made by a wayward electric guitar was tearing a hole in the chilly night air. Polly stood next to him at the sink, and he pointed at the ramshackle house on the other side of the trees. "It sounds like someone's torturing a cat."

The real-estate agent grimaced. "It does, doesn't it?"

He pulled his head back inside and shut the window. "I'm going to have to think about it."

She followed him through the house. Reaching the front door, she grabbed the knob, then stopped. "I can have a talk with him, if you'd like. Ask him to turn it down."

"Who?"

She opened the door, and the screaming guitar invaded the quiet interior. "The moron who likes to play his music so loud."

"You know him?"

"Name's Ricky Smith. He's my ex-husband. He likes to play his stereo loud enough to wake the dead. Especially his Stevie Ray Vaughan bootlegs."

Somewhere in the woods a dog was howling. Throughout the neighborhood other screaming mongrels joined in. Unsnapping her purse, Polly dug out a Kleenex and began to blow her nose. Suddenly the guitar stopped being a guitar, the CD player stuck on a screaming high note. The neighborhood mongrels shredded their vocal chords, and Valentine realized she was crying. He touched her arm.

"You going to be okay?" he asked.

"Who knows?" she said.

They returned to the kitchen. Hiding in the ancient Frigidaire was a can of Miller Lite. Polly poured it into a tall paper cup, which she tapped against Valentine's water glass. While crying, she had inadvertently wiped away her mascara and makeup, and now resembled an eighteen-year-old, her eyes puffy and soft.

"Sorry about the waterworks," she said. "Ricky and I didn't part on the best of terms. We dated in high school; I dumped him, thought he was a jerk. We got back together a few years ago. I thought he'd changed, or that I could live with him, or whatever. Stupid me. Any idea what it's like being married to someone who's convinced he's a born loser and has no self-esteem? It's like watching someone circle a drain. I finally dumped him."

"Did he always play the stereo so loud?"

"Yes. I thought it was cute in the beginning, like he was rebelling against something. When I complained he gave me earplugs."

"Any kids?"

"I couldn't see him as a father. I think that was what drove us apart. He didn't have the backbone."

"You still talk?"

"We went to this marriage counselor after we split up. Slippery Rock being a small town and the two of us having to cross paths just about every day, the counselor suggested we keep a dialogue going, you know, keep things civil. Hah! All we did was vent our spleens at each other. One night we had drinks at the Holiday Inn and I ended up punching his lights out."

Her cup was empty, and Valentine watched her search the refrigerator for more beer.

"Any regrets?" he asked.

"Yeah. I wish I waited until he had some money to divorce him."

Valentine didn't say anything, and watched her slam the refrigerator hard.

"He stuck me for ten grand when we split up," she explained.

69

"Oh," he said.

"Ricky's rich now. He won a million bucks out in Las Vegas, and this afternoon I heard he picked a fifty-thousand-dollar lottery ticket, if you can believe that. But to tell you the truth, I don't think all the money in the world could get us back together. Ricky isn't the type of cat that's going to change his stripes, know what I mean?"

He walked Polly to her car. As she was climbing in, her cell phone chirped, and she answered it while firing the engine up. "Hey, Kimberli. Yup, everything's fine, I'm just leaving. Thanks for checking up. Bye-bye."

Valentine took a step back from the car. The Holiday Inn in town wanted a hundred and thirty bucks a night for a room. With all the hidden taxes and charges, it would come to a hundred and fifty bucks easy. Times the four nights he expected to be here was six hundred bucks. Taking his wallet out, he removed six crisp hundreds, then tapped on Polly's window with his knuckle. The window came down, and she stuck her head out, an expectant look on her face.

"Here's six hundred for the first month's rent," he said.

"You want the place?"

"It will do."

"There's also a security deposit," she said.

"For what? The house is practically falling

down and there's nothing worth stealing. Six hundred, and that's my final offer."

He shoved the money into her hand. She considered it for a moment.

"You've got a deal," she said. "You want me to call Ricky, tell him to turn the music down? He will if I ask him."

"He won't get mad?" Valentine asked.

"Oh, he'll yell and scream, but that's typical."

"Why don't you give me his phone number? He starts yelling, I'll go over and punch him in the nose."

She giggled, the alcohol giving her voice a little squeak. "It's 555-1292."

He memorized the number and watched her back down the drive. Growing up with a drunk for a father, he'd learned to hate what alcohol did to people, and he brusquely motioned for her to come back. She drove back to her original spot and lowered her window.

"You forgot to give me the keys to the house," he said.

CHAPTER 8

While his father was getting settled in Slippery Rock, Gerry was traveling to Gulfport, Mississippi, determined to find Tex "All In" Snyder and have a talk with him.

It had been a long day. He'd flown from Key West to Atlanta that afternoon, taken an eight-seater to Hattiesburg, Mississippi, and rented a car. By the time he'd actually gotten on the highway, it was growing dark, and he'd wisely gotten in the right lane. A lot of tall white trucks were on the highway, and they roared when they passed him.

He found a radio station that wasn't country, and jacked the volume up. He was tired, but it was a good tired. His father had bailed him out, given him fresh wings. He'd never been in prison, so he didn't know what it was like to get sprung. But he had a feeling that the euphoria he was feeling right now was something real close.

He looked at himself in the mirror. That morning, at Yolanda's suggestion, he'd gotten his hair cut. He liked to wear it longer than most, and his wife had reminded him that he was heading into Dixie, where Yankees were not always welcome. So he'd gotten his ears lowered, and decided he liked the way it made him look.

He turned his attention back to the highway. It ran north-south, with a fifty-foot median planted with hundred-year-old pines. The night seemed very big, the stars illuminating the farthest corners of the universe. It was too good not to share, and he flipped open his cell phone and called his wife.

An hour later, he passed a junior college, then a milling operation where acres of forty-foot-long trees stood adjacent to the highway. Next was a large store that sold nothing but Bibles. Then he passed a town that consisted of one building that housed two restaurants, and a state trooper's car hiding in the shadows looking for speeders.

The highway eventually dead-ended at a beach-front marina and amusement park. Beneath the glare of a full moon, the park had a ghoulish, otherworld quality that reminded him of a horror film called *Carnival of Souls*. Hanging a right, he drove to a brightly lit casino named Dixie Magic and found a space in the crowded lot.

He was about a quarter mile from the front doors, but that was okay. His legs were stiff, and he stretched his hamstrings as he walked. He'd never been to Mississippi, and his father had explained the deal to him. By law, casinos couldn't be on Mississippi soil, so several local businessmen had dug out huge craters of beach-front, flooded them with water you wouldn't swim in, and floated barges whose interiors were giant casinos. To lessen the cheesy effect, the barges were covered in blinking lights and garish neon.

He crossed the metal gangplank with a bounce in his step. Find Tex, have a chat, and go home to his wife and beautiful baby. It didn't get any easier than that.

At the front door, a security guard counted him with a clicker. The barge could hold only a certain number of passengers, and a running count was kept of everyone inside.

"Busy night?" Gerry asked.

"Every night's busy," the guard said.

Gerry pushed open the glass door, and the smell almost knocked him over. Adrenaline and cheap aftershave, a thousand cigarettes, free booze. The smell of a few thousand people compressed in a tiny space, gambling. For years, people swore that the casinos pumped extra oxygen through the air vents to keep players going, but it wasn't true. The games kept people going.

He caught the eye of a cute change girl, and learned the poker tournament was on the second floor. He made his way to a bank of elevators. Down in Key West, his father had given him a videotape of Ricky Smith's winning streak, and he'd watched it with Yolanda. Ricky Smith had played poker with Tex Snyder for twenty minutes and won two hundred grand. He'd made Snyder look like a chump. Surely Snyder would have some interesting thoughts on what happened. The challenge would be making him open up.

Gerry got on a crowded elevator. On the way up, he found himself checking out the other haircuts. He fit right in. Great.

The poker tournament was in the casino's card room and was being filmed by a cable station for a later showing. Tournament poker was the rage on TV and, according to his father, was creating a whole new legion of suckers. Anyone could enter, and as Gerry started to walk in, he noticed the guy by the entrance. Black, six-two, a soul patch on his chin, his black shirt hanging outside his pants, disguising his massive girth. Stepping forward, he placed his forefinger on Gerry's shoulder. It was as big as a blood sausage.

"Your name Gerry Valentine?" he asked.

"That's me," Gerry said.

"My name's Lamar Biggs. I run the casino's security. You're not wanted here. I'm going to show you out. If you try to resist, I'll hurt you."

Gerry flashed Lamar his best smile. "Au contraire. That's been cleared up. If you call Bill Higgins at the Nevada Gaming Control—"

"Au what?"

"Au contraire. It's French. It means, on the contrary."

"So you just told me in French that I'm an idiot," Lamar said, his eyes narrowing.

"I told you that it's been cleared up," Gerry replied stiffly.

Lamar tried to squeeze his shoulder, and Gerry instinctively pulled back. It took all the sting out of whatever nerve Lamar was trying to pinch, and the big man looked surprised. Then his face hardened into a piece of granite, and with his head, he indicated the EMERGENCY EXIT sign. "That way," he ordered.

Gerry did as told. Walking down the stairway, he felt Lamar's hot breath on his neck. He'd had onions for dinner. Gerry's father had told him not to get upset with heads of security who had bad attitudes. Usually, it meant they'd been ripped off and needed to release some anger. At the first-floor landing Gerry stopped and stared straight up. What looked like a water sprinkler hung from the ceiling. It was only a few inches long and covered in tiny hair.

"What's that?"

"A bat," Lamar said. "Barge is filled with them. Rats, too. Keep walking."

"That's why you have this stairway closed except for emergencies, huh?" Gerry said. "Never show them the inside of the sausage factory."

"The what?"

76

"The sausage factory. It's an old expression. It means, don't—"

Lamar gave him a push. "I don't care what it means. Keep walking."

Gerry had a good idea what was coming next. Outside, Lamar took him to the parking lot to a spot Gerry guessed wasn't being watched by the cameras. He saw Lamar pull back his sleeves.

"Having a bad day, huh?"

Lamar grunted something under his breath and threw a punch at his face. Gerry wasn't good at judo like his old man, but he knew a couple of moves. Ducking the big man's fist, Gerry grabbed his wrist and within seconds spun Lamar around and held his arm firmly behind his back. He hadn't liked being pushed in the stairwell, and gave Lamar's arm a little extra twist. Lamar grimaced and muttered, "Okay, okay."

"We need to get something straight," Gerry said. Holding Lamar's wrist with one hand, he dug out his cell phone and said, "What's the number of your surveillance control room?"

"Why? You want to call them and embarrass me?"

"No. I just want to clear something up."

Lamar gave him the number. Gerry punched it in, stuck the phone up to Lamar's face, and said, "Tell whoever answers the phone to go to your desk and look through your mail for a letter from the Nevada Gaming Control Board."

A woman with a Southern accent answered, and

Lamar told her to go to his office. She came back a few moments later.

"Sorry, Lamar, but I can't find any letter."

"Tell her to try your e-mail," Gerry whispered in his ear.

"Try my e-mail," Lamar said.

"Got it," the woman said a few moments later.

"Read it to me," Lamar said.

"It's from William Higgins, director of the Nevada Gaming Control Board," the woman said. "It says, 'It has been brought to my attention that several casinos in Las Vegas recently sent out a warning regarding an individual named Gerry Valentine. This warning was sent in error. Gerry Valentine is not a casino cheater, nor is he a card counter. He is employed by his father, a highly regarded gaming consultant named Tony Valentine. Please disregard this warning. Thank you.'"

"When was this sent?" Lamar asked.

"Yesterday. This is the guy you just pulled off the floor, isn't it?" the woman said.

Lamar hesitated, clearly at a loss for words. In his ear, Gerry whispered, "Say, 'That's right. Guess I'll have to let him go.'"

Lamar glanced at him over his shoulder. Something resembling a smile crossed his lips. He repeated the words to the woman, then said good-bye. Gerry killed the connection and released Lamar's wrist. The big man turned around, shaking his arm.

"Thanks for doing that," he said.

"Anytime," Gerry replied.

The problem with running a casino off a barge, Lamar explained when they were sitting in his office, was that there were weight restrictions. To allow more passengers to gamble, the owners had cut down on the amount of surveillance equipment, leaving Lamar and his staff at a disadvantage when it came to catching cheaters and card counters.

"We get ripped off a lot," Lamar said, fingering Gerry's business card. "Lots of small stuff, but it adds up. So what's this Grift Sense?"

"It's my father's consulting firm."

"I figured that out," Lamar said. His office was the size of two phone booths. The woman with the drawl came in without knocking, placed two steaming cups of coffee on the table, then left. "What does it mean?"

"It's the ability to spot a hustle or a scam. It's like a sixth sense."

"That's what you and your old man do?"

Gerry had never nailed a cheater in his life, but he saw no reason to tell Lamar that. "That's right. A lot of casinos put us on retainers. We look at video-tapes of suspected cheating, and sometimes even live feeds from the casino floor."

"How'd you learn?"

"My father was an Atlantic City casino cop for twenty-five years."

Lamar clicked his fingers. "That's where I heard

the name. How long you been working for him? Couple of months?"

There was a twinkle in his eye, but Gerry knew a challenge when he heard one. "Look, friend. My father is the best there is. But I'm no slouch. You're getting ripped off? Hire us, and if we don't figure out what's shaking, we'll give you your money back."

Lamar laughed under his breath. "Cut the sales pitch. I'll give you the business if you can answer a simple question for me."

"What's that?"

"I get scammed a lot. But one scam is pissing me off. We're getting ripped off the same two times a month. We don't know how, or where. We just know our take is short about four grand twice a month."

Lamar ripped the tops off a handful of sugar packets and dumped them into his coffee. Gerry sipped his drink while trying to hide the smile on his face. Of all the questions Lamar could have asked him, he had picked one that Gerry actually knew the answer to. Looking his host in the eye, he said, "Based upon what you just told me, I'd say it's an inside job."

Lamar glared at him while mixing his coffee with the eraser end of a pencil. "Give me a break. How can you draw that conclusion based upon what I just told you?"

"You're short the same two times a month?"

"Correct."

"Every month?"

"Yeah, so?"

"Is it right before payday?"

Lamar leaned back in his chair and gave Gerry the same thoughtful look he'd shown out in the parking lot. "You know something? I think I could learn to like you."

CHAPTER 9

Valentine sat in a rocking chair on the screened porch of his new house and stared at the forest that was his backyard. The night was chilly, and he wore his overcoat buttoned to his neck. He'd downed a gallon of Diet Coke during the drive, and didn't think he could fall asleep if his life depended on it.

Stevie Ray Vaughan's music continued to blast out of Ricky Smith's house. Valentine had decided that he liked it; the music had an earthy quality that struck him as real. And he liked the man's singing voice. It was raw and powerful.

A few minutes past midnight, Ricky Smith's stereo stopped playing. Valentine watched the windows in Ricky's house go dark. He tried to imagine what it had been like for Polly to be married to such a clown. His own marriage had lasted more than forty years. The secret had been compromise and more compromise. Ricky sounded like he didn't know the meaning of the word.

The forest came alive with hoots and cries that he never heard down in Florida. Back home, it was mostly frogs and crickets and an occasional dog. The sounds he was hearing now were wilder. He leaned forward in his chair, trying to place them.

Then he heard the footsteps and sat up straight in his chair. They were in the forest and coming toward the house. He decided it was kids returning from the woods and felt himself calm down. It was a perfect place to drink beer.

The backyard was a hundred feet wide. Then the forest began. The footsteps were close, and he imagined the kids were directly behind the first stand of trees. He strained his eyes to see them. It was too dark to make out anything but vague shadows.

"This the house?" one of them asked.

"That's the one," another replied.

"You positive? I don't want to hit the wrong one."

"That's the one. Fucker's in there."

The voices weren't coming out of kids' mouths. They were adults, male, and had hints of Spanish accents. They also spoke like tough guys, each syllable laced with a threat. Valentine started to push himself out of his chair and heard it loudly creak.

"What the hell was that?" a third voice said.

"We've been made," a fourth voice said.

"You think so?"

"Shut up," the first one said.

Valentine felt his heart doing the funny thing it

always did when he got scared out of his wits. His gun was in his suitcase on the other side of the house. He could call the police on his cell phone; only, he hadn't gotten the house's address from Polly. His earlier conversation with Mabel suddenly hit home. *Stop thinking about Ricky jumping out of the burning hotel.* In other words, look at it like any other crime. Only, he hadn't, and now he was screwed.

His other option was to run out the front door. It would buy him some time, and right now, he needed as much of that as he could get. He pushed himself out of his rocker and heard his cell phone ring. It was sitting on the side table, and he stared at the illuminated caller ID. Gerry, calling from Gulfport. He cursed silently.

From the woods came whispering. It was in Spanish, and he tried to pick up a few words that he knew. They were debating what to do. They outnumbered him, but no one wanted to go first. He'd never met a tough guy with an ounce of courage, and these jokers were no different.

He looked around the porch for something to defend himself with in case they rushed the house. In the corner sat a mop in a bucket. He'd found other cleaning utensils around the house and guessed the last cleaning person had just up and left. He went and picked up the mop. It had an adjustable handle that allowed the user to squeeze the water out without having to bend over. He had an idea.

He waited until his cell phone stopped ringing, then took the mop and jerked the handle down the throat of the mop two times. He did it hard. It sounded similar to a shotgun being pumped. He walked to the edge of the screen and stared at the spot in the darkened forest where he believed the four Spanish men stood.

"I hear you sons-a-bitches out there," he called out in his best hillbilly accent. "I'll shoot the first one of yah that steps foot on my property. You hear me?"

The words almost sounded comical; only, he had a feeling that these guys didn't know the difference. The question was, would they call his bluff, or would they run? More whispering came out of the trees. He thought about easing backward off the porch and making his way toward the front door, when he heard the men start to walk away. They'd bought the act, hook, line, and sinker. He smiled to himself. He couldn't wait to tell Mabel about this one.

In the forest he heard a small animal running through the brush. One of the guys said something excitedly in Spanish. His words were followed by the *bang, bang* of a small-caliber firearm. Valentine dropped to the floor.

"Cut that shit out," the first voice said.

One of the men laughed wickedly.

When they were gone, Valentine ducked inside the house and got his gun from his suitcase. It was a Glock pocket rocket. People who purchased them did so with the intent of carrying them around. He needed to start doing that, or go home and enter the shuffleboard league near his house. He ventured outside the front door and got the flashlight from the trunk of his Honda. It was the kind favored by foot cops, and big enough to double as a weapon.

He walked around the house and into the backyard. It was peaceful again, and he walked to the forest with the gun's barrel aimed at the shadows. Entering the darkness, he flicked the flashlight on and saw its yellow beam cut a wide swath in the brush. He found the footpath and walked down it, trying to make as little noise as possible.

He found the dead rabbit in the middle of the path. Its body was still warm, and he examined the entry point of the bullet. It had gone through the back of the neck and was small enough to be a .22. Tough guys didn't carry .22s. Kids did.

He felt the air trapped in his lungs escape. Had they been planning to rob the house? That was the logical explanation, and he decided to go with it. But it didn't mean he wasn't going to be careful. Arming himself was a good start.

The next morning, he awoke at dawn, just like he had every day of his adult life. Splashed water on his face and brushed his teeth, then threw on last night's clothes and went outside.

It was always coldest before dawn and there was frost on the grass. He went into the garage and found a shovel propped against the wall. Going into the forest, he found the rabbit just as he'd left it. He lifted its limp body with the shovel.

He found a shady spot in the backyard and laid the rabbit down. Then he dug a hole a few feet down. The ground was hard and unforgiving, and sweat dotted his brow. The older he'd gotten, the more he'd come to appreciate the sanctity of life, even that of dumb animals. *Stupid damn kids,* he thought.

He laid the rabbit in the hole and covered it with dirt. With the toes of his shoes, he patted the mound down, then found a stick in the forest that resembled a cross. He plunged the stick into the mound, crossed himself, and went back inside the house.

CHAPTER 10

Rising before dawn, Ricky Smith threw on a track suit and headed out the door, his trusty Doberman by his side, the dog enjoying this new habit his master had acquired. His name was Thor, and although he technically belonged to Ricky's ex-wife, Thor had run away from her and back to Ricky so many times that she'd given up trying to make any claims on him. "Keep him!" she'd screamed into the phone the last time they'd spoken. Ricky had hung up, laughing his head off.

His feet quickly found the familiar trail through the woods, the matted leaves glistening from yesterday's rain. Right after he'd come back from Las Vegas he'd started jogging, determined to shed the extra fifty pounds he'd been lugging around since high school. He'd started out slow, huffing and puffing, but after a few days tiny wings had sprung from his heels, allowing him to keep up with Thor's medium-paced trot.

Hank Ridley's woods backed up onto Ricky's two acres, and as Ricky jogged down the path, Ridley's falling-down barn became visible through the trees.

A chemical in the shingles made them glow under the sunlight, and Ricky saw his rotund neighbor coming around the path, a joint palmed in his hand. Hank's dog, a shaggy mutt named Buster, exploded through the trees and stopped dead upon seeing Thor. The two dogs sniffed tails, checking out what the other had for dinner, then started wagging.

"Morning, Hank," Ricky said. Wherever Hank went, an aromatic fog of marijuana followed. He'd never been arrested, nor asked to curb his egregious behavior, and Ricky was one of the few in town who knew why: Hank's family still held the lease on the land on which the police department was built.

"Morning, Ricky," Hank said, exhaling a blue cloud. "How's the rat race?"

Hank did not read the paper or watch TV and, like Roland, knew nothing of Ricky's recent good fortune. It had kept their relationship normal, and Ricky said, "Not so bad. Yourself?"

"Can't complain. Ever read any Walt Whitman?"

"Just *Leaves of Grass* back in junior high."

"Didn't make much of an impression, huh?" The joint dropped from Hank's hand, and he ground it into the wet path. In Hank's world there were people who read poetry and those who didn't. "Didn't know if you'd heard the latest, but we've got a new neighbor."

"Someone rented the Muller place?"

"Yeah. Guy named Tony Valentine. Rumor is, he's a retired cop writing his memoirs."

The wind was blowing easterly, carrying the pungent smell of Hank's breath away. Slippery Rock's grapevine had many drums, and strangers didn't stay that way very long.

"You talk to him?"

"Naw, but your ex has. She rented him the house."

Ricky was getting cold standing still, the sun hanging like an ornament in the crisp blue sky. Talking about Polly always put him in a funk, and he shrugged. Hank snapped his fingers, and Buster exploded out of a bush, all out of breath.

"I'll keep you posted once I find out what he's up to."

"You think he's up to something?" Ricky asked.

"Why the hell else would someone come to Slippery Rock?"

"Thanks, Hank."

Ricky took a long cut home, his legs having grown stiff from standing too long. He ran down a seldom used path, the steep descent made treacherous by the wet leaves. Clumps of mud flew up from his heels, and he found himself surfing down the hill with Thor by his side. At its bottom, he hung a sharp left and got onto a paved road.

A minute later he passed the old Muller place. A beat-up Honda Accord with Florida plates was parked in the drive. It was early May, and from what he'd seen on the Weather Channel, the weather in Florida was letter perfect. Slippery

Rock was anything but perfect, with lots of rain and leftover cold winter air. Hank was right. It was a strange time of year for someone from Florida to be visiting.

Only after he had showered and was drinking coffee at the nook in his kitchen did Ricky give it any more thought. Polly had obviously checked the guy out. She checked out all her potential clients. If she thought Valentine was snooping around, would she have deliberately rented him a house nearby?

Going to his study, he booted up the computer on his desk and got on the Internet. He went to Ask Jeeves, typed in Valentine's name, then hit Search. A split second later, he was staring at a menu of Internet articles that included Valentine's name. The first item immediately caught his eye. The guy had a Web site called Grift Sense.

Ricky went onto the site. Valentine ran a consulting business and helped casinos around the world catch cheaters. The site included articles he'd written for *Casino Times* on the subject and a long list of satisfied clients. Ricky leaned back in his chair. The Mint had sent Valentine to Slippery Rock, convinced Ricky had cheated them.

"Thanks, Polly," he said.

The alarm clock in the kitchen buzzed. He went and turned it off, then fiddled with the radio on the kitchen table until he found WADU. He pumped up the volume as they played a roadhouse boogie of Stevie Ray Vaughan's "Love Struck

Baby," the supercharged twelve-bar shuffles getting Ricky's toe tapping. WADU was public, and therefore at the mercy of those who gave it money. Upon receiving Ricky's promise of a generous donation, the station manager had been more than willing to review a list of his "favorite artists" as well as the "time of day" that Ricky usually tuned in. According to a blurb he'd seen in the paper, the station had put out a call for Stevie Ray's old bootlegs. He could hardly wait to see what they turned up.

Thor came into the kitchen followed by Miss Marples. She, too, had refused his ex's company, tearing up so much furniture that Polly had appeared on his doorstep one day and handed her over, not a word spoken. Miss Marples was old and slept in most mornings, asking to be fed whenever she awakened, and Ricky opened the fridge and got the Friskies Senior dinner that was precut into bite-size pieces. The cat rubbed against his legs and arched its back.

With a soft moan, Thor settled down in the corner. Miss Marples usually left food, which ended up in Thor's stomach. Ricky slid into the nook with his cup of coffee in one hand, the cat food in the other. Putting his cup down, he slid the food onto his ex's former spot, then slapped his hand on the table, indicating it was okay for Miss Marples to come up. With age had come bad hips, and Miss Marples hit the table edge with her belly, her back end dangling in space. Ricky lifted her onto the table, where she promptly knocked over his coffee.

He watched the steaming black liquid sweep toward him. He had nothing to stop it with, and not enough time to get out of the way. Just a split second, really, so he sat very still and watched the coffee split into two distinct streams as it hit a bulge in the table and poured down the floor to either side of him. Not a drop touched his left leg, nor his right. The cat, who had not touched her food, stared at him quizzically.

Lucky me, he thought.

CHAPTER 11

Valentine found instant coffee in the cupboard, boiled water, and fixed himself a mug. It tasted horrible, but that was okay. Not every cup was going to be perfect.

He sipped his drink while thinking about Lucy Price. He'd met her by accident while doing a job in Las Vegas. She was a degenerate gambler and not the kind of person he normally gravitated to. Only, Lucy had ignited a spark in him; an emotion he'd thought long-dead had flickered to life. So he'd given her some money and tried to help her.

She'd taken the money and gone on a gambling bender. First she was up—at one point, her winnings had totaled more than a hundred fifty thousand dollars—then down, then up again. Feeling invincible, she went to Bellagio and blew it all on the hundred-dollar slot machines. The casino's staff treated her like a princess and showered her with attention until her money ran out. Then, they turned a cold shoulder.

Devastated, Lucy got her car from the valet and drove away. Five blocks from the casino, she jumped a concrete median on Las Vegas Boulevard and broadsided a rental car filled with British tourists. One died.

Lucy was arrested and charged with vehicular homicide. Her trial was scheduled to begin in a few days. She was facing hard time and was terrified of going to prison.

Valentine put his empty mug into the sink and stared out the window at the forest behind the house. Giving Lucy money had been a terrible mistake. He'd set into motion a series of events that could not be fixed. It was a nightmare he couldn't wash from his mind.

At precisely eight o'clock, he powered up his cell phone. He hated his cell phone almost as much as he hated screaming brats on airplanes. But he had to use one to stay in business. To compromise, he turned his phone on only at certain times of the day. So far, it seemed to be working out okay.

He had a message in voice mail. It was Gerry, the prodigal son. He hoped Gerry's trip to Gulfport was going okay, and that he hadn't gone and done something stupid. His son had been doing stupid things since early adolescence. Gerry believed there was such a thing as a fast buck, and two months ago, that belief had nearly cost him his life. Gerry swore he'd learned his lesson, but Valentine had a feeling that only time would truly tell.

"Hey, Pop, guess what?" his son's voice rang out.

"I think I got us a new client. It's a floating casino in Gulfport called the Dixie Magic. I met the head of security last night. I sort of went out on a limb and said I'd help him nail some employees who are stealing from him. Problem is, I'm not sure what I'm looking for."

Valentine swore into the phone. Didn't Gerry know not to go around bullshitting people like that? The casino business was small. If Gerry got caught with his pants down, every casino manager from Atlantic City to Reno would hear about it.

"So here's the deal, Pop. The money *isn't* being stolen from either the hard-count or soft-count rooms. Lamar, the head of security, has cased them both. So it has to be coming off the tables. They only have one craps table and one roulette wheel, but more than sixty blackjack tables. My guess is, it's coming off a blackjack table."

"Brilliant," Valentine said.

"The shuffling procedures here are pretty rigid, and the players can't touch their cards, so the cards probably aren't being manipulated. That leaves an employee either stealing chips from the tray, or stealing chips from other players. That's as far as I've gotten. So I was wondering . . . would you mind calling me and giving me some hints of what to look for? I'd really appreciate it, and so would Lamar."

Valentine took the cell phone away from his ear and stared at it. What about Tex Snyder? Had Gerry bothered to locate him yet? Wasn't that why

96

he'd sent Gerry to Gulfport? He angrily dialed his son's cell number.

"Hello . . ."

"Get out of bed," Valentine said.

"Pop, is that you?"

"No, it's an impersonator. Rise and shine."

"It's an hour earlier here," his son protested. "It's still dark outside."

Valentine told himself to calm down. His son had gotten a new client. That was a good thing, so why was he barking at him like a junkyard dog? Because he'd been pissed off since Lucy Price had entered his thoughts, and needed to vent his anger on someone before he popped a blood vessel and had a stroke.

"Sorry," he heard himself say.

"No, that's okay," Gerry replied, sounding more awake. "I need to get up and call Yolanda. Thanks for calling me back."

"You're welcome. You said in your message that the Dixie Magic is losing money to insiders. Based upon what you told me, I have a couple of theories of what's going on. Get something to write with. I'll tell you everything you need to know to help your friend Lamar."

"Great. Did I tell you I think he wants to hire us?"

"Yeah," Valentine said. Then added, "Good going."

Valentine had decided that the Dixie Magic was getting ripped off by chip scams. They were practically undetectable and a favorite among employees looking for quick money. So he spent twenty minutes explaining to his son how they worked.

Before casinos had surveillance cameras in the ceiling, dealers who wanted to steal chips simply handed off a stack to an accomplice while paying off a winning bet. So long as the boss wasn't looking, the theft was invisible.

Then, eye-in-the-sky cameras had come along. Part of surveillance's job was to watch dealers paying off customers. If an overpayment or "dumping" was detected, the dealer was terminated on the spot and often prosecuted.

But some cheating dealers had gotten clever and devised techniques to steal chips while fooling the cameras. Valentine had seen many during his years policing Atlantic City's casinos. They were like magic tricks. They happened in front of your nose; only, you couldn't see them, unless you knew what to look for.

He spoke in a slow, relaxed tone to his son, pausing occasionally when he thought Gerry was getting behind. His son was smart; he'd just never applied himself. Someday, Gerry would start using the brains God gave him, and the world would be a better place.

"That pretty much covers it," Valentine said. He heard the unmistakable clicking of poker chips on the line. "What are you doing? Practicing?"

"Got a stack of ten green chips right here," Gerry

said proudly. "It's amazing how deceptive these scams are."

Green chips were worth twenty-five bucks apiece. His son didn't have two nickels to rub together, and was traveling on money his father had given him.

"What are you doing with those chips?" Valentine said.

"Pop, it's not what you think."

"You're supposed to be hunting down Tex Snyder, remember? Come on, Gerry, get with the program."

The line grew silent.

"That woman out in Vegas still calling you?"

Valentine rubbed his face with his hand. "Yeah. Is it that obvious?"

"She's got you climbing up the walls," his son said. "She's a stalker, Pop. You need to get your cell number changed. Maybe she'll get the hint and leave you alone."

The front door bell rang. It was a cheap sound, as if someone had replaced the bell with a joy buzzer. He told his son good-bye and got off the line.

Valentine recognized Ricky Smith the moment he opened the front door. Ricky's picture had been splashed across every TV news show in the country: a sloppy, boyish grin offset by eyes always looking somewhere else. He was a self-professed geek who liked to eat junk food and as Valentine stepped onto the front stoop, Ricky stuck out a big paw of a hand and said, "Welcome to the neighborhood. My name's Richard Smith, but everyone calls me Ricky. I live two houses away."

"The guy with the loud music," Valentine said.

Ricky flashed a sheepish smile. "Yeah. Hope it didn't keep you up."

"Only half the night. You like the blues?"

"I like Stevie Ray Vaughan," Ricky confessed. "Lucky for me, Stevie Ray recorded just about everything—rock, blues, rockabilly, surfer music, acoustic—so it never gets tiring."

"Except for your neighbors," Valentine said.

Ricky let out a laugh that caused his whole body to shake. On the surveillance tape from the Mint, he had acted like a zombie, and no emotion had registered on his face as he'd beaten the casino silly. In real life he was playful and animated, with the face of a kid who's just gotten caught stealing a cookie out of a jar.

"So, listen," Ricky said, "I wanted to invite you to the May Day Annual Fair. It's being held down at the local high school. There's lots of good food, and exhibits from the school, and it's a great way to meet your neighbors."

"Right now?"

"Yeah. It goes on all day. I'd be happy to drive you."

Valentine considered the offer. He needed to meet people in town, and establish who he was, and put them at ease when he came around later and started poking his nose where it didn't belong. Only, something was wrong with Ricky's offer. Guys didn't drive the welcome wagons in most neighborhoods. Women did. Ricky was up to something. Valentine saw him look at his watch.

"They're having a drawing at the fair at eleven," Ricky explained. "You can't claim the grand prize if you're not there."

"What is it?"

"An all-expenses-paid trip to Hawaii."

"Think you're going to win?"

Ricky took out his wallet and removed a brown ticket with five numbers printed on it. "I bought this ticket before I went out to Las Vegas and won a million bucks. I figure if I'm going to win that trip, now's the time."

Valentine looked at the numbers on the ticket, then into Ricky's pale blue eyes. Ricky made it sound like a given. Valentine realized his neighbor was challenging him. That was why he'd come to the house and rang the bell. He'd found out who Valentine was and why he was visiting Slippery Rock. He wanted Valentine to see it himself and decide.

"Let me get my jacket," Valentine said.

CHAPTER 12

Slippery Rock High School was a rambling one-story structure nestled behind a stand of poplars and pines. A colorful banner announced that today was the May Day Annual Fair, Come One, Come All. The parking lot was nearly full, and as Ricky parked his Lexus in the last available space, he explained how different buildings had been added on as local townspeople had passed away and willed their money to their favorite departments.

"It's sort of a tradition," he said, killing the engine.

For a long moment they sat silently. In the nearby woods, a deer with two fawns lifted its head to stare at them. Its mouth was full of leaves, and it munched away, convinced they posed no threat.

"Which department are you going to will yours to?" Valentine asked.

"The art department. It was the only class I ever really liked. I wanted to be a commercial artist, but my parents drummed it into my head that it was a bad career choice." He looked at his watch, then popped open his door. "Better hurry. The drawing is in five minutes. Don't want to miss winning the big prize."

As Valentine followed him across the lot, he remembered Mabel's remark about Ricky running from one game to another at the Mint, like he was on some kind of timetable. It had sounded suspicious as hell; only, what if he really was on some kind of lucky streak? Wouldn't there be some type of urgency behind it?

Going inside, they walked down a long hallway scuffed by years of running kids and into a gymnasium with a raised stage at one end of the room. It was filled with hundreds of people huddled around exhibit tables that had been pushed against the walls. On the other end of the room, volunteers sold hot dogs and hamburgers at the cafeteria's food stations, with all the proceeds benefitting the school. Ricky tapped the face of his watch.

"Made it with a minute to spare. You want something to eat?"

"A drink would be fine," Valentine said, following him over to the food stations. A stern-faced woman wearing a hairnet smiled at Ricky as they approached. Without having to be told, she took an Orange Crush soda from a chest and said, "What will your friend have?"

"Diet Coke," Ricky said.

Valentine felt his face burn and watched the woman take out a sixteen-ounce bottle of his favorite drink and unscrew it with a twist. How had Ricky found that out? He'd been in the news-papers a lot the month before; probably one of them had mentioned it after they'd run out of interesting things to say. Ricky had really done his homework.

"Thanks," Valentine said to the woman.

The sound of someone tapping a finger on a microphone shushed the room, and everyone turned to face the stage. In its center stood a guy in his mid-thirties wearing a carnival barker's outfit: porkpie hat, paisley bow tie, and a red sports jacket that looked a size too small for his lean, angular body. He spoke with a loose smile on his lips.

"Good morning, folks, my name's Vernon Hudsinger," the barker said.

"We know what your name is," someone in the crowd called out.

"I bet you do! It's my privilege to officially welcome you to the annual Slippery Rock May Day Fair. Sorry for the cloudy day, especially after this rotten winter. Which is why the grand prize of this year's festival drawing is most appropriate. A week's paid vacation at the fabulous Mauna Kai resort on the beautiful island of Oahu. Let's give a big Slippery Rock thank-you for the folks at Tripp Travel for donating this fabulous prize."

Half the people in the cafeteria clapped their hands. The other half stomped their feet. The sound reminded Valentine of a hockey game. It lasted for about three seconds, and then everyone stopped on cue. Then there was a hush and everyone started laughing.

"What did I miss?" Valentine said.

"It's an old tradition," Ricky said.

"Now," the barker continued, "let's get this show on the road. I'm sure all of you know how this works. Our own town librarian, Mary Alice Stoker, is going to come out with a paper bag filled with Ping-Pong balls. I'm going to roll up my sleeve, and stick my hand down inside that bag, and pull out five Ping-Pong balls. Each Ping-Pong ball has a number printed on it. If the five numbers I pull out match the five numbers on your ticket—and remember, they can be in any order—you win the grand prize. If no one hits five, the person who has four numbers wins, or three, or two, or I just do it over. Although I don't think that's ever happened before." He stepped back, and through the backdrop said, "Hey, Ms. Stoker, we ever have a do-over before?"

"Not that I can recall," a voice behind the stage called out.

"So there you go," the barker said. Walking to center stage, he pulled off his jacket as Mary Alice Stoker made her appearance to a smattering of applause. The librarian was white-haired, smartly dressed in a floor-length dress, and had perfect posture. Holding a brown paper bag between her hands, she was the picture of small-town grace.

Vernon dropped his jacket on a nearby chair,

then rolled back his sleeve. For effect he wiggled his fingers, and a bunch of people in the crowd laughed. "And now, ladies and gentlemen," he said, "let me introduce my helpers. Come on out, kids."

Five kids who couldn't have been more then ten came trotting out and got a huge round of applause. The boys wore ties and jackets, the girls Sunday dresses, their hair done up in bows. Standing in line, they smiled nervously at the audience as video cameras whirred.

"Ready, kids?" Vernon said. "Okay, here's the first number."

Sticking his hand into the bag, Vernon shut his eyes and swished his hand around for a moment, then pulled a Ping-Pong ball out and handed it to his first helper. The little boy stared at the Ping-Pong ball.

"Tell them the number," Vernon whispered to him.

"It's a number six," the boy said loudly.

The kid's parents burst into applause. Ricky, who'd been swigging his soda and laughing at everything Vernon had said, pulled his ticket from his pocket and shoved it a foot away from Valentine's face.

"One down, four to go," he said.

Valentine stared at the six in the center of the five numbers. He looked back at Vernon and saw him pull a second Ping-Pong ball from the bag. Valentine's eyes were still pretty good when it came to distances, and he saw the number on the Ping-Pong ball clearly. It was a twelve. Valentine stared at the twelve on Ricky's ticket.

"I'm so hot I'm steaming," Ricky said.

The next number was twenty-three. It was also on Ricky's ticket. By the time the fourth and fifth numbers were drawn, Valentine had already accepted that Ricky was going to win. It was obvious he and his friend had rigged the game, and the locals were too naive to realize it.

"You should be ashamed of yourself," Valentine said when Ricky raised his hand to acknowledge he had won the jackpot.

Ricky's face turned bright red. He lowered his arm stiffly, the winning ticket clutched between his fingers.

"Are you accusing me of cheating?" he said loudly, drawing stares.

"Tone it down."

"Are you?"

"I sure am," Valentine said through clenched teeth. "I wasn't born yesterday."

"No, you were born five hundred years ago," Ricky shouted at him. "The people in Las Vegas sent you, because they don't believe I won my money legitimately. They think I'm a cheater. They don't believe in luck. And when someone comes along who is lucky, they try to destroy him."

People were staring and acting uncomfortable. Ricky pointed at the stage. "We've been holding that drawing since before I was born. No one cheats. You think there's something smelly going on, come up and prove it."

The crowd parted, and Ricky marched up to the stage. Valentine felt angry stares rain down as he followed him. They climbed the stage together, and Ricky addressed the five little kids. One at a time, they came over and handed Valentine the Ping-Pong balls they were holding.

"Here you go, mister," the last little kid said.

Valentine examined the five balls. They appeared normal. He went over to the librarian and peered down inside the bag. Easily a hundred Ping-Pong balls were inside of it, and he pulled out a handful and stared at the numbers printed on them. Each number was different. He compared them to the five winning balls in his hands. They were the same size and had the same smooth texture, ruling out Vernon somehow being able to pull them out by touch from the bag. That was how the scam *had* to be done; only, no evidence supported it. The five winning balls were exactly the same as the others. He glanced at the librarian, wanting to ask her a question, and saw her stare right through him. He felt a catch in his throat. She was blind.

"So, what do you say?" Ricky asked, standing next to the barker on the other side of the stage. "Is the game clean, Mr. Valentine?"

"Yes," Valentine said.

"Could you say that a little louder? I don't think everyone could hear you."

Valentine shifted his gaze to the audience. He was

ready to swallow his pride and tell the hometown crowd that he'd spoken out of turn and that the game wasn't rigged. But then his eyes fell on the camera crew standing in the front. The crew consisted of a cameraman, a soundman, and a breathless female reporter with her hair tied in a bun. He hadn't seen them from the back, and saw the soundman point a large mike in his direction.

Valentine exited stage left and within seconds was behind the safety of a curtain. He heard Ricky exhort the crowd into another raucous Slippery Rock cheer. They clapped and stomped their feet, mocking Valentine all the way to the parking lot, where he stood in the cold, wondering how he was going to get back home.

CHAPTER 13

L amar had rented the basement of a restaurant for Gerry's meeting with the Dixie Magic's surveillance team. The team consisted of twenty-one employees, who split three eight-hour shifts between them. The casino had shut down for an hour, to allow the TV crew filming the poker tournament to do a number of shots and interviews inside the casino. Heavily armed security guards followed the crew's every move, giving Lamar the freedom to pull his staff for a quick off-site meeting.

"Okay, listen up," Lamar said, standing at the front of the room. "As you all know, the casino is getting ripped off. The gentleman standing to my left is Gerry Valentine, a partner in the firm Grift Sense, whose specialty is catching casino cheaters. Gerry has come to the conclusion that the stealing is taking place at the tables in the form of chip scams. He's going to give us a demonstration of this unusual art, and then take questions."

Lamar relinquished the floor, and Gerry stepped up to a table in the room's center. On it was a piece of green felt and a tray of chips similar to those used by dealers inside the casino. As he stepped up to the tray, he glanced at the faces in the crowd. Two women, the rest men, all in their thirties, all giving him hard looks, like they resented him waltzing in and telling them how dumb they were. His father had warned him about this. Casino surveillance people were territorial, just like cops. *Be humble*, his father had said.

He had inherited two things from his father. The first were his dark Italian looks, which he hadn't liked as a kid but liked as he'd grown older. The second was his memory, which was close to photographic. Working off the script his father had given him, he said, "Good morning. Thanks for having me. There's an old expression: Everything that's old is new again. Chip scams have been around a long time. But they get the money, and that's all cheaters care about."

A man in the back row smothered a yawn. *A joke*, Gerry thought. He should have gone against his father's advice and opened with a joke.

"There are three basic chip scams. Each involves the dealer in cahoots with a player. I'm sure you all know what that means."

Now he was getting mean looks. Of course they knew what *cahoots* meant.

"I should also explain something. These scams are difficult to detect using surveillance cameras. Bosses on the floor *can* see them, but they're usually looking the other way when they happen. Know why?"

His audience had turned to stone. Out of the corner of his eye, he saw Lamar staring at him like he'd grown two heads.

"The reason is because the dealer's accomplice uses a prearranged set of signals to tell the dealer if the boss is watching the table or if he isn't. Cheaters call this *giving the office*. The accomplice uses two signals: *stop* and *go*. Smart teams change signals every hour, making it impossible to read them."

Gerry kept his eyes moving as he spoke. He'd read in an airline magazine that this was the best way to address a crowd. He saw Lamar look at his watch, and felt sweat start to trickle down his spine. *Dump the script,* he thought.

Taking four green twenty-five-dollar chips from the tray, he placed them into his left hand. He crumbled his fingers and showed the chips were gone. He'd been heavy into magic as a kid, and saw every face in the room light up. He showed them the four chips finger-palmed in his right hand. Then he placed them in a stack on the felt.

"Let's pretend this is my accomplice's bet. He wins his hand, and I move to pay him off. But before I pay him off, I size his bet."

Gerry scattered the four chips on the felt. Only, now there were five. He pointed at the fifth chip. "Any of you see where that came from?"

"Your sleeve?" someone called out.

"No. I palmed it out of the rack," Gerry said.

112

"Then I added it to my accomplice's bet. This is called *sizing in high.* I pay the player off, and we steal fifty dollars of the house's money. This is hard to detect because every action looks normal."

He demonstrated the scam two more times. Once slow, and once at regular speed.

"Show us another," a black guy in the back of the room said.

"Sure," Gerry said, giving him a smile. The black guy didn't smile back. He had a hard face and wore a navy blazer with faded elbows. The jacket was hanging partially open, exposing the shoulder harness and gun strapped beneath his armpit. Gerry swallowed hard. Casino employees weren't allowed to pack guns unless they were guards. Maybe this guy had some kind of special permit.

Gerry picked up four green chips and split them into two piles. He placed them on the felt. "Another common scam is to use a losing bet to cap a winning bet. The dealer picks up the losing bet and pretends to put it in the tray. In fact, he clips the chips between his fingers and immediately adds them to the winning bet." He turned his palm over, showing the clipped chips. "If the bets are small, this is hard to detect."

The black guy said, "Do it again."

Gerry obliged him. This time, the man nodded approvingly. Gerry snuck a glance at his watch. Fifteen minutes had passed. It felt like an hour.

"The third common chip scam occurs when the accomplice asks for change," he said. "It's common for players to throw high-valued chips down and ask for them to be changed into chips of lower value. The dealer picks up the chips and adds chips palmed in his hand. He always adds enough chips to make the stack even. That way, he can break it into two even piles, which looks nice for the camera."

Gerry placed six green chips on the felt, then demonstrated the move, adding two additional green chips in the act of cutting the stack into two piles. From the front, it looked like a magic trick, the chips instantly growing before everyone's eyes, and he saw the unfriendly looks leave their faces.

"Those are the three basic chip scams," he said. "There are countless variations, but all rely on these same elements. Distraction, signals between the accomplice and the dealer, and a boss on the floor looking the other way. Any questions?"

A dozen hands went up. Lamar pointed at one of the females in the group. She was pretty, had flaming red hair, and looked French. Gerry assumed she was from Louisiana, and saw her flash a sly Southern smile.

"Yes, Isabelle," Lamar said.

"How do we catch these sons of bitches?" she asked.

Isabelle leaned forward in her chair. So did everyone else in the room. Gerry thought back to the phone conversation with his father. His old man had a theory about what was happening at the Dixie Magic, and Gerry decided it was time to return to the script.

"Lamar said you're losing four grand, twice a month," Gerry said. "Most chip teams steal four hundred a session. That's about ten plays. Any more would draw heat.

"Divide four hundred into four thousand, and that gives us ten teams. That's a lot. My guess is, they're all working together. They may even have a member who serves as the 'turn.'"

"What's that?" Isabelle asked.

"The turn's job is to turn the floor boss's attention away from the action. It usually comes in the form of a question. Turns are usually attractive females or older people with hearing problems."

"Why hearing problems?"

"Because it forces the floor boss to repeat everything he says."

His father had promised Gerry that at some point in his presentation, he would win the group over. Gerry had taken his words as fatherly encouragement and was pleasantly surprised when he saw everyone start smiling and nodding.

"The next question is, how do you identify the team?" he went on. "You have sixty blackjack dealers on every shift, and you have three shifts. Which ten dealers are dirty?" He paused, and let his eyes glance across their faces. "What you look for is some other connection. Perhaps they all live in the same apartment complex. Or they worked together before, or served in the military. There *has* to be a link."

"Why is that?" Lamar asked.

"Because the hardest part of working in a team is trusting your partners. That trust has to be there from the start. Nearly all cheating teams have some type of shared past."

A dozen more hands shot up. Gerry realized he had run out of things to say and glanced at Lamar. As if reading his thoughts, the head of surveillance came up beside him and placed his hand on Gerry's shoulder.

"I think this was very illuminating and has given us a lot to work with in catching these folks. What do you say we show Gerry our appreciation?"

And with that, his audience burst into long and loud applause.

Lamar drove Gerry back to the Holiday Inn. Lamar had held up his end of the bargain and arranged through the casino for Gerry to meet Tex "All In" Snyder, who was also staying at the hotel. Pulling up to the front entrance, Lamar said, "Well, here's where we part ways. I appreciate you taking the time to do this. I hope your meeting is worth it."

Gerry started to get out of the car. He had expected Lamar to mention hiring his father's firm and was disappointed that he hadn't. Then he remembered the guy at the meeting who was packing a gun. He got back in, looked Lamar straight in the eye.

"You're a cop, aren't you?"

Lamar stuck his tongue in his cheek. "Why do you say that?"

"Because I just spoke to a roomful of cops."

"How do you know that?"

"Because there wasn't a fat one in the bunch. And one of them was packing heat. They're working for you, aren't they?"

"Maybe," Lamar said. "You see a lot."

Gerry looked through the windshield at an orange tour bus disgorging a gang of elderly passengers. He'd seen them leaving the hotel for the casino, all hearty and full of pep. Now, they looked tired and beat up. *Not a winner in the bunch,* he thought.

"You have a real problem, don't you?" he said.

"Yes," Lamar said.

"How many games are getting ripped off?"

Lamar took a deep breath, as if considering whether or not he should talk about it.

"From what we can tell, all of them," he said quietly.

"Blatant stealing like what I described?"

Lamar nodded. The last of the tour bus junkies walked past the car. A white-haired woman was all smiles and chattering up a storm. None of her friends were listening to her. She must have won a jackpot, Gerry guessed. He started to get out of the car again, then glanced at Lamar a final time. "Let me know if we can help."

"I'll do that," Lamar said. "Good luck with Tex."

"Am I going to need it?"

CHAPTER 14

Valentine got a man in the parking lot of Slippery Rock High to give him a lift back to his rented house. At least one person in town hadn't been there for Ricky's shining moment. Then he took his Honda into town and bought a ham-and-Swiss sandwich at a deli. It was a real deli, and not located inside the bowels of a supermarket like the delis back home in Florida. The sandwich filling was easily an inch thick, what they used to call a Dagwood. He ate the sandwich at the kitchen table while drinking a homemade lemonade he'd also bought at the deli. It was a little tart and had the kind of taste you could never get out of a bottle. He drank it slowly, thinking about the public embarrassment he'd endured that morning. Ricky had played him like a fiddle.

He went outside onto the screened-in porch. The furniture was covered in plastic, and he peeled a protective sheet off a love seat and made himself comfortable. The porch was in the shade and very cold, and he felt his head clear. His thoughts went back to Ricky holding the winning ticket in front of his face an hour earlier. Why had Ricky done that? He thought about it for several minutes before the answer came to him. Because Ricky didn't want him to think he had somehow printed the ticket after the fact. Ricky had wanted to establish the numbers. Which meant the barker had somehow manipulated the selection of the five Ping-Pong balls. There was no other logical explanation.

He heard a loud banging coming from inside the house, followed by a man's voice. He went inside and walked through the house to the front door. The voice sounded familiar, and he jerked the door open and saw Ricky jump back.

"Hey, don't hit me," he said, flashing his court-jester grin.

"Should I?"

He stood on the steps, still smiling. "You were pretty pissed when you left the school."

"You set me up."

"Me?" Ricky put his hand over his heart. "Scout's honor, I did no such thing. You just don't want to believe what you saw is real. You're a skeptic."

"So why the house call? You want to rub it in?"

"No, no," his visitor said. "I came to make peace. I don't want you thinking I'm some kind of crook. I know that's what you deal with every day; I went on your Web site. But I'm not a crook. Never broke a law a day in my life. I want to convince you of that."

"There's only one problem," Valentine said.

"What's that?"

120

"You *are* a crook."

Stepping onto the stoop, Valentine jabbed his forefinger hard into Ricky's chest. "Tell me something. When you were on your streak at the Mint, why didn't you try the slot machines? They have a progressive jackpot worth ten million. Why didn't you take a shot at that?" He could see the gears grinding inside Ricky's head. "I'll tell you why. Because you couldn't rig a slot machine. Practically nobody can. So you avoided them."

"Slots are for idiots, that's why I didn't play them," Ricky said, slapping Valentine's hand away. He was blushing and acted like his feelings had been hurt. He stuck his hands into his pockets. "You have a real serious anger issue, you know that?"

"So I've heard. Now what do you want?"

"Another chance."

"To do what?"

"Convince you that this isn't a scam, that I really am lucky."

"You going to make me look like a fool again?"

"No," Ricky said.

Valentine burned a hole into Ricky's face with his eyes.

"That's a promise," Ricky added.

"You just buy this?" Valentine asked, sitting in the passenger seat of Ricky's Lexus a few minutes later. The car had more amenities than most third-world countries, and he counted twenty-six different buttons on the dashboard and his door.

"I bought it with the money I don't have," Ricky said with a derisive laugh.

"You mean the Mint's money?"

"That's right. I've got an unlimited line of credit everywhere I go in town. It's like being king for a day, every day of the week."

They began to descend a steep hill, and Valentine listened but could not hear the car's gears shift as they reduced speed. It was a hell of a car, and it reminded him that he was going to need new wheels someday soon. He'd been putting off thinking about it, not wanting to jinx the car he had. So far, the philosophy was working just fine.

"I want to explain something about my lucky streak," Ricky said when they reached the bottom of the hill and the road flattened out. "If I'm drawn to something, I go to it. If not, I don't. I can't just sit down at a slot machine and expect to win."

"Unless you're drawn to it," Valentine said.

"That's right."

"Let me guess. A little voice tells you."

Ricky bit the words about to escape his lips. He was trying not to be a jerk, and it was killing him. Valentine, on the other hand, could be a jerk whenever he wanted to, and said, "There was one flaw to the Ping-Pong scam this morning. Want me to tell you what it was?"

Ricky flashed a village-idiot grin. "Oh, pray tell, do."

"There were a hundred Ping-Pong balls with numbers in that bag. What do you think the odds of you getting all five on your ticket were?"

"I have no idea," Ricky said, staring at the road.

"More than seventy-five million to one. Which is the same as walking out of your house, and being struck by lightning twice. Get it?"

"No. What's your point?"

"My point is, if you got four out of five, I could buy that. But not five out of five. There's a name for what you did. It's called the too-perfect ending. It screams fix. You and your barker friend and whoever else is involved messed up."

Ricky blew his cheeks out. They were on a highway, driving away from town, and Valentine glanced at the dashboard and realized they were doing eighty. It didn't feel that way, the car insulated from everything on the outside except the fleeting scenery.

"And based on that, you're calling me a cheater."

Valentine hid the smile forming at his lips. It was the second time that Ricky had used that word. He leaned back in his seat and didn't respond. After a minute he saw Ricky point at a green highway sign. They were crossing into South Carolina.

"Our exit is a few miles ahead. South Carolina legalized betting on horses last year. I'm going to pick some winners." He smiled and added, "Don't worry. For some reason, I'm never one hundred percent when it come to the ponies. I guess even luck has its problems with stupid beasts."

The Off Track Betting parlor was a few miles across the state line. From the distance, it resembled a black outhouse with tinted windows. Valentine's father had frequented OTBs back in New Jersey, and he could still remember the night his old man had lost his paycheck before his mother could get her hands on it. She had cried for hours.

He followed Ricky inside the building. The parlor was packed with unshaven, chain-smoking men staring at a wall of four-color TVs showing racetracks around the country. Ricky waved at the men, and got dull looks in return.

"Guess you didn't pick any winners for them, huh?" Valentine asked.

"You think they'd listen?" he said, wiping his nose on the sleeve of his coat.

"Probably not," Valentine admitted.

"Probably not is right. I could pick winners all day, and they wouldn't notice."

Valentine followed him to the far end of the room. Three skinny, sallow-faced men sat behind barred windows and took bets. Valentine wasn't sure who was worse-looking—the people who frequented OTBs, or the people who worked in them.

"You know why they wouldn't notice?" Ricky

said, peeling off his jacket. "Because they all have a system or a premonition or a hunch that tells them how to bet. They think luck is going to wave a magic wand over them, and they're going to get rich."

Throwing the jacket over his arm, he approached the betting window. The teller pushed a racing slip through the bars, and Ricky picked up a pencil while staring at the names of the horses. In a matter of seconds he circled the names of three horses for a race at Belmont Park in New York and pushed the slip back through the bars. From his pants pocket he extracted three crisp hundred-dollar bills. He shoved them through the bars into the teller's hands.

"Those three horses to show," Ricky said.

Valentine watched the teller places the three bets. To show meant that Ricky would win money if the horse came in first, second, or third. It was a safe bet, except the three horses Ricky had picked were long shots. The odds were heavily against him winning any money at all.

They crossed the room to the TV sets to watch the race. The room was a smoker's paradise, and Valentine found himself struggling not to grab a pack out of the nearest guy's hand.

"You a punter?" Ricky asked.

It was an English expression for a gambler, and Valentine shook his head. "My father was. He lost all our money."

"And the son was forever cured," Ricky said. He

pointed at a TV set in the center of the wall and said, "That's us."

Valentine stared at the set. Belmont Park near Queens, New York, was one of the most respected thoroughbred tracks in the world. He remembered once hearing about a race that was fixed by a jockey at Belmont. Somehow, the track stewards had found out the moment the race was about to start. Instead of letting the horses run, they'd shut off the power to the starting gate and offered refunds to everyone who'd placed a bet. Ricky Smith might somehow rig a casino game or a high-school lottery, but he wasn't capable of rigging a race out of Belmont. No one was.

The race was a mile and a half long. There were nine horses, a crowded field. Valentine had memorized the numbers of the horses Ricky had picked. As they came out of the gate, all three horses started strong. Ricky broke out in a crazy dance, drawing the ire of his fellow bettors.

"Sorry, guys," he said. "Just working my mojo."

At the mile marker, Ricky's horses were lined up in a row and fighting for the lead. In fourth place was the favorite, a horse named Four Leaf Clover. The jockey had run a poor race and allowed himself to get boxed in. His horse had the speed; he just couldn't properly use it.

A cry went up among the other bettors. As Four Leaf Clover faded from the picture and Ricky's three picks crossed the finish line, they tore up their tickets and stomped their feet. Ricky was oblivious to their pain and started doing a faithful rendition of the twist. Valentine saw a bettor ball his hand into a fist, and instinctively stepped between him and Ricky.

"I wouldn't do that if I were you," Valentine said.

"Your friend's a flaming jerk," the man growled.

"I'm not arguing with you there," Valentine said.

Ricky had shut his eyes and was rolling his head like Stevie Wonder. He was making fun of them, and the men quickly surrounded them. They had wolflike looks on their faces, as if they were planning to tear Ricky up and devour him.

"Cut it out," Valentine told him.

Ricky's eyes snapped open. Seeing the situation he had created, he stuck his leg out and gyrated like Elvis Presley.

A door banged open on the far side of the room. The teller who'd taken Ricky's bet stuck his head out. "Knock it off!" he exclaimed.

Ricky kept doing his crazy dance. The teller marched across the room and shoved Ricky's winnings into his hand. Then he pointed at the door.

"Get the hell out of here."

Ricky was still gyrating as Valentine dragged him out the door.

CHAPTER 15

Gerry stopped at the Holiday Inn's front doors. Looking over his shoulder, he saw Lamar give a short nod. He nodded back and watched Lamar drive away, then went inside.

The lobby floors glistened from a recent mopping. If there was one thing he liked about the south, it was how clean people kept things. The bank of elevators was next to the reception area. As he started to push the call button, an elevator's doors opened.

A beautiful young woman came out and swept past him. She wore tight black pants and a clinging red blouse. Her gaze met his, and she flashed a coy smile. She was a few eyelashes short from being a supermodel, and Gerry watched her cross the shiny lobby in her stiletto heels, pausing at the glass doors to steal a glance over her shoulder. The look was just long enough to be an invitation.

He got in the elevator and pushed a button for the top floor. As the doors closed, he turned and saw the woman still looking his way. Before Yolanda, he would have stopped to talk with her.

Now that he was married with a kid, that talk would take on a different meaning. It would be like chatting with the devil, and he didn't need any of that in his life right now.

Tex "All In" Snyder was staying in a suite. The door was ajar, and Gerry peeked inside. A maid's cart sat in the center of the living room. The place looked like a crazy New Year's Eve party had just taken place, with stuff hanging from the walls and light shades tilted to one side. He spotted Tex sitting on a couch, talking on a cell phone. His trademark black ten-gallon Stetson sat in his lap. Looking up, he quizzed Gerry with a frown.

"Who're you?" he asked.

"Lamar's friend," Gerry replied.

"Who's Lamar?"

"Head of security at the Dixie Magic."

"Oh, right." Into the phone he said, "Well, I'm sorry I pissed you off, lady, but that's life." Hanging up, he barked in Spanish at the chambermaid, and she stopped her cleaning and left the room, shutting the door behind her. Tex pointed at a chair directly across from the couch. "How about a little liquid libation?"

Gerry waved off the invitation and took the seat. Tex smoothed out his thinning hair with his fingers, then stuck his hat on like he was about to be photographed. He was in his late sixties, with a face as rough as rawhide and gray eyes that could pierce steel. Lowering his voice, he said, "Know what the hard part about being a celebrity is?"

"No."

"Watching your mouth. That lady on the phone, she's the mayor of the town I was born in. A week ago, a newspaper reporter asked me if there was anything unusual about the place. I said that the most unusual thing was that the population never changed. Every time a girl got pregnant, some guy always left town."

Tex slapped his knees and guffawed. Gerry started to laugh, then saw Tex's face turn dead serious.

"The mayor caught wind of it, and now she's threatening to drag my name through the mud if I don't apologize. Guess I eventually will. Then again, maybe not." Tex rose from the couch and pulled an ice-cold beer out of a bucket sitting on the wet bar. Turning, he caught Gerry's eye. "Sure you don't want one?"

Gerry stared at the dripping beer bottle. His father had told him no drinking on the job, and he reluctantly said, "Thanks, but no thanks."

"Suit yourself." Tex returned to the couch. "So, what can I do for you? Lamar was a little vague on what you wanted to talk to me about."

Gerry removed his wallet and handed Tex his business card. While the older man studied it, Gerry said, "My company has been hired by the Mint in Las Vegas to look into Ricky Smith's winning streak. We want to be sure everything is on the up-and-up. The Mint asked us to talk to you and get your feelings on what happened."

"Your father's Tony Valentine?"

"That's right."

"Heard his name when I played in Atlantic City." Tex put the card on the coffee table, then lifted his eyes. He had his poker face on. His features were stone hard, his eyes as friendly as a snake's. "It's like this, son. I got beat by a guy on a lucky streak. Ricky Smith doesn't know shit about cards, but sometimes that doesn't matter in poker."

"Could he have been cheating?"

Tex smirked. "Fat chance."

"You don't think you could be cheated at cards?"

Tex gave him a look. "*No.* Ever hear the joke about the four Texans playing poker? One turns to the other and says, 'I just saw Billy Bob deal off the bottom.' And the other says, 'Well, it's his deal.' Everyone cheats where I'm from, son. I've seen every scam and greasy hustle that's ever been invented. I would've known if Ricky Smith was cheating me."

Gerry leaned forward in his chair. "My old man has an expression."

"What's that?"

"There's a paddle for everyone's ass."

Tex drew back in his chair. He picked up his bottle and took a long swig of beer. Then he put the bottle back on the ring it had left on the table, and pointed at the door.

"Get out," he said.

★ ★ ★

131

Gerry went to the door. His father had told him to charm Tex. He wondered what his father had expected him to do. Tickle his ass with a feather? He turned to look at the older man. "Was she any good?"

The beer bottle froze an inch from Tex's lips. "Who's that?"

"The hooker you had before I came up. I made her in the lobby."

"I don't know what—"

"She was beautiful. Like a-thousand-dollars-an-hour beautiful. Nobody else in this dumpy hotel can afford her."

"You're grabbing at straws, boy."

Gerry took a step back into the room. Tex hadn't denied it, and Gerry said, "Hookers that work hotels make their johns meet them in the lobby and escort them out. That way, they can't get arrested for pandering. This hooker didn't have an escort. You didn't want to risk being seen with her. Mr. Celebrity."

Tex lowered his beer bottle. He shot Gerry a school-yard look, as if sizing him up. He pointed at the chair Gerry'd just vacated. "Sit down," he said.

"Why should I?"

The older man broke into a smile. "Because I think I like you, boy."

Tex went into the bedroom and came back with a leather bag that he dropped on Gerry's lap. It was heavy, and the leather was old and cracked. Gerry peeked inside. Stacks of brand-new hundreds stared back at him.

"How would you like to make a quick fifty grand?" Tex said, returning to the couch.

The little voice inside of Gerry's head told him to get the hell out of there. Only, he could not stop staring at the money. Fifty grand would put him and Yolanda out of debt. He told the little voice to shut up and dropped the bag onto the floor. "Doing what?"

"You know what a money farm is?"

Gerry shook his head.

"It's a sucker who's got more cash than common sense. There's one playing in this cockamamie poker tournament. Guy named Kingman. Made his fortune building trailer parks. I'm playing him this afternoon in a private game. There's an empty seat."

"So?"

"I want you to be my partner," Tex said.

"Is the game rigged?"

Tex smiled like he'd just said the funniest thing in the world.

"Now don't disappoint me by talking stupid," he said.

Tex drained his beer and let out a prolonged belch. The gambling world was replete with stories of well-oiled suckers who'd lost millions to world-famous poker players. The suckers were often cheated—usually by simple scams like marked cards, or professional dealers who were in fact mechanics. The suckers were allowed to win a few hands, then led to the slaughter. They were always square when it came to paying up. The money meant nothing, and later they could tell their friends that they'd played head-to-head with one of the greats.

Gerry stared at the bag lying on the floor. Half of the stacks had tumbled out. The money was singing its siren song, drowning out every single promise he'd made to his wife and to his father and to his priest in the past month.

Tex went to the minibar and stuck his hand into the bucket. This time, he pulled out two beer bottles. He came over and handed Gerry one. He clinked his bottle against the one he'd given Gerry.

"Partners?" he asked.

Gerry stared at his reflection in the bottle. The face he saw was the old him, Gerry the mover. *Just one quick score,* he thought, *that's all this was. Just one.*

"Okay," he said.

CHAPTER 16

While Ricky drove one-handed down the highway while adjusting the volume on the Stevie Ray acoustic set coming out of the radio's multiple speakers, Valentine stared at the winning racing slip lying on the seat between them. In his hurry to throw Ricky out, the clerk at the OTB parlor had mistakenly given the slip back to Ricky, along with his winnings.

Valentine picked up the slip and stared at it. The slip was telling him something. Namely that he was beaten. He had no idea how Ricky had picked the winners. And he was sure Ricky hadn't cheated.

He knew this because of the amount of money Ricky had won. Eight hundred thirty-six dollars and eighty-seven cents. If Ricky had somehow fixed the race, it would have meant bribing all three jockeys, plus other jockeys, stewards, and handlers. It would have taken a lot of money, and as a result, the payoff would have had to be huge. Eight hundred and change was small potatoes. He glanced across the seat at the younger man.

"You know, I might be willing to go along with

135

this if you didn't act like such a world-class jerk," Valentine said.

Ricky's eyes remained glued on the road. "Is that what's got you ticked off?"

"Yeah. Those guys in the OTB parlor wanted to kill you. You acted like a real asshole to them."

"Everyone around here's an asshole. Why should I be any different?"

"Set an example. Show some class."

"Whether you know it or not, I did those guys a favor."

"How do you figure that?"

"Do you know why people gamble? I'm not talking about your weekend schmo who bets in an office pool. I mean your die-hard guy who bets the rent on a roll of the dice, or bets the ponies every day. Know why he does it?"

Valentine had heard plenty of reasons as to why people gambled. For the entertainment, the thrill, and the adrenaline rush were three at the top of the list. But he sensed Ricky was going down a different path, and shook his head.

"They do it to punish themselves."

That was a new one. Valentine smiled, saying nothing.

"Think about it. They bet their money, and most of the time, they *lose*. Everybody loses in the end. Am I right?"

"Yes."

"Which means that they go into it *knowing* they're going to lose. They *know* the house has an edge that they can't overcome. But they still gamble away their money."

"Maybe they think—"

"That this time will be different?" Ricky said. "Fat chance, brother. Deep down, they know they're going to get beat."

"How can you know that? Everybody has dreams."

Ricky snorted derisively. "Did you look at those guys in the OTB parlor? They were wearing the same clothes they had on yesterday. They wear the look of losers because they *are* losers."

"So why are you doing them a favor?"

Ricky's face lit up. "So, you're accepting my argument."

"It has its points."

"Glad you think so. I'm doing them a favor by reminding them how cruel Lady Luck can be. I drive up in a seventy-thousand-dollar car, make one wager, and walk away a winner. There's a lesson if I ever heard one."

"Which is what?"

"Life sucks, and then some guy rubs your face in it."

Valentine realized Ricky was being serious. It was a sad philosophy, and he shifted his gaze so he was staring at the highway.

The outskirts of Slippery Rock was like a thousand other small towns, the landscape littered with strip shopping centers and flat-roofed fast-food franchises. Ricky bought two sixteen-ounce coffees from a McDonald's and drove around the outskirts of town for a while. Several times drivers in other cars waved at him, but he did not wave back.

"You always so antisocial?" Valentine asked.

"Didn't know them before, don't want to know them now," Ricky said, blowing the steam off his cup. "I mean, why do people think they *want* to know you just because you're rich? Christ, the phone calls alone."

"People harassing you?"

"You could call it that, yeah."

Something clicked in Valentine's head. He'd assumed the four Spanish guys in the forest last night were looking for him. Had they been looking for Ricky and gotten the house wrong? It would have been easy to do in the dark.

"Any of them Spanish?" he asked.

Ricky turned his head to stare at his passenger. A long moment passed. Valentine pointed at the highway. "Watch the road, will you?"

"No," he said.

"You don't want to watch the road?"

"None of them were Spanish."

The highway was entering a curve, and the Lexus drifted into the next lane. Valentine reached over and straightened the wheel with one hand. Ricky returned his attention to his driving. After a moment he glanced at his watch and cursed.

Valentine felt the car accelerate. A sign that said 60 MPH flew by. The Lexus was doing at least eighty. "What's the hurry?"

"I promised my buddy Roland Pew I'd meet him at the Republic National Bank at two," Ricky explained. "We won a lottery ticket together yesterday. The check is in both our names. I have to endorse it with him."

"The bank's open on Saturdays?"

Ricky nodded. "It's a Slippery Rock tradition. The manager is coming in to congratulate Roland. His name is Highland Moss."

"This must be a big occasion."

Ricky nodded. "Roland's going to open an account with his share of the money. He's had a hard life. It's the first time anyone in his family has had a savings account."

"So the manager agreed to come in on a Saturday and help him do it."

"That's right."

"I thought you said everyone around here was an asshole," Valentine said.

The Republic National Bank was a one-story concrete bunker with a single drive-in and no ATM. A sign on the lawn gave the daily mortgage rate. Beneath the rate were the words NO POINTS. They got out and Ricky locked the car doors with the key. He headed toward the bank's entrance with Valentine beside him.

"There are some decent people around here," Ricky admitted. "Highland Moss is one. Roland Pew is another. So's Max Bookbinder."

"Who's he?"

139

"He's the ex-principal over at the high school." He caught Valentine's look and said, "Let me guess. My antisocial ways would have precluded me from liking an ex-principal."

"Did I say that?"

"No, but you were thinking it. Max is a great guy. A few weeks after Polly and I busted up, she spent the weekend with Max. Guy's old enough to be her father. Sure enough, I hear about it, just like everyone hears about everything in this jerkwater town." They had reached the front door, and Ricky rapped on the glass. "So I run into Max in the produce department at the supermarket. I've been working on this line for days, and I ask him, 'Hey, Max, how do you like secondhand goods?' I mean, I say it real loud. Without batting an eye, Max tosses a grapefruit into his cart and says, 'You wouldn't have known it, Ricky. You wouldn't have known it.'" Ricky broke into a smile. "I mean, it hurt, but Christ, he'd been working on his lines, too, you know?"

"You've got some warped sense of humor," Valentine said.

"Thanks."

The bank's front door was darkened by a curtain. Above the door hung a tasseled banner. These were Golden Savings Days, the banner proclaimed—INVEST NOW IN SIX-MONTH CDS. A white-haired guard pulled the curtain back. He tried to wave them away.

"That's Claude," Ricky said under his breath.

"Single-handedly supports every titty bar in the county." He raised his voice. "Hey, Claude, let us in!"

"We're closed," Claude said through the glass.

Ricky pointed at a beat-up bicycle parked beside the front door. "I'm here to help Roland Pew open his account. He needs me to cosign the check."

Claude turned his head, and Valentine guessed someone inside the bank was talking to him. When he turned back, he was frowning. He reached for the giant key ring hanging from his belt, then hesitated. Ricky banged the glass with his palm.

"Come on, Claude. Open up."

Claude unlocked the door. His movements were stilted. As they went inside, he closed and locked the door behind them. The bank's interior was as cold as a meat locker. On one wall were three teller stations; on the other, a row of desks where officers conducted business. On each desk was a blotter, a phone with multiple lines, and a computer. The chairs behind the desks were empty.

Valentine followed Ricky to a desk that had a plaque with Highland Moss's name on it. The phone on the desk was blinking wildly, all four lines on hold. Valentine heard an alarm go off inside his skull. He turned around, his eyes sweeping the room. The teller stations were also deserted, and he spied the contents of a woman's pocketbook strewn across the floor. A lipstick, some coins, gum, and a pocket calendar.

Shit, he thought.

He heard someone cough and glanced over his shoulder. Behind Highland Moss's desk was a large curtain. From behind it stepped a tall, gangly man with a black ski mask pulled over his face. He was dressed like a scarecrow, the knees of his jeans gone, his red flannel shirt caked with dirt. From his right hand dangled a .357 Magnum revolver.

"Arms in the air," the scarecrow said.

Valentine and Ricky raised their arms into the air. Swallowing hard, Ricky said, "Where's Roland?"

"He a friend of yours?" the scarecrow asked.

"Yeah."

"Roland's right here."

The scarecrow snapped his fingers, and Roland Pew emerged from behind the same curtain. A handsome kid, wearing his Sunday clothes. *Probably one of the happiest days of his life until he'd stepped through that door*, Valentine thought. The scarecrow shoved Roland forward, then pointed at the floor. "Get on your knees. You, too, Claude."

For a long moment, no one moved. The scarecrow waved the .357 menacingly in their faces. "Don't make me shoot you," he said.

The four men slowly sunk to the floor.

Ricky could not stop staring at Roland. It was the first time he'd seen the kid he used to babysit not look cool. Roland had called that morning, said the check had come overnight express for their lottery ticket, and that he'd deposit his half this afternoon and wanted to celebrate tonight over a few beers. He'd never sounded happier.

"You boys in the wrong place . . . wrong time," the scarecrow informed them. "Shouldn't have gotten out of bed this morning. Stayed home, watched *Oprah*."

The scarecrow was trying to sound tough. Sweat poured down his face, and he wiped furiously at his brow with his free hand. Ricky's mother, who'd died at an indecent age of ovarian cancer, had taught him that God sometimes took people to crossroads. The paths were always clearly marked: some good, some bad, the choice always a free one. The scarecrow's path was obviously not what he'd expected.

The circular steel door that led to the vault banged open, and a second masked robber entered the room. He was shorter, heavier, his clothes spotted with blood, and he dragged a leather satchel stuffed to overflowing with the bank's money across the tile floor.

"Who the fuck are these guys?" the shorter robber screamed. "You weren't supposed to let anyone in!"

"They were banging on the door," the scarecrow said.

"So?"

"I was afraid they'd call the cops. You know, on a cell phone."

"What a goddamned handicap you are," the shorter robber swore.

Ricky heard a funky noise. Roland's stomach was making barnyard noises. First his stomach sounded like a pig, then a chicken, then a horse. Had Ricky known of this talent, he would have asked his friend to demonstrate years ago.

Ricky looked up. The bloodied robber had stopped in the middle of the floor and was staring murderously at Roland like he knew him. And Roland was staring back like *he* knew the robber.

"Hey, Beasley," Roland said. "Fancy seeing you here."

"My name's not Beasley," the shorter robber snapped. "Shut up!"

"How long's it been? A couple of years?"

"I said shut the fuck up."

Then Roland did the bravest thing Ricky had ever seen. His friend rose from the floor and took a step forward. "Come on . . . it's me, your old pal Roland."

Beasley pulled a sawed-off shotgun from the leather satchel and waved it in Roland's face. "Get back on your knees, goddamn it."

Roland took another step forward. "Let us walk," he implored. "You and I been tight a long time."

"Shut the fuck up, will you?"

"We'll tell the police you had masks on—"

"I said shut up, Roland."

"Claude will say the same thing," Roland told him. "So will Ricky. And I'm sure we can get this other guy to go along. Won't you, mister?"

"Sure," Valentine said.

"You had masks on," Roland said. "We didn't recognize you."

"Shut the fuck up, Roland," Beasley shouted at him. "There ain't no turning back now."

Roland shook his head. "You *can't* kill us."

"I sure can," Beasley said, somehow able to rationalize his own barbarism. His breath had turned foul and gave the air a pernicious stench. "Things happen because they're supposed to, and there's nothing anyone can do about it. Call it nature, or Fate, or God's will. So get on your knees. Right fucking now."

Roland wouldn't do it. Instead, he held his palms out, begging for mercy. Ricky could see that Beasley was getting tied up in knots, and wondered what tied him to Roland. Maybe they'd shot hoops in high school, or gone deer hunting in the fall, or just hitched up every once in a while and chugged beer. Friendships in these parts ran as thick as blood, usually lasted a lifetime.

"My mind's made up," Beasley replied. "This is my one chance to climb out of life's great shit hole. All I want is a little taste of paradise." He glanced at the scarecrow for reinforcement. "Ain't that right, Larry?"

The flame called hope lit up the scarecrow's eyes, and he nodded enthusiastically. "We're going to be eating cheeseburgers in paradise."

"You got that right."

"Come on, Bease," Roland pleaded with him.

"You and I broke the law before. This will be no different. I never ratted you out."

"Get on your knees," Beasley roared at him.

Ricky realized they were all about to die and fought the overwhelming urge to pee on himself. Roland held his ground, refusing to kneel.

"You're a frigging coward," Roland said, making his last stand. "No more hamburgers for me! No more sunsets, or drive-ins, or one-on-one behind the school. Never going to see my baby born because of you."

Beasley couldn't take any more. Stepping forward, he kicked Roland in the balls.

Roland bent in half, hugging himself. After a moment he straightened, tossed back his shoulders, and defiantly stuck out his tongue. "Fuck you, Bease," he said.

Beasley stuck the barrel of his shotgun in the space between Roland's eyes.

"Close your eyes," he ordered Roland.

"No."

"Do as I tell you!"

Roland wouldn't do it, his eyes growing as large as saucers. Beasley stepped back, his eyes filled with murderous rage. "Take him out, Larry," he told the scarecrow. "Put a bullet in his head, and we can get out of here."

"Me?" his partner squeaked.

"Yeah, *you*. You let them in."

"But—"

"No buts. Just do it."

Clutching the .357 with both hands, the scarecrow shut his eyes tightly and tried to blow a hole in the side of Roland's head.

"I . . . can't . . . do . . . it."

"I said shoot the stupid son of a bitch."

"I can't . . ."

"Do it!"

The scarecrow opened his eyes. "I've never shot nobody," he whimpered.

"Don't you want a new life?" Beasley screamed at him. "Cheeseburgers in paradise, remember?"

"Yeah . . ."

"Then for Christ's sake, blow the motherfucker away!"

The scarecrow steadied his aim, the muzzle of the .357 a foot from Roland's head. "Sorry, buddy," he whispered.

It wasn't supposed to be like this, Ricky thought. Everyone was supposed to end up happy and rich. That was the plan. But Beasley and the scarecrow were past reasoning with, their murderous minds made up. Ricky wanted to tell them that he had the cash and he'd be happy to share it with them, just leave his poor buddy alone; only, the sound of the bullet leaving the chamber stopped him cold.

Roland's head snapped back. Ricky waited, expecting him to crumble. Only, Roland didn't crumble. Instead it was the scarecrow who went down. A dime-size hole had appeared at the spot in his mask where his eyebrows met, and put everything behind it in a scramble. Framed by the black ski mask, his eyes registered great surprise.

The second gunshot was equally loud. It tore a hole in Beasley's jaw and lifted him clean off the tiled floor. He stayed that way for an instant, legs splayed spastically in the air, his shotgun discharging and blowing out the fluorescent lights. When he landed, he bounced as if made of rubber. Then the toes of his work boots began to rattle, and the spirit left his body. The ceiling fire sprinkler let out a shrill whistle. Within moments the bank's interior was drenched by a dull, steady rain.

CHAPTER 17

Claude the guard struggled to rise on the slippery bank floor, his arthritis making his hips sing. He'd been watching his life flash by like an old silent movie when the first shot had snapped him awake. He knew the sound of a .357, and that wasn't it.

He went to where Beasley and the scarecrow lay on the floor and checked each man for a pulse. Both were dead as doornails. Just to be safe, he pried the guns from their fingers and deposited them on Highland Moss's desk. He'd once caught a baby shark on a fishing trip. It was dead when he went to take the hook out, yet still managed to bite his hand. Evil, he'd learned, was capable of some mighty strange things.

He glanced at Ricky Smith and the older guy holding the gun. For the life of him, Claude could not figure out where the gun had come from. One moment the older guy's hands were behind his head; the next, he's holding a piece. Claude had guessed the robbers were wearing Kevlar vests beneath their shirts, which anybody could buy these days. The older guy had figured this out, too, and drilled them both in the face.

And the way he'd popped them. Lightning fast, without flinching. That was something that did not come naturally. It was practiced, and usually for good reason. Claude felt a hand on his shoulder, and glanced at Ricky Smith.

"Where's Hi Moss?" Ricky asked.

Claude pointed at the door that led to the vault. Beasley had dragged Hi Moss and two bank employees back there five minutes ago. Then, they'd heard a muffled gunshot.

"They're all in there," the guard said.

Highland Moss was fading fast when Valentine and Ricky Smith reached him, the floor of the bank's vault pooled with his dark blood. His two employees were crying their eyes out, and Valentine led them out of the vault, then returned to find Ricky kneeling next to Moss.

"Hey, Ricky," the bank manager said weakly. "Long time no see."

Ricky said something in reply that sounded like a squeak. Tears were streaming down his cheeks, and his face was ashen.

"You run across Beasley?" the bank manager whispered.

Ricky found the strength to answer him. "He's dead. Mr. Valentine shot him."

"What about his partner?"

"Mr. Valentine got him, too."

Moss gave Valentine an approving look. Then said, "Before he shot me, Beasley said something about being voted off the island. Made it sound like it was the reason he was robbing the bank. Any idea what he meant?"

Ricky swallowed hard and shook his head.

"Me neither." Moss blinked, then blinked again, and a layer of his self seemed to float away. His breathing grew shallow and his chest caved in slightly, and Valentine braced himself for what was about to follow. Ricky knelt down beside him.

"Anything I can do," Ricky whispered. "Anyone you'd like me to call?"

The bank manager thought about it, then shook his head.

"Not enough time," he whispered.

By the time the EMS crew arrived, Moss's tenure on Earth was over. As the medics swarmed into the vault, Valentine and Ricky went back into the bank with the employees. The overhead sprinklers had shut off, and they found two dry seats to sit on.

Ten Slippery Rock police officers arrived a few minutes later. Both genders of officers were built like gladiators, with pumped-up bodies and the bad attitudes that seemed to accompany people who spent too much time in the gym.

The musclehead in charge was a sergeant named Rod Gaylord. He was in his mid-forties, had an abundance of freckles, and acted like he'd never been around a homicide scene before. Valentine watched him and his team pick up the weapons on Highland Moss's desk, then touch the victims' bodies. They were destroying the crime scene, not that he thought any of them knew what that meant. Gaylord grabbed the bank guard and started to pull him outside. Valentine got up and walked toward the two men.

"Get back in that chair, mister," Gaylord said, pointing a finger at him.

"But—"

"No buts. I'll question you when I'm good and ready."

"I need to talk to you," Valentine insisted.

"I said sit down," the sergeant snapped.

Gaylord looked nervous as hell. Like he knew this was the defining moment of his career and he was about to blow it. From his pocket Valentine removed the Glock he'd used to shoot the robbers and handed it to the sergeant.

"I shot them," he said.

Gaylord stared at the gun like it was an alien baby. His heavily freckled face turned bright red. Looking at the guard, he said, "I thought you shot them."

"No, sir," Claude said. "It was Mr. Valentine here."

Gaylord turned the gun over in his palm. To Valentine he said, "You got a license for this, mister?"

Valentine got the license from his wallet and

handed it to him. He went to the firing range twice a week and practiced fast-drawing from his ankle holster, always hoping he'd never have to put the skill to use.

"That was some fine shooting," Gaylord said.

"I got a little lucky."

"Two bullets, two dead men. I wouldn't call that luck. What brings you to Slippery Rock?"

A television news team was at the front door banging on the glass. Valentine watched the sergeant wave them away. Telling Gaylord he was here on a job would not add anything to the sergeant's day. This was his town, and he'd be offended that Valentine hadn't checked in with him. So he used the same lie he'd told Polly. "I'm a retired cop. I'm writing my memoirs."

"You don't say. Got a publisher?"

That was fast. "Not yet," Valentine said.

"I need to question Claude here, then ask you some questions. Don't go running away, you hear?"

The sergeant said it with a slight smile on his face, but there was no smile in his voice. He pointed at a chair, and Valentine dutifully crossed the room and sat in it.

Praying there were no troopers on the highway, Polly floored the accelerator of her Acura Integra. That morning, her life had seemed to be getting back on track. She had a new boyfriend, and her career selling real estate for Century 21 was finally

153

taking off. It had taken her a long time to feel really independent, not just financially but also in her head, and with a single phone call she'd seen it all fall apart.

She'd been in a closing when her mother had called. Retired with nothing to do, her mother called when she was bored, creating emergencies to get her daughter on the line. Polly had grown tired of it, and she'd snatched the phone out of her assistant's hand. "What's up?"

"Did you hear the news?" her mother asked.

With which Polly had gotten royally pissed. She wasn't going to make it in real estate by being momma's little girl. In a cold voice she'd said, "Look, Mother, can't this wait until later? I'm in a closing and they're ready to sign—"

"Your ex-husband walked into a bank robbery this afternoon. There were a pair of robbers. Somehow they got shot to death. I just thought you'd want to know."

"Ricky? In a bank robbery? Are you sure?"

"Yes, honey. It's all over the radio and the TV. One of the robbers killed Hi Moss. I'll let you go."

"Is Ricky okay?"

"Yes, dear. Ricky's fine."

Polly had hung up the phone and put her hand over her mouth. It was like she'd been told one of her brothers had nearly died. Only, it wasn't one of her brothers, it was her lousy prick of an ex-husband. Yet it did not stop her from bursting into tears.

154

The highway's narrow two-lane blacktop had turned blurry, and Polly swiped at her eyes and punched the gas. *Been Down So Long It Looks Like Up to Me.* That was the name of a funny book she'd given Ricky for his birthday once, and he'd laughed when she'd threatened to have it framed and hung over the mantle. They'd had their share of good times; they'd just been overshadowed by the bad.

She drove around Slippery Rock High School and spotted Max Bookbinder shooting hoops with a gang of men twenty years his junior. Max dribbled with mercurial ease, the ball flying from hand to hand, through his feet and behind his back, feats she didn't know he was capable of. He feinted his way to an easy two points, then dropped a line on his younger teammates. A howl of laughter ensued.

She parked in the lot, found an opening in the fence, and walked toward the courts. Her right heel sunk in the mushy field, her ankle twisting painfully. The native ground had the consistency of quicksand, and she slipped off her pumps, shoved them into her purse, and finished the walk in her stockings.

Max Bookbinder, Slippery Rock High's ex-principal reincarnated as a gym teacher, shuffled over. Polly had enjoyed her fling with him, enjoyed their friendship even more. At his retirement party he'd told everyone that he was looking forward to teaching gym, for now when he told the kids what to do, they'd listen to him. Out of politeness he tugged off his Red Sox cap. A few wispy strands of hair stuck straight up. Kissing her on the cheek, he said, "How's life treating you?"

"I've been better. Yourself?"

"Terrific. Started hitting the pavement again. Two miles every morning." He pounded his chest, apelike. "Feel like a kid."

"I need to talk to you."

"Sure. What's wrong?"

Polly sensed he hadn't heard the news. In a soft voice she said, "There was a robbery at Republic National Bank this afternoon. My ex was there. The robbers shot Hi Moss, then someone shot them."

Bookbinder looked at her incredulously.

"Hi was killed," Polly said.

Bookbinder hid his face in his baseball cap. He had put in thirty years as a teacher and administrator and had seen half the town pass through his school. Putting his cap back on, he turned to the gang shooting hoops and let out a primal yell.

"Hey, guys, I'm outta here."

Bookbinder walked Polly to her car. At the fence he offered his hand as Polly wiped her feet and slipped her pumps on.

"When I heard the news, I cried," she said.

"For Hi?"

"No. I mean, yes, I cried for Hi. But I also cried for Ricky. I imagined him being shot and it broke my heart. I can't explain it."

"Can't explain what?"

"I *hate* him."

"You were married and you loved him once," he said. "You shared things; you had a history and your own language. All married couples do. You missed those things."

"How did you know that? I never told you—"

"You didn't have to. I was married once myself."

"Does this mean I still love him?"

"You make it sound like a curse."

"Oh my God, you have no idea what it was like."

A Mustang convertible filled with teenagers sped by. Bookbinder stuck his face against the fence and barked out one of the boy's names. Instantly the car slowed to a snail's pace. At his retirement party he had given a speech and summed it up pretty well. Kids were the affirmation of life; being around them, he found that hope was not easily extinguished and dreams impossible to dismiss. Turning to her, he said, "What are you going to do?"

"I honestly don't know."

"That's not like you, Polly."

"*I don't,*" she insisted.

Bookbinder stuck his hands in the pockets of his sweats and looked at the ground. "You know, Polly, I've known Ricky a long time, and he isn't as bad as you make him out to be."

"Ricky isn't bad?"

"That's right."

"Oh, Max," she shrieked. "Come on!"

CHAPTER 18

Gerry Valentine returned to Tex Snyder's suite at the Holiday Inn at four o'clock that afternoon. He'd showered and shaved, and in the pocket of his sports jacket was the money Tex had staked him to play in his friendly little game.

Tex had the whole thing worked out. He'd bribed the hotel into bringing an authentic felt card table to his room, then stocked the place with top-shelf liquor and bowls of nuts and chips and a humidor filled with Cuban cigars. He'd turned it into a guy's hangout, and all for the purpose of fleecing Kingman, the trailer park magnate.

Kingman was already into the Scotch when Gerry arrived. A native of Chicago, Kingman was a short, thick, disagreeable guy worth a cool hundred million bucks. He lay on the couch in such a way that no one could share it with him. He grunted when Gerry introduced himself.

Three other players drifted into the suite and introduced themselves. Bill, Bob, and Phil. No last names. Gerry guessed they were also "friends" of Tex.

They sat down at the card table, and Tex suggested they play Texas Hold 'Em. It was the most popular poker game in the world. It was also played on television in tournaments where players "exposed" their cards to the camera. As a result of these shows, millions of people thought they knew how to play. Professionals had a name for these new players. They called them suckers.

Kingman was definitely a sucker. He quoted the odds after each hand was played, and told other players when he thought they were bluffing. Bill, Bob, and Phil told him he was right every time, further convincing Gerry they were stooges. Kingman also continued to drink as he played. He was as raw as they came.

Gerry played conservatively for the first hour. Tex had told him to fold most of his hands and had explained that he wanted Gerry "in the game" later on, when Kingman was led to the slaughter and the two men scammed him.

Tex's scam was as easy as they came. During a hand, he would give Gerry a prearranged signal. He would take a cigar out of the humidor, but he wouldn't light it up. He'd just chew on it for a while.

That was the cue for Gerry to start raising the bet. It meant that Tex had a cinch hand and was convinced he was going to beat Kingman. But Tex didn't want to scare Kingman away, so it was Gerry's job to lure him in. After a few rounds of

159

betting, Gerry would drop out of the hand and let Tex take over.

Card hustlers called this *playing top hand*. His father had told him that it was used by many of the world's top players to fleece suckers. What made it so deceiving was that the person doing the raising never knew what his partner was holding. He simply did as told.

But Gerry also knew something else. Playing top hand wasn't infallible. Texas Hold 'Em had three rounds—the flop, the turn, and the river. The sucker might draw a miracle card on the river and win all the money. It happened all the time.

Somehow, Gerry didn't think Tex was going to let this happen.

An hour later, room service brought hamburgers and milk shakes to the suite. It wasn't the kind of grub that Gerry would have used to feed a millionaire, but Kingman dived into the food like it was his last meal. Tex had obviously done his homework.

The suite had two bathrooms. While Bill, Bob, and Phil took turns using one, Gerry went into Tex's bedroom to use the other. Only, the bathroom door was shut. From behind it, he could hear a low beeping sound. Gerry put his ear to the door. The sound was familiar. A hearing aid. Plenty of folks in his neighborhood in Florida wore them. When the batteries went low, they emitted a low, shrill noise.

Smiling, Gerry pulled his head away from the door. Tex was wearing a hearing aid. That explained how he could be so confident that he'd beat Kingman. Tex wasn't just playing top hand. He was also playing *the peek.*

The peek was the oldest con known to card cheaters. A hidden accomplice would peek at a player's cards and secretly communicate them to the table. Sometimes the peek was a hole drilled into the wall, or someone staring through a window with a pair of binoculars. Before the mob had been run out of Las Vegas, it had taken place at every card room at one time or another. And it was still a favorite among people who ran private games.

Tex came out of the bathroom tucking in his shirt.

"Got your battery fixed?" Gerry asked.

"Not so loud. How much you got left?"

"Twenty-five grand."

"Good. Keep it up."

Gerry glanced at the doorway leading into the room where they were playing. Kingman was on the other side, talking with Phil. He was slurring his words and had spilled ketchup on his pants. All the money in the world couldn't stop him from making a jackass of himself.

"Why don't you just play him straight?" Gerry said under his breath.

"Think that would work?"

"The guy's a loser."

"Sometimes losers get lucky," Tex said, walking away.

Gerry went into the bathroom and locked the door behind him. Putting the toilet seat down, he powered up his cell phone and had a seat. He felt a tug at his conscience and rubbed the bridge of his nose with two fingers. Tex was one of the best card players in the world. He didn't have to be cheating Kingman; he could beat him ninety-nine times out of a hundred. But it was that one freak time he was afraid of. It just didn't seem right.

He'd been working on the excuse he was going to tell Yolanda for not calling. They had a pact about him calling, and she would be angry that he'd broken it. He started to dial the number at his house when his phone let out a chirp, indicating he had a message.

He went into voice mail and retrieved it. The message had come in at two o'clock and was from Yolanda. He felt his face burn, feeling like he'd already been caught. They hadn't had a fight since the baby had been born. It had been the best two months of his life.

"Hey, Gerry, where are you?" he heard his wife say. "I'm sure you're busy and everything, but I missed hearing from you."

Gerry felt the tension leave his body. Yolanda wasn't mad.

"Anyway," she went on, "there's someone here who misses you and wants to talk to you. Hold on for a second, okay?"

He listened as she juggled the phone while saying something that he couldn't quite hear. Then he heard the unmistakable sound of his daughter's laughter. His wife was holding Lois up to the phone and was tickling the soles of her little feet. That was the spot that always got her laughing. Gerry stared at the bathroom floor, envisioning his daughter on the other end.

It lasted for a few more seconds, and then Yolanda pulled his daughter away and came back on. "Well, isn't that something. She was crying her head off a moment ago. Then I told her I was calling her daddy, and she brightened up. I just wanted you to know that we're thinking about you and hope you come home soon. Don't we, honey?"

His daughter let out a peal of laughter, and Gerry guessed Yolanda was tickling her stomach, another weak spot. He heard his wife say good-bye, and then the connection went dead.

A knock at the door brought him back to the real world. He cracked it and saw Tex staring anxiously at him. "You fall in?" the old poker player asked.

"What's wrong?"

"We started. It's time to take Kingman to the cleaners."

"I need to talk to you," Gerry said.

"Can't it wait?"

"No."

Gerry shut the door. He'd put the cell phone on the sink, and he ran the cold water and splashed a handful into his face. Then he took a hard look at his reflection in the mirror. He'd flown to Atlantic City last month to see his family priest, Father Tom. Spent four hours in a confessional spilling his guts and trying to cleanse his soul. He'd been fucking up since he was a teenager, and hearing everything he'd done come out of his mouth had been the most excruciating thing he'd ever put himself through. But it had been worth it.

He slipped the cell phone into his pocket and went out. Tex was standing nervously beside the door. There was spittle at the corners of his mouth, and his eyes were dilated.

"What's wrong?" he asked under his breath.

"I'm backing out of our deal," Gerry said.

"What the hell you talking about?"

"You heard me. Get Phil or Bob or Bill to do it."

"But they're pencil dicks. They'll freeze up."

"I can't help you there."

"But we had a deal."

Gerry took the money Tex had staked him out of his jacket pocket and shoved it into the older man's wrinkled hands. "Kingman is a chump. Beat him fair and square."

"So what if Kingman can't play? Why does that bother you, boy?"

"It's like stealing from a little kid."

"So?"

Gerry shuddered. Thank God he hadn't gone

through with this. It would have been a road from which there would have been no turning back. He started to walk away. Tex grabbed him by the arm.

"You running out on me?"

"Call it what you want."

"Boys get whipped in Texas for doing that."

"We're not in Texas."

Tex clenched his teeth. They were crooked and badly discolored from years of tobacco stains. Through them he said, "You're making a huge mistake, Gerry. I'm giving you a chance to reconsider. Go into that room and help me take Kingman's money. I'll give you the fifty grand when we're done, and you can go back to your life and I'll go back to mine. What do you say?"

He was smiling, like the world would be a better place if Gerry just saw things his way. He was a phony through and through, and Gerry realized how much he disliked him.

"I'd rather be a dog in Korea," Gerry said.

Riding in the elevator to his floor, the enormity of what he'd done hit Gerry in the head like a shovel. He could use that fifty grand to get the wolves away from his door. He owed a lot of money and didn't have much coming in. Fifty grand would have wiped the slate clean. The elevator stopped and opened its doors. As he stepped out, he considered going back upstairs. Kingman would never miss the money. How could that be a crime?

He heard his cell phone beep and removed it from his pocket. Yolanda's message was still in voice mail. He hit play, then stuck the phone to his ear and listened to his daughter's laughter. Someday, he was going to have the same influence on her that she was already having on him. It was scary to think about, and he went to his room, knowing he'd made the right decision.

CHAPTER 19

Sergeant Rodney Gaylord didn't like the answers Tony Valentine was giving him. Call it a good cop's sixth sense. But since he couldn't figure out what it was he didn't like, he kept his feelings hidden, fearful of looking stupid.

That was Gaylord's greatest fear—looking stupid. Because he'd once taken steroids to build muscles and had developed a hair-trigger temper, his co-workers had stuck him with a mean nickname. They called him Time Bomb. Gaylord had been a cop his whole life, and took pride in the way he ran Slippery Rock's finest. He deserved better, or so he thought.

It was almost five. He stood at his desk, typing up his report of the bank robbery. Tony Valentine sat in the seat next to his desk, blowing on a cup of coffee. The guy could sure down the caffeine. Gaylord reread the report still in his typewriter, trying to put a finger on his suspicions. Something didn't sit right. Valentine wasn't telling him the whole truth. Slippery Rock did some tourism business, but generally it was folks from Atlanta and Charleston that came here, mostly to antique shop or hike in the hills. Visitors from Florida were rare, and he had a hard time believing Valentine had come here to write his memoirs.

"Talk to me about Hi Moss," Gaylord said, turning off his typewriter.

Valentine sipped his coffee. "I told you everything that happened."

"I know, but something's got me stumped. You said Hi Moss told you that Beasley said he'd gotten voted off the island. Hi said he thought this was why Beasley was robbing the bank. What do you think that meant, voted off the island?"

"It's from a TV show," Valentine said.

"Did Hi tell you that?"

"No, I remembered it a little while ago."

"Which show?"

"*Survivor.*"

Gaylord felt his face burn. He religiously watched the tube every night and had seen *Survivor* more times than he cared to remember. Usually it was with a beer clutched in his hand, his eyes glued to the attractive women in bathing suits who were always contestants. "What do you think Beasley was talking about?" he asked.

"Well, I'd imagine he got thrown out of some group and he was sore about it."

Sore. A real Yankee expression. Gaylord consulted his notes lying on his desk. He'd asked Ricky Smith the same question earlier and gotten the same response. He wondered if it was one of those things

168

he'd never get to the bottom of. Out of the corner of his eye he saw Valentine shift uncomfortably in his chair.

"We'll be done in just a second," the sergeant said. "One other thing's got me scratching my head."

"What's that?"

"Both Larry and Beasley had their weapons drawn, yet neither got a shot off. You were kneeling on the floor, they were standing, yet you managed to shoot both men in the face. What are you, a trick-shot artist?"

"No."

"Then how do you explain it?"

"I was desperate."

"That's it?"

"And I got lucky."

Gaylord gave him a hard stare. It just wasn't ringing true. Killing one bank robber he could accept, not two. The odds of that happening were simply out of this universe. He went to the door and said, "You want another cup of coffee?"

"I thought you said I could leave," Valentine said.

"I just need to check something out," Gaylord replied.

Gaylord shut the door behind him on the way out. Standing for long stretches made his back sore, and he paced the hall outside his office. He could tell that Valentine was starting to get annoyed. He was definitely acting uncomfortable.

If he started leaning on him too hard, it might blow up in Gaylord's face.

Maybe Valentine *had* gotten lucky. Gaylord was starting to slide in that direction, for no better reason than he had nothing to go on but a hunch. The fact was, Valentine had foiled a bank robbery. He had done a heroic thing, and as a result Roland's baby would have a daddy and Claude would get free lap dances for the rest of his life and Ricky Smith would solidify his reputation as the luckiest man in Slippery Rock. A happy ending if Gaylord had ever heard one.

At the hallway's end was a conference room with a coffee machine. He fished two quarters out of his pocket and went inside. Two of his deputies were in the room, chowing down on hoagies while staring at a TV set sitting on the desk. Gaylord stared at the black-and-white picture on the screen. "What are you watching?" he asked.

"The videotape of the bank robbery," one of the deputies replied.

Gaylord pulled up a chair without saying a word to either man. On the screen he saw the two masked bank robbers pointing guns at Ricky, Roland, Valentine, and the guard, who were kneeling on the bank floor. The film was grainy and had no audio. The camera was also at a bad angle, and Valentine was partially out of the picture.

It was an incredibly tense scene. The bank robbers yelled at their hostages, then they yelled at each other. Then, out of the blue, the two bank robbers were lying on the floor with bullets in their heads.

"Play it again," Gaylord said.

One of the deputies rewound the tape and started it over. It happened amazingly fast. First there were two bank robbers, then there were none.

"You should sign him up, sergeant," the other deputy quipped. "That guy's the Nolan Ryan of pistol-shooting."

Gaylord made the deputy replay the tape a third time while staring at his wristwatch. Based upon his less-than-scientific calculations, Valentine had drawn from an ankle holster and shot the two robbers in slightly less than two seconds. It sent a chill through him. He was willing to bet his paycheck that no retired cop in America could handle a gun like that.

Back in his office, he found Valentine reading a newspaper he'd fished out of the trash. Gaylord tapped him on the shoulder, and Valentine dumped the paper into the basket and rose expectantly.

"You're free to go," Gaylord said. "I may want to question you some more, so I'm requesting that you stay in town until our investigation is finished."

Valentine headed for the door. Gaylord could not help himself and said, "Take my advice, and stay out of trouble."

Valentine stopped at the door, a look of concern on his face.

CHAPTER 20

Valentine went downstairs to the reception area, expecting to find Ricky Smith waiting for him. Ricky had promised to give him a ride back to the house he was renting. Instead he found a handwritten note awaiting him on the receptionist's desk.

> *Hey Mr. Valentine,*
>   *Sorry to leave you high and dry, but I had to go home.*
>   *A deputy will give you a lift, if you want.*
>   *Thanks for saving my life.*
>
>   *Ricky*

Valentine crumpled the note and tossed it into a trash basket. He'd saved Ricky's life and the kid couldn't hang around and take him home. That was gratitude for you. Through the front doors he spied rays of sunlight peeking through the clouds. It was the first decent weather he'd seen in days, and he asked the receptionist how far his house was from the police station.

"About two miles as the crow flies," she replied.

"What if the crow's walking?"

She gave him directions, and he headed out the door. The late afternoon air was crisp and clean, and he crossed the street and found a footpath beside the main road that led into town. The path was well-worn, and he settled into a comfortable pace. It had become a beautiful day to be outdoors, and with each step, he felt himself start to calm down.

He walked with his hands stuck in his pockets, thinking about Beasley and the scarecrow. He'd killed seven people in his life, including them. Each time, it had punched an invisible hole in him that had been slow to heal. Most cops he knew could walk away from a killing without any regrets. He couldn't. He would think about Beasley and the scarecrow for a long time, wondering if he could have handled it any differently.

A mile into his walk, a pickup truck pulled up alongside him. He heard it slow down and stopped walking. Then he glanced at the driver. It was a middle-aged woman with her hair tied in a bun. She stared at him anxiously, and he realized he recognized her. She'd served Ricky soft drinks in the cafeteria and known that Ricky liked to drink Orange Crush.

The truck braked to a halt. The road had four lanes, and no other vehicles were in sight. Valentine took his hands from his pockets and waited expectantly. The woman stared at him while clutching the wheel. She looked scared out of her wits.

173

"Hello," he said.

She continued to stare, as if frozen in space.

"Can I help you?" he asked.

Her breath fogged the side window. She shook her head.

"Do you want to tell me something?"

She glanced in her mirror to see if anyone was coming, then rolled down her window. "This is a small town," she said, making it sound like a curse.

"Am I in danger?"

She hesitated. "You should leave. For your own good."

"Am I in danger?"

"I've told you all I can."

"Look, we're going the same way. How about you give me a ride?"

She hesitated. She had a kind face, and he remembered the easy repartee she'd shared with Ricky that morning. He stepped into the road, thinking that if he got in the truck, she might open up and tell him what was on her mind. She shook her head, and the truck quickly sped away. Standing still had gotten him chilled, and he started walking again.

One of the curses of the retired was dredging up childhood memories. Valentine had read this in a magazine published by AARP. According to the writer, the elderly spent too much time dwelling on stuff that had happened when they were kids. It was a hard trap to avoid, considering all the free time retired people had on their hands, and the writer had suggested that his readers take up a hobby, like collecting stamps.

The article had annoyed the hell out of him. Since moving to Florida, he'd found himself thinking about his childhood often and had come to the conclusion that dredging up childhood memories was just another of life's natural stages. You grow old, slow down, and look over your shoulder at where you've been. It wasn't a trap, and nothing was wrong with it.

He often thought about his father. Dominic Valentine was a drunk and had abused his wife. At age eighteen Valentine had thrown him out of the house, and they'd never gotten along after that. Yet what Valentine remembered about him now was his father's honesty. His father believed it was wrong to steal or take anything that didn't belong to him. It was a lesson that he'd instilled in his son, one that Valentine was grateful for.

He stopped walking. He could see Slippery Rock up ahead, and slipped into the forest by the side of the road and stood beneath the shadow of a giant oak. Fishing a pack of Life Savers from his pocket, he popped one into his mouth.

For a while, he watched the comings and goings in town. In the daylight it looked smaller than it had at night. He tried to guess how many people lived here. Nine thousand? Probably less. Atlantic City, the town he'd been born and raised in, was also small. His mother had liked to say that gossip was the local currency, with everyone in town knowing everyone else's business. He guessed Slippery Rock wasn't any different.

His thoughts drifted to Ricky Smith. He was a local fixture; the woman in the cafeteria had known what kind of soda he drank. And Ricky knew everyone, as well; he'd pegged Roland Pew's bicycle sitting outside the bank that afternoon.

This is a small town.

What was the woman in the pickup truck trying to tell him? That everyone in town was connected to Ricky in some mysterious way? It sounded far-fetched, yet she had acted genuinely scared.

He rested his head against the tree, its bark cold against his neck. Closing his eyes, he felt like he was falling through a bottomless hole, and put the palms of his hands against the tree for support. All his life, he'd been having epiphanies, strange little moments in time when his brain suddenly saw truth where only questions had been before. He was having an epiphany now, and Ricky's incredible string of luck suddenly took on a whole new meaning. To an outsider, Ricky winning the lottery and a drawing for a trip to Hawaii and a horse race looked like a miracle. But to the locals, it didn't look like a miracle at all. Instead of making a fuss over him, they were accepting it. Anywhere else, they would have been throwing palm fronds at his feet and treating him like a saint.

Not here. Not once had Tony seen anyone in

town come up to Ricky, whack him on the back, and tell him how amazing his lucky streak was.

But why?

Only one good answer came to mind. The locals knew something about Ricky that he didn't. They knew what was going on.

This is a small town.

Valentine opened his eyes and realized he had his answer. The key to the puzzle was right here in Slippery Rock, and he walked out of the forest determined to find it.

CHAPTER 21

Gerry figured it was time to leave Gulfport. He'd done like his father had asked, and talked to Tex Snyder. The fact that it had turned into a dead end was too bad, but he couldn't do anything about it.

He checked out of the Holiday Inn a few minutes after six. He hadn't eaten much that day, and had been eyeing the flashing neon sign on the restaurant directly across the road from the casino. BEST STEAKS IN THE SOUTH. He was in the mood for a big bleeding piece of meat, even though his old man would probably holler when he saw the charge come through on the credit card. What the hell.

He ended up ordering a sixteen-ounce T-bone with hash browns and string beans smothered in butter on the side. The meat was tenderized in something that would probably give him stomach cancer in ten years, but he didn't care. He'd crossed a major bridge in his life today. He'd walked away from temptation. It was worth celebrating.

The meal made him want to sleep, and he

ordered a double espresso. By the time he got on the road it was seven-fifteen and his eyelids felt like they were nailed to his forehead. He'd made a hotel reservation in Hattiesburg, and planned to get up first thing in the morning and catch a commuter flight back to Atlanta, then home to Tampa.

He drove to the run-down beachfront marina and hung a left on Highway 49. In his mirror he watched the marina's lights slowly fade. He'd heard that Donald Trump had expressed an interest in the marina, then backed out. Gerry guessed it was because the Donald didn't like the way gambling was run in Mississippi. The state had a conscience when it came to gambling, and had put limits on how much locals could wager; five hundred dollars for two hours was the maximum. They'd initiated the rule as a result of a rise in personal bankruptcies, and it had worked great. Gerry had decided he liked that. It kept things sane.

The speed limit was sixty-five. He drove a mile below it through the outskirts of Gulfport. The other good thing was that the state was pouring the proceeds from the casinos into public works and schools. Like the Indian reservations, they were doing something constructive with the money. He liked that, too.

After an hour he passed the town at the bend with the Bible store and noticed a state trooper's car hiding in the shadow of two small restaurants.

179

A few miles later, the smell of freshly cut pine trees invaded the car. His headlights caught the pine-milling operation up ahead. Acres of forty-foot-long trees lay on the side of the highway, waiting to be turned into two-by-fours. He filled his lungs with the great-smelling air.

He saw headlights come up from behind him. A Jeep, going way over the speed limit. Gerry shifted into the right lane. The Jeep moved over as well and got on his bumper. It had its brights on, and Gerry put his mirror down to cut the glare. He didn't like how close the Jeep was, and punched his accelerator.

The cars separated, then the Jeep caught up. Where in hell was the state trooper when you needed him? Gerry heard a loud bang. The flash of a rifle being discharged was quickly followed by his car lurching to one side, its left rear tire blown to bits. Gerry hit the brakes and saw the Jeep swerve to avoid slamming into him. He accelerated and heard another loud bang followed by someone in the Jeep cursing.

This time when he hit the brakes, he put his foot straight to the floor. The rental screeched a hundred yards down the highway before it came to a halt. The Jeep couldn't brake that hard without flipping over. It flew past him on the highway, then slowed down and did a hasty U-turn.

Gerry looked up and down the highway. He was in the middle of Mississippi nowhere. On one side of the road was a barren field. On the other, the pine-milling operation. He drove the car over the median, crossed two opposing lanes of traffic, and looked for a place in the logs that he could drive the rental through. Behind him he heard three men's coarse laughter. They sounded like good old boys.

He found an opening in the logs and drove through it. It was just wide enough for his car. Then he had an idea. Braking, he threw the rental into reverse, then opened his door and jumped out. He started to run as the rental went backward. He heard it hit the Jeep.

"Shit," a good old boy screamed.

"He's getting away," another shouted.

"Out of the car," the third yelled.

Gerry ran down an aisle of stacked trees. They were stacked with spaces between them, and he saw his assailants on the other side, running alongside him. Each had a pump shotgun, a big belly, and a ponytail. What had happened to the old days, when guys with long hair stood for peace, love, and understanding? He saw one of them stop, aim, and fire. The blast flew by Gerry's head.

Up ahead he saw another opening in the logs. He was doomed: Those good old boys would run through and shoot him and that would be it. Gerry couldn't believe it. He'd finally gotten his act together, and now he was going to die.

His eyes saw a green and white metal sign. It

was positioned next to the logs, and its lettering glowed in the moonlight. DANGER!! DO NOT TOUCH!

"There's an opening," one of them yelled.

"He's mine," the second screamed.

"No, he's mine!"

Gerry felt his feet sprout wings. He reached the glowing sign before any of his pursuers reached the opening. Groping around in the dark for the thing that the sign didn't want him to touch, his fingers latched onto a metal handle. He grasped it with both hands and looked through the space in the logs at the three bear-size men. They had stopped and were smiling like it was a rabbit they'd cornered and not another human being.

He yanked hard on the handle. A mighty roar followed as the forty-foot-long trees became disengaged from the metal cables holding them together. One of his pursuers screamed.

Gerry stood motionless. The space between the trees did not immediately close, and he watched as two of the men were instantly crushed. The third got a running start and was halfway across the highway when the trees caught up with him. He was knocked down like a bowling pin and carried along, his body banged and smashed.

The trees spread out evenly across the highway. Gerry waited until they'd stopped rolling, then walked over to where the first two men lay. Both had died with looks of surprise on their faces. He wanted to feel happy that they were dead; only, he didn't. All he'd wanted was to get away. He hadn't wanted to crush the life out of their bodies. It had just worked out that way.

He crossed the road and stopped where the third man lay in the middle of the road. The man was hanging on by a thread, the whisper of life in his eyes. His shotgun was still in his hand. Gerry kicked it away.

"You . . . ," the dying man moaned.

"Who sent you?"

". . . gonna . . ."

"Tell me."

". . . die . . ."

He shut his eyes, and Gerry saw his chest cave in and realized he was passing into the great beyond. The wind, which had been blowing forcefully from the gulf, suddenly died off, and for a long moment time seemed to stand still. Gerry stared into the dead man's face. Then he walked to the side of the road and surrendered his dinner.

The rain came back with a vengeance during his walk home, and Valentine peeled off his soaking wet clothes as he passed through the front door of his rental house and headed straight for the shower.

When he emerged ten minutes later, his skin was tingling and he felt refreshed. In the refrigerator he found the half-eaten sandwich from yesterday, and sat down at the kitchen table with a can of Diet Coke to wash it down. Since his wife had died, he'd been eating sandwiches for dinner and keeping crazy hours and basically living like a kid in a college frat house. Mabel was constantly scolding him about it, and out of deference to her, he picked up his wet clothes lying in the foyer when he was finished, and threw them in the washing machine in the basement. Then he dug out his cell phone and called his neighbor.

"How's it going?" he asked when she answered.

"Oh, Tony, I've done something really stupid," she replied.

Valentine sincerely doubted it. Mabel was one of the sharpest people he'd ever known. She rarely blundered, and when she did make a mistake, she was a master at fixing it.

"Let me guess," he said, walking up the creaky basement stairs. "You wiped out the database in my computer."

"That will *never* happen again," she said. "No, this was just stupid. But I'm still ashamed."

Reaching the first floor, he walked through the foyer to the kitchen and halted. A white envelope lay on the threadbare rug in the foyer. He'd had a visitor while he was downstairs, and he opened the front door and stepped onto the porch. It was still raining buckets. In the distance he faintly saw a kid on a bicycle pedaling furiously up a hill and out of sight.

"It must have been a doozy," he said, closing the door. He picked up the envelope off the floor and went into the kitchen.

"I was in your study going through today's mail, and I got distracted and without thinking . . . oh, this sounds like such a senior moment."

"Come on," he said, dropping the envelope on the kitchen table. "What did you do? The suspense is killing me."

"I ate your hundred-thousand-dollar candy bar."

"My what?"

"The 3 Musketeers bar that Ron Shepherd in Canada sent," his neighbor replied. "It came in yesterday's mail. Shepherd said it was for your collection of crooked gambling equipment, so I figured it must be important, even though I didn't know how it worked. Well, like a dope, I absent-mindedly tore off the wrapper and took a huge bite out of it. When I realized what I'd done, I nearly got sick."

Valentine put his hand over his mouth. He'd helped Ron with the case over a year ago. A casino in Canada suspected its gift-shop manager of stealing from customers. Ron had sent him a video-tape of the manager at work, and Valentine had quickly made the scam. Later, he'd learned the manager was stealing a hundred thousand dollars a year. It had to be a record, and he'd asked Ron to send him the candy bar after the trial so he could add it to his collection. He could not believe it now resided in his neighbor's stomach.

"Is that laughter I hear coming out of your mouth?" Mabel asked.

"Sorry."

"I get the feeling I haven't totally ruined your day."

"The image of you biting the end off, then realizing what you'd done—"

"Stop it," she scolded him.

"Sorry."

"So now that you've had a good chuckle, please explain what makes this candy bar so special? It certainly didn't taste like it was worth a hundred big ones."

"How much did it taste like it was worth?"

"Stop it!"

"Sorry. The manager kept the candy bar on the counter, next to where customers put items to be rung up. If a customer put down four items or more, he added the candy bar to the total. If someone looked at the receipt and questioned him, he pointed at the candy bar and said, 'Didn't you want that?' The person would say no, and he'd apologize and give them their money back. It looked like an honest mistake, so no one ever reported it."

"How much did the candy bar actually cost?"

"A buck."

"You're saying he did this a hundred thousand times a year?"

"Yeah. He had hundreds of customers a day. He cooked the books to hide the theft."

"So what you're saying is, I could have replaced the candy bar with one I bought at the grocery, and you wouldn't have known the difference."

This time Valentine couldn't help himself and burst out laughing.

"What's so funny?" she said.

"That's something I would do," he told her.

"Oh my, would you look at the time?" his neighbor said. "I'm off to the movies. Mustn't let my one free day go to waste. Ta-ta."

Valentine started to reply, but the phone had gone dead in his hand.

He retrieved the envelope he'd found in the foyer and opened it. Mabel probably hadn't liked being strung along like that. He promised himself to make it up to her when he got home. The envelope contained a white sheet of stationery, with the faint scent of women's perfume. He'd never liked things that were left anonymously. If the author wouldn't look him in the face, why should he believe what was written on a piece of paper? His let his eyes scan the page.

WE MET THIS MORNING. I WOULD LIKE TO TALK TO YOU. MEET ME IN THE HIGH SCHOOL LIBRARY TOMORROW. FRONT DOOR OF SCHOOL WILL BE OPEN. WALK TO BACK, TAKE A LEFT, GO TO END OF LONG HALL. 9:00.

He found himself shaking his head. A clandestine meeting in the school library on a Sunday morning? It didn't get any more spellbinding than

187

that. He guessed the woman in the pickup had finally gathered the courage to talk to him. He smothered a tired yawn. The day had finally caught up with him.

The lumpy bed in the master bedroom felt surprisingly comfortable. He lay down in his clothes and stared at the ceiling. Sometime tonight he was going to wake up in a cold sweat. It had happened every time he'd shot someone. He would then lie awake and replay what had happened, just to reassure himself that he'd made the right decision. Sometimes, he'd drift back asleep. But most of the time, he'd do ceiling patrol.

As his eyes closed, he thought about Gerry. They hadn't talked all day. He wondered how Gerry's meeting with Tex Snyder had gone. He guessed Gerry hadn't learned much. Otherwise, he was sure his son would have called.

He was still thinking about it as he drifted off to sleep.

CHAPTER 22

Gerry's insistence on not giving a statement until he had a lawyer did not sit well with the two highway patrolmen who appeared on the scene ten minutes later. The three dead men were locals; Gerry was a New Yorker recently transplanted to Florida. One of the patrolman wagged a finger menacingly in Gerry's face.

"You better start talking, boy," he declared.

"Not until I have a lawyer," Gerry said.

So they cuffed his wrists and threw him in the back of their cruiser and eventually drove him to the Harrison County jail. On the way they passed several sprawling industrial plants and a refinery. The patrolmen continued to give him a hard time, and Gerry lowered his head and stared at the floor. His father had once told him that cops usually followed their first impressions. He obviously hadn't made a good one here.

The jail was three stories of generic yellow brick topped by razor wire. Inside, the patrolmen turned Gerry over to a tobacco-chewing plainclothes detective in a three-walled cubicle. The detective asked questions—current address, date of birth, arrest record—while hawking gobs of spit into a trash can. Gerry felt his stomach turn over.

"So you've been arrested for selling drugs," the detective said.

"Pot. When I was a kid. It was a little bag."

"How little's little?"

"A quarter ounce."

"Where was this?"

"Atlantic City. It's where I'm from."

"How old were you?"

"Fifteen."

"Fifteen-year-olds in Mississippi drive cars and get married," the detective said.

Gerry got his drift. The detective told him to stand up. They walked down a corridor to where fingerprinting equipment was shoved into a corner. The detective unlocked Gerry's handcuffs and did his prints, rolling each finger carefully on the inkpad and then on the form. Then he did them again in weird groupings; four fingers together, both thumbs, until Gerry's fingers were so black he couldn't see the nails. The detective gave him a paper towel and a plastic spray bottle and led him to the bathroom.

"Don't be long," he said.

"How long's long?" Gerry asked him.

Gerry thought he saw the detective crack a smile. Next stop was the mug-shot room, which also served as the snack room. The detective bought a Butterfinger bar from the candy machine while Gerry got a front and side shot taken by a techie.

190

"I need you to e-mail those shots to me," the detective said.

"I'm kind of backed up," the techie said.

"This can't wait. I need to send them to the NCIC."

The techie shot Gerry a look. "Okay," he said.

Gerry was back in the detective's cubicle when he remembered what NCIC stood for. National Crime Information Center. The tobacco-spitting detective was going to send his prints and mug shot to a law enforcement database to see if Gerry was wanted for any other nefarious deeds. He glanced at the clock hanging from the wall: 3:00 A.M.

"How long is this going to take?" Gerry asked.

The detective was staring at his computer screen like a kid stares at a test with questions he's never seen before. Without looking away, he said, "Depends if I can ever get this stuff to send. Once they get the information, who knows? They get pretty backed up on weekends."

"Give me a hint."

The detective's head jerked away. "One more wiseass remark out of you, and I'll toss you in the holding pen."

Gerry felt himself uncontrollably shudder. The holding pen on a Saturday night would consist of the worst scum Gulfport had to offer. With the way his luck was running, someone in there would be related to the three guys he'd just killed.

"Sorry."

The detective grunted and resumed looking at his computer screen.

"I don't want to be a jerk, but you haven't let me call a lawyer," Gerry said.

"That's because there ain't no lawyers working on Saturday night," the detective said, spitting in the trash. "First thing tomorrow morning, you can call as many lawyers as you want."

Gerry had not seen the detective take the tobacco out of his mouth before eating his candy bar. He felt like he was going to get sick again. He needed some fresh air and something cold to drink. But most of all, he needed to stop feeling scared.

"Can I call a friend in town?" Gerry asked.

"Who's that?"

"Lamar Biggs."

The detective turned from the computer. The look in his eyes was pure disbelief. Gerry sensed that he had crossed some imaginary line, and hurried to explain. "I did a job for him today. The Dixie Magic is having a problem with some employees stealing chips. I explained to his crew how the scam is working. That's what I do." He pointed at his wallet sitting on the detective's desk. "My card's in there."

The detective took out his business card and read it. "You did a job for Lamar?"

"That's right."

"Why the hell didn't you say so?"

★   ★   ★

192

Valentine awoke from a deep sleep to hear his cell phone ringing in the kitchen. The luminous clock beside his bed said 3:00 A.M. The only reason people called at night was because something awful had happened. He pushed himself out of bed.

Walking was a struggle. With age came certain dependencies. Eight hours of sleep a night was one of them. He sat down at the kitchen table and picked up his cell phone. His head felt like a balloon, and he stared at the phone's face. The caller ID said UNKNOWN. Gerry, he decided. His son called whenever he felt like it.

"What's up," he said by way of greeting.

"Tony? Is that you? Oh God, I'm so happy you finally answered your phone."

It was Lucy Price. He closed his eyes and took a deep breath.

"Are you still there? Please don't tell me you hung up."

"If I hung up, I couldn't tell you," he said.

Lucy laughed shrilly, and he realized she'd been drinking. The cold metal of the phone seeped into his hand. He could not talk to Lucy without seeing her face. She bore a strong resemblance to his late wife, who he missed more than anyone in the world. So he'd allowed himself to get to know her. A stupider mistake he'd never made.

"I had to call you. I'm sorry if I've bothered you," she said.

His eyes went wide. Now she was laying on the guilt.

"What do you want? What's wrong?"

"How did you know something was wrong?"

"Because it's three in the morning," he said, his voice rising.

"Oh God, you're right. I always get the time change mixed up. A terrible thing happened today, and I just needed someone to talk to. You have been so . . . supportive."

More guilt. Raised Catholic, he could ferret out the guilt in every sentence. He leaned back in the chair. "I'm listening."

Lucy loudly blew her nose. "I went to the Holsum Bread building today to buy bread, and there's this cashier I've gotten friendly with named Ashli. Real nice girl. Ashli says, 'Well, it's been nice knowing you, Lucy. We're closing down.' I went and got the manager and he confirmed it. The building is being converted into upscale condos called Holsum Lofts. I went out to my car and started crying."

"Because they're closing down the bread company?"

"Yes."

"So buy your bread someplace else."

"This is different. This is the Holsum Bread company."

Then Valentine remembered. During a trip Valentine took to Las Vegas, a Nevada Gaming Control Board agent had taken him by the

Holsum Bread building on West Charleston. The agent had explained that this was where every down-and-out Las Vegas gambler bought day-old bread to feed themselves and their families. If they were really desperate, the agent said, they got free two-day-old bread from the Dumpster in back.

"I know it sounds pathetic," she went on, "but Holsum was a last resort. No matter how bad things got, you could always go there and get bread. And now they're going to replace it with a chi-chi high-rise."

She blew her nose again. He realized that was all she wanted to tell him. He stood up and cleared his throat. She'd lost everything in the past month—her money, her car, and probably her freedom—and he wondered if she'd finally hit bottom. Was Lucy finally ready to come to grips with her life?

"Maybe it's a sign," he said.

"What is?"

"The Holsum Bread building being torn down."

"A sign from who?"

He thought about it and said, "From God."

"Is that supposed to be a joke?"

"No," he said. "You've hit the end of the line, Lucy. You need help. You always thought you could still buy bread and feed yourself, but that option is gone. God is telling you this is it. Take his advice and get some help."

"But—"

"No buts. Just do it. And don't call me until you do."

"But I'm going to court in a few days. *I'm afraid.*"

Valentine felt something as big as a baseball catch in his throat. He wanted to help her; only, helping people didn't work when they refused to help themselves. Sometimes, it actually made things worse.

"Good-bye, Lucy," he heard himself say.

CHAPTER 23

At eight forty-five Valentine drove to Slippery Rock High School and parked by the front entrance. He had never gotten back to sleep and felt stiff climbing out of the car. It took only a few bad nights for his body to start feeling old.

At a minute before nine he went inside. Schools were empty places without kids, and he listened to his own footsteps as he walked down a tiled hallway to the library. The note had said last door before the cafeteria. He stopped at this door and rapped with his knuckles.

"It's open," a women's voice said from within.

He pushed the door open and stuck his head in. Five kids looked up at him. They ranged in age from about fifteen to about nine, and had books open in front of them.

"Over here," the voice said.

He followed the voice across the room. A handsome white-haired woman sat at a desk in the corner. "Sorry," he said. "I must have the wrong room."

"This is the right room," she said. "Please come in."

Valentine stepped into the library and shut the door behind him. The kids had stopped looking at him and gone back to their studying. Crossing the room, he realized that he recognized her. It was Mary Alice Stoker, the blind librarian he'd met at the Ping-Pong drawing the day before. She had sent the note.

"Please sit down," she said.

He pulled up a chair. An item on her desk caught his eye. It was a picture of her skiing, taken before she'd lost her vision. She couldn't see it anymore, but others could.

"I had hoped to meet with you alone," she said, "but the children's parents called and asked me to open up. Finals are in a few weeks, and they need to use the reference library. I'm sure you understand."

He nodded, then felt his face burn with embarrassment.

"Of course," he said.

"Good. If we keep our voices low, I'm sure they won't hear a thing."

He pulled his chair up a little closer.

"My hearing isn't what it used to be," he admitted.

Surprise registered on her face. "If you don't mind my asking, how old are you?"

"Soon to be sixty-three."

"Really. With all that's happened, well, I just assumed—"

"I was young and strapping?"

Her hand came up to her mouth. It was too late, and her laughter escaped. The five kids jerked their heads in her direction.

"Now you've really got them confused," Valentine said.

"Are they staring?"

"Afraid so."

"The town drums will be beating this afternoon."

Valentine leaned back in his chair and laughed softly. She was an easy person to be around and seemed at peace with her situation. Maybe if he was good, she'd explain her secret.

"I'd like to tell you a story," she said. "Do you mind?"

"Not at all."

"I used to have a favorite little boy. By the time he'd reached the sixth grade he'd read every book in this library. He could also recite Shakespeare by heart and the Preamble to the Constitution and anything else he put his mind to. He was brilliant; only, he came from a terrible family situation. Parents always drinking and fighting and getting thrown in jail. He came to the library to escape. I used to open up on Sundays for him, too.

"One day, right after he turned thirteen, he disappeared. The police thought he'd been kidnapped, and there was a frantic manhunt around the state. All the women in town cried when he wasn't found. I think I cried the hardest.

"Eleven months later, he was found in a sleepy town in the Florida Panhandle. He hadn't been kidnapped as everyone thought. He'd gone and run away with a carnival.

"The carnival people were gypsies. They'd adopted him and had him working for them. They'd dyed his hair dark and given him a new name. When he came back to Slippery Rock, he was a different person. They hadn't molested him or abused him or anything like that. But they'd changed him."

She folded her hands and put them in her lap. Tears welled at the corners of her sightless eyes. The memory was so painful that her chest heaved up and down. Valentine felt like he'd sat down in the middle of a movie and didn't know what was going on.

"You don't understand, do you?" she said.

"No," he said.

"That little boy was Ricky Smith."

One of Valentine's first jobs as a cop in Atlantic City had been to drive a carnival out of town. It hadn't been an easy assignment. The same carnival had been coming to town ever since he could remember. They would rent an empty lot for the summer and set up their colorful tents and old-fashioned midways. They offered games where people could win prizes, and sometimes they had entertainment, as well. Right after Labor Day they would pack up and head down south. Watching them leave had always made him feel sad.

At first he had wondered why the carnival had

to be run out. The Atlantic City Boardwalk also featured games and entertainment, and no one gave their owners a hard time. It didn't seem right, so he'd gone to his superior and asked him.

His superior was a hard-ass named Banko. Normally, Banko would have chewed him out for not following orders. But he'd seen something in Valentine's eyes that told him an explanation was warranted. So Banko had sat him down and explained.

"The carny people that come to Atlantic City are coldhearted thieves. Their games look the same as the Boardwalk games, but they ain't. They're crooked. Know why?"

Valentine shook his head. The carnival people had always been nice to him, and he was having a hard time believing Banko.

"Because they have to make a living, that's why," Banko snapped. "The carny people are here for two months. They're only open at night. It's not like the Boardwalk, which is always filled with customers. People go to the carnival once or twice. If one-tenth of them won prizes—like those big stuffed animals—the carny people would go broke. So they rig the games so nobody can win."

"But I've seen people win," Valentine blurted out.

"You've seen pretty girls win," Banko replied.

"What do you mean?"

"Only pretty girls win."

"What do you mean?"

201

"It's good for business. A pretty girl walking around a carnival carrying a giant stuffed panda? It's gonna make everyone smile." He put his hand on Valentine's shoulder. "These people are rotten to the core. They offer acts on the midway. Sword swallowers, the world's tallest man, Hilda the Bearded Lady. Some of them are pretty good. And the carnival people only charge you twenty-five cents admission. Bargain of the century, right?"

"Right," Valentine said.

"Well, it's a ploy, a con. The reason they charge you any admission is because they want to see inside a guy's wallet. Guys always bring money with them to the carnival, especially if they're on a date or have kids. The guy selling the tickets sits on a high chair and rips tickets off a spool. But what he really does is stare into wallets. If a guy has a lot of dough, he signals to another carny guy in the crowd.

"That guy walks up behind the pigeon and draws a mark down his back with a piece of chalk. He does this as he bumps into him. The pigeon never feels it.

"The pigeon is now a target for a pickpocket. He gets cleaned out, and his wallet gets returned without him knowing it. That way, if he goes to the police with a beef, they'll see he still has his wallet and figure he just blew the money."

Valentine tapped his fingers on Mary Alice Stoker's desk. He could remember the conversation with

Banko like it was yesterday. It had been like learning there was no Santa Claus. And now the librarian was telling him that Ricky Smith had spent nearly an entire year with bad carnival people.

"How was Ricky different when he came back?" he asked.

"He wasn't a little boy anymore. I guess you could say he'd lost his innocence."

"Did he get back with his parents?"

"They split up, and then Ricky moved in with his aunt."

"Did you have much contact with him?"

She shook her head. Behind her desk was a window that faced the forest. A deer stepped into the picture, watching him out of the corner of its eye as it munched on the grass.

"Ricky stopped coming to the library," she said. "He started cutting classes and never carried books in school. Somehow he still managed to get straight A's."

"Think he was cheating?"

"A lot of the teachers suspected it, but they couldn't prove it."

"What do you think?"

"He was cheating."

Valentine stared over her shoulder at the deer. It was eating nervously, and he guessed it had gotten used to coming by and not getting any response out of Mary Alice.

"Any other suspicious behavior?"

The blind librarian nodded. "Ricky had a friend named Stanley Kessel who also came from a broken home. Stanley was a gambler. Got caught several times in school running card and dice games. Got expelled in his senior year and never returned."

"And they hung out together."

"Bosom buddies."

"Are they still friends now?"

"Stanley went to New York five years ago, became a stock broker, and made a killing in the market. I'm told he and Ricky are still friends."

"Did you know Stanley personally?"

"Yes. Stanley was slime. My blindness is caused by a degenerative eye disease that started twenty years ago. The week I lost my vision, Stanley came into this room and stole forty dollars from my purse. I was here."

There was a harshness in her voice that he hadn't heard before. Stanley Kessel had stuck an invisible knife in her and probably hadn't even realized it. Valentine reached across the desk and placed his hand onto hers. She smiled thinly, and he left his hand there.

"Ms. Stoker, we're done," a little voice said.

Valentine glanced over his shoulder. The five kids who'd been buried in their books a moment ago were now standing behind them in a row. They had funny smiles on their faces, and he slowly withdrew his hand.

★   ★   ★

Mary Alice introduced the children to him. "This is Kristen, David, and Annie Buchholz, and Sara and Terry Williams," she said. "Children, say hello to Mr. Valentine. And, David, if you're wearing your baseball cap, please take it off."

The kids stuck out their hands and said hello. They stared at him like he had two heads, and Valentine made them repeat their names as he shook their hands. Each one carried a book, and he recalled how difficult it had been to get Gerry to study back when he was in school. Terry Williams, who looked about thirteen and had a mop of dark hair, stepped forward. "Ms. Stoker, we were wondering if Mr. Valentine could show us something."

"And what might that be, Terry?" the librarian asked.

"Well, we all went on Mr. Valentine's Web site yesterday, and there's all this cool stuff about casino cheating and crooks. On the Web site, it says that Mr. Valentine goes to casinos and gives demonstrations."

"Yeah," Annie piped up. "And we want to see some."

"Cheating?" the librarian said.

"Yeah!" the five kids replied in unison.

"I have a deck of cards," Terry said brightly, producing a dog-eared deck of Bicycles from his pocket. Handing them to Valentine, he said, "They're all there. I counted."

Valentine saw Mary Alice Stoker shift uncomfortably in her chair and guessed she was having visions of five more children being corrupted. He considered showing the kids a simple trick or two, but realized she wouldn't be able to see. Then he had another idea.

He made the kids pull up chairs so they sat around him in a semicircle. He took the deck from Terry and removed the rubber band encasing the cards. Then he held the cards on his outstretched palm. The five children stared at them.

"I'm not going to show you any cheating. Do you know why?"

Disappointment appeared on their faces, and they shook their heads.

"Because cheating is a crime. It's no different than stealing. But I know something about these playing cards that few people know. Want to hear it?"

They slowly nodded.

"Okay. No one knows who invented playing cards. Some people believe they were invented by medieval magicians who concealed all sorts of occult symbolism into the different pictures." Valentine turned the cards faceup and spread them between his hands. "The cards are evenly divided, with twenty-six red cards and twenty-six black. This symbolizes day and night. Then there are the four suits: clubs, hearts, spades, and diamonds. What do you think these stand for?"

David, the boy with the baseball cap, said, "The four seasons of the year?"

"That's right. How did you get so smart?"

The kids were all smiling now. Valentine upjogged all the jacks, queens, and kings and pointed at them. "Okay. There are twelve picture cards in the deck. Do any of you know what they stand for?"

"The twelve months in the year?" Sara said.

"Very good. Now, here's a tough one. There are thirteen values—ace through the king. What do these stand for?"

The kids acted stumped. Then a lightbulb went off over Terry's head.

"The thirteen lunar cycles?"

"Right. Now, here's an easy one. What do the fifty-two cards stand for?"

"The fifty-two weeks in the year," Kristen said.

"That was an easy one. Okay, here's the last one, and it's a doozy." He leaned forward and lowered his voice. "If you were to add up the values of all the cards in a full deck, counting the joker as one, what do you think you'll get?" The kids looked at each other and shook their heads. Out of the corner of his eye he saw Mary Alice nodding in approval. He said, "You'll get exactly three-hundred and sixty-five, the number of days in a year."

The kids looked at one another. "That's really cool," Annie said.

Valentine squared the deck between his palms. He had big hands, and they completely obscured the cards. When he opened his hands a moment later, the deck had disappeared. He removed them from his jacket pocket with a faint smile on his face.

"Show's over," he said.

The kids left the library chattering among themselves. Valentine offered to give Mary Alice a lift back to wherever she lived. She declined, saying a friend was coming by later to take her home.

She escorted him down the empty hallway to the entrance of the school. She walked without a cane, and he thought how nice it was that she worked in a place that her memory still remembered. She stopped a foot before the front door.

"I know this might sound strange," she said, "but you aren't the man I expected you to be."

He stared through the glass cutout in the door. His car looked lonely in the empty parking lot. He tried to imagine how a blind person would envision him.

"Did I live up to your expectations?"

A startled look registered across her face. She reached out, groping to find his arm. Her fingers found his wrist and squeezed it. "I thought you would be some kind of brute," she said. "I was wrong. You're a caring man beneath the tough exterior. You can help us."

"You think so?"

"Yes, I most certainly do."

"Help you how?"

"By straightening out this mess." With her free hand, Mary Alice made a sweeping gesture. "First

Ricky wins all that money in Las Vegas, then he comes home and starts winning lotteries and sweepstake drawings. And then the robbery at the bank. That mess."

"You think they're connected?"

She released his wrist. "Yes. I just wish I could tell you how."

Valentine watched her walk away. Her steps reverberated down the hallway, and when she was safely back in the library, he went outside and started up his car.

CHAPTER 24

Lamar Biggs sprung Gerry out of the Harrison County jail at 5:00 A.M. He was dressed in jeans and a Mississippi State sweatshirt and had a haggard look on his face. Every cop in the place knew him, confirming Gerry's earlier suspicions that Lamar was not casino security but in fact involved in some area of law enforcement.

"Explain to me what happened during your drive," Lamar said.

Gerry stared out the windshield. They were on the major east-west artery of I-10, six lanes of superhighway that shot traffic from Florida to west Texas. It was an industrial wasteland, and white dust jumped up from the road with each passing car. He found himself wishing he was back home with his wife and baby daughter.

"Three good ole boys ran me off Highway 49 near the pine-milling factory," he said. "They had shotguns and were trying to kill me. I got desperate and pulled a lever that said *do not pull*. It released about a hundred logs and killed them."

Lamar mumbled under his breath. He drove like

a New York cabbie, his body hunched forward, his chin a few inches off the wheel. He took an exit and five minutes later pulled down an unmarked dirt road. They came to a handsome, two-story shingle house hidden behind a stand of trees. Lamar pulled up the driveway and killed the engine.

"You live here?" Gerry asked.

"Yeah. I figured it was the safest place to bring you."

Gerry stared at him. "What am I hiding from?"

"My wife is making breakfast," Lamar said. "Let's have something to eat first, and then I'll explain what's going on."

The smell of grilling sausage greeted them as they entered the house. The dining-room table had two place settings, and his host pointed at one of the empty chairs. Gerry dropped into it. Taking out his cell phone, he powered it up and checked for messages. Yolanda and his father had called, both sounding worried as hell. The door leading to the kitchen swung open, and Isabelle, the lady from Louisiana he'd met the day before, entered with two steaming plates of food. She served them, all the while smiling at Gerry.

"I heard you've had a rough night," she said. "Hope this helps."

Gerry stared down at his plate. Grits, sausage, a pile of scrambled eggs with green stuff mixed in, and two steaming-hot biscuits. That was one of the things he liked about the South. No one was ever on a diet. He dug in.

"Those three boys you killed were the Dubb brothers," Lamar said, pushing back from the table when he was done. "They're hit men for the Dixie Mafia."

Gerry dropped his fork on his plate. "There's Mafia in Mississippi?"

"Yeah. They're not Eye-talian. But that's what they call themselves. You done?"

Gerry nodded, and Lamar stacked their plates and took them into the kitchen, then returned with a pot of coffee. He filled Gerry's cup without being asked, then his own. Sitting, he said, "Before the casinos came, Mississippi was the poorest state in the Union. Jesse Jackson once likened it to Ethiopia. The Dixie Mafia ran the crime. Mostly drugs, like crank and blow and amphetamines, but also prostitution and small-time gambling. They even sold ruckus juice now and then."

"What's that?"

"Moonshine. Then the casinos came. It wiped out their gambling dens overnight. Over time, it began to eat into their other operations, as well. Their customer base started to dry up." He shook a toothpick out of a container on the table and worked it between his gums. "Now, what I'm going to tell you is not to be repeated."

"Okay," Gerry said.

"The Dixie Mafia has infiltrated the Dixie Magic

and probably a couple of other casinos in town, as well. They're stealing a lot of money. It's their last stand, so to speak."

Gerry understood the gravity of what Lamar was saying. If word got out that Mississippi had organized crime figures working in its casinos, the state's gambling business would be ruined overnight. It would affect everything from health care to education.

"How do you figure in this?" Gerry asked.

"I run the enforcement division of the Mississippi Gaming Commission," Lamar said. "Isabelle and everyone you saw in that room yesterday works for me. My job is to figure out how the Dixie Mafia is cheating the casinos, and put everyone involved behind bars."

"Wow," Gerry said.

"Wow is right. Now, I need to ask you a question, and I want you to come clean with me."

Gerry stiffened. "Sure."

"What the hell happened between you and Tex Snyder yesterday?"

The truth, Gerry knew, could be your best friend or your worst enemy. It all depended upon how it came out of your mouth. He put his elbows on the table and lowered his voice. "Tex asked me to help him fleece a sucker in a poker game yesterday afternoon. He offered me fifty grand. I'd be lying if I told you I wasn't tempted."

"But you said no."

"That's right. I said no and walked out on him."

Lamar worked the toothpick between his teeth and gums. "That explains a lot."

"Why, what happened?"

Lamar smiled thinly. "From what we can figure out, the sucker got lucky and beat Tex for a few hundred big ones. The problem was, Tex wasn't playing with his own money. He was playing with the Dixie Mafia's money."

Gerry felt like he'd been jabbed with a cattle prod. "Did they—"

"Go after him? Oh, yeah. The Dubb brothers beat Tex to within a few inches of his life. He's lying in the hospital in critical condition. My guess is, Tex told them that you ran out on him and screwed up his scam. That's why the Dubbs went after you."

Gerry stared into the depths of his coffee and took a deep breath. If Yolanda hadn't put his daughter on the phone, he probably would have gone along with Tex and fleeced the sucker. And that would have put him in cahoots with a group of organized criminals.

"Am I a marked man?"

"You are until we catch the last Dubb," Lamar said.

"There's another brother?"

"No, he's the father. Name's Huck. He was behind the beating of Tex. He let his sons go after you." Lamar rose from the table, came back with a mug shot. "You can keep this."

Gerry stared at Huck Dubb's mug shot. He was

in his mid-fifties, wore bib overalls, and looked like a hillbilly with his scraggily beard and visible nose hair. Gerry slipped the picture into his shirt pocket.

"The police are going to need you as a witness," Lamar said, "so here's what I'd like to suggest. You can stay here with me and Isabelle. We'll make sure no harm comes to you, and you can enjoy some more good home cooking."

"How long are you talking about?"

"Three, four days, tops."

"That's all?"

"The law works quick here."

Gerry considered it. If Lamar's position with the Gaming Commission was anything like the enforcement directors in other states with casino gambling, he was incredibly powerful. So powerful that he could tell the police to stick Gerry in a seedy motel and watch him round the clock. Offering to put him up was beyond the call of duty. "I'm happy to help," Gerry said. "I appreciate the hospitality."

Lamar smiled with his eyes. "There is one thing I'd like to ask in return."

"You mean there's a catch to eating Isabelle's wonderful cooking?"

"Afraid so. The Dixie Magic is getting ripped off badly. I need you to look at all the games, see if you can spot anything. It would really help."

Gerry took another deep breath. Telling Lamar he was an expert on casino scams had just bitten

215

him in the ass. Would he ever stop lying to people? He doubted it; he'd been doing it too damn long. With his father's and Mabel's help, he guessed he could figure out what was going on.

"Be glad to," he said.

Isabelle did not permit smoking in the house, and Gerry went out behind the garage and lit up. As he brought the match to his face, he saw that his hand was shaking. He'd nearly gotten himself in a whole lot of trouble. But somehow, for some reason, he'd been spared. He wondered if it had something to do with going to confession with Father Tom last month. Coming clean had been the hardest thing he'd ever done. But it was going to be harder to stay clean. He knew that now, and it scared him.

He removed Huck Dubb's mug shot from his shirt pocket and stared at it. How had Huck reacted when he'd learned his three boys had gone to the big double-wide in the sky? *He's probably looking for me right now*, Gerry thought.

He powered up his cell phone. He hadn't talked to Yolanda since killing the Dubbs. He hadn't known how to explain to her that he'd just killed three men, even though it was in self-defense. He'd disappointed his wife too much to drop this on her. So he decided to wait until he got back home. He knew it was shitty, but it was the only way he could handle it.

CHAPTER 25

Mabel unlocked the front door of Tony's house and was punching the code into the security system when the phone in the study rang. She didn't like coming in Sunday mornings, but when Tony was out of town, there was no other choice. Casinos around the world did big business on Saturday nights and, as a result, were more susceptible to cheaters than any other day of the week.

The security system accepted the code and beeped. She walked down the hallway to the back of the house. Entering the study, she heard the phone stop, then immediately start ringing again. She guessed the caller was using speed dial to call back and was desperate.

"Grift Sense," she answered cheerfully.

"Do you do psychic readings?"

It was Tony. She lowered her body into the chair behind the desk. "Just tarot cards and tea leaves."

"No palm reading?"

"Afraid not. I once had a man read my palm. He told me I had a wet future and spit in my hand."

She heard him laugh. It was an infectious sound,

and she realized that he hadn't been doing enough of that lately. She guessed it was because of that damn woman in Las Vegas, Lucy Price. Every time Lucy called, it put Tony in a terrible mood.

"Heard from Gerry?" he asked.

"Yolanda talked to him last night," Mabel said. "Gerry met with Tex Snyder but didn't learn anything. He was on his way home."

"Tex didn't think he was cheated?"

"No," Mabel said. "Is that bad?"

"It's the one part of the puzzle that doesn't make sense. Games can be rigged. But cheating a world-class poker player is different."

Mabel stopped reading e-mails. "So you think Ricky Smith is a cheater?"

"Let's say I'm getting warm," he said.

Tony's computer sat on the desk, and Mabel scrolled through his e-mail messages. Over a dozen casinos had contacted him since yesterday. Normally, Tony would ask her to read the messages to him. He was more than warm, she decided.

"I need you to take a road trip and do some snooping for me," he said. "Feel up to it?"

"Today?"

"Yeah. Take Yolanda and the baby with you. Make an outing out of it."

"Well, aren't you just filled with wonderful ideas. Next you'll be telling me to pack a picnic. Now, where exactly am I going?"

"To the land of make-believe," he replied.

★ ★ ★

At noon, Mabel pulled out of her driveway in her Toyota Tercel, drove half a block, and pulled up in Yolanda's driveway. To her amazement, Yolanda came outside a few seconds later, holding the baby in one arm, the car seat in the other. Mabel had never known a new mother to ever be on time to anything. Yolanda strapped the baby in, then jumped into the front seat.

"Let's roll," she said.

Mabel stared at her. "Are you auditioning for Superwoman?"

"Why, is something wrong?"

"New mothers are always late. It's a tradition."

"I talked to Gerry earlier, and he got me so excited," she said, a smile lighting up her face. "He's going to be staying in Gulfport a few more days. The Mississippi Gaming Commission is asking him to help them with a case."

Mabel backed down the drive. "You sound happy he isn't coming home."

"Oh, no. I miss him terribly. It's just . . ." Yolanda struggled for the right words. "I've always wanted Gerry to be engaged in something. I think working for his father is going to turn out great."

Mabel handed her a sheet of paper lying on the seat. It was driving instructions she'd printed off an Internet site called MapQuest. Yolanda's eyes scanned the page. "Is this where we're going?" she asked.

"Yes. The little town of Gibsonton. It's about an hour's drive."

"What's in Gibsonton?"

"Carnival people," Mabel said.

Gibsonton was eight miles south of the interstate and smack in the middle of nowhere. The town barely resembled one, with a few businesses and mom-and-pop restaurants lining a deserted street, and a trailer park at the far end of the road. It was like many central Florida towns—sleepy and small—and Mabel found herself feeling mildly disappointed. She'd loved going to carnivals as a child and had envisioned the town having men walking around on stilts and jugglers on every corner. Yolanda pointed at a building on the other side of the street. A hand-painted sign said SHOWTOWN BAR & GRILL.

"Let's go in there," she suggested. "I need to change the baby's diaper."

Mabel pulled into the lot and parked by the front door. The drive had taken less time than she'd expected, and it was only twelve-thirty. Bars and restaurants weren't allowed to sell alcohol on Sundays until after one, and she had a feeling that no one would be inside. Maybe they could get a bite to eat and wait for the regulars to arrive.

The Showtown was your average watering hole, with a long water-stained bar and a few tables scattered around the room. It was deserted save for two men—the bartender, a rail-thin man in his sixties sporting a goatee, and a dwarf sitting on a bar stool, nursing a glass of tomato juice. They both said hello.

"Good afternoon," Mabel said, sidling up to the bar. The backlit mirror was covered with post-cards, most of them showing traveling circuses and sideshows. The dwarf courteously removed his hat, and a butterfly flew out of its folds. He cackled with laughter.

"My name's Brownie, and this here's Little Pete," the bartender said. "How can we help you ladies?"

"I was trying to get some information about a carnival that used to run out of Panama City," Mabel said, "and was hoping one of you gentlemen could help me."

Little Pete glanced over his shoulder. "Gentlemen? Who walked in?"

"You'll do," Mabel told him.

The dwarf smiled and so did the bartender.

"Hey," Yolanda said from the other side of the room.

Mabel turned from the bar. "What's wrong, my dear?"

"This door to the ladies' room isn't a door."

The room's light was poor, and Mabel squinted at where Yolanda was pointing. There was a door to the men's room, and beside it, a door to the women's room with a brass plaque. Yolanda was pushing on the women's room door, but it wasn't budging.

The baby was crying, her mother losing her

patience. Mabel crossed the room, assuming the door was locked. Only when she was a foot from it did the illusion stop. It was a painting. The shadowing and detail were so exact, it tricked the eye into believing it was a door.

"It's around the corner," Brownie called out.

"What a bunch of practical jokers," Yolanda said under her breath, hurrying away.

Mabel saw the men at the bar smiling at her. Little Pete pointed at her head.

"Your hair," he said. "It's come undone."

Mabel touched her hair. She liked to wear it up. She saw the dwarf pointing at the mirror on the far wall. She went to it and stared at her reflection. A startled sound escaped her lips. Her reflection wasn't there. But everything else in the room was.

She reached out and touched the mirror. It was another illusion made from paint. The room's furnishings were faithfully reflected in it, including the mop bucket on the floor and the silver napkin dispensers on the tables.

"I'm impressed," she said, looking at the two men. Brownie's smile said he was the culprit, his eyes laughing. She started to cross the room, and Little Pete pointed at the floor.

"Watch out!"

Mabel looked down at the open manhole, complete with toppled cover. She instinctively stopped and touched the cover with her foot. Another painting. She shook her head in amazement. It didn't matter that she knew it was a fake. Her brain still told her to be careful, and she gingerly stepped over it to the delight of the two men.

Back at the bar, she slapped the water-stained counter. "I think that deserves a drink. How are you in the ginger ale department?"

Brownie found a ginger ale in the cooler and poured it into a tall glass filled with ice. "On the house," he said.

"What do you call these paintings?" Mabel asked, taking a long drink. "I've never seen anything like them."

"Trompe l'oeil," he replied. "That's French for 'trick of the eye.' They keep things lively. Hope we didn't offend you and your friend."

"Not at all," Mabel said. "I like to be fooled."

Brownie and Little Pete were both retired sideshow performers, and they talked about their lives when Yolanda returned and joined Mabel at the bar, the baby sleeping in her arms.

Brownie called the sideshow a detour of shock and wonder. He and Little Pete had crisscrossed the country with circuses and carnivals for more than forty years. Brownie had started as a teenage clown, making himself up with shaving cream and lipstick. Little Pete informed them that he personally hadn't needed any makeup.

"As I got older, I became a talker," Brownie went on. "That's the guy who stands outside the tent and prods the crowd, called the tip, to buy a ticket. We used to have a bally—that's a small stage—where one or two acts would perform for free to get the crowd's attention. I also acted as a gazoony. That's the guy who put up and took down the show."

"You must have been awfully busy," Mabel said.

"When I was working, I slept five hours a night. I loved every minute of it."

Mabel removed a piece of paper from her pocket. It had her notes from her phone conversation with Tony. She pretended to consult them. She had a feeling that Brownie would talk all day if she let him. "Did you ever run across a carnival out of the Panhandle?" she asked. "It was run by a family of gypsies. This was about twenty years ago."

Little Pete said, "Could be the Schlitzie carnival. They were gypsies."

"They were criminals," Brownie said. "Ran crooked games and stole money from people left and right." He looked at Mabel. "That who you looking for?"

Mabel glanced at her notes. Tony had said the gypsies had brought Ricky Smith into their fold when he was a teenager, and taught him the tricks of their trade. She couldn't think of anything more harmful for a young man.

"Yes, I think so," she said.

"They were bad eggs. If I remember correctly, the mother and father got deported, and the carnival disbanded. This was about—"

"Fifteen years ago," Little Pete said, having captured the butterfly beneath a glass. Taking his cap off, he deftly picked the glass up off the bar and shook the butterfly out. It landed in his cap, which he immediately placed on his head.

"How long do they last?" Mabel asked.

"This one's going on six weeks," the dwarf said.

Mabel consulted her notes. Tony had been fooled by a lottery drawing and had decided that the method was something that Ricky Smith might have learned during his carnival days.

"Last question," she said. "A friend of mine was fooled by a lottery he saw. He thinks the drawing was rigged. It used Ping-Pong balls." She looked up at Brownie and Little Pete. "Does this ring any bells?"

"Ping-Pong balls?" Little Pete said. "Did she say Ping-Pong balls?"

"I believe she did," the bartender replied.

Little Pete jumped out of his chair and onto the bar. His balance was off, and he nearly fell, then instantly righted himself. Mabel guessed there was more than tomato juice in his glass. She watched him run down the bar to the end. He grabbed a brown paper bag sitting on the top of a refrigerator. He kept his back to her, hiding his actions. When he returned, he was holding the bag in his outstretched hands.

"Take a look inside," he said, "and tell me what you see."

Mabel peeked inside the bag. Yolanda looked as

well. The baby hadn't made a sound, God bless her. The bag was filled with white Ping-Pong balls. Each one had a number printed on it in block lettering. Little Pete shook the bag for effect.

"All right, ladies and little girl, I want you to watch close. My dear friend Brownie is going to pull five balls out *with his eyes closed*. And I, the all-knowing, all-seeing Little Pete, am going to tell you which ones before he does. Ready?"

Mabel looked at Yolanda. "You watch his left hand, I'll watch his right."

"Got it," the younger woman said.

"The numbers nine, fourteen, twenty-three, thirty-five, and forty-seven. Those are the numbers which Brownie will pull from the bag. Nine, fourteen, twenty-three, thirty-five, and forty-seven."

Brownie unbuttoned his shirt sleeve and tugged it back to his elbow. His arm was covered in blue-black tattoos of mermaids and battleships. A navy man, Mabel guessed.

Closing his eyes, Brownie stuck his arm into the paper bag and removed a ball. It had the number twenty-three written on it.

"Twenty-three! Call me a genius. Everyone else does!" Little Pete said.

Brownie pulled out two balls at once. Numbers nine and fourteen.

"The daily double! How does he do it? Nobody knows!"

Grinning, Brownie pulled out a fourth ball. Number thirty-five.

"Someone start a religion after this man," the dwarf said. He stared at Yolanda with a devilish grin on his face. Then he offered her the bag.

"Go ahead, take out the last one. Number forty-seven."

"But I don't understand how the trick works," Yolanda protested.

"That doesn't matter," Little Pete said.

Clearly perplexed, Yolanda handed Mabel her sleeping baby, then rose a few inches off her seat and stuck her arm into the paper bag. Suddenly her facial expression changed, and it took a moment before Mabel recognized the look. Yolanda was in the know.

She withdrew her hand and handed Mabel ball number forty-seven.

"How did you do that?" Mabel exclaimed.

CHAPTER 26

It was noon when Valentine heard the doorbell ring. He'd decided that renting the house in Slippery Rock was one of the stupidest things he'd ever done. Everyone knew exactly where to find him. The front door had warped from all the rain, and he had to jerk it open. On the stoop stood Sergeant Gaylord. He was in his uniform, hat in hand.

"Sergeant Gaylord. What a pleasant surprise."

Gaylord shot him an unfriendly look. "I normally don't work Sundays, but seeing as I've got three dead men lying in my morgue, I'm clocking extra hours. Mind if I come in?"

"What's this about?"

"You, my friend."

Valentine ushered him into the kitchen and offered him a chair. Then he brewed a fresh pot of coffee with the coffee-maker he'd found in the pantry. He'd never known a cop to refuse a cup of joe, and Gaylord did not let him down. Tempering the drink with several teaspoons of sugar, the sergeant took a sip and winced.

"That's mighty strong. You a caffeine junkie?"

"Afraid so."

"Everyone's got an addiction. Be happy yours is legal." The sergeant took a bigger sip this time, and it made his eyes widen. "Here's the deal, Tony. I called around and checked you out. You're not in Slippery Rock writing your memoirs."

Valentine guessed Gaylord was the last person in town to figure that out. He said, "Kind of obvious, huh?"

"Just a little." Gaylord loosened the knot in his necktie. "So here's the deal. I want you to come clean with me. I need to know why you were in that bank with Ricky Smith. Now, understand, I'm not accusing you of anything. But I need to know the truth. And if I think you're lying, I'm going to haul you in under suspicion. Understand?"

Valentine nodded. He'd put Gaylord in a bad position by not coming clean with him yesterday. It was disrespectful, and they both knew it. He took a gulp of coffee and told the sergeant the real reason he was in Slippery Rock.

At first, Gaylord didn't say much. There didn't appear to be much going on behind his dull green eyes. Small-town cops were notoriously dumb; below-average IQs were a requirement among many police departments, the belief being that someone with brains wouldn't be interested in sitting in a patrol car all day. Ripping open a pack of gum, the sergeant stuck three sticks into his mouth and began to vigorously chew. When Valentine was finished talking, Gaylord said, "Want a piece?"

"No thanks."

He put the gum away. "So you think Ricky may be staging all this stuff, making himself look like he's the world's luckiest man?"

"That's my theory," Valentine said.

"But you don't have any proof."

"No, sir."

"But you have a motive," he said, working his gum hard.

Valentine shook his head.

"Sure you do. Ricky's trying to be something that he's not."

"What do you mean?"

Gaylord put his cup in the sink, then returned to his chair. "That's the motivation behind most robberies. The robber wants the money because he thinks it's going to change him in some life-altering way. It's his ticket to the big time."

The coffeepot was still on. Valentine refilled his cup, thinking back to the robbery at the bank. "Sort of like Beasley and the scarecrow."

"Exactly."

Gaylord removed a spiral notebook from his back pocket and stared at his notes. "Just before you shot them, Beasley told his partner they were going to be eating cheeseburgers in paradise. That's a line from a Jimmy Buffet song. My wife is a Parrot Head, has all his CDs."

"Is that what they call his fans?"

Gaylord nodded. "I listened to the song last night. You know what it's really about?"

"No."

"The song is about dreams."

Valentine sipped his coffee. Mary Alice Stoker had told him that she thought Ricky's lucky streak and the bank robbery were somehow connected. Now Gaylord was inferring the same thing. He wasn't seeing the connection and put his cup on the table. "Maybe I'm missing something, but what does that have to do with Ricky Smith winning everything in sight? The bank robbers didn't act like they knew him."

Gaylord flipped his notebook shut and slapped it on the table. There was a spark behind his eyes now. "I honestly don't know. But my gut tells me they're connected. Beasley and the scarecrow didn't have arrest records. Something drove them to do what they did." Glancing at his watch, he said, "My wife is going to kill me," and pushed himself out of his chair.

"She making you lunch?"

"We're going out. It's our anniversary."

Valentine followed the sergeant outside to his car. Gaylord had his keys out. As he started to get in, an SUV passed on the road. The sergeant watched it like a hawk, then said, "See that car? Brand-new Lexus SUV. Owner is a housepainter. Set him back forty-five thousand bucks."

"I hear they're nice cars," Valentine said.

Gaylord shot him a funny look. "Know how many new cars I've seen in the past week? An even dozen. BMW, Mercedes-Benz, Lexus, even one of those crazy-looking Hummers. I've worked here sixteen years and never seen that many new cars."

"Are the people who're buying them connected?"

"Nope. Just a bunch of locals. They're going to the bank and taking out loans."

Valentine felt himself stiffen. *They were buying on credit, just like Ricky Smith.*

"Not just for cars, either," the sergeant went on. "People borrowing money to buy plasma-screen TVs and motorcycles and putting additions on their houses. If I didn't know better, I'd think Slippery Rock was single-handedly trying to jump-start the economy."

Valentine's cell phone rang. He took it out and flipped it open. It was Gerry.

"My son," he told the sergeant.

Gaylord climbed into his car, then lowered his window. He held out a paper bag, which Valentine took from him and looked inside. It contained his Glock.

"Thanks."

He watched Gaylord drive away and felt himself shiver. He'd come outside without his overcoat and was already regretting it. The old adage was true: People from the north were always cold, people from the south always warm.

"How's it going?" he said to his son.

"Not so great," Gerry replied. "I'm still in Gulfport."

Valentine went into the house and slammed the door behind him. The reception on his cell phone instantly got better. "How much did you lose?"

"What do you mean?" his son said, sounding hurt.

His ass hit the chair hard. Gerry had come into this world kicking and screaming and had been causing headaches ever since. "How much did you lose in the casino? That's what you're calling about, isn't it?"

"No, Pop, it's not. Three brothers tried to execute me outside Gulfport last night. They're in the Dixie Mafia. I dumped some logs on them and killed them. I'm staying in Gulfport until the police arrest their father. He's in the Dixie Mafia too."

Valentine felt his heart racing out of control. He could hear real fear in his son's voice. When he opened his mouth, he heard the same fear in his own.

"Why did they try to kill you?"

"Tex Snyder asked me to help him cheat a sucker. I turned him down. Turns out Tex was working with these guys."

"You doing okay?"

His son took a deep breath. His voice sounded

like it was going to crack. Valentine wished they were in the same room so he could throw his arms around his son's shoulders and comfort him.

"No," Gerry said.

CHAPTER 27

Huck Dubb felt an invisible knife stab him in the heart. He stood in the basement of the Harrison County morgue, staring at his three sons lying side by side on slabs. Their naked bodies were covered in purple bruises, their heads twisted unnaturally to the side. He'd heard the news and rushed over. He had to see it with his own eyes.

He touched each of his boys. Their skin had turned cold and clammy. He'd never believed in God and believed in him less now. God wouldn't rob a man of his three sons all at once. Not even a man as bad as him. He looked at the walleyed orderly who'd let him into the morgue. His name was Cur. Huck had run moonshine with his daddy years ago.

"Cover them," Huck said.

Cur draped black sheets over the three boys. Huck reached out and touched each of them again. Last Sunday, they'd gotten together and drunk whiskey on the front porch of his house. Their combined weight had caved the porch in and killed his best hunting dog. His sons had laughed like hell. He withdrew his hand.

It wasn't fair. One of his boys dying he might be able to live with; not all three. He looked at Cur. "What you hearing?"

"I'm hearing it was an Eye-talian that killed 'em," Cur said, shuffling his feet as he spoke. "Named Valentino or something."

Huck felt the knife give his heart another stab. Valentine was who he'd sent his boys to kill. "Where's Valentine, in the county jail?" he asked.

"Nuh-uh," Cur said, still doing his little dance. "Lamar Biggs sprung him."

"The niggah with the casino commission?"

"Yeah. I hear he's a mean one, that Lamar. I hear he'd kick a baby in the ass."

Huck spit on the floor. Lamar Biggs was a college-educated colored boy. He couldn't think of anything he hated more. "Know where this baby-kicker lives?"

Cur's head bobbed up and down. "You gonna go get Valentine?"

"What the hell do you think?" Huck said.

"Gonna kill him?"

"What the hell do you think?"

"Biggs, too?" Cur looked up. "I hear he's got a pretty, white wife."

"Him, too," Huck said.

Cur smiled crookedly and told him how to get to Lamar Biggs's house.

Huck went out to his Chevy pickup, took his shotgun off the gun rack, made sure it was loaded, and with it sitting on his lap drove to Lamar Biggs's place. The truck was brand-new, with cushy leather and all the fancy stuff, yet had cost no more than the Chevy truck he'd bought six years ago. The salesman had explained that everything was made in Mexico, then assembled here. Huck hadn't liked that. Mexicans were as bad as blacks; he didn't want his money going into their pockets. Then he'd driven the truck for a while and decided he could live with it.

Halfway to Lamar Biggs's house a thunderbolt hit him. Any black man who lived with a white woman in Mississippi had serious firearms in his house. Huck didn't want to be outgunned, and did a hasty U-turn in the middle of the road.

Huck's own house was on the northern end of Gulfport near the industrial plants. He had no neighbors. The stench from the pollution kept the civilized folks away.

Ten minutes later, he drove down the single-lane dirt road and pulled up the driveway. The house was actually a double-wide with a facade tacked on to make it look like a real house. It wasn't much to look at, but Huck liked it. The obscure location made surveillance by the police impossible, unless they decided to watch him by satellite.

His girlfriend's lime-green Mustang was parked on the front lawn. Her name was Kitty, and she slung drinks at a honky-tonk called Junebugs. Parking beside her car, Huck saw a new dent in the driver's door. Drunks propositioned Kitty all the time. Those that didn't like being turned down took their frustration out on her car.

"Where you been?" she asked as he came in.

"None of your business," he said.

Kitty lay on the couch beneath a blanket, the TV on so loud it made the room shake. "Well, excuse me. You having a bad day?"

"Lost my boys," he said, heading toward the bedroom in back.

"Try looking in the bars," she called after him. "They're usually there."

Huck shut the bedroom door behind him. Got on his knees and pulled the cardboard box out from beneath his bed. Pulled out the AK-47 and began stuffing his pockets with ammo. He'd drive up to Biggs's house, jump out, and start shooting. The AK-47 would shoot right through the walls, probably go right through the damn house. Anything inside would die. He started to leave, when another thought struck him. If he killed Biggs or his wife, he'd have to leave town for a while. He'd need money, and began to search through the drawers of his dresser for any spare cash.

"Goddamn woman," he swore angrily.

Kitty had cleaned him out. She claimed she'd been clean for five weeks, but Huck knew she was lying. Kitty would swallow or smoke or stick up her nose anything that would get her high. Then she'd lie on the couch and clean out the refrigerator. As a result, he'd started taking precautions. Picking the AK-47 up off the floor, he went into the front of the house.

"Hey," she said, "where you going with that thing?"

"Squirrel hunting. Where's the stash box?"

"On top of the TV. I smoked the last of the pot." She silenced the TV with the remote, then rose from the couch with the blanket draped around her shoulders. "Say, you got any money? We need groceries."

Huck stared at her and felt his anger boil up. Damn woman was a leech. She'd spend all his money until he was tapped out and then find herself another sugar daddy.

He grabbed the stash box off the TV, turned it upside down. A pack of rolling papers and a hash pipe hit the floor. Sticking his hand into the box, he pulled out the false bottom and removed a thick wad of hundred-dollar bills. Kitty shrieked.

"You been holding out on me!"

Huck pointed at the couch. "Shut up and sit down."

"Why didn't you tell me you had money?"

"You heard me."

Kitty drew the blanket farther around herself and sat down. A little-girl pout appeared on her lips. "It's not fair. You're going to hit the bars with your sons and leave me here."

"My boys are dead," he said.

She looked up, startled. "What?"

"You heard me. I need to enact a little payback. I may have to disappear for a while. The police come looking for me, you don't know nothing, understand?"

"Dead? All three of them? How can that be?"

Her eyes were glassy; she was high on something, and it wasn't pot. Probably speed someone had given her at Junebugs. Long-distance truckers came in, plied the girls with pills. Huck peeled two hundred-dollar bills off his wad and tossed them at her. She tried to grab them out of the air and missed by a foot. She retrieved them from the floor.

"Thanks, Huck."

"What are you going to say if the police come?"

"Nuthin'. I ain't saying nuthin'." She opened her blouse and stuffed the bills down between her breasts. It was another bad habit she'd picked up at Junebugs. "I washed your clothes. They're in the dryer, case you need them."

Huck looked at her. "I'll call you when I can."

She nodded woodenly.

"You gonna be okay?" he asked.

"I guess," she said.

Huck got his clothes out of the dryer. Rolled them in a ball and heard Kitty raise the volume on the TV. She'd live here until her money ran out, he guessed.

"Hey," she called out. "Come here and look at this."

"No time," he said, stuffing his clothes under his arm.

"We're on TV!" she exclaimed.

"What you talking about, girl?"

"The house is on the TV," she said. "I changed the channel, and we're on TV."

Huck went back into the living room. The TV was a big-screen he'd bought on sale at Sears. He'd had the worst time getting it through the front door. He stared at the picture of his house and the two cars parked on the lawn. The clothes under his arm hit the floor.

"What channel you on?"

"One of the satellite ones," she said.

He threw open the front door and stuck his head out. Everything looked the same; then his eyes settled on the telephone pole sitting in his yard. A white transformer can was sitting on top of the pole. Kitty shouldered up next to him. Huck pointed at the can.

"When did they install that?"

"Yesterday. Telephone crew came by. They were here a while. Is the camera in that?"

"Yeah. It's a pole pig."

She let out a cry. "Don't go calling me names!"

"I ain't calling you names. It's a pole pig."

"Stop that!"

Huck ignored her and raised the AK-47 to shoulder height. Pole pigs were law enforcement's newest toy, the can hiding a high-resolution camera with a telephoto lens. A microwave video transmitter sent the video signal from the camera to a receiver up to a mile away. The can probably had a leak in it, and the leak was getting picked up by the antenna on top of his house. He got the can in his sights and pulled the trigger.

The can shot blue flames. He went back inside and stared at the blank screen on his TV. Then he looked at Kitty. She was crying her eyes out.

"You're a piece of shit," she said.

Huck threw her in the bathroom and propped a chair against the door. Outside he could hear sirens, and guessed the police had been waiting for him to come home. He ran outside through the back door. His sons' four-wheelers were parked in back. He got one started and made its engine bark. Then he ran back inside.

Through the front window he saw four police cruisers burning down the road. He busted out the glass with the barrel of the AK-47 and started shooting. The front cruiser took the hit in its engine and spun crazily off the road. The other cruisers pulled off as well. Huck went to the bathroom door.

"Lie on the floor," he said.

"Don't leave me," she wailed.

He went outside and jumped on the four-wheeler. Miles of dirt trails twisted through the woods behind his house. He drove down one for a minute, then pulled off. In the distance he could hear staccato bursts of gunfire, and imagined the police shooting his house up. The local cops were cowards. They usually hid behind their cruisers and shot blind. He put Kitty's chances of surviving at fifty/fifty.

"Good luck, baby," he said, and drove away.

CHAPTER 28

Valentine spent an hour on the phone talking to Gerry. He wasn't sure it did any good. Killing the murderous Dubb brothers had ripped a hole in his son's psyche.

Valentine knew the feeling too well. Television and the movies distorted how the act of killing another human being actually made you feel. There was nothing glorious or heroic about it, and there never would be.

"Pop, I need to go," his son said. "Lamar just got a call from the local police. The Dubb brothers' father is on the loose, and Lamar wants to take me to a more secure place."

Valentine pushed himself out of the chair he was sitting in. He didn't want his son to hang up. His boy's situation had reminded him that there were more important things in life than figuring out how casinos got ripped off. "You keep yourself glued to Lamar Biggs's side," he said. "You don't know who in that town Huck Dubb knows."

"I will," his son said.

"You tell Yolanda any of this?"

"Not yet. I wanted to do it in person. Like you used to with Mom after you had to shoot someone."

Valentine had always wondered if his son had learned anything from him. It was nice to know something had sunk in.

"I'm going to leave my cell phone on," Valentine said. "Call me anytime you want to."

"You're going to leave your cell phone on?" Gerry said, feigning astonishment. "That's a first. I'm alerting the media."

And a smart mouth. Gerry had learned that from his father as well.

Hanging up, Valentine went into the living room and browsed through the books left by the previous owners. An entire set of the *Encyclopaedia Britannica* lined one shelf, their spines yellow with age. He pulled out the edition with the word *Atlas* printed on its spine. In the very front was a four-color map of the United States. With his thumb, he measured the distance between where he was in North Carolina to where Gerry was in Mississippi. It was about five hundred miles. His paternal instinct told him he needed to go.

He'd left his cell phone on the kitchen table and now heard it beep. Someone had left a message. He guessed it had come in while he was talking to Gerry. He went into the kitchen and retrieved it, and heard Mabel's cheerful voice.

"Yolanda and I just had the most marvelous time

245

with two flatties in Gibsonton," his neighbor said. "That's slang for carnival people. And guess what? They taught us how the Ping-Pong trick works! I'm not surprised it fooled you. Call me at home when you get a chance, and I'll be happy to explain how it's done."

Valentine erased the message and then dialed Mabel's number. He realized he was smiling. He was always explaining scams and cons to her and could tell she enjoyed knowing something that he didn't.

"Let me guess," he said when she answered. "A four-year-old kid could figure it out."

"Oh, not at all," his neighbor said. "In fact, I don't think I would have figured it out myself. The Ping-Pong ball hides the secret."

He sat down at the kitchen table. "Okay, I give up. What secret?"

"Five of the Ping-Pong balls are frozen ahead of time. Those are the winning numbers. The audience can't tell that the balls are frozen, because they're white to begin with. The person who pulls the balls out of the bag simply grabs the cold ones."

Which meant that the barker at the high school was part of the scam. The smile faded from his face. But what about Mary Alice Stoker? Was she involved, or just a patsy, chosen because she was blind and wouldn't know that frozen balls were in the bag?

"But the balls weren't cold when I examined them," he said.

"That's the other clever part of the scam," she said.

He waited and heard her breathing on the line.

"Uncle," he said.

"Uncle?"

"Yeah. I give up. What's the other part?"

"The balls warm up in a person's hand," his neighbor replied, sounding delighted with herself. "It takes about ten seconds for the plastic in the ball to return to room temperature. It's an old carnival trick."

"I bet it is," he said.

"Oh, I also got the skinny on the gypsies that ran the carnival Ricky Smith lived with. They were called the Schlitzies, and they were real crooks."

Valentine felt his face grow warm. *And so are a bunch of other people in this town.* From the front of the house he heard a frantic banging and realized someone was at the front door. He went into the hallway and put his face to the glass cutout in the door. No one was there.

"That's funny," he said.

"That the Schlitzies were crooks?" his neighbor said.

"Sorry. I was just talking out loud."

"Well, I need to run. I've got lasagna baking in the oven, and Yolanda is coming over later for dinner. You take care of yourself."

"You, too," he said.

The phone went dead in his hand. He killed the

connection when the frantic banging started again. It was so loud it nearly made him jump. He jerked open the door to find a young girl with a ponytail standing on the stoop. Out in the driveway lay a bicycle.

"Mr. Valentine," she said breathlessly. "Please help."

Valentine crouched down so they were eye to eye. It was a trick he'd learned when he was a street cop and had to talk to a kid. It immediately set them at ease. The girl was about twelve, tall and blond, and wore a navy sweatshirt that said ASPIRING SHOPAHOLIC. It was funny; only, there was nothing but fear in her eyes.

"What's your name?"

"Elizabeth Ford. Everyone calls me Liz."

"Who do you want me to help, Liz?"

"Ms. Stoker."

He gently placed his hand on her shoulder. "Has she been hurt?"

She was breathing hard and nodded her head.

"Did she send you?"

"She doesn't know," she said.

"Take a deep breath and tell me what happened."

"I went to her house. She was going to help me with a book report for school. I usually let myself in through the back door. There's a key under the mat. I went into the kitchen and heard voices in the living room. I pushed the door open and looked inside."

Tears raced down her cheeks. Valentine held her steady. "You're a very brave girl. Now tell me what you saw."

"There were four men in the living room with Ms. Stoker. They had accents. They were threatening her. She was sitting in a chair, and they were standing around her. One of the men was breaking things—"

"What kind of things?"

"I don't know," she said. "I was scared."

"I know you were. What were the men saying?"

"One of them was threatening Ms. Stoker. He kept telling her she had a big mouth and that he'd hurt her if she said anything else. Ms. Stoker tried to talk back, but the man kept poking her in the shoulder with his hand. Finally she tried to say something, and . . ."

"And what?"

"He hit her in the face with his hand."

Liz was really crying now. Valentine drew her into his chest and held her until the sobs subsided. He could remember it like it was yesterday: His old man getting drunk and slapping his mother around. The memory had only grown more vivid as he'd gotten older. "What did you do then?" he asked.

"I hid in the pantry. I heard the men leave and ran into the living room. Ms. Stoker was sitting in her chair crying. I asked her what she wanted me to do. She told me to go home and forget what I'd seen."

"But you came here instead."

She swiped at her eyes. "I heard you liked her."

Valentine pushed himself up so he was standing. "You're a smart kid, you know that?"

"Are you going to help Ms. Stoker?"

"You bet I am," he said.

CHAPTER 29

Liz gave him instructions to Mary Alice Stoker's house, then pedaled away on her bike. The blind librarian lived near the high school. Valentine had wondered how she got to work every day, and now he knew. She walked.

From the kitchen he got his Glock and ankle strap and put them both on. He planned on retiring the gun once he got home. But not a minute before.

He made the tires squeal backing down the driveway. If Mary Alice was being threatened for opening her mouth, then he was in danger as well. Braking the car, he reached down and drew the Glock from his ankle and laid it on his lap. Then he drove to Mary Alice's house with one eye on his mirror.

As the high school came into view, he weighed calling Sergeant Gaylord and giving him a heads-up. Gaylord had made it clear he wouldn't tolerate any more nonsense. Mary Alice's street was directly behind the school, and Valentine pulled down it with the phone clutched in his hand.

But he didn't make the call. Mary Alice had told

Liz not to call the police, and he had no right to ignore her request. He laid the phone on the seat and searched for her address. He found her house at the street's end—a simple two-story with peeling paint and a wraparound porch with a swing—and pulled into her driveway. Slipping the Glock into his pocket, he climbed out of the car.

Standing at the front door, he started to knock, then hesitated when he heard footsteps on the other side of the door. "It's Tony Valentine. May I come in?"

"I was in the middle of something," she said through the door. "What do you want?"

"I need to return an overdue book."

There was a long silence. The four men had scared the daylights out of her. That was why she wasn't opening the door. He knocked again, this time a little more forcefully.

"What do you want?" she asked again.

"Your permission."

"To do what?"

"Beat up the four guys who threatened you."

The door jerked open, and she stood silhouetted in the doorway. She wore a floor-length denim dress and had her hair down. Something hard dropped in his stomach. A hideous purple bruise marred the right side of her face. She held an ice pack in her outstretched hand, letting him see what they had done to her. He silently followed her inside.

★   ★   ★

252

His eyes canvassed the living room. Liz had said the four men had broken things while threatening Mary Alice. He didn't see any evidence of that.

"Elizabeth Ford told you," she said, sitting on the couch.

He drew up a chair and sat across from her. "That's right. She said four men were threatening you."

"It was a misunderstanding."

Valentine stared at the bruise on the side of her head. It was a beauty. "I've discovered that kids are good barometers when it comes to bad people. These guys sounded scary."

"I told you, it was a misunderstanding."

"Liz said one of them hit you."

"She has an active imagination."

"How did you get that bruise?"

"I fell down earlier when I was outside. Blind people do that sometimes."

He drew back in his chair. There was real defiance in her voice. The friendliness she'd shown that morning had evaporated, and he sensed that she didn't want him in her house.

"Would you like me to leave?"

"You're very perceptive," she said.

He rose and put the chair back where he'd found it. He started to walk to the door and heard something crunch loudly beneath his shoe. His eyes found a tiny piece of porcelain lying on the rug. Kneeling, he picked it up with the tips of his fingers.

"What are you doing?" she asked.

"Wondering why you just lied to me."

She shuddered. "I'd like you to leave. I was taking a nap. Please go."

"No," he said.

A swinging door led him into the kitchen. He went to the sink and started pulling open the large cabinet doors beneath it. She followed him uncertainly into the room.

"What are you doing? Please stop whatever it is you're doing."

"No," he said again.

The back door was ajar. He opened it and stepped outside. A short flight of wooden stairs led to her garden. The garden was meticulously kept, with three rows of red, white, and yellow roses. They were all in bloom. Her babies, he guessed.

At the foot of the stairs he spied a cardboard box. He walked down the steps and picked up the box with both hands. It was heavy, and he felt its contents shift. He walked up the stairs and went into the house, dropping the box onto the kitchen table. Mary Alice jumped.

"You're a lousy liar," he said.

"Please don't be angry with me as well."

He peeled back the lid. Inside the box were porcelain statues that had been shattered into tiny pieces. One of the pieces was a little boy's head, and he held it on his palm and stared at the painstaking detail that had gone into its creation.

"You collect these?" he asked.

She fumbled pulling a chair out from the kitchen table. Then she sat in it. "Yes. They're from a town in Germany called Meissen. There's a shop in Palm Beach that used to sell them. Every year I would save up my money and treat myself to one."

"How many did you have?"

"Twenty-two. I gave each one a name."

He put the head back into the box and closed the lid. Her other babies, he guessed. He pulled a chair out from the table and sat down beside her. He reached over and put his hand on her arm. A wall of resolution rose in her face.

"I would prefer if you didn't touch me."

He withdrew his hand. "When did I become the bad guy?"

"My friends in town called me. They told me what you did."

"What did I do?"

"You shot the two bank robbers in cold blood. They were trying to talk their way out of it, and you shot them. The casinos sent you. You're some kind of hit man."

A porcelain bowl filled with white candy sat in the center of the table. He stuck his hand into it. Some of it was hard, while other pieces were soft. He put some into his mouth and chewed. It was sweet and disgustingly good.

"Do you know Roland Pew?" he asked.

"I taught Roland to read," she replied.

He took the cordless phone off the counter and

called information, got Roland's number, and punched it in. Roland's familiar voice answered on the second ring. Valentine handed Mary Alice the phone. "Roland was there during the robbery," he said. "Ask him to tell you what really happened."

Valentine ate the entire bowl of candy while Mary Alice talked to Roland. She made him repeat himself a number of times, and Valentine guessed she was comparing his version of things against that of her friends. She hung up shaking her head.

"I can't believe my friends lied to me," she said.

"Maybe someone lied to them," he said. "This candy is absolutely delicious. You've got to give me the recipe."

She broke into a faint smile. Her hand reached across the table, and Valentine realized she was trying to touch him. He put his hand on top of hers and left it there.

"I'm sorry I doubted you," she said. "I hope you weren't offended."

"I'll get over it."

"The candy is made from peanuts, raisins, and Golden Grahams cereal. Put everything in a small garbage bag, then add melted chocolate, melted peanut butter, and a cup of confectioners' sugar. Shake the bag hard, and you're done."

"It's addictive. What do you call it?"

"White Trash."

He repeated the recipe to himself. He was lousy

in the kitchen and would have to entice Mabel to make up a batch. "Did you know the four men who threatened you?"

"Their voices were unfamiliar."

"Spanish accents?"

"Yes."

"They told you to stop talking to me, didn't they?"

"Yes. They said you were responsible for all the horrible things that were happening."

"Which one of them hit you?"

She shook her head, this time smiling.

"I really did fall down when I was outside," she said.

Stuck to Mary Alice's refrigerator was a list of important phone numbers, along with names of friends and family. The phone numbers were printed in English and in braille. He studied it for a few moments, then said, "Do you have any friends nearby you could stay with? I think it would be best if you got out of Slippery Rock for a few days."

"I have a cousin in Brevard. It's ten minutes away."

"I'd like to drive you, if you don't mind."

"That's very thoughtful of you," she said.

Ten minutes later Mary Alice was sitting in his car, her suitcase in the trunk. He hated taking her away from her house and the things she knew, but saw no other way to protect her. As he was backing out, his cell phone rang. He picked it up and stared at the caller ID.

"For the love of Christ," he muttered under his breath.

"What's wrong?"

It was Lucy Price, the last person in the world he wanted to talk to right now. He flipped the phone open and punched the power button. The phone went dead in his hand.

"Nothing," he said.

"You killed the power on your phone."

"It was someone I didn't want to talk to. How do I get to Brevard?"

"Who might that be?"

He had reached the end of her driveway. He didn't know which way to go and threw the car into park. There was suspicion in her voice, and he said, "It was a woman I met in Las Vegas last month. I tried to help her. It didn't work out. Now she calls me ten times a day."

"How did you try to help her?"

"If you don't mind, I really don't want to talk about it."

"I do mind," she said stiffly. "I'm letting a strange man drive me someplace. I want to know who you are, or I'll get out right now and go back in my house."

She crossed her arms in her lap. She impressed him as someone who'd wait all day to get a straight answer. He killed the engine and turned sideways in his seat. "Her name is Lucy Price.

She's a degenerate gambler. She's addicted to slot machines and owes money all over Las Vegas. I felt bad for her and gave her twenty-five thousand dollars to help her out."

The figure made her head snap. "Seriously?"

"Yes. She isn't a bad person; she just has this horrible problem. So I gave her the money."

She looked puzzled, and Valentine watched her run her hand over the seat, then the dashboard, then the panel of the door. She shook her head.

"This is an old car, isn't it?" she said.

"It's a '92 Honda Accord."

"You're not a rich man, are you?"

"I make a decent buck, but no, I'm not rich."

"So you gave her the money out of the goodness of your heart."

"I guess you could put it that way."

"So why are you now shunning her? It doesn't add up."

Valentine felt the air escape his lungs. He didn't want to go down this road. It was painful, and thinking about it would only ruin his sleep tonight, his dreams tortured by Lucy's problems and his own troubled conscience. As if reading his mind, Mary Alice reached across the seat and grasped his arm. She gave it a healthy squeeze.

"Please answer me," she said.

He had never liked talking in cars, and they got out and walked to her porch. The swing looked inviting so they sat in it. He stared at the maple tree in her front yard and tried to gather his thoughts. A big fat crow sitting on a branch stared back at him.

"When I first became a cop in Atlantic City, I thought part of my job was helping people," he said. "I grew up there, so most of the people I came in contact with I personally knew. They were my friends, so I tried to help them work their problems out."

"Instead of arresting them."

"Exactly. One day, my supervisor took me aside. His name was Banko, and he liked to do things by the book. He told me I was making a mistake, that I needed to stop."

"Did you listen to him?"

"Not at first. Then one day, something happened that changed my mind. Two cops I knew got called to a domestic disturbance. Their names were Manley and Hatch. I'd known them since grade school. Good guys. The disturbance was between a girl and her boyfriend. The girl was trying to break up, and the boyfriend was taking it hard. He was threatening her, so a neighbor called 911.

"Manley and Hatch entered the house, and the boyfriend got belligerent with them. Right then, they should have cuffed him, read him his rights, and thrown him in their cruiser. That's what that situation calls for. Only, they didn't. Manley put his hand on the kid's shoulder and tried to talk some sense into him.

"The boyfriend was crazy angry. He worked

construction, and his tools were sitting on the table. He reached down and picked up a ball-peen hammer."

"What's that?"

"It's a special hammer used to beat metal into shape. He smacked Manley in the face with it. Manley's nose practically came off and was hanging on the side of his face. Hatch drew his gun and shot the kid through the heart."

"Does that make Manley wrong?"

"Yes."

"Please explain why."

"Manley's intentions were good, just like mine were when I interceded in disturbances. But the fact is, if Manley had cuffed the boyfriend like he was supposed to, he wouldn't be walking around today with a steel rod in his face, and the kid would still be alive. Sometimes the best thing is to arrest a person and stick them in jail. Sure, it's rock bottom, but that's a place some people need to go."

Mary Alice folded her hands in her lap. "Is that where Lucy Price needs to go?"

"Yes."

"But you gave her twenty-five thousand dollars. Surely that helped her."

"It only made things worse," he said. "I had this selfish dream that by giving her the money, she'd get her life back in order and we'd get together. Instead, she took the money and went on a gambling binge. When it was over, she was broke.

She got so despondent, she left one of the casinos and ran her car over the median of Las Vegas Boulevard. She hit another car and injured several tourists. One died."

"Do you blame yourself for that?"

"Yes."

"And you honestly believe that she'd be better off if you hadn't given her the money."

"I don't know if Lucy would be better off or not," he said. "I just know that someone wouldn't have died."

The crow started cawing at him. It was like being heckled from a crowd, and Valentine fished a coin out of his pocket to throw at it. Before he could, Mary Alice stood up from the swing. She did it suddenly, and his legs shot out from the sudden shift in weight. She marched across the porch to the front door of her house, then turned to face him.

"Goodness is never a sin," she said.

He stared at her, his face burning.

"Shame on you for thinking so," she added.

"Don't you want me to take you to Brevard?"

"No," she said.

She went back inside and shut the door behind her. He heard the dead bolt being thrown. It was a humiliating sound, and he sat for a long moment and let the crow berate him. Then he got her suitcase from the trunk and put it on the front mat.

CHAPTER 30

At three-thirty Sunday afternoon, Lamar pulled his car into the parking lot of Dixie Magic, found one of the few remaining spaces, and killed the engine. The casino was doing brisk business, and Gerry stayed low in the passenger seat.

"You think I'll be safe here?"

"I'm not putting you inside the casino," Lamar said. He pointed at a construction trailer at the rear of the lot. "I'm putting you there."

Gerry stared at the trailer. It was covered in aluminum siding, and an air conditioner hanging from a window was dripping water. It looked like a pit.

"Why there?"

"That's command central," Lamar said. "Come on."

Lamar took his gun off the seat and slipped it under his belt. They got out and crossed the lot, with Lamar standing between Gerry and the road.

Lamar knocked three times on the trailer door, paused, then knocked three times again. The door popped open, and a blast of cold air greeted them. They went in, and Lamar closed the door behind them and locked it. Gerry was wearing a short-sleeved shirt and felt himself shiver.

"We keep it this cold so the humidity doesn't ruin the equipment," Lamar said.

Gerry stared at the tables cramming the trailer's interior. They contained dozens of video monitors stacked atop each other, and machines that generated the date and time on a tape. There were also phones and log books and plenty of empty coffee cups. Watching the video monitors were two guys Gerry remembered from his lecture the day before. Both men turned in their chairs and said hello.

"We set up command central a few weeks back," Lamar explained. "It lets us watch the action inside the casino without anyone knowing it."

Gerry stared at the monitors. "Discover any more cheating?"

Lamar scratched his chin. "Well, that's where I was hoping you could help us."

"Help you how?"

"You know, like you did with the chip scams."

"You want me to figure out how you're getting ripped off?"

"Only if you want to," Lamar said.

Gerry felt breakfast turn over in his stomach. He'd watched videotapes of cheaters from his father's library and had always been stumped. His lying was going to be the death of him one day. "Sure," he said.

★   ★   ★

264

Lamar's two men were named Kent and Boomer. Both had played football for Ole Miss and were likable guys. The only problem was their shoulders. Sitting between them, Gerry felt like he was wedged between two boulders.

Kent and Boomer had both worked for the Mississippi Gaming Commission for ten years and were knowledgeable about gaming security. Both men understood that the best way to detect a scam was to figure out which table was the problem, then work backward. His father did this all the time. He called it Logical Backward Progression.

They had isolated which tables were losing the most money in the casino, and determined that this was where the majority of cheating was taking place. The problem areas included a craps table, a roulette table, and a blackjack table. They had videotaped these tables for two days and were watching the tapes in slow motion in an effort to determine how the money was being stolen.

Gerry stared at the monitors while sipping a cup of bitter coffee. Watching videotapes was about as stimulating as watching paint dry. Knowing someone was stealing made it a little more interesting, but not by much. More than once his father had caught him switching channels when he was supposed to be studying casino tapes.

"We've watched these damn tapes forward and backward and still can't see what's going on," Kent said, biting off the end of a candy bar. "It's frustrating."

"It's probably something simple," Gerry said.

Both men glared at him. So did Lamar, who stood in the corner.

"They can be the hardest ones to detect," he added.

"Like the chip scams you showed us," Boomer said.

"Exactly. Chip scams are considered the lowest form of stealing, yet they cost casinos millions a year."

The three men stopped glaring at him. A short silence followed.

"So what are we missing?" Lamar said.

Gerry didn't have a clue. Only, it was too late in the game to admit that and not get run out of town. Then he had an idea. He'd call his old man. "I need to look at these tapes in privacy for a little while. Would you mind if I used your office?"

"Gonna go consult your crystal ball," Lamar said.

"Something like that."

"Be my guest." Lamar led him to his corner office. It was dark and about as inviting as a cave, and contained a desk with a computer and a phone. Lamar turned the computer on and told Kent to send the feeds from the video monitors they were watching to his computer. Seconds later, a matrix appeared on the computer screen, with the different feeds showing in each of the matrix's boxes.

"There you go, sport," Lamar said, showing himself out.

Gerry shut the door behind him. Getting behind the desk, he took his cell phone out and powered it up. As he punched in his father's number, he was suddenly seized by a sense of panic. His father had promised a dozen times that he'd start leaving his cell phone on, but so far, it hadn't happened. His old man was a dinosaur when it came to technology. *Come on, Pop, surprise me,* he thought as the call went through.

"When the hell are you going to stop lying to these people?" his father said after Gerry told him what was going on. His father rarely swore. And Gerry couldn't remember the last time he'd sworn at *him.* Not that he didn't deserve it. But his father had somehow always shown restraint.

"Is something wrong, Pop?"

"I just had a blind librarian tell me what a bum I was for avoiding Lucy Price," his father said. "Do you think I'm a bum for avoiding her?"

Gerry stopped staring at the matrix on Lamar's computer screen and shifted his eyes to the wall. His father sounded upset. Lucy Price was bad news. Gerry had discussed her with Mabel, and they'd both decided that the best thing his father could do was get Lucy out of his life. She was drowning and was only going to pull down his father with her.

"You bailed her out already, Pop. You gave her a chance to redeem herself. That's all you can do with someone like that. The rest was up to her, and she blew it."

"You really think so?"

"Yes. So don't go flogging yourself over it."

"Is that what I'm doing?"

"It sure sounds like it."

His father took a deep breath. "Okay. Thanks for listening. Now, tell me what you're seeing on these video monitors."

Gerry shifted his gaze to the computer screen. He couldn't remember ever giving his father advice before. "Where do you want me to start?" he said.

"Start with the procedures they're using at each of the games," his father said. "That's usually how table games get scammed."

"What do you mean?"

"Crooked dealers and croupiers will change a procedure. The change usually doesn't look like much, but it's enough to help them hide how they're stealing money. They'll use the new procedure for a while to see if it creates any suspicion. If no one says anything, they start the scam. Hustlers call this *putting the eye to sleep.*"

"Huh," Gerry said.

"You know, I already told you this once before."

"You did?"

"Yeah, about three weeks ago. I guess you weren't listening."

Gerry swallowed hard, then described to his father what he was seeing on the screen.

★ ★ ★

Ten minutes later Gerry walked out of Lamar's office with his chest puffed out and a shit-eating grin on his face. He'd been able to nail each scam just by listening to his father and staring at the matrix on Lamar's computer. His old man could be a bear sometimes, but he never let you down.

Kent and Boomer separated their chairs and gave him space to sit. Gerry took the seat and pointed at the monitors. "Where do you want to begin?"

Lamar was standing in the corner. "You figured out all three of them?"

"Sure did."

"Well, paint me blue and call me Quincy. Okay, start with the roulette scam."

A monitor in the center of the table showed roulette. Kent hit some strokes on his keyboard, and every monitor in the trailer switched to show the same thing.

The roulette table was crowded with people. Gerry pointed at the croupier, a guy with a pasty complexion and an ill-fitting tux. It was his job to control the game, spin the wheel and throw the ball, and collect bets at his end of the table. Gerry said, "The croupier is part of the gang. He's changed a procedure at the table, which is letting his partners past-post."

"You mean they're betting after the ball drops," Lamar said.

"That's right. Before the wheel slows down and the ball starts to drop, the croupier is supposed to wave his hand over the layout and say 'No more bets.' That way the people watching through the eye in the sky know the betting is over.

"Well, this croupier isn't waving his hand over the table. If you watch the tape, you'll see that he's *saying* it, which is why it hasn't caught the attention of the security people on the floor. But the people manning the eye in the sky can't hear him because there isn't any audio on their tapes. The croupier is giving his partners a chance to see where the ball is going to fall, and place a late bet."

Kent and Boomer stared at the monitors. After a minute Kent spotted the past-poster. It was a man sitting in a wheelchair at the table's end. He was hugging the table and slipping late bets onto the layout.

"Right in front of our noses," Kent said.

"How's the craps scam working?" Lamar asked.

Gerry glanced at him. "Let me guess. You've got a bet with Kent and Boomer that I won't figure them all out."

Lamar bit his lip and didn't reply. Kent and Boomer burst out laughing.

"How much?" Gerry said.

"Twenty bucks," Kent said.

Gerry looked at him. "Twenty between the two of you, or twenty each?"

"Twenty each," Boomer said. "Lamar is a gambling man."

"What's my cut?" Gerry said.

The two ex-football players stopped laughing. "What do you mean, your cut?" Kent said.

"If I win, you win. *Comprende?*"

Kent shrugged. "How about ten bucks?"

"Each?"

Now it was Lamar's turn to laugh. "Man strikes a hard bargain."

Kent and Boomer looked at each other. "Okay," Kent said.

Gerry turned back to the monitors. Kent typed in a command, and the screens showed the craps table where the stealing was taking place.

"The craps scam is similar to the roulette scam, in that it exploits the fact that there's no audio being captured on the casino floor. The craps dealer and a partner are pulling off verbal scams. They're pretty basic, but very effective.

"The craps table is crowded with players, and they're making lots of noise. The partner comes over to the table and throws his money down. He tells the craps dealer what his bet is. Only, no one at the table hears him. There's so much noise, no one can. The craps dealer says, 'Money plays,' indicating the bet has been accepted. The dice are thrown. Whatever the outcome is, the craps dealer pays the player off as if that was his bet."

Gerry pointed at the craps dealer on the video monitor. They watched in silence as he paid a player off for a bet that was never made. The payoff was several thousand dollars, and Lamar let out a groan.

"You owe us twenty bucks, each," Boomer told him.

"He still hasn't explained the blackjack scam," Lamar reminded him.

The blackjack scam was Gerry's favorite of the bunch. It employed an ordinary box of Kleenex and a dealer with a head cold. His father had called it the Runny Nose scam. He glanced over his shoulder at Lamar. "Want to make another bet?"

"No thanks," Lamar said.

Above the door was a monitor that showed the outside of the trailer. Standing outside was a fat guy in bib overalls, holding an automatic rifle. The fat guy raised the rifle to his shoulder and took dead aim at the trailer.

"Duck!"

A fusillade of bullets ripped through the aluminum walls. It happened so fast that no one moved. Lamar, Kent, and Boomer let out moans and fell to the floor. Gerry touched himself. He had an angel sitting on his shoulder and was unhurt.

In the monitor he saw the fat guy reloading. Lamar saw it too. He was lying on the floor, holding his bleeding arm. He drew the gun from behind his belt buckle, then offered it to Gerry.

"You've got to stop him," Lamar said.

CHAPTER 31

Someone had once told Mabel that the month of May was beautiful wherever you went. Not just in the United States, but all over the world.

It was certainly true in Florida. The air was warm but not too humid, the grass and vegetation blooming everywhere you looked, the days longer and more fulfilling. She sat on a rocker on her front porch, taking it all in. The trip to Gibsonton had been fun, but now she was exhausted. She put in long hours working for Tony. Usually she enjoyed it, but sometimes it also wore her out.

A FedEx truck came down the street and stopped in front of Tony's house. FedEx delivered on Sundays, but you had to pay them through the nose. It was probably a videotape from a casino that had lost a bundle of cash. It seemed to be happening more and more, despite the break-throughs in technology that were available, like facial-recognition databases and digital cameras that could photograph a pimple on an elephant's behind. Because casinos generated so much cash, they attracted the worst that society had to offer.

Like Tony was fond of saying, it wasn't a matter of *if* a casino was going to have problems, it was a matter of *when*.

She signed for the package, then watched the truck pull away from the curb. Moments later, she saw Yolanda come out of her house with the baby in her arms. Yolanda looked harried, and Mabel saw that she had on mismatched slippers. Mabel pushed herself out of her rocker and walked down the path to the sidewalk in front of her house.

"Is everything all right?" she called across the street.

Yolanda shook her head. "No."

"Is this about Gerry?"

"Yes."

"Give me a minute."

Mabel went inside, made sure the teakettle wasn't boiling on the stove, then grabbed her keys and hurried out the door. It had bothered her that Gerry hadn't come home right away from his trip to Gulfport. Something about his reason for staying had sounded fabricated. Reaching Yolanda's house, she let herself in.

She heard Yolanda in the kitchen, talking in Spanish on the phone. As she walked down the hallway, Mabel glanced into the different rooms. Each was spotless, with not a single child's toy or piece of child's clothing lying on the floor. Mabel was convinced that Yolanda would one day surrender to motherhood, but so far it hadn't happened.

In the kitchen she found Yolanda sitting at the table, the baby struggling in her lap. Mabel took the baby from her and felt its heavy diaper. She went into the master bedroom and changed her.

"It's my mother in San Juan," Yolanda called out. "She's had a premonition about Gerry."

"Is he in trouble?"

"Yes."

Yolanda's mother had this uncanny ability to see into the future and predict when bad things were about to happen. By having a son-in-law like Gerry, she was going to be busy for a long time. Mabel finished changing Lois's diaper and returned to the kitchen. "What did he do?" she asked.

Yolanda was saying good-bye to her mother, which could take anywhere from ten seconds to a full minute. Finally she hung up. "My mother had a dream while she was taking a siesta this afternoon," Yolanda said, taking the baby from her. "In it, she saw Gerry being pursued by a man who looked like a bear. My mother said Gerry took something from him."

Yolanda's lips were trembling. Mabel didn't believe in psychics, or the frauds on TV who claimed to communicate with the dead; only, Yolanda's mother's premonitions somehow always came true.

"This isn't good," Mabel said. "Have you called Gerry and asked him to come clean?"

"No," Yolanda said.

Mabel glanced at the cell phone sitting on the table. So did Yolanda. Her mother had spooked her, and Mabel watched her bring the baby to her chest and rock her.

"Would you like me to call him?" Mabel asked.

Yolanda kissed the top of Lois's head with her eyes closed.

"Would you please?" she asked.

Gerry stared at the monitor above the door of the trailer. In his hand was Lamar's gun. The fat guy—who he guessed was Huck Dubb—was having a problem loading his automatic rifle. Gerry wanted him to lower the rifle's barrel a little bit more. Just another foot, and Gerry was going to open the door and blow his head off.

"He's got an AK-47," Lamar said, lying on the floor. His right arm was spurting blood, and he was holding his other hand over the wound. "Their barrels heat up if you fire too many rounds at once."

Gerry glanced at Kent and Boomer. They had dragged themselves over to the corner and were tending to each other's wounds.

"You need to take him out," Lamar said.

"I know," Gerry said.

"Better turn the safety off."

Gerry found the safety and flipped it off. In the monitor, Huck Dubb was cursing and banging his rifle with the palm of his hand. Gerry heard his cell phone ring, and jerked it out of his pocket.

It was Yolanda, calling from the house. He hit talk.

"I love you," he said. "Call you right back."

He killed the power and put the phone away. Then he jerked the door open and stepped outside the trailer. There was a small platform, then three steps to the pavement. Huck stood twenty feet away, not seeing him. He aimed at Huck's chest and squeezed the trigger. The gun barked, and Huck spun like a top, the rifle flying out of his hands. Gerry watched it slide beneath a parked car and felt the weight of the world lift from his shoulders.

Huck fell against a car and brought his hand up to his head. Blood was spurting from his ear, and Gerry realized he'd winged him. He went down the steps and saw Huck start to back away. Gerry motioned for him to stop. Huck kept backing up.

"I'll shoot you," Gerry said.

The side of Huck's face was sheeted in blood. Huck spit at Gerry.

"You killed my boys," he said.

"You shouldn't have sent them after me."

"You a cop?"

Gerry shook his head. In the distance he could hear an approaching siren.

"Fuck you," Huck said.

Huck did a one-eighty and took off at a dead run. Gerry aimed at his back. He started to squeeze the trigger, then hesitated. From the trailer he heard Lamar yelling at him to do it. He thought of the faces of the Dubb boys as he dumped the logs on them. He'd seen in their eyes the stark terror that accompanies the realization that your life is about to end. He didn't want to see that look ever again, and lowered his arm.

"Aw, shit," he heard Lamar say.

Two ambulances and half the Gulfport police force showed up a minute later. A posse of cops went to hunt down Huck, while the three wounded men were put on gurneys and taken to the hospital. Gerry rode in the ambulance with Lamar.

"You should've shot him," Lamar said.

"You ever kill anyone before?" Gerry asked him.

Lamar shook his head.

"Then shut up," he said.

Gerry turned his eyes away as a medic treated Lamar's wound. He felt something being pressed into his hand, and looked down to see Lamar handing him his cell phone.

"Call Isabelle, would you? Tell her what happened."

Gerry made the call for him. Isabelle had already heard the news. The employees who they suspected of cheating were being rounded up. She made Gerry put Lamar on. He put the phone next to the big man's lips and saw him whisper something to her, then say good-bye. Gerry put the phone back to his own mouth. "Isabelle, I need you to do something for me." To Lamar he said, "Which blackjack table was I watching before?"

"Table seventeen."

"Isabelle, make sure you confiscate the trash can beneath blackjack table seventeen. It will be filled with used tissues."

She agreed, and the line went dead. He saw Lamar smile at him.

"Used tissues?"

"That's right."

"Still want to win that bet, huh?"

"Twenty bucks is twenty bucks," Gerry said.

CHAPTER 32

Valentine was still steaming over Mary Alice's remark when Bill Higgins called him late Sunday afternoon. She'd made him feel absolutely rotten, and he'd known her exactly one day. Woman were amazing that way, the power they yielded far greater than they knew.

"You forget about me?" Bill asked.

Just what he needed: more guilt. No, he hadn't forgotten about Bill. He just didn't have anything solid to tell him. He now remembered why he liked to keep his cell phone turned off. It allowed him to lead a normal life.

"I'm on the case," Valentine said. "Casino bosses biting at your heels?"

"They're calling me on the carpet tomorrow afternoon," Bill said.

"I thought your meeting wasn't until Friday."

"So did I. The Associated Press won't leave the story alone. They're hounding the mayor's office and the convention and visitors bureau for closure. Did you know that Ricky Smith hired a public relations firm in New York?"

"With whose money?"

"That's what I'd like to know."

Valentine was sitting on the rocker on the screened porch of his house, staring at the forest. In Florida, a forest was another name for an overgrown swamp; here, it was maples and pines and vegetation that didn't have alligators hiding behind it. "My gut tells me Ricky Smith is as crooked as a corkscrew," he said. "Problem is, I can't prove it."

Bill breathed heavily into the phone. He'd worked for the Gaming Control Board for thirty years; finding another job at this stage of his life wouldn't be easy. He said, "I stumbled upon something strange earlier."

"What's that?"

"The night Ricky beat the Mint, I interviewed all the floor people. Everything seemed on the square. It occurred to me that I hadn't talked to anyone in the surveillance control room. I read their log sheets, and no one reported anything suspicious while Ricky was winning, so I didn't take it any further. But I figured, what the hell, I should talk to these folks, feel them out."

"And you found something."

"Yeah. There were two techs watching the craps table. They got a call from the floor ten minutes before Ricky started to roll the dice. A floor manager thought two rail birds at the table might be stealing other players' chips."

Rail birds were bystanders who watched the action but never played. Casino people hated them, but there was no way to get rid of them. It was a free country.

"The rail birds were standing at opposite ends of the table," Bill went on. "The techs watched them. They didn't see any stealing, but you know, that stuff is almost invisible."

"Sure."

"So one of the techs calls downstairs and gets a cocktail waitress to approach them. She tells them that if they're staying in the hotel, she'll get them free drinks. They said yes and volunteered their names. She called upstairs and passed the names to the techs. They contacted the police and the GCB to check if either had a criminal record."

"Did they?"

"No, both were clean. But here's the good part: When I interviewed the techs, one of them pulled the names off a sheet and gave them to me."

"Anyone we know?"

"Frank Barnes and Clayton McCormick."

Valentine racked his memory. "Never heard of them."

"They're both from Slippery Rock, North Carolina," Bill said.

"Must be friends of Ricky."

"That's what I figured. But then I remembered something. Ricky told me he'd come to Las Vegas alone."

Valentine jumped out of the rocker and in the woods heard a small animal scurry through the leaves for cover. The epiphany he'd had the day before came back to him. *This is a small town.* It should have dawned on him that if people in the town were willing to help Ricky Smith rig lotteries and fix horse races, they might also be willing to step on a plane and go to Las Vegas and help him work his magic out there.

"Barnes and McCormick were staying at the Mint," Bill said. "They came out that morning and left the next day."

It was like the trees had parted and Valentine could see clear through the forest. Every time he'd watched the tape, he'd watched Ricky. That was a mistake. He needed to be watching the other players at the table. He felt the heady rush that came when a puzzle began to come together.

"I'll call you right back," he told his friend.

Valentine went into the bedroom, pulled his suitcase from beneath the bed, and removed a copy of the videotape of Ricky Smith. In the living room he popped the tape into the VCR beside the TV. The VCR made a sound like it was regurgitating, and he thought it had eaten the tape. Then the TV flickered to life.

He fast-forwarded the tape to Ricky's streak at craps. Ricky had rolled the dice fifteen times and beaten the house every time. The odds were about the same as stepping outside and being hit by lightning. He watched the tape, then called Bill back. "I've got the tape of Ricky frozen on the screen of my TV. Which guys are Barnes and McCormick?"

Bill described them to a T. Both were in their mid-thirties, with thinning hair and growing paunches. They stood at opposite ends of the craps table. As Ricky threw winner after winner, they jumped up and down and whooped their fool heads off.

"You said Barnes and McCormick stayed at the Mint," Valentine said.

"That's right," Bill said.

"Same room?"

"Yes."

Valentine pulled a footstool up to the TV. That was the clue he needed. Barnes and McCormick were friends. Friends didn't stand on opposite ends of a craps table. They were part of a gang. They had purposely done something suspicious to get the floor manager to call upstairs and ask for them to be watched. That was their role in the scam.

"Let me think about this," he said.

"I'll be right here," Bill replied.

The house soon grew dark and the temperature dropped. Valentine remained frozen in front of the TV. The only thing moving was his finger on the remote control. The tape would end, and he'd rewind and watch the craps shooting over again. Fifteen rolls, fifteen winners. He still couldn't make the scam. He realized that he'd grown to despise Ricky, if for no other reason than that his cheating ways had kept him here, and away from more important things. His cell phone rang. It lay on the floor between his feet. He looked down at the caller ID. It was Bill.

"Any luck?" his friend asked.

"Not yet."

"I had a brainstorm," Bill said.

Valentine stared at the screen. It felt like a portal to another universe. "What's that?"

"I called the convention and visitors bureau and got them to contact all the hotels in town. I asked them for the names of everyone from Slippery Rock who was staying in Las Vegas that weekend."

Valentine tore his eyes away from the screen and stared at the phone illuminated in his hand. "And?"

"You're not going to believe this."

"Try me."

"There were twenty-six of them. I've got their names right here."

Valentine froze the picture on the screen. If people in Slippery Rock wanted to gamble, they could visit Biloxi or hit one of the Indian casinos in North Carolina. He counted the number of players standing around the craps table, cheering Ricky on. There were twenty-six on the nose. He hit play and watched the dice fly down the table and everyone cheer.

"For the love of Christ," he said.

"What?"

"*Everyone's involved.*"

Valentine felt like an idiot. The clue he'd been searching for was right in front of his nose. Ricky had learned his trade in a carnival. With carnival scams, everyone was involved. It was what made the illusion so believable.

"What do you mean, everyone?" Bill said.

"Players, employees working the table, even the floor manager," Valentine said.

"*What?*"

"It's a big charade. They're miscalling the dice, Bill. That's why the floor manager called upstairs. He asked surveillance to watch both ends of the table to insure that the camera for the game stayed at a wide angle. On the tape, we see the dice fly down the table, but we're not seeing the outcome. What we're seeing is the crowd and employees' reaction to Ricky throwing sevens or elevens, or making his point. But he isn't. The crowd is just making us believe he is."

"Wait a minute," Bill protested. "I saw the stick man pull the dice back with his stick three times. He did it slowly. I saw that Ricky had rolled sevens."

"That's right. Ricky rolled sevens legitimately three times. So the stick man pulled the dice back slowly so the camera could see it. The other times, the stick man kicked the dice over as he retrieved them. That way, the camera couldn't see the total."

Bill whistled through his teeth. "I've never seen anything like this. Have you?"

"No."

"So how do we convict them without a videotape we can show in court?"

Valentine killed the VCR and went onto the porch. No jury in Nevada would convict someone of cheating without videotaped evidence. It didn't matter if the prosecutors had loads of circumstantial evidence; the locals hated the casinos and paid them back whenever they could. He stared at the eerie sheen the moon had cast over his backyard.

"You don't," he said.

"You're saying I should let them skate?"

"Afraid so. No tape, no case."

"What do I tell the casino owners?"

"Tell them you saved them a million bucks. You have probable cause to keep Ricky's winnings. I'll crack one of the other scams, and you'll have enough evidence for an arrest. They should also fire the employees who were involved and get them banned from working in the gambling industry again. It's not the punishment they deserve, but it's better than nothing."

The plaintive wail of Stevie Ray Vaughan's guitar ripped a hole in the otherwise peaceful night. Ricky was thumbing his nose at the neighborhood again. He liked to do that. And he obviously liked to corrupt people; especially his friends. And when things had gotten hairy, he liked to send his thugs out and terrorize blind librarians. Opening the screen door, Valentine stepped outside and began walking across the yard toward Ricky's house.

"I need to have a talk with my neighbor," he said. "I'll call you later."

CHAPTER 33

There were times when Valentine was happy he was no longer a cop. He'd liked the work and the sense of balance it had brought to his life, but the rules had sometimes confined him. Especially when dealing with bad people.

He approached Ricky's house from the rear, the music so loud it made his head hurt. The song sounded familiar. Stevie Ray doing Jimi Hendrix's "Manic Depression," the chords etched into his brain from hearing it so many times when he was a cop. His partner at the time had called it the drug dealer's national anthem.

Ricky's house was built by a weekend carpenter, with an addition that did not mesh with the original structure, and mismatched shingles on the roof. There was a back door, and he stared through the glass into the kitchen. An aging Doberman and a cat were huddled in the corner. Both animals looked frightened, and he saw a pool of urine on the floor.

He tried the knob. The door was unlocked. He cracked it open and saw the dog and cat jump forward, wanting out. He opened the door fully. Both bolted past him.

He went in and smelled something burning in the oven. He turned the heat off, then pulled the oven door open. A TV dinner lay smoldering inside.

The music changed to Stevie Ray playing an instrumental with a big-band accompaniment. Valentine loved big band; but, this was too damn loud. He went to the swinging door that led to the next room, opened it with his finger. Through the crack he spied Ricky collapsed on a chair in the dining room. He wore jeans and a ratty T-shirt and was staring at the floor.

"No," Ricky said.

A muscular guy wearing black pants and a black turtleneck stepped into the picture. He looked Cuban, late thirties, with his hair greased down like an old-time hoodlum. His hand cradled Ricky's chin and lifted his head up. With his other hand, he slapped Ricky in the face.

"You're going to do what I tell you," he shouted over the music.

"No, I'm not, Juan," Ricky said.

"You don't have a choice," Juan shouted.

Ricky looked up, his face defiant. *"It's over."*

Juan looked across the dining room. Three other Cuban macho men were holding up the wall. "You hear that? Ricky said it's over."

"Ha!" one of them said.

Valentine pushed the door open a little more.

Judging by the bulges beneath their shirts, the Cubans were packing heat. Lying on the floor were hundreds of shattered CDs, and he guessed this was Ricky's prized music collection. They were giving him the same treatment they'd given Mary Alice. He let the door close and walked through the kitchen and out the back door. Heroes, he'd learned long ago, were dead people who got elementary schools named after them. He'd call Gaylord and let him deal with this.

Out on the lawn he found the Doberman waiting expectantly. He let the dog sniff his hand and heard a loud pop, followed by shouting.

He spun around. The house had gone completely dark, and he guessed a fuse had blown. *Serves you right for playing the music so damn loud,* he thought. In the kitchen he heard someone banging around in the dark.

"The fuse box is out back," a man said. "I saw it when we came in."

"So go flip the switch," another said.

Valentine looked for someplace to hide. With the moon out, he was going to be easy to spot, and he ducked beside the house and held his breath. Moments later, one of the Cubans came out the back door and headed straight to where he was standing. Valentine pressed his back to the house, feeling ridiculous. Yet somehow it worked: The man didn't see him.

They were the same height, the Cuban heavier and about thirty years younger. Opening the fuse box, he squinted at the switches beneath the moonlight, then glanced at Valentine standing a few feet away. Reaching out, he placed his hand on Valentine's arm like he was some trick of his imagination and not real.

"Hey," he said.

Valentine took his hand and bent the fingers back. Groaning, the younger man sunk to the ground. Valentine kneed him in the jaw, and he fell backward and lay still on the ground.

"What's the holdup?" another man called from the house.

Valentine grabbed the Cuban's arms and dragged him around the house. He heard the back door bang open and the other man step outside.

"Just flip the fucking switch," the man said. "Is that so hard?"

Valentine came around the side of the building just as the man reached the fuse box. Valentine hit him flush on the jaw. The man did a crazy dance across the yard, and the Doberman tackled him. He went down hard.

"Good dog," Valentine said. He went to where the second man lay. Out cold. He pulled up the man's sweater and, to his surprise, saw a cell phone where he'd expected to see a gun. He quickly frisked him. The guy wasn't armed.

He ran around the building and frisked the first guy. He wasn't armed, either. That changed the balance of things. Kneeling, he drew the Glock from his ankle holster, then went to the fuse box and flipped the down fuse. The house instantly came back to life.

He marched into the kitchen and straight into the dining room. Ricky was still sitting in the chair, looking dazed. Valentine pointed the Glock at his two tormentors.

"Arms in the air, girls."

Juan and the other man froze. Then, slowly, they reached for the ceiling. Valentine led them across the room to a small closet. "I hope you two like each other," he said.

They reluctantly squeezed themselves into the cramped space. Valentine shut the door and propped a chair up against it. Then he went to the front door and opened it. A black SUV with tinted windows was blocking Ricky's Lexus from leaving.

"Out the back door," he told Ricky.

They went outside, and the Doberman instantly jumped on its master.

"You see my cat?" Ricky asked.

"Cat's fine," Valentine said.

Valentine considered marching straight over to his house and calling Gaylord, but then decided that was a bad idea. If the Cubans decided to follow, they could surround the house. "You know the trails in the woods?"

"Like the back of my hand," Ricky said.

"Lead the way. And don't do anything stupid."

"Like what? Tell you your mother dresses you funny?"

Valentine stared at him. Ricky's face was swollen, his lips and nose bloodied. Usually those were things that lent people sympathy. Valentine shoved him forward and saw Ricky wince like he'd been kicked.

A hundred yards into the woods, they heard a commotion. Valentine glanced over his shoulder as the back door to Ricky's house burst open. Juan and his friend had broken free. Juan was cradling a rifle in his arms while his partner screamed at him.

"For Christ's sake, put that thing down."

"I'm gonna kill that fucker," Juan said. He stared into the darkened forest. "I can hear them rustling around out there. Hey, boys—think we can't hear you? Think again!"

Valentine grabbed Ricky's arm and pulled him behind a tree. He could feel his heartbeat kicking against his chest and the adrenaline pumping through his veins. The two Cubans were standing beneath the back-door light and made easy targets. He went into a crouch, raised his Glock, and aimed at the center of Juan's chest.

"Please don't shoot him," Ricky whispered.

"Why shouldn't I?"

"They're just a bunch of mutts."

"What does that—"

"They're not going to hurt us."

"They roughed you up pretty good."

"I deserved it," he whispered.

"That rifle could do some damage."

"He'll probably shoot his foot off with it."

Valentine watched Juan and his friend argue back and forth. If Juan hadn't been holding a rifle, it would have been comical. They had the physical mannerisms that gangsters had been using in movies for years. What was missing was the guts to pull it off.

"These guys related?" Valentine whispered.

Ricky nodded in the dark.

"Cousins?"

"Yeah," Ricky said, "how did you know?"

Valentine had grown up with a slew of cousins and thought he recognized what was going on. Juan was acting tough to impress his cousin. If he didn't, his cousin would later give him shit for it. Valentine lowered his Glock. Ricky was right; the only people they were probably going to hurt were themselves.

The Doberman pinned to Ricky's side curled its upper lip and emitted a fierce snarl. Ricky put his hand on the dog's snout and clamped it shut.

"You hear that?" Juan said.

"It was just an animal," his cousin said. "Come on, let's beat it before the cops get here."

"They're right out there. Come out here, you fuckers!"

His cousin tugged at his sleeve. "Come on."

Juan shoved him aside. Taking a step forward, he raised the rifle to shoulder height and began shooting. Valentine pulled his head behind the tree while cursing his missed opportunity. Bullets tore through the trees on either side of them. It sounded like a heavy rain and was punctuated by a dozen sleeping animals waking up and darting for cover. After a few moments the shooting subsided. Valentine glanced up at Ricky and saw him hugging the tree and sobbing.

CHAPTER 34

Valentine reached up and pulled Ricky down beside him. "No more advice," he said.

Then he stuck his head around the tree and stared at the house. Juan was hitting the rifle with the heel of his palm like it was jammed. The two Cubans he'd sucker punched were on their feet and encouraging Juan to give it up. Juan was having none of it.

"I'm going to get him if it's the last thing I do," Juan said.

Again Valentine aimed at Juan. He aimed directly at his heart and started to squeeze the trigger, then hesitated. Killing Juan didn't change the situation. They had a rifle, and he had a handgun. Any of the other three could pick up the rifle and come after them. Then he had an idea and aimed at the light above the back door. It was illuminating the entire backyard. He fired twice and hit the bulb with the second shot. The backyard turned dark.

He jumped to his feet. "You first."

With the Doberman nipping at their heels, they

ran down a well-worn path. Valentine stopped after a few hundred yards to see if anyone was following them. The only sounds he heard were animals chattering nervously in the forest. With his hand he found Ricky's arm.

"You okay?"

Ricky swallowed hard. "Yeah. Sorry about that."

"Who lives nearby?"

"Hank Ridley."

"Think he'll let us use his car?"

"If I ask him, sure. Where are we going?"

"To the police."

Valentine dropped his hand, expecting Ricky to lead the way. But the big lug just stood there and wrestled with something he wanted to say. The words refused to come out, and finally he spun around and took off through the woods.

A minute later they emerged onto a large backyard with a bamboo tiki hut sitting in its center. Hank Ridley's house sat on the other end of the property, a shingle farmhouse with a brick chimney and large weather vane. An American flag with the stars replaced by a peace symbol hung across the front porch. They crossed the lawn, and a motion-sensitive floodlight momentarily blinded them. Ricky started to climb the steps to the porch, then stopped.

"Hank's pretty heavy into the reefer, okay?"

Valentine said okay. Potheads didn't bother him the way drunks did. He guessed it was because he'd had little interaction with them as a cop.

Potheads didn't batter their spouses or fight in bars; they just hung out at home, ate sweets, and melted into the furniture.

Ricky rapped loudly on the front door. From within came the strains of rock 'n' roll music. Ricky put his ear to the door. "*Dick's Picks.* Grateful Dead, Tampa, Florida, December 1973. The 'Here Comes Sunshine' track on this set was really awesome."

"What's *Dick's Picks*?"

Ricky's foot was tapping the beat on the porch as if he'd forgotten what had brought them here. "A guy named Dick Latvala collected bootleg Grateful Dead recordings and released the good ones with the band's permission. There were thirty-one CDs in all."

"Does Hank have every one?"

"You bet."

The front door opened, and a marijuana fog enveloped the front porch. A heavyset, bearded man in his late fifties emerged. He was dressed like the last of the Beat Generation and wore ratty shorts and a tie-dyed T-shirt. He seemed oblivious to the chilly weather, and offered the burning joint in his hand to Ricky. Ricky shook his head, and Hank offered Valentine the joint like it was the most natural thing in the world.

"He's an ex-cop," Ricky said.

Hank's bloodshot eyes went wide, and he tossed the joint into his mouth and snapped his lips shut.

Then he started to gag like the joint was burning his head off.

"I said ex!" Ricky exclaimed.

Hank swallowed the joint anyway. He smiled loosely at his visitors.

"You into poetry?"

Valentine realized the question was directed at him. "I just started reading Billy Collins."

"Man after my own heart. I'd invite you in and show you my collection, but there are illegal pharmaceuticals lying around. I'm sure you understand."

"Of course."

"We need to borrow your car," Ricky said.

Hank dug the keys out of his shorts and tossed them in the air. Valentine grabbed them before Ricky could. He watched Hank spin around and walk straight into the doorjamb with his face. He bounced like he was made of rubber and went inside.

"He always so messed up?" Valentine asked as they walked around back.

"That's pretty straight for Hank," Ricky replied.

Hank's car reeked of reefer. It was an ancient Checker Cab that Hank had bought from a dealer in Chicago over the Internet. The seats reminded Valentine of an old school bus, and he got behind the wheel and fired up the engine. Taking the Glock from his pocket, he laid it on his lap. Ricky made the dog sit on the floor in back, then strapped himself in.

"Tell me how to get out of here."

Ricky pointed at the gravel driveway. "Go out that way. At the top of the hill, hang a left. We're going to have to pass my place to go to town."

"Is that the only way out?"

"In a car, yeah."

Valentine didn't like it. If the Cubans were waiting, they might follow them and start shooting. He said, "How far is your place?"

"About half a mile."

Valentine killed the cab's headlights and rumbled down the road. The engine sounded like it was about to hit the ground, and he had a feeling that the Cubans would hear them even if they didn't see them. The road was on a steep incline, and he killed the engine and left it in neutral. The cab rolled silently down the hill.

They passed Valentine's rental house, then came upon Ricky's place. The black SUV sat in the driveway, its front end pointing toward the street. Beneath the moonlight Valentine could see exhaust coming out of the muffler.

"That's them," Ricky whispered fearfully. "Gun it."

Valentine considered it. They'd get a jump on the Cubans, but that was all they'd get. Even an SUV weighted down by four men could catch this clunker. He brought the cab to a stop in the middle of the road. Taking the Glock off his lap, he lowered his window and took aim. He thought about putting a bullet through the SUV's engine, then realized the Glock wasn't powerful enough to do that.

"Oh, Jesus, can't we just get out of here?" Ricky said.

Valentine shook his head. He had to assume that the Cubans had scoped out the neighborhood and knew that this was the only escape route. He had to stop them right now or risk never talking to Mabel or chewing out Gerry or changing his granddaughter's diaper again.

"No," he added for emphasis.

"You going to shoot them?"

Valentine nodded. "Does that bother you?"

"Yeah. I never bargained for this."

"You know these guys?"

"Yeah."

"Close your eyes."

"Why?"

"Just do as I say," Valentine said.

Ricky brought his hands up to his eyes. It was something a little kid might do. Valentine turned and stared at the SUV idling in the driveway. He rested his left forearm on the windowsill and balanced the Glock on it. The SUV's windshield was dark, and he had to imagine where the driver was sitting.

An ember of light appeared. The driver was smoking a cigarette. It made a nice target, and he put it into the Glock's sight and squeezed the trigger.

The gun barked. Then the SUV's windshield

imploded. As the glass fell inward, the Cubans screamed and dived to the floor. Except for the driver. It was Juan, and he remained strapped in his seat, the burning cigarette glued to his lower lip. The bullet had whacked him in the forehead. Like the boys in the bank, he'd never seen it coming.

Valentine started the cab's engine and floored the accelerator.

"You can open your eyes now," he said.

CHAPTER 35

For a guy who'd just gotten shot in the arm, Lamar was all smiles at the Gulfport hospital. He joked with the nurses and doctors in the emergency room and with Gerry, who'd ridden in the ambulance with him.

"Know why the police can't solve redneck murders?"

Gerry shook his head.

"The DNA's all the same, and there are no dental records."

His demeanor was no different when Isabelle showed up. With a smile he pointed at Gerry and said, "Huck was shooting at *him* and winged me and Boomer and Kent instead. Take this boy to the casino and put some dice into his hands!"

Isabelle somehow found it in her to smile. "The police think Huck's hiding with relatives. They're going to search every trailer park until they find him." She glanced at Gerry. "You need to lay low."

"I thought that was what I was doing," Gerry said.

"Out of sight. We'll keep you at the house with a police guard."

Gerry nodded. The doctor was stitching up Lamar's arm. The bullet from Huck's rifle had torn out a slice of flesh that would probably never grow back. Gerry felt his stomach turn over and saw Lamar wink at him.

"You bring the trash can from the casino?" Lamar asked.

Isabelle reached into the floppy bag slung over her shoulder and produced a small metal trash can filled with used tissues. She handed it to Gerry. "This came from table seventeen. The casino has been losing a lot of money there."

Gerry took the trash can and pushed aside the top tissues with his fingers. The dealer obviously had a real bad cold. On the bottom of the can were fifteen playing cards, just like his father had said. He stuck the can under his arm and thanked her for bringing it.

"I need to go back to the casino," she said. "A detective named Clarkson will come by later and take you back to the house. He also wants to ask you some questions about Huck Dubb."

"I don't know anything about the guy," Gerry said.

"Maybe not. But Huck knew where to find you. Clarkson is trying to figure out how. He'll try to jog your memory, if that's okay."

Gerry had been wondering about that himself. The parking lot had been empty when he and Lamar had gone into the trailer, yet Huck had somehow tracked him down.

"Sure."

"Good. I'll see you back at the house."

She gave her husband a smooch on the lips and left. Lamar stared at the spot where she'd been standing and smiled. Gerry didn't think he'd ever seen a greater love in a man's eyes than was in Lamar's. After the nurses and doctor were gone, Lamar said, "First time I met Isabelle, she was wearing a red blouse in the casino. I explained to her that the surveillance cameras see right through red fabric, and the boys upstairs were admiring her. Know what she did?"

Gerry shook his head.

"She found out how long I'd been on the job. It was my first day. So she knew I hadn't been watching her. I asked her out the next week." He pointed at the trash can. "You still think you're going to win that bet?"

"Sure do," Gerry said.

Lamar yelled through the curtains separating them from Kent and Boomer.

"Hey, boys, get your wallets and get in here. It's showtime."

It was a miracle that all three men's wounds were superficial. They knew it, and exchanged plenty of good-natured ribbing and high-fiving. Then Gerry made them take their money out, and the laughter subsided.

Gerry got a second trash can and carefully removed the tissues from the can Isabelle had brought from the casino. When he was done, he pointed at the handful of playing cards lying in the bottom of the casino trash can. He said, "See these cards? They're from the blackjack game at table seventeen. They're all babies."

Babies were low-valued cards, the twos through sixes, and favored the house.

"How do you know that without looking at them?" Lamar asked.

"It's how the scam works," Gerry said. He shook the can, and the cards flipped faceup. As he'd predicted, they were all babies. "Here's the deal. The dealer is required to spread all the cards faceup on the table before he starts. That way, the players—and the cameras—can see that all the cards are there. If any high cards were missing, the house's edge would be unbeatable. If babies were missing, the players would have the edge.

"So the dealer starts with all the cards. But he has a cold. So he puts a box of tissues on his table. That's his shade."

"His what?" Boomer asked.

"Shade. It's a hustler's term for misdirection. The dealer is palming babies out and dropping them in the wastebasket. He palms them when he's putting cards into the discard tray. Then he grabs a tissue to blow his nose. The tissue hides the palmed cards. He drops the tissue and the cards into the wastebasket."

"So he's shorting the shoe so it favors the players," Kent said.

"Exactly."

"Looks like we win forty big ones," Boomer said.

Lamar was examining the can and didn't appear ready to give in. "Just hold on a second. Every night, the blackjack dealers are required to count their cards. I've personally supervised them. Table seventeen has never come up short. If the dealer is palming babies out, why didn't it show up in the count?"

There was real skepticism in his voice. Gerry smiled. "The dealer adds them back."

"How?"

"As he counts, he drops some on the floor. At the same time, he kicks the can over. He picks up the cards he dropped and adds the babies."

"What if they've got snot on them?"

Gerry's smile grew. "I guess he blames it on his cold."

Lamar rolled his eyes. Kent and Boomer started braying like mules, and Lamar reluctantly handed them his money.

"Isabelle tells me you're an authority on casino cheating," Clarkson said.

They were standing outside the hospital, Clarkson a smoker and needing a fix, Gerry joining him because he suddenly needed one as well, the events of the day having caught up to him like a tidal wave that he could no longer outswim. Clarkson was in his thirties, tall and broad-shouldered, and looked every inch a cop.

"My father's the authority. I'm just learning the ropes."

Clarkson exhaled two purple plumes through his nostrils. Gerry liked the way his answer had come out. And it wasn't a lie.

"Any idea how Huck Dubb found you so easily?" the detective asked.

There was an accusing tone in his voice. *He thinks I called him*, Gerry thought. It was perfect cop logic. The trailer was a hideout; no one outside of the police and the Mississippi Gaming Commission agents knew about it. No one, except Gerry.

"I didn't call him, if that's what you're thinking."

Clarkson smiled; only, it wasn't a smile. More a widening of his mouth as he sucked in a monster cloud of smoke. "Did you call anyone else?"

"My father. I was stuck on a scam that Lamar had showed me, so I called him, and he doped it out for me."

There it was again: the truth. It didn't hurt nearly as much as he thought it would.

"Nobody local?" Clarkson asked. "Like the hotel or something?"

"Nope."

"Your father nearby?"

"Slippery Rock, North Carolina."

Clarkson used the dying cigarette to light another. "Might your father have called someone?"

"We have our disagreements, but nothing like that."

Clarkson grimaced at the stupidity of what he'd just said. The cell phone in Clarkson's pocket rang. He pulled it out and flipped the phone open. "Detective Clarkson, at your service." He listened for a moment, then cupped his hand over the mouthpiece. "It's Isabelle. She's getting takeout from Best Steaks in the South and wants to know what you'd like."

Gerry found himself grinning. He had eaten there last night and assumed that *Best Steaks in the South* was their slogan. He thought back to the menu and tried to pick the least expensive thing. For all he knew, Isabelle was paying for it.

"Hamburger, medium rare, onions," he said.

Clarkson relayed his order, then asked for the same, well done. Gerry watched him say good-bye and put the cell phone away. Then he stared out at the hospital parking lot. It was a crystal-clear afternoon, the sun mirrored in each of the cars' rooftops. His father had told him he sometimes had epiphanies and was able to make sense out of situations that seemingly had none. Gerry realized he was having one now and that his fingers and toes were tingling.

He looked at Clarkson. "I just figured it out," he said.

"What's that?" the detective asked, grinding out his butt.

"How Huck Dubb knew where to find me."

Clarkson got in his face. "How?"

"I had dinner at Best Steaks in the South last

night. After I left, the Dubb brothers tried to kill me. Someone in the restaurant called them. That same person saw me go into the trailer today and called Huck."

"But you said the parking lot was empty when you entered the trailer."

"It was."

"Then how did this person see you? I've been in that restaurant plenty of times. There aren't any windows."

"There's a surveillance camera on the corner of the building," Gerry said. "I saw it last night. The rat in the restaurant is pointing the camera across the street at the casino. He saw me go into the trailer and called Huck."

Clarkson gave him his best aw-shucks smile. "Damn! You sure you weren't once a cop?"

Gerry shook his head. He watched Clarkson whip out his cell phone and call his superiors. Within a minute, he'd arranged to have the steak house raided. The tingling sensation in his fingers had not gone away, and Gerry stared at his hands. Then he realized what it was: No one had ever mistaken him for a cop before. He imagined his mother up in heaven, looking down and smiling at him.

CHAPTER 36

Huck Dubb was sitting in the study of his grandma's house, staring at her computer. He'd bought it for her last Christmas and used it to send and receive e-mail. Most of the men he ran with had similar setups. They had computers at relatives' houses, and nothing was in their own names. His grandma entered the study. She'd been wearing a bathrobe and slippers for the past ten years of her life. She was holding a fried steak sandwich on a paper plate.

"Eat this," she insisted. "You're looking puny."

"Don't want it," he said.

"Don't talk back to me, boy. I said, eat it."

His grandma had practically raised him and his retarded brother; disobeying her was an insult to all the sacrifices she'd made. He took the sandwich and bit into it. The effort made his wounded ear hurt. He'd rubbed cocaine on it, and the pain had gone away. But that was the little pain. The big pain was still raging out of control inside of him.

"You want some iced tea?" she asked. "I made it extra sweet."

"Do I have a choice?"

"*Huck.*"

"Love some," he said.

She shuffled out, and he resumed staring at the computer. On the screen was a live feed from the surveillance camera outside Best Steaks in the South. The camera had pan/tilt/zoom lenses and was focused on the parking lot across the street. His cousin Buford, who owned the restaurant, had been sending him the feed for weeks. What Huck was hoping for was a repeat—Gerry Valentine coming back to the trailer, and Huck jumping into his car and going and shooting the son of a bitch.

Two sedans pulled up to the restaurant. Four cops jumped out of each. They drew their sidearms and entered the restaurant in single file. Huck's cell phone rang. He stared at the caller ID. It was Buford.

"You watchin' this?" his cousin asked.

"Yeah," Huck said. "Where you?"

"In my office at the restaurant, staring at my computer. What am I gonna do?"

"Get a lawyer."

"They're gonna call me an accomplice. They're gonna kick my balls in. You shouldn't have sprayed that trailer, you stupid son of a bitch."

"He killed my boys," Huck said.

Buford slammed down the phone so hard that Huck jerked it away from his head. On the computer, he saw a cop break off from the group.

Climbing onto the fender of a car, the cop started to dismantle the camera. Huck rose from his chair and snapped the suspenders keeping his overalls up. "Shit," he said.

"*Huck!*" his grandma bellowed from the kitchen. She was deaf in one ear and couldn't hear out of the other, yet somehow heard through walls when Huck swore.

"Sorry, Grandma."

"No swearing in this house. Not while I'm alive."

"Yes, ma'am."

"Come in here quick. I've got something for you."

He crossed the small house in a funk. If they were sending eight cops to close down Buford, they probably had a small army guarding Gerry Valentine. He'd blown his chance to kill the man who'd killed his boys. His ear was hurting from where he'd been shot, but it didn't hurt nearly as much as his heart.

He found Grandma in the kitchen holding a tall glass of iced tea. Having something from her kitchen was her cure for whatever ailed you, and he took a big swallow. The drink was so cold it made his fillings hurt.

His retarded brother, Arlen, sat at the kitchen table, eating a bowl of frosted corn flakes. Their mother had done drugs, and Arlen had paid the price. Arlen lived in an alternative universe. When everyone was sleeping, Arlen was awake; when everyone ate dinner, Arlen ate breakfast. Physically, the brothers were about the same and had worn each other's clothes all their lives. It had been easy, being they were rarely awake at the same time. He petted Arlen on the shoulder and saw him lift his bovine eyes.

"What you want?" Arlen asked suspiciously.

Huck had once stolen dessert from Arlen and had never been forgiven.

"Just checking up. How you doing?"

"Breathing," Arlen said, clutching his spoon.

"How'd you like to go on a trip? Leave Gulfport for a few days."

"Dunno."

Huck knelt down beside him. He glanced at Grandma stirring a pot on the stove. In a low voice, he said, "I need you to help me. I need to pay a man back. I'm gonna kill his family. I think they live someplace down in Florida. I need you to help me kill them."

"Kill 'um how?"

"Guns and knives," Huck said.

"Can I watch?"

"Yup."

A spark of life flickered behind Arlen's eyes. Huck had taken Arlen to jobs before. The prospect of seeing someone shot or sliced open always brought his brother up from his stupor. His spoon hit the bowl of cereal with a loud *plunk*!

"When?" he said.

Huck had always known that the life he'd led and the things he'd done would one day catch up with

315

him. It was the reality that all criminals lived with, the hot wire that ignited their blood. So he'd prepared, and buried jars of money in different places around town, each stuffed with thousands of dollars in crumpled hundred-dollar bills. He'd buried two jars in the backyard of Grandma's house, and he dug them up with a garden hoe, then unsealed them while Arlen stood beside him, holding a flashlight.

"We're rich," Arlen said.

Huck shoved a hundred dollars into his brother's hand and saw his face light up. Then Huck went inside the house and dumped the jar onto the kitchen table. Grandma was standing at the counter peeling potatoes and stared at the money.

"It's yours," Huck said.

"What for?"

"I'm buying your car."

"Car ain't worth that much," she said, throwing a handful of peeled spuds into the vat of boiling water sitting on the stove. "Go ahead and take the car. I don't use it none. You can give it back to me when you get back."

"I may not be getting back," he said.

She took a handful of potatoes out of a paper bag and started the process over. "You fixin' to stay in Florida for a spell?"

"Don't have much choice. Police looking for me."

"Summers down there are mighty long. You gonna send Arlen back?"

"Yeah. He never liked the heat."

"Well, okay," she said.

He went outside and backed her ancient Ford Fairlane out of the garage. Popping the trunk, he got a pair of illegal short-barreled shotguns from her tool shed, along with a metal strong box filled with ammunition. Arlen had gone into the house and emerged wearing his camouflage hunting vest with his collection of rubber knives and plastic toy guns. He jumped into the passenger seat and slapped his hands on his knees. Huck stared at him.

"You say good-bye to Grandma?"

Arlen frowned the way he did when he was reminded of his own stupidity. It was a sad face, almost a pout. "No," he sputtered.

"Think we should?"

"Guess so."

Huck got out of the car and led his brother back into the house. Grandma was at the counter fixing peanut-butter-and-banana sandwiches. They were Arlen's favorite thing in the whole world. She put four into a bag along with a Thermos of iced tea. Then she handed the whole thing to Arlen, took her grandson's head into her hands, and kissed him good-bye.

CHAPTER 37

The visitor parking lot of the Slippery Rock police station was empty, and Valentine parked beside the front door of the darkened station house, then jumped out, went to the door, and loudly knocked. It was a single-story concrete building with as much personality as a sewage treatment plant. When no one answered, he went back to the car.

"Stay here," he told Ricky.

Ricky lowered the wad of Kleenex pressed to his nostril. It had started bleeding right after they'd driven away from his house. "Where the hell am I going to go?"

Valentine leaned on his opened door. During the drive over, Ricky had refused to say why the Cubans were at his house, beating the daylights out of him. Valentine had saved Ricky's life twice in the past two days, yet they were no closer than the moment they'd first met.

"Just stay put, okay?"

"Sure thing, Sarge."

Valentine went around the back of the station house and saw a clunker parked in the employee

318

lot. He banged on the back door, and a Hispanic woman appeared behind the steel-meshed glass, looking shaken up. She shook her head to indicate that she wasn't opening the door come hell or high water. He went back around the building and got into the car.

"No one's here," he said.

"It's Sunday night," Ricky said. "Whoever's on duty is probably on a call or getting something to eat at McDonald's."

"Who's going to answer if I call 911?"

"An operator over in the other county. She'll call whoever's on duty and give him the message."

Valentine turned the key in the ignition and fired up the engine. He'd wanted to get Ricky someplace safe, and the police station had seemed the best choice. He backed out of the lot and pulled onto the street, but not before first looking in both directions. The road was quiet. He wondered if the Cubans had been smart enough to bring a backup car with them. Most professional crews usually had one.

"I need to put you someplace safe," he said.

"You got me," Ricky said.

"I was thinking about dropping you at your ex-wife's."

Ricky jerked his head so hard that the dog sleeping in back lifted its head. "Are you nuts? Polly and I can't be in the same room together."

"She still cares for you. She showed me my house and couldn't stop talking about you." He glanced at his passenger. "Not all of it was pleasant, but there's something still there."

"Wow, this is great. First you save my ass, now you're trying to save my failed marriage. Is there anything you can't do?"

If Ricky hadn't been bleeding, Valentine would have backhanded him in the face.

"Where does she live?"

"I'm not telling you," Ricky said.

"You want me to call information, and call her and make you look like a fool?"

Ricky threw the bloodied Kleenex to the floor and buried his head in his hands.

"I can't believe this is happening," he said.

Dressed in a bathrobe, Polly Parker stood on her wraparound front porch when Valentine pulled down her gravel driveway a few minutes later. He'd gotten her number from Ricky and called her, and she'd offered her house as a safe haven without a moment's hesitation. He had been right. The thread of love was still there.

Polly's house was small and quaint, with enough Southern charm to grace the pages of a magazine. Before getting out of the car, Ricky scrubbed his face with his shirt sleeve. It was like watching a kid going on his first date. As he climbed out, the dog bounded out of the backseat and moments later was in Polly's arms, getting hugs and kisses.

"Oh, my God," Polly said as Ricky climbed onto the porch. "What happened to your face?" She glared at Valentine coming up from behind. "Did you do that to him? Did you?"

"Some hoods came to the house and beat me up," Ricky said. He jerked his thumb in Valentine's direction. "Mr. Wonderful saved me."

Polly gently pushed the dog away. She was wearing Garfield slippers and was a foot shorter than her ex. Reaching up, she touched his damaged face.

"You just can't stay out of trouble, can you?"

Ricky pulled his head away like he'd been slapped. "Don't start in, okay? He's bad enough. I don't need any more."

"Oh, Ricky, come on."

"What do you mean?"

"I mean grow up and put it behind you. I have."

He looked down at his feet. "I'm . . . sorry."

She slid her arms around his waist and held him. "Why don't you come inside, and I'll clean you up and make you a sloe gin fizz, and you can sit in front of the TV and not worry about anything. What do you say?"

A long silence followed as Ricky seemed to wrestle with her offer, his eyes still staring downward. And then it hit Valentine what was going on. Ricky had kept Polly in the dark. She wasn't one of the gang of people in Slippery Rock involved in whatever crazy scheme he had going on. He'd protected her by not telling her. It said a lot of things about him as a man, but most importantly, it told Valentine that Ricky knew what he'd done was wrong. Otherwise, he would have had no reason to hide it from her.

"I'd like that," he said.

Polly started to lead him into the house. She turned when they were both in the foyer and looked at Valentine. "You're welcome to join us. I'm sorry I was so short with you."

"Thanks, but I need to run," Valentine said.

Ricky turned to stare at him. Panic had returned to his eyes.

"You going to the police?"

"I sure am," Valentine said.

Not knowing his way around Slippery Rock, Valentine retraced his steps back to the police station and, finding the parking lot empty, drove back to his house. On the way, he started to punch in 911 on his cell phone, only to stop when he realized that he would have no way of knowing if the cop who replied to his call was also involved in Ricky's scheme. So he called information instead and asked for Rodney Gaylord's number. As he suspected, it was unlisted.

"I need you to do me a favor," he told the operator. "Please call Sergeant Gaylord and tell him Tony Valentine needs to speak with him. Tell him I'm at my house, and he should drive there right away. Okay?"

The operator was young and didn't like being told what to do. "I'm not supposed to do that. It's against the rules."

"Tell him I just shot someone, and I figured he'd want to know," Valentine said.

"You serious, mister?"

"Dead serious."

He drove back to Ricky's house. As he expected, the black SUV was gone. He pulled into Hank Ridley's driveway a few minutes later. Hank had looked pretty stoned a half-hour ago, and Valentine guessed Hank was spinning in the ozone by now. Leaving the keys on the front door mat, he put his ear to the door and heard blaring rock 'n' roll bleeding through the grain. It was another bootleg of the Grateful Dead. The band sounded horribly out of tune. Maybe it sounded good to Hank.

Valentine traipsed through the woods back to his house, stopping every fifty feet to listen to the sounds of the forest. In his eardrums he heard a steady beating sound, then realized it was his heart. He came to a stump and sat down on it.

His thoughts drifted to Juan. He'd hated shooting him, but he hadn't seen any other choice. Back when he was patrolling Atlantic City's casinos, he'd rarely drawn his firearm, much less used it. Guns were dangerous in crowded places. But having been a street cop, he also knew that guns never settled problems. They simply ended things.

For the hell of it, he took his pulse. Eighty-eight beats a minute. Normally it was seventy. He stood up and walked down the path toward his house.

★ ★ ★

Sergeant Gaylord was waiting for Valentine in the driveway of his rental house. He was dressed in blue jeans, a threadbare sweater, and sneakers. His eyes were puffy, and his hair looked like he'd stuck it in a blender.

"Give me your gun," he said.

Valentine removed the Glock from his ankle holster. Gaylord examined the gun and shook his head. "One bullet?"

Valentine didn't understand what he meant.

"You shot him with one bullet in the head."

Valentine felt the air escape his lungs. "That's right."

"You're pretty damn good at that." Gaylord locked the Glock in the trunk of his vehicle. Then he said, "Show me where."

Valentine walked him down the road to Ricky's house while explaining what had happened and why he'd chosen to shoot Juan in Ricky's driveway. Gaylord stared at him intently in the dark. More than once the sergeant stumbled on the uneven road.

"Ricky tell you why they were beating him up?" Gaylord asked.

"No, sir."

"And Mary Alice Stoker stonewalled you as well?"

"Yes."

"You think this has something to do with the scam at the Mint?"

Valentine met his gaze. It was the first time he'd

heard Gaylord imply that he thought Ricky was a cheater. "I sure as hell do," he said.

They halted at Ricky's driveway. Gaylord said, "Stay behind me," and walked a few yards ahead of him while asking Valentine to point out where the vehicle had been parked. They came to the spot, which was directly in front of the garage. Gaylord pointed at a spot in the grass. Valentine stood there and watched the sergeant remove a small flashlight from his pocket and flyspeck the area. He took his time, and Valentine felt himself shiver as the chilly night area knifed through his clothes.

After a minute, Gaylord went into a crouch. Sticking the flashlight into his mouth, he plucked several things off the ground and placed them on his outstretched palm. Rising, he came over to where Valentine stood. Valentine stared at several tiny shards of tinted glass and the butt of a cigarette. It looked odd, and he picked it up and gave it a whiff. Reefer. The men in the van had been smoking a joint when he'd shot them.

"Looks like they cleaned up after themselves," Gaylord said.

They had also cleaned the interior of Ricky's house. No broken or damaged CDs on the living-room floor, the furniture back in its proper place. Even the pool of urine left by the dog in the kitchen was gone. Gaylord dug into the trash and, finding nothing, went outside and looked in the garbage cans beside the garage. Ricky's destroyed CD collection was nowhere to be found.

"You said they shot at you," the sergeant said.

Valentine stood on the back lawn and re-created what had happened. Gaylord looked through the grass for shell casings from Juan's automatic rifle but found none. He took a cell phone out of his pocket and called for backup. They went inside and sat in Ricky's kitchen.

"What do you think's going on here?" Gaylord asked.

Valentine shook his head. He had no earthly idea.

A uniformed cop named Farnsworth appeared fifteen minutes later. He was a handsome guy and all red in the face. Valentine wondered where he'd been rousted from.

"Watch him," Gaylord said.

Farnsworth took Gaylord's seat. The sergeant went outside and slammed the door. Through the kitchen window Valentine watched him enter the woods with the flashlight in his hand. Feeling the weight of Farnsworth's stare on his face, he shifted his eyes.

"I saw the video of you shooting the bank robbers," Farnsworth said. "Where'd you learn to shoot like that? Army?"

Valentine shrugged and resumed looking through the window. The images of Beasley and the scarecrow were gradually fading from his mind; in a few weeks, they'd be gone and would resurface only during bad dreams or those times when life got him down.

"I meant it as a compliment," Farnsworth said.

"Thanks."

"I've never had to shoot anyone," he admitted.

"You're damn lucky."

Gaylord emerged from the woods ten minutes later. In one arm he held Ricky's cat. He entered the kitchen and let the cat slip out of his grasp. It scampered over to its food bowl. He came over to the table, reached into his pocket, and dropped several small objects on the table.

"I found those in the woods," he said.

Valentine picked the objects up and examined them. They were rubber bullets.

CHAPTER 38

"Sweet dreams," Isabelle said into the phone. They were in the kitchen of her house, Gerry drinking a cup of decaf at the kitchen table, Clarkson in the other room watching ESPN, two cruisers parked outside on the street. Isabelle blew a kiss into the phone and hung up. To Gerry she said, "Want a refill?"

"That would be great," he said.

She joined him at the table, and he saw the glimmer of a tear in her eye. He remembered the first time his father had gotten shot and how his mother had reacted. It was like someone had invisibly torn her in half.

"Lamar wants to know if you've spent the money you won off him," she said.

"I haven't had time."

"I think he was joking," she said, spooning sugar into her cup.

Clarkson let out a yell. Gerry looked into the next room and saw the detective throw his arms into the air as his team scored. It was nice to see he had his priorities straight.

"Lamar really likes his job, doesn't he?" Gerry said.

"Loves it," Isabelle said.

"This won't slow him down?"

She shook her head. "I think he saw it as another badge. Not one he wanted, but one he'd wear if it happened."

"What kind of badge?"

She glanced at the living room, not wanting Clarkson to hear her. She had a sultry look that was in her genes. Part French and who knew what else. In a soft voice she answered him. "When Lamar was sixteen, he went into a convenience store in Gulfport to buy a loaf of bread and some milk and got himself arrested. Spent a whole night in jail. Got thrown in a holding cell with a bunch of hard cases. They scared the shit out of him. Worst experience of his life, to hear him tell it."

"What did he do?"

"I told you. He bought a loaf of bread and some milk."

Gerry felt like she was baiting him. He tried to imagine a scenario where a sixteen-year-old black kid could innocently enter a store and get arrested, and came up with air.

"Was it a case of mistaken identity?"

Isabelle shook her head. "It was nine-fifty in the evening. The store closed at ten."

He chewed on the information for a little bit.

"Was the store in a bad part of town?"

"Yes. The store owner had been robbed several

329

times. It always happened when he was closing up. That's when there was the most money in the till. He saw Lamar and thought he was getting robbed again, so he pressed a buzzer beneath the counter and called the cops. And all because Lamar was big and black."

Gerry said, "Is that why he went into law enforcement?"

"Yes. The first day on the job with the Casino Commission, you know what he did?"

"No."

"He went back to that convenience store and had a chat with the manager."

Isabelle's cell phone rang. It was down inside her pocketbook and sounded like a tiny bird trying to escape. She dug the phone out and stared at the caller ID.

"Speak of the devil."

She said hello to her husband, then went silent for a moment. She handed the phone across the kitchen table to her guest. "He wants to speak with you. Says it's urgent."

Clarkson drove Gerry to Gulfport Memorial Hospital. One cruiser led the way, while another followed them. Clarkson said it was risky going out, but Gerry didn't care. He was not one to ignore a dying man's request. They went inside and were met by a white-haired doctor with a kind face, holding a clipboard clutched to his chest. The doctor looked saddened by what had happened.

"He was doing fine a few hours ago," the doctor said. "Then suddenly everything started to slip. I don't like to give people death sentences, but I'm afraid I had to tell him. I asked him if he'd like us to call anyone, and he asked that we track you down."

"Did he say why?" Gerry asked.

"No. I don't think he has any immediate family. He wrote *None* in the box that says *Next of Kin* on his admittance application."

They took an elevator up to the top floor of the hospital. It had rubber floors and walls and felt like the interior of a space ship. Gerry followed the doctor down the hallway past the nurses' station to the ICU. At the doorway the doctor pulled back.

"Call me if you need anything. There's an intercom by the bed."

Then he was gone. Gerry swallowed hard and stuck his head into the room. It was a single, with a bed against the wall and a bunch of tubes running into the patient. Tex "All In" Snyder stared back at him with drooping eyes. He looked one foot in the grave, his face ashen. His hand popped up out of the sheet like something in a horror movie. He beckoned Gerry closer, his lips moving up and down. Gerry pulled up a chair and sat beside the bed.

"Hey, Tex, how's it going?"

"I'm dying," he whispered.

Tex tried to reach across the bed. Gerry took his hand with both his own.

331

"You want me to do something for you?"

Tex nodded.

"Name it."

"You got religion in that bathroom yesterday, didn't you?" the old gambler said, his voice hoarse. "You went in ready to rob that sucker with me. When you came out, you'd changed. What happened?"

Gerry told him about getting the message from his wife and how the sound of his daughter's laughter had cleared his head and driven away the bad decisions he'd made. Tex nodded approvingly when Gerry was finished, then motioned for the water bottle sitting on the night table. Gerry placed the flexible straw beneath Tex's lips and watched him drink.

"I have a half sister in St. Augustine," Tex said when he was done. "Haven't seen her in twenty years. I want her to get some money I have stored away."

"Where is it?"

"In a safe-deposit box. Her name is on the box. She doesn't know it."

"You want me to contact her for you?"

"Yes. I would be forever in your debt."

Gerry got a pad and pencil from the nurses' station and wrote down the location of the safe-deposit box and the box number, then Tex's sister's name and her last known address. He told Tex he'd be able to find her even if she'd moved, the Internet being what it was. Tex reached beneath his cotton pajamas and removed a thin gold chain hanging around his neck. From it dangled a safe-deposit key. He started to give it to Gerry, then hesitated. "Promise me you'll do it," he said.

"You have my word," Gerry said.

"Please don't rob me."

"How much money are we talking about here?" He saw Tex glare at him and said, "What I'm asking is, should your sister bring a bag?"

"A million and a half dollars."

Gerry blew out his cheeks. A small fortune for a sister Tex hadn't laid eyes on in twenty years. He tore the sheet off the pad and stuffed it into his pocket. Then he took the key out of Tex's hand. He saw Tex stare at him like he'd just made the worst decision of his life.

"Please don't rob me," he said again.

"I'm not going to rob you," Gerry said. "But I want you to come clean with me."

"About what?"

"Did Ricky Smith really beat you at the Mint that night?"

Tex flashed the weakest of smiles. " 'Course not."

"You let him win?"

"His partner paid me to lose. Slick guy from New York. I said sure. Good for business." Gerry didn't understand. Tex motioned him closer to the bed. "It's like this, son. I'm a cheater. Problem is, if I win all the time, nobody will play with me. So I lose sometimes to lesser players. Word gets out that I'm getting old and not what I used to be. The suckers think I'm easy pickings and come looking for me."

The exertion got him coughing, and Gerry grabbed the water bottle. He thought back to the videotape of Tex and Ricky playing. Neither had shown their cards at the same time. Usually that meant one player was bluffing. That wasn't the case here. Tex had thrown away winning cards and let Ricky steal the pot.

"How much did this guy from New York pay you?"

"Ten grand."

"Did he have a name?"

"Stanley." Tex's eyes darted across the room. Gerry turned around in his seat and saw Clarkson standing in the doorway. The look on his face was not a happy one. He motioned with his hand, and Gerry rose from his seat. Tex grasped the cuff of Gerry's shirt sleeve.

"Swear on a stack of Bibles you'll contact my sister."

"I already told you I would."

"I don't trust you."

Gerry looked into Tex's face, and their eyes locked. *Then why did you ask for me to come here?* he nearly said. He put his lips to the dying man's ear.

"Too bad," he said.

Clarkson took Gerry into the hallway. In a hushed voice he said, "Huck Dubb and his retarded brother showed up at the Holiday Inn a half hour ago. Huck asked the receptionist on duty to tell him what room you were staying in. The receptionist told him you checked out yesterday. Huck didn't believe him. He and his brother tore the place up."

"Did my coming here get you in trouble?"

"Yes. I need to get you back to Lamar's house, pronto."

"I need to say good-bye to Tex."

"Your life is in danger. We're got to leave right now."

The detective took Gerry's arm and began to drag him down the hall. As they passed the nurses' station, a piercing alarm went off. The nurse on duty stared at a monitor on her desk. She jumped up, ran down the hall, and disappeared into Tex's room.

Gerry looked at the monitor. A flat line was tracking across the screen. Tex was gone. Gerry crossed himself, then got onto the elevator with Clarkson.

CHAPTER 39

Gaylord wasn't nearly as stupid as he acted. After Valentine examined the rubber bullets, Gaylord pulled a chair up and made Valentine repeat what had happened. He took copious notes and made Valentine clarify points that bothered him or didn't make sense. It was an old cop trick, designed to trip up a suspect. The sergeant obviously didn't believe Valentine's story.

When Valentine was finished, Gaylord picked up the phone and called Polly Parker's house. He asked for Ricky and spoke to him for several minutes. The questions he asked were the same ones he'd asked Valentine. He jotted down Ricky's answers, keeping his pad tilted. When he was done he said good-bye and hung up. The look on his face was one of confusion.

"What's he saying?" Valentine asked.

"Four Cubans he used to know showed up on his doorstep, said he owed them money," Gaylord said. "They roughed him up and broke some of his stuff. Then you showed up and saved the day."

"What about the guy I shot in his driveway? Did he mention that?"

Gaylord slapped his notepad on the table. "Ricky said you told him to shut his eyes. He heard you shoot your gun but didn't see anything. That true?"

Valentine shook his head. Did anyone deal in the truth in this goddamned town? "Yes," he said.

"So there aren't any witnesses?"

"No."

"No witnesses and no body." Gaylord rose and picked up his notepad. "I wish like hell I knew what was going on here. My gut says you're telling the truth, but I don't have anything to corroborate what you're saying. Understand?"

"Yes, you don't have a case."

"Not yet."

Valentine looked into his face expectantly.

"I like to work off assumptions," the sergeant said. "I'm going to assume you're telling the truth and that you shot someone earlier tonight. Which means there's a body, and that body needs to be dealt with. I'm putting an all-points bulletin out to every police precinct within five hundred miles of here, asking them to be on the lookout for a man shot between the eyes."

"Assuming they dump the body."

"Ricky said the SUV they were driving was rented. They'll have to dump the body before they drop the rental off. My guess is, they'll do it sooner than later."

His thinking was sound, and Valentine stood up. "What do you want me to do?"

"Stay put. I'll call you in the morning."

"Thanks for taking my side in this."

"It's the only one that makes any sense," Gaylord said.

Leaving Ricky's house, Valentine crossed the yards to his own. Ricky's cat was at his back door, pawing the wood. He guessed the owner of the house had once fed it. He let the cat in and searched the shelves of the kitchen pantry. He found a box of cat food that had expired a few weeks ago. He poured some into a dish and put it on the floor. The cat didn't seem to mind.

He'd put his cell phone on the table, and noticed it was blinking. He had a message. He retrieved it and heard the sound of his son's voice. He listened to the message twice. He was happy to hear that Gerry had gotten Tex Snyder to open up and admit he'd participated in a scam. But he wasn't happy to hear that Huck Dubb was still on the loose. He erased the message and called his son back.

"You okay?" he asked.

"Yeah," his son said. "I'm back at Lamar's house. You never told me how dangerous your business was."

Valentine settled into a chair and felt the cat rubbing against his legs. Reaching down, he rubbed its head. "Something you said in your message didn't make sense. Huck Dubb and his brother went to the Holiday Inn looking for you, right?"

"That's right."

"But Huck already knew you'd checked out. He sent his boys after you, remember?"

There was a long pause on the line.

"Maybe he forgot," Gerry said.

"I don't think so," Valentine said.

Another long pause. If his son was going to work in this business, he needed to use his head for something else besides growing hair.

"I give up," Gerry said.

"Huck knew you stayed at the Holiday Inn. He and his brother went there looking for something else."

"Like what?"

"How about the card you filled out when you registered?" Valentine said. "Every hotel asks for it. You give them your name and address. They send it to their corporate headquarters, put you on a mailing list."

"You think that's what he was after? You think he's going after my family?"

"You killed his boys. Yes, he's going after your family."

"Oh, Jesus, Pop. Jesus Christ."

His son sounded like he was ready to cry. He had wanted to join his business in the worst way. Was he having second thoughts?

"I'll call the Palm Harbor police and alert them," Valentine said. "You need to call Yolanda and tell her to move across the street to my place until Huck gets hauled in."

339

"Shit," his son said.

"What's wrong?"

"The card I filled out at the hotel had two boxes. One for home, the other for work. I put your address in that one."

Valentine silently counted to five. He kept a PO box, which he'd told Gerry to always use. Obviously, his son hadn't listened.

"Tell Yolanda to go down the street to Mabel's house."

"You think Mabel will be okay with that?"

"She will if you ask her nice."

Valentine hung up, then called the Palm Harbor police department. He'd lived in Palm Harbor for two years and had tried to ingratiate himself with the local cops without becoming a pain in the ass. So far, it had worked pretty well, and the cop he spoke to promised to send a cruiser to Gerry's house. He also promised to call the Gulfport police and make sure they coordinated their efforts. It was all Valentine could ask for.

He went to the bedroom, pulled his suitcase from beneath the bed, and started packing. If a deranged Mississippi redneck wanted to do his family harm, he needed to be there and deal with it, even if it meant breaking the promise he'd made to Gaylord to stay put.

He looked at the luminous face of his wristwatch. Nearly eleven. If he left now, he could hit the highway when it was empty and speed home. He figured the trip at ten hours max. He guessed Huck was also driving, but would stay away from main highways to avoid any highway patrol that might be looking for him.

In the hallway he found his heavy coat, and threw it over his shoulders without buttoning it. He looked around the house, wondering if he'd left anything. If he had, it would probably come to him when he was on the road.

He was pulling open the front door when he saw a pair of headlights pierce the darkness. A vehicle was coming down his driveway. He slammed the door shut, and for a moment considered running. If it was the Cubans, he needed to hide in the woods.

The car stopped halfway down the drive. He looked through the cutout in the door and saw an interior light come on. He squinted and realized it was Gaylord. He opened the closet door, and shoved his suitcase inside. Then he pulled his coat off and threw it on a peg. He heard a knock and pulled the door open. Gaylord stood on the stoop.

"We found the body," he said.

CHAPTER 40

Mabel was ready to nab a cheater, when she heard someone at the front door. "It's me," Yolanda called out.

Mabel glanced at the clock on Tony's desk. Nearly midnight. Normally she'd be in bed by now, nibbling on licorice and reading a book. But tonight was different. Tonight she was going to nab the invisible chip thief.

Employee theft was a problem in every casino. Perhaps it was the vast amounts of money the employees saw flow by each day. Or maybe it was the long hours and miserable pay. Tony often said that casinos offered the last factory jobs in America.

The Palace in South Africa was getting ripped off by an employee. One hundred dollars was disappearing from the roulette table every night. The casino was sure that it was an inside job. Tony had given her the job a week ago, with the promise of a bonus if she could detect the cheating. So she'd stayed up late and glued herself to the computer.

"I'm coming," she said, pushing herself out of the chair.

She found Yolanda on the stoop, the baby asleep in her arms.

"Gerry called from Mississippi. He said a man named Huck Dubb is coming to Florida to kill me and my baby."

"What?" Mabel ushered her inside and shut the door. "Do the police know?"

Yolanda nodded. She looked remarkably composed. "Yes. They don't think this man will get here until tomorrow. He's driving, so they've set up roadblocks on the highways. They're sure they'll get him, but Gerry doesn't want me taking any chances. Would it be okay if the baby and I stayed with you?"

Mabel put her arms around the younger woman. Yolanda was doing her best to act brave. "Of course you may. You can use the guest bedroom. Did you pack anything?"

"I left the house right away," Yolanda said. "Gerry told me to."

"But you said this man wouldn't get here until tomorrow."

"Gerry said he has a lot of friends. He might even have friends here in Florida."

Mabel looked into her face. Yolanda's eyes were puffy, and she wore no makeup. Had she been sleeping when Gerry had called? She gave her a gentle hug.

"Let me go and shut off Tony's computer. Then we can head down to my place."

★   ★   ★

343

Sitting at Tony's desk, Mabel started to shut down the computer, when her eyes froze on the screen. The roulette game at the Palace was in full swing, with a dozen players making bets. So much money was on the layout, it was hard to watch the employees. But Mabel's eyes had locked onto one. It was the banker, whose job was to collect losing bets and pay out winning ones. He sat in front of a huge tray of colored chips. When he leaned forward to collect a bet, his necktie hung over the tray and his elbow pressed down on it.

"Gotcha!"

She called the Palace and got the general manager on the line. Mabel said, "Mr. Valentine asked me to call you. The banker just stole a black hundred-dollar chip. It's hidden behind his necktie with a piece of double-sided Scotch tape."

"Mr. Valentine is sure?" the general manager asked.

"Positive."

Mabel heard a click on the phone. Yolanda came in and stood beside her. Two men appeared on the screen and lifted the banker cleanly out of his chair. Casino people called this giving someone the jerk. One of them turned the banker's necktie over and exposed the stolen chip. Mabel clapped her hands in delight.

"Gerry also said that Huck Dubb might come to Tony's house," Yolanda said when they were standing on the stoop and Mabel was locking the front door.

"Meaning we shouldn't come back here until he's caught," Mabel said.

"Yes."

"What kind of person is this Huck Dubb?"

"Gerry said he's part of the Dixie Mafia. Gerry did something to him, and Huck tried to kill him. He didn't succeed, so now he's coming after us."

Mabel went back inside and got Tony's Sig Sauer. Then she flipped the security system on. As she relocked the door, she tried to imagine the kind of person they were dealing with. If Huck Dubb was driving here from Mississippi hell-bent on revenge, Gerry must have done something awful to him. Which meant Huck wasn't going to leave if he discovered Yolanda wasn't home. The police might catch him, and they might not. Leaving her and Yolanda to fend for themselves.

"That's not good," she said. "How about some homemade lentil soup?"

Yolanda smiled. "Sounds great."

It was a moonlit night, and they walked down the block to Mabel's place and let themselves in through the front door, the house filled with the heavenly smells of that afternoon's cooking.

The lentil soup tasted better the second time around. Lois was a little angel and remained asleep in her mother's arms. Yolanda and Mabel sat in the living room and spooned the soup into their mouths while staring at the window that watched the street. A police cruiser passed by and stopped outside Yolanda's house. A uniformed cop got out and walked around the property with a flashlight in his hand. He returned to his vehicle and drove away. Several minutes passed.

"I don't like this," Yolanda said.

"The soup?"

Yolanda displayed her empty bowl. "Being helpless. Sitting here waiting for something to happen. Acting like unemancipated women."

"Is that what we're acting like?"

"Yes. What are we waiting for? We should be doing something to protect ourselves."

"We are. We're hiding."

"That makes us victims, doesn't it?"

Mabel stared at the Sig Sauer lying on the couch. She supposed Yolanda was right. She refilled their bowls in the kitchen. Coming back to the living room, she said, "What are you suggesting we do? Set a trap for Huck Dubb?"

"That's what Tony or Gerry would do. They know Huck is coming, so they'd use that to their advantage. They'd think a step ahead and ambush him."

Mabel stood at the window and spooned hot soup into her mouth. The police cruiser reappeared, and she glanced at her watch. Fifteen minutes had passed since the cruiser's first visit. A lot of bad things could happen in fifteen minutes.

Yolanda was right. They needed to take precautions, or risk becoming a sound bite on the

346

evening news. That was all murders were good for these days.

She sat down beside the younger woman. Yolanda had a funny look in her eyes, and Mabel realized she had something specific in mind.

"Are you going to tell me what you're thinking?"

"I think we should call the men we met in Gibsonton," Yolanda said.

"You mean Brownie and Little Pete?"

"Yes. I think they can help us."

CHAPTER 41

Valentine led Gaylord into the kitchen and fixed a pot of coffee. The sergeant fell into a chair, his body language indicating that the last thing he wanted to be doing on a Sunday night was dealing with a murder. That was the problem with homicides. They always came at the wrong times.

Valentine excused himself, went into the bathroom, and called Mabel's house on his cell phone. His neighbor answered and, hearing the concern in his voice, quickly assured him that she, Yolanda, and his granddaughter were safe and sound.

"We're taking precautions," Mabel said. "Don't worry."

"I'll be home as soon as I can," he said.

When he returned to the kitchen, the coffee had finished brewing and Gaylord had laid several folded sheets of fax paper out flat on the kitchen table. Valentine saw yellow highlights on every page, along with notes written in meticulous script in the margins. The sergeant waited until he had a steaming mug in his hand before speaking.

"You mind my asking you a personal question?"

"What's that?" Valentine said.

"Why go back to work after retiring? The money?"

"My wife died. She used to keep my social calendar."

The sergeant stared into the depths of his drink. "There's a message there, isn't there?"

"It's nothing you can prepare for," Valentine said.

Gaylord looked up at him. "The loss of a spouse?"

"Loneliness."

The sergeant put his mug on the table. He hadn't even tasted it. Picking up the fax paper, he read from it. "The manager of a 7-Eleven about fifty miles north of here found a body behind his store an hour ago. The victim was a Hispanic male, late thirties, about six feet tall and a hundred and ninety pounds. He'd died from a gunshot to the forehead. The policeman who arrived on the scene said the victim was still warm when he touched him."

"No ID?"

"No. His pockets were picked clean. And get this. His fingerprints were gone. Burned away with some type of acid."

"They didn't take out his teeth, did they?"

"I already figured out who he is." Something resembling a smile crossed Gaylord's face. He probably got the opportunity to solve a real crime about once a year. He picked up his mug and sipped his coffee, extending the moment. "I figured the guys who dumped him weren't driving around with acid in their car. I contacted the major credit-card companies and asked them to pull up any recent purchases of acid at any home improvement or auto-parts stores in the past few hours. I cast a net of a hundred miles from the 7-Eleven."

And hit pay dirt, Valentine thought. Since 9/11, credit-card companies had become one of law enforcement's biggest allies. If a cop knew a suspect's purchasing patterns, he could follow the suspect across town or across the country.

"I got a number of hits," Gaylord went on, "but one stood out. A man named Angel Fernandez purchased a can of boric acid at a Home Depot about thirty miles from the 7-Eleven a few hours ago. He also bought cleaning fluid. He paid for the items on his Visa card.

"Now here's the interesting part. The credit card was a corporate card issued to employees of a company called AGM. Stands for Asset Growth Management. They're out of New York."

"Sounds like a brokerage house," Valentine said.

"They are. I got Visa to send me the names of the other AGM employees who have cards."

Gaylord spun one of the faxes around. It was from Visa and contained the names of fifteen people. One name had been highlighted in yellow: Juan Rodriguez. "You said the guy you shot was named Juan, so I assumed this was him."

"Did you check to see if he had a record?"

Gaylord handed him another fax. It was a rap sheet for Juan Rodriguez and included a grainy mug shot. It was the same guy Valentine had shot in Ricky's driveway.

"He's a drug dealer," Gaylord said. "Works out of Miami, connected to several cartels in Colombia. You shot a real bad dude."

Valentine felt the invisible knot in his chest loosen. Gaylord was telling him to forget the rubber bullets; he'd shot a menace to society. He pointed at the remaining faxes on the table. "Can I look at these?"

"Be my guest."

Valentine read the page with the names of the AGM Visa cardholders. His eyes locked on a name at the top. "Stanley Kessel," he said. Gaylord read it upside down.

"Doesn't ring any bells."

"Was he before your time?"

Gaylord shot him a hurt look. "What's that supposed to mean?"

"Stanley Kessel is from Slippery Rock. He's a childhood friend of Ricky Smith's. Mary Alice Stoker said Stanley once stole money from her purse. Said he was a bad apple."

Gaylord gave it some thought. Had his brain been an engine, Valentine imagined he would hear the gears shift. "Stan Kessel. Yeah, I remember that little weasel. In his senior year, he got caught stealing the answers to the SAT tests. They had

351

to cancel the tests in the whole state. I heard he moved to New York, made a killing in the stock market."

"Does he have family here?"

"His parents are long gone."

"His name is at the top. My guess is, this is his company. Why do you think he sent four thugs to intimidate Ricky Smith?"

"Because Stanley's involved."

"Has to be," Valentine said.

As a kid, Valentine had admired a man in his neighborhood named Ralph Coker. He was a plumbing salesman and always drove nice cars. Coker's son Eddie and Valentine had played together. One day, Eddie had taken Valentine to his father's office. There had been a desk and a phone. Nothing else. "Where's your father's chair?" Valentine asked.

"They don't give him one," Eddie said. "They want him out selling."

Gaylord's office at police headquarters reminded him of Ralph Coker's. A desk, a phone, a computer, and no chair. There was a chair against the wall, and Valentine guessed it was for guests. He sat in it while Gaylord worked his computer. The sergeant's thick fingers were a blur across the keyboard. The computer responded with beeps and funny noises that, put together, resembled music.

Gaylord went into NCIC, a national registry of criminals that every law enforcement agency in the country could access. He typed in Stanley Kessel's name and hit enter.

"Don't you ever sit down?"

"Yeah. In the car and in front of the TV. This is exercise."

NCIC came up with nothing. Gaylord went to Google and again typed in Kessel's name. This time, he got a number of hits, and Valentine watched him scroll down the list, then select one and click on it with the mouse.

"You were right," Gaylord said. "Kessel is the president and founder of AGM. I found a story from the *Wall Street Journal* about him. Says he's a self-made millionaire. Specializes in market making, whatever the hell that is."

"That's a broker who takes companies public on the stock market."

"Must be lucrative."

Valentine leaned back in his chair. He felt the cold concrete wall seep into his neck. It cleared his head and let him see the real picture. Stanley Kessel was a smart guy who'd started his own company. Ricky Smith was a loser who stayed home and played loud music. Stanley was running the show, not Ricky.

"How many miles from here did you say they dumped the body?" he asked.

Gaylord lifted his eyes from the computer screen. "Fifty. Why?"

"Can you do a record search of the nearby towns?"

"Sure. What am I looking for?"

A house on the edge of town, or a large apartment. Someplace where the larcenous citizens of Slippery Rock could congregate and practice ripping off a casino. Every gang had one.

"A place in Stanley Kessel's name," he said.

CHAPTER 42

Stanley Kessel owned a house on a two-acre lot on the outskirts of Slippery Rock. Or rather, his company did. Gaylord knew the place but hadn't been there in years.

"Can't believe he's been right here under my nose and I didn't know it," Gaylord said as they drove down a dirt driveway. The house was on a dead-end street with no streetlight. Gaylord killed the engine of his car and sat perfectly still. It was nearly one A.M. He'd gone to a judge's house and gotten him to sign a search warrant.

He started to climb out, then glanced sideways at Valentine. "Stay here."

"You don't know what you're looking for," Valentine said.

"You don't think I'll recognize cheating equipment if I see it?"

"You don't know what cheating equipment is."

Gaylord's chin sagged. "So what do you suggest I do?"

"Deputize me. Then I can't taint the crime scene."

Valentine could tell that Gaylord wasn't thrilled

355

with the idea. He raised his right hand, just to goad him. Gaylord shook his head and swore him in.

They got out and stared at the house in the darkness. It was practically falling down, with a patchwork shingle roof and shutters hanging on one hinge. The front porch creaked unhappily as they stepped on it. Gaylord put his face to the glass cutout in the door. Finding it locked, he said, "Step back."

"You going to kick it in?"

"No, I'm going to blow it down."

Valentine smiled. It was the first funny thing he'd heard the sergeant say.

"Try the back door," he suggested.

"Why?"

"It's obvious no one used the front much."

Gaylord mumbled under his breath and walked off the porch. He was packing the weight but could put it into high gear when he needed to. As they came around the house, a motion-detector light went off, the bright orange light shining directly in their faces.

It took a moment for Valentine's eyes to adjust. When they did, he saw that the lawn behind the house was littered with broken refrigerators. Gaylord shook his head.

"The town will pick this stuff up, free of charge."

Valentine got close to the machines and realized his eyes were playing tricks on him. They were slot and video-poker machines with their guts ripped out. *The gang wanted to steal a jackpot but couldn't figure out how,* he thought.

Gaylord tested the back door and found it locked. He punched out a pane of glass with the butt of his automatic and stuck his hand through.

"Hold on," Valentine said.

"You think there's something behind the door?"

"You said Kessel was a weasel. You want to put your life in a weasel's hands?"

Gaylord stepped away from the door. "No."

Valentine went into the garage behind the house and came out with a piece of rope. He tied the rope around the doorknob, then walked into the yard. He handed Gaylord the end, and the sergeant gave it a sharp tug. The door banged open, followed by a loud *thwap!* An arrow flew through the back door. Its path took it directly between where Valentine and Gaylord were standing. Both men heard its whistle as it flew by their heads.

The arrow went into an oak tree in the backyard with such force that Valentine could not pull it out without snapping it in two. Drawing his sidearm, Gaylord said, "Thanks for saving my life," and marched into the house. Valentine saw a light come on and followed him into the kitchen. It was a square room with a yellowing linoleum floor. Sitting in the room's center was a crossbow strapped to a metal chair. Tied to the trigger was an bungee cord, which was also tied to the back door.

Valentine had never seen a crossbow except in the movies. It was a fierce-looking weapon. He decided he'd be happy if he never saw one again.

He cased the downstairs. The rooms were sparsely furnished and covered with a coat of dust. The upstairs was the same, with box springs lying on the bedroom floors. Returning to the kitchen, he said, "I didn't find anything. Does this place have a basement?"

"What kind of question is that?"

"I live in Florida. We don't have basements."

"I'm sure it's got one."

"Then it must be hidden, because I can't find it."

Gaylord banged on the walls. Inside the pantry he found a hollow wall and pried it open with his fingernails. Cold air blasted their faces. He stuck his head into the space, then found a light string and tugged on it. A naked bulb came on. Valentine peeked over his shoulder and saw a stairway descending into the basement. Gaylord started to go down, and Valentine touched the sergeant's shoulder.

"Can I go first?"

"Let me guess. You don't want me touching anything."

"If you don't mind."

Gaylord let him go first. The air in the basement was extremely cold, and Valentine felt a chill go through his body that went straight to his toes. At the bottom of the steps, he paused to stare and felt the sergeant bump into him.

"Pay dirt," he said under his breath.

The basement resembled a small casino. On one wall was a blackjack table with two chairs; in the room's center, a roulette table and betting layout; on the far wall, a regulation-size craps table. On the floors around each of the tables were dozens of chalk Xs. Gaylord pointed at them and said, "Looks like a dance recital."

Valentine went to the blackjack table. It had been bugging the hell out of him that he couldn't figure out how Ricky had won every single hand of blackjack he'd played at the Mint. He'd never met a scam he couldn't figure out, and he'd decided that it was because it was a tape.

So he stood a few feet away from the blackjack table and just stared. There were only two chairs, one for Ricky and one for someone else. He remembered back to the tape. An elderly woman with white hair was at the table. She had fronted Ricky his initial stake. Was she also involved?

He stared at the table for a full minute. Everything looked normal, except the pack of Lucky Strikes sitting on the right side of the table. If he remembered correctly, the elderly woman had smoked like a chimney. He stared at the position of the cigarette pack. It was directly beneath the shuffle machine. The Mint used shuffle machines at their blackjack tables, as did many Las Vegas casinos.

Shuffle machines sped the games up and made them more profitable.

Valentine had never liked shuffle machines for the simple reason that cheaters could also get their hands on them. The one on the table was called a Shuffle Master. It could shuffle eight decks of cards at once. It also had a unique feature. After the decks were shuffled, the Shuffle Master inverted their entire order, one card at a time. The machine did it at lightning speed, but the inversion was still visible if you stuck your nose to the face of the machine. Or if you stuck a camera beneath the machine.

He picked up the pack of Lucky Strikes. It looked normal, but felt heavy. He popped the lid and stared at the miniature camera inside. Then he examined the top of the box. The camera's eye was part of the bull's-eye pattern on the front.

Hanging from one of the chairs was a lady's handbag. He opened it and found a receiving device inside. He heard Gaylord come up from behind him.

"What did you find?"

Valentine handed him the pack of Lucky Strikes. "The camera inside the cigarette box recorded the order of the cards inside the shuffle machine. The information was sent to a computer. The computer had a software program that calculated how to play the cards so that the house would lose every hand."

"How's that possible?"

"Ricky constantly switched the number of hands he played. One round, he played one hand; the next he played three. The software program told him to do that."

"How did he get the information?"

Valentine tapped the chair with the woman's handbag. "The lady sitting next to him received the information. All she had to do was stare into her handbag. She communicated to Ricky with some kind of code."

"Is the dealer involved?"

"The dealer doesn't have a clue," Valentine said.

"And they practiced it all right here in Slippery Rock," the sergeant said. "Well, this should be enough to convict Ricky of cheating."

"It won't convict Ricky of anything. There's nothing illegal about owning crooked gambling equipment. The crime is bringing the equipment into a casino."

Gaylord shot him an exasperated look. "So what do we do?"

"Find something that *will* convict him."

Valentine crossed the basement to the roulette table. He spun the wheels and set the ivory ball in motion. The most common way to beat roulette was by gaffing the wheel. This was done by creating a bias in the wheel that would favor one side over another. The other method was to gaff the pocket walls, called frets. Some frets would be gaffed so they'd be more likely to reject the ball, while others would accept the ball more easily. On the betting layout he saw a stack of yellow legal pads. Picking one up, he stared at the rows of figures and mathematical calculations covering the page. In exasperation he dropped the pad on the table.

"Not good?" Gaylord asked.

"They're using visual prediction."

Gaylord shouldered up beside him. "Guess that isn't illegal either, huh?"

He shook his head. "It's an advantage strategy that predicts the outcome without any outside assistance. The player mentally calculates the ball and wheel speed to estimate where the ball will drop from the ball track. Then, based upon bounce swing—"

"What's that?"

"An estimate of how many pockets the ball will bounce after it falls. Each wheel is different. So is each dealer who spins the ball. Anyway, the player takes that into consideration and makes his prediction of which numbers are most likely to be winners."

"How could Ricky Smith do that?" the sergeant said. "He's not that smart."

"Ricky didn't. Another player did," Valentine said. "That player checked out that wheel days or weeks before. He recorded hundreds of wheel spins and wrote down profiles of the different dealers." He walked around the table and stood behind the roulette wheel. "That player stood here, did the math, and signaled to Ricky which numbers to bet on. Ricky then quickly bet those numbers."

"You've seen this before?"

"Yeah. It only works if the player doing the predicting is sharp." Valentine tapped the yellow pads on the table. "This guy."

"You think that was Kessel's role? He was real smart in school."

"Then why did he steal the SATs?"

"Like I told you, he's a weasel."

Valentine already knew how the craps scam worked and did not bother to examine the table. Instead, he stood in the room's center and scratched his chin. Nothing he had found was going to put anyone in jail—except the crossbow, and it was going to be hard to prove who put that in the kitchen.

"Hey, look at this." Gaylord was standing on the side of the room beside the furnace. He'd found a door and had his fingers on the knob.

"Hold on," Valentine said. He went upstairs and got the rope. They repeated the door-opening drill, but stood at an angle from the opening. This time, nothing came flying out. Gaylord went in and flipped on the light.

The room was unfinished, with walls made of packed dirt and an uneven concrete floor. In its center was a table that held two TV sets. A chair sat in front of the table, a remote on the seat. Valentine picked up the remote and pressed the power button. Both TVs instantly came to life. On one set was a commercial; on the other, a female newscaster talking sports. Valentine stared at them, not seeing any connection.

His eyes fell on the thirty-gallon garbage bag leaning against the wall. It was the same kind of bag he used at home, with a built-in tie at the mouth of the bag. He crossed the room and untied the top. Inside he saw a few thousand used scratch-off lottery tickets.

"All right," he said under his breath.

"What?" Gaylord asked.

He extracted a handful of tickets. "Ricky won a fifty-thousand-dollar lottery jackpot, didn't he?"

"Yeah, a few days ago. Let me guess. He found a winning ticket and figured out a way to cover over the circles."

"There you go."

"Ricky then gave the ticket to his friend, who worked at a convenience store," Gaylord said, "and was planning to repurchase the ticket and then show everyone he'd won a jackpot. Only, he decided to let Roland Pew in on the action."

"Why do you think he did that?" Valentine asked.

"They're old buddies."

Valentine slung the garbage bag over his shoulder. As he started to walk out of the room, he saw Gaylord standing in front of the twin TVs. A horse race was showing on both sets. It was the same race, only being run at different times, the horses at different portions of the muddy track.

"I've seen this channel before," Gaylord said. "It's on cable. It shows nothing but horse races and equestrian events. My teenage daughter loves it."

Valentine watched the race end on one set, then watched it end on the other, all the while counting silently in his head. Seven seconds between endings.

"You know what this means?" Gaylord asked.

"It's how you rig a horse race," he said.

CHAPTER 43

They left Stanley Kessel's house at one-thirty. Valentine had Gaylord drive to the Off-Track Betting parlor where Ricky had picked winners the day before. In the backseat of the car was the garbage bag of used lottery tickets they'd found inside the house. Gaylord was convinced that it was evidence, and Valentine was too tired to argue with him. Ricky had bought a bunch of tickets, found a $50,000 winner, and re-covered the scratch-off spots with a similar-looking substance. There was no crime in that.

They stopped at an all-night convenience store and got coffee. It was really strong. When their cups were empty, Valentine explained to Gaylord why the tickets weren't evidence. This time, the sergeant got it.

"So where does that leave us?" Gaylord asked when they were back on the highway.

"We need to find evidence that Ricky scammed the OTB parlor. Otherwise, we don't have a case."

They did not speak for the rest of the drive. Valentine had dealt with a lot of brilliant criminals, and Stanley Kessel was heading for the top of the chart. He didn't leave meaningful clues, or evidence that would hold up in court. That was the difference between the average criminal and the pro. The pros rarely went to jail.

They crossed the state line and pulled into the OTB parlor's parking lot. A low-slung car was parked in the back of the lot. The vehicle was rocking to the beat of love, and Gaylord pulled a flasher off the floor and stuck it on his dashboard. He turned it on while hitting his siren. Two half-dressed adults bounced up in the seats.

"Make him take you to a motel," the sergeant yelled out his window.

The car sped away. Gaylord parked in front of the parlor and killed his headlights. Valentine got out and walked to the front door. He stood on his tiptoes and tried to see the roof. The moon was taking a powder behind some clouds, and he couldn't see anything. He returned to the car and asked Gaylord for a flashlight.

"It's in the trunk. I'll pop it for you."

Valentine walked around to the trunk and took out the flashlight. He twisted the light on and walked up to the front door. Shining the light on the roof, he ran the beam back and forth several times. He saw only one antenna. He went back to the car.

"Mind if I climb on the hood of your car? I need a better vantage point."

"Go ahead. But take your shoes off, okay?"

Valentine slipped his shoes and socks off and climbed onto the hood. This time, he focused the flashlight's beam on the spot where the antenna was. A thick black wire protruded from the roof. He swore and climbed down.

"They beat us here," he said, getting in the car.

"They destroyed the evidence?"

"Yes." He punched the dashboard and watched the indentation slowly vanish. It was a perfect metaphor for what was happening. He knew how Ricky had scammed every single game, and he couldn't prove a damn thing. "I need more coffee."

"You think that's going to make you think better?" Gaylord asked.

"Yes."

"You think there's something you missed?"

"Maybe."

"Why don't you sleep on it? Maybe in the morning—"

"By tomorrow they'll have destroyed every piece of evidence there is. If you want to pack it in, I'll drive you home."

"I was only suggesting—"

Valentine turned sideways in his seat. "Suggest something else."

"Like what?"

"Like a solution."

"What do you mean?"

"How would you handle this case if it was yours?"

Gaylord chewed it over all the way to the convenience store. Valentine had decided that the guy wasn't stupid, just stuck in a crummy system that wouldn't let him use his brains for anything besides typing reports. As Gaylord pulled into the lot, he slapped the wheel.

"Got it," he said, a triumphant smile on his face. "We go after the woman who helped Ricky with the blackjack scam. She's an accessory. Stick the computers we found at the house under her nose and turn the steam on."

Valentine found himself smiling. Out of the mouths of babes and police sergeants came the most amazing things. He tried to recall the woman at the blackjack table. White hair and cigarettes was all he could pull up. She'd passed Ricky dozens of signals. That took hundreds of hours of practice. And trusting your partner. Only, that had to come naturally.

"She's a relative," Valentine said.

Gaylord stared at him. "You think so?"

"Positive."

"That first cup of coffee must still be working."

Sitting in the convenience store's parking lot, Valentine called Bill Higgins at home on his cell phone. Normally, he tried not to call Bill at home and ruin his evenings. In the end, it was only casinos' money they were talking about, and usually that could wait until the next day. But this was different. He had to assume that Ricky had contacted the woman who'd helped him cheat at blackjack and alerted her to what was going on. Bill needed to grill her, before she had a chance to work on her story.

"Her name is Helen Ledbetter," Bill said.

"You know her?"

"I interviewed her last week. She's a retired bookkeeper, used to work for the casinos. You really think she was involved?"

There was real doubt in Bill's voice. Had Helen Ledbetter served him coffee and something to eat and won him over? She's rehearsed her role in the scam and probably rehearsed being interviewed by a policeman as well.

"Let me put it another way," Valentine said. "She's the only lead we have. And if you can't link her to Ricky Smith, we don't have a case."

"And I'll probably end up losing my job," Bill said.

"Correct."

"I'll need a search warrant," Bill said. "Considering I don't have any evidence, I'm going to have to do some tap dancing before a judge. This is going to take time."

"How much?" Valentine said.

"Give me until early tomorrow morning."

Valentine filled two sixteen-ounce Styrofoam cups with coffee and walked to the front of the convenience store. Gaylord was shooting the breeze with the manager, a turbaned Middle

370

Easterner with a permanent smile plastered on his face. As Valentine put the cups on the counter, he saw Gaylord glance at the doughnuts sitting in a cardboard box beside the cash register. What did marketing people call that? Point of purchase. Valentine picked up a napkin and plucked a pair oozing with purple jam.

"These too," he said. "My treat."

"Would you like some cigarettes?" the manager asked as he rang up the items.

"How did you know I smoked?"

"Sergeant Gaylord said you were a policeman," the manager replied.

"Do all cops smoke?"

"All the ones that come into my store do."

"I'm trying to quit."

"Nicotine gum perhaps?"

Valentine threw up his arms in defeat. The manager's smile grew, and he added a package of nicotine gum to his items. Taking out his wallet, Valentine extracted a ten-dollar bill and handed it to him. As he waited for his change, he glanced at his money. He was running low and would need to find an ATM soon. He took the change from the manager and tucked it into his billfold, then noticed a piece of paper he hadn't remembered seeing before.

He pulled it out and stared at Ricky's racing slip from the OTB parlor. Printed on it was the date and time of the race and the three winning horses Ricky had picked. Ricky had wagged the slip in his face, then left it on the seat of the car. Valentine guessed he had subconsciously known the slip would come in handy and had stuck it into his wallet. Putting the slip to his lips, he kissed it.

"Did you win the lottery?" the manager asked excitedly.

"Close enough," Valentine said.

CHAPTER 44

Huck and Arlen Dubb were driving across the Florida Panhandle when Arlen said he had to pee. It was growing light, and they were on a desolate stretch of highway called I-10. The highway bisected the northern part of Florida and stretched into two time zones. They had left Gulfport four hours ago and hadn't pulled over once, Huck fearful of being seen by some rent-a-cop who had nothing better to do than look for wanted criminals.

"Can't you hold it in?" Huck asked.

"Nuh-uh," Arlen said.

Forty-eight years old, and Arlen's brain had never grown past the second grade. Huck reminded himself of that every time he got angry with Arlen. Huck picked up the thermos off the seat and poured the last of Grandma's iced tea out his window. Handing it to his younger brother, he said, "Do it in this. It will save time."

Arlen scrunched his face up. "Nuh-uh."

"Why not?"

"I gotta do both."

"Why didn't you say that in the first place?"

"Didn't want to."

Huck reined in the urge to curse him. He pushed the car over the speed limit. After a minute a sign flashed by. Rest stop, two miles.

"Hold on, little bro," he said.

Arlen had his pants undone before he was out of the car. He ran to the brick building that housed the restrooms and hit the door hard with his shoulder, then disappeared.

Huck got out and stretched his legs. His ass felt like it had melted and become part of the car seat. He walked around the grounds and saw a bunch of signs planted in the grass. One was a welcome from Jeb Bush. Another said a twenty-four-hour guard was on duty. He looked for the guard, didn't see him, then looked for the guard's car. The lot was empty. It didn't feel right.

He walked down a concrete path to the edge of the building, lit up a cigarette, and in the flame's temporary light stared across the grounds. A police cruiser materialized before his eyes. It was sitting in the shadows beside the exit. Was the cop hiding, or taking a snooze?

Huck got back into his car and tapped his fingers on the wheel. The cop hadn't put his lights on. Maybe he was asleep. Or hadn't seen them. Or didn't care. Arlen came out a few moments later munching on a candy bar and hopped in.

"Put your seat belt on," Huck said.

Huck pulled out of the rest stop and got on the

highway. He put the car up to the speed limit but didn't go over it. A minute later a car appeared in his mirror. Then another, the two vehicles driving side by side. They'd been spotted.

He floored his accelerator. He watched the two cars disappear from his mirror, then glanced at the dashboard. He was flying at one hundred miles per hour. Arlen clapped his hands like a seal.

Up the road a few miles was a suspension bridge that Huck thought was the prettiest man-made thing he'd ever seen. It hung over a steep valley of trees and rushing water. Passing over it, they would go from the Central time zone into the Eastern. No police would be on it—too risky for a roadblock. The roadblock would be on the other side. Flashing lights appeared in his mirror. In the distance, but gaining.

"You see the bridge that's coming up ahead?" he said.

Arlen nodded enthusiastically.

"There's going to be a roadblock on the other side. Cops. I'm going to have to ditch the car. You remember what to do if that happens?"

"Cops?"

"Yeah. You want me to tell you again?"

"No, I remember."

"You sure?"

Arlen's head bobbed up and down. Huck steered with one hand and dug out his wallet. He tossed it to Arlen and saw him dig for the money and his credit cards.

"Leave me some," Huck screamed at him.

"How much you want?"

Damn little shit, already acting like everything in the wallet was his.

"Enough to get by," Huck said.

The suspension bridge loomed in his windshield. It looked eerie at night. During one of his moonshine runs years ago, he remembered thinking that by crossing it, he was actually going back in time. A lot of crazy thoughts had gone through his head. Like all the things he'd do differently with his life, if he had the chance.

He hit the bridge doing one ten. Halfway across he put his brights on. There was no roadblock on the other side. He felt a momentary sigh of relief and relaxed his foot on the accelerator. Then he saw the faint outline of four cruisers parked sideways on the highway. They were a half mile up the road. He wondered why they'd picked that spot. Maybe they'd been fearful that some redneck would come burning over the bridge and plow right into them. In his mirror the cruisers behind him were gaining. He looked at his brother. "Hold on to something."

Arlen wrapped his arms around his chest.

"Not yourself, you idiot. Hold on to the car!"

Arlen grabbed the door handle. Up ahead, the cruisers simultaneously turned on their headlights and their bubbles, the highway awash in light. Huck flashed his brights at them. When he was close enough to see their faces, Huck spun the wheel to his left and jumped onto the grass median. It was risky: Parts of the median had deep culverts, but it was a chance he had to take.

He heard the tires grind on the dirt. He flew past the roadblock and saw the flash of a shotgun blast. It missed them. Sons of bitches couldn't hit an elephant.

His right rear tire exploded, and the car sagged to one side. He jerked the wheel to his right and got back on the highway. In his mirror he could see the cops jumping into their cruisers and giving chase. He guessed he had a minute on them.

"I'm going to ditch the car," he said. "I'm going to run one way, you run the other. *Don't run after me.*"

"I won't," Arlen said.

"Do you remember what to say if the cops nab you?"

"Yeah."

"You sure?"

Arlen tapped his finger on his skull. "I got it burned in my brain."

Two thousand miles away, Helen Ledbetter climbed out of bed and threw her bathrobe on. For thirty years, she'd risen every morning at six thirty and gone to work. Being retired, she'd expected her inner clock to start letting her sleep in. So far, it wasn't cooperating.

She ate a bowl of sugar-coated cereal. A couple

of times she glanced at the phone on the counter. The little red light was blinking, indicating she had a message. She muted the ringer when she slept, and sometimes forgot to turn it back on. She'd put her name on the National Do Not Call Registry, but sneaky telemarketers found clever ways to call her. "We're conducting a survey," was the usual opening line. Or the company was one she "did business with" and wanted to let her know about a "special offer."

When she was finished eating, she put her dishes in the sink, then punched the play button on the phone.

"Aunt Helen, this is Ricky calling," her nephew said. "I've got some bad news. A detective the casinos hired is onto us. He's here in Slippery Rock. It's only a matter of time before he figures out the blackjack scam."

Her rump hit her chair hard. *"No,"* she said aloud.

"You have to run," her nephew went on.

"No," she shouted at the phone.

"I'm going to wire you five thousand dollars. It's the last of my money. You need to get out of Las Vegas. I'm sorry to be telling you this."

Helen Ledbetter's vision went blurry. Five thousand dollars? Ricky had promised her more than two hundred thousand dollars. She'd gotten brochures for everything she wanted to buy and spread them across the living-room floor. One night, she'd even danced in front of them.

"Call me when you get this. Please."

She felt paralyzed and stared at the answering machine. Ricky had said it *couldn't* go wrong. And what was the harm of taking money from a casino? They swindled their patrons all the time with false promotions.

Finally she found her legs and walked into the living room. The brochures were stacked in a neat pile on the coffee table. She'd put Post-its on the pages that contained the things she wanted to buy. Taking the brochures into the kitchen, she threw them into the trash compactor while cursing silently to herself.

She was packing a suitcase when she heard a car's wheels on the driveway. She went to the window and parted the curtains with her fingers. Light streamed out, and she saw two middle-aged men in a black Impala. The one behind the wheel was familiar-looking. As he got out, she realized it was Bill Higgins, the director of the Nevada Gaming Control Board who'd interviewed her.

She ran to the hall closet and pulled out the purse with the miniature camera she'd used to scam the Mint. The camera was sewn into the purse, so it couldn't accidentally fall out if dropped. Ricky had told her to throw the purse off the Hoover Dam. Helen had agreed but hadn't done it.

She ran into the kitchen and shoved the purse into the trash compactor. The front doorbell chimed. She hit the button and went to the back door. The second man was standing on the stoop.

"No, no, no," she shouted at him.

His cold eyes met hers. He put his silver badge to the glass. "Please let us in," he said politely.

Helen ran back into her bedroom and locked the door behind her. Ran around the room with her hands on her head. She knew what they did to cheaters in Nevada; she'd seen it countless times in the casinos she'd worked in. They dragged them into court in handcuffs, convicted them, and put them in prisons like Ely, which were living hell. Cheating a casino was a felony because you were also stealing from the state. The average sentence was four and a half years.

She heard her back door being kicked in. Sat on her bed and cried.

"Ms. Ledbetter," Bill Higgins said through the door.

"Go away!"

"Ms. Ledbetter, please open the door."

She was going to federal penitentiary. She would live in a cell and do what other people told her to. She was seventy-three years old and was going to lose her freedom. She could not imagine a more horrible fate.

She went to the room's rear window. It faced west and looked out onto the desert. Every day she took a long walk in the desert, even when it was hot as an oven. It cleared her head and gave her thoughts a special clarity. And now she was going to lose that.

"Please, Ms. Ledbetter," Bill Higgins said.

There was a shelf above the window. She took the revolver from it and pressed the barrel to her temple. Squeezing the trigger was not nearly as hard as she'd imagined.

CHAPTER 45

"We lost our witness," Bill Higgins said. Valentine closed his eyes and felt his spirits sink. It was eight in the morning, and he was sitting in the kitchen of his house with Gaylord, sucking down coffee. They'd stayed up and traded war stories while waiting for Bill to call. "Don't tell me she got away," he said.

"She put a gun to her head."

Valentine felt his stomach roll over. That made nine dead people in three days. And for what? A million bucks that Ricky Smith hadn't even collected.

"We searched her house," Bill said. "She's Ricky's aunt on his mother's side. I found some letters in a desk and an album with Ricky's picture in it."

"Any evidence we can use in court?"

"No. She put her purse into the trash compactor before we could get to her. It crushed the miniature camera she used in the scam into a thousand pieces."

Bill sounded like he was hurting. No cop wanted to cause a suicide. Helen Ledbetter taking her own life would eat at Bill, just as the three men Valentine had killed would eat at him. Opening his eyes, he said, "I'm sorry this happened."

There was a pause. Then Bill said, "What are you going to do now?"

Valentine removed Ricky Smith's winning OTB slip from his pocket. He'd been praying that Bill would haul in Helen Ledbetter, and she'd crack and turn evidence on the rest of the gang. Then he'd be able to leave Slippery Rock and go home. Only, life didn't always work out the way you wanted it to. "I'm going to ask the sergeant who runs this town to arrest everyone who's involved," he said.

"Do you have enough evidence to do that?" Bill asked.

Valentine stared at the slip. Every crime had at least one flaw. The slip was Ricky's, and it was going to put a whole bunch of people in jail for a long time. "Yes. But first I need you to do something for me."

"Name it," Bill said.

Gaylord drove Valentine to the police station in his car. It was a four-door Volvo, and Valentine found himself appraising the vehicle. It had a powerful engine and plenty of amenities, but something felt wrong. Then he realized what it was. The car was meant for a family, which meant that if he bought one, Gerry would abscond with it.

They went inside and found the deputy at the front desk flirting with the cleaning lady. Valentine wanted to ask him where he was a few hours ago, but decided he'd already stirred up the pot. They went into Gaylord's office, and the sergeant shut the door. Paper was coming out of the fax machine, and Gaylord pulled the cover page from the tray and read it. "It's from your friend in Las Vegas."

"How many pages is he sending?"

"Twenty-seven, including the cover."

Valentine removed the five sheets already in the fax tray. Each was a bill from a Las Vegas hotel with a person's name on it, along with how many days they'd stayed in the hotel, what they'd spent, etc. Bill was faxing the names of everyone from Slippery Rock who'd been in Las Vegas when Ricky scammed the Mint.

Valentine handed the sheets to Gaylord. As more sheets came through, Valentine passed them to him. By the time the machine had spit out twenty, the sergeant was sitting in a chair and the blood had drained from his face.

"I know these people," he said, sounding shaken. "I go to church with them and my kids attend the same schools and my wife's in the PTA with . . . aw, shit, what am I saying?"

"You're saying they're your friends."

The sheets were clutched in the sergeant's hand. "My best friends."

Valentine went into the next room and got

another chair. He came back and shut the door, then sat next to the sergeant. "I can leave you out of this. It will take me longer, but I can. I don't want to ruin your life."

The last of the sheets had come through. Gaylord pulled them out of the tray. His eyes fell on one, and he groaned. "My kid's pediatrician." He put the sheets on his desk and tiredly rubbed his face with his hands. "Let me ask you something. How much time are these folks looking at? A year, maybe two?"

"Try four and a half in the federal pen," Valentine said.

"What?"

"They all committed felonies."

"But Ricky didn't collect the money."

Valentine saw the pleading look in Gaylord's eyes. Nevada had the harshest laws in the country when it came to cheaters, with conspiracy to steal from a casino as bad as the act itself. Those twenty-six names sitting on Gaylord's desk—along with perhaps their spouses and friends—were guilty of conspiracy to defraud. They were toast.

Gaylord leaned forward in his chair. His beard had come out, and he looked like he was about to become a werewolf. "I read in the paper a few weeks back about a casino in Las Vegas that had rigged a promotion. They had a raffle and gave away a Mercedes-Benz, a ten-thousand-dollar chip, and a five-thousand-dollar chip. They rigged the raffle so that some high rollers who'd lost a lot of money won the prizes. You hear about that?"

Valentine nodded, wondering where this was going.

"The Nevada Gaming Control Board fined the casino a million bucks, which is a chunk of change. Only, this casino is making a quarter-billion dollars a year. Two of the upper management guys who rigged the game went on to other jobs. The third got promoted."

"What does this have to do with anything?" Valentine asked.

"You work for these people."

Valentine nearly said *no*. But it was true. He was here in the casinos' employ, even though he hated every last one of them.

"That's right."

"Well, how about we do something similar here?" Gaylord suggested. "We make the people who were involved pay a fine, or do some other kind of community service, provided they give you enough evidence to nail Stanley Kessel and Ricky Smith. Those are the two you want."

Valentine thought it over. Gaylord was asking him not to rip the guts out of Slippery Rock. For every person he put behind bars, a great many more would suffer. And all because they'd let some fast-talking scumbags talk them into scamming a casino.

"You're on," Valentine said.

They shook hands on it. Valentine picked up the

stack of faxes from the desk and handed them to him. "Pick out the person in this group who you can talk into helping us."

Gaylord pulled out the pediatrician. His name was Dr. Russell McFarland. "Russ has too much to lose. He'll do whatever you want."

"Let's go see him," Valentine said.

Gaylord could be a world-class prick when he wanted to be, just like most good cops. He put the screws to Russ McFarland the moment they were behind the closed doors of McFarland's office. The doctor worked out of a renovated house a quarter mile from town. It had polished wood floors and was filled with expensive furniture.

McFarland was about what Valentine had expected. Mid-forties, nice clothes, expensive haircut, living high on the hog. Maybe the HMOs had taken a bite out of his income and he'd decided to join Ricky's gang. Valentine was sorry it was Gaylord putting the screws to him. He hated rich people who cheated. They had the best that life had to offer, yet somehow it was never enough.

"I'll do whatever you want," the doctor said, his voice trembling.

"Even rat out your friends?" Gaylord said.

"Yes. Just don't tell my wife. She thinks I was at my high-school reunion."

Gaylord dropped the stack of faxes on McFarland's lap. Then he told the doctor what he wanted done.

"You want me to call *all* of them?" McFarland said.

Gaylord slammed his fist on the desk. The doctor jumped an inch out of his chair, then reached for a phone book on the shelf.

"You learn fast," Gaylord told him.

CHAPTER 46

It took McFarland an hour and ten minutes to call every person in the stack of faxes. When he was done, he was sweating through his clothes. In between calls, he'd admitted he had a twenty-two-year-old mistress in L.A. who visited him in Las Vegas twice a year.

Valentine was sitting on the edge of the desk. Once, he'd gone to the door and glanced into the waiting room at the gang of little tykes and their mothers waiting to be seen. It had made him that much angrier at the guy. Long ago, he'd accepted that there were people in the world who were rotten to the core. He just didn't want them to be people who dealt with children. He saw McFarland hang up the phone.

"That's the last one," the doctor said.

Valentine remained where he was. McFarland looked around the room. A frightened look crossed his face when he realized Gaylord had left to take a leak.

"Stop looking at me like that," McFarland said, tugging on his collar.

"How am I looking at you?"

389

"Like I was something you scraped off your shoe."

"I want you to tell me something."

"I did what you asked. Get out of my office."

Valentine came around the desk and put his hand on the back of McFarland's chair. Before the doctor could protest, Valentine spilled him onto the floor, then put his foot to the small of his back.

"What do you want?" McFarland said, his face kissing the wood.

"I want to know what kind of doctor you are."

"I'm a pediatrician."

"That's not what I mean."

"I'm a good doctor. I just screwed up."

"Think you'll screw up again?"

"No, no. Never." He looked at Valentine with one eye. "I promise."

"While you're cleaning up your act, lose the mistress."

McFarland started to protest, then caught himself. "Okay."

Gaylord came into the room, rolled his eyes, and immediately walked out. Valentine lifted his foot and followed the sergeant outside to the car.

They went to the town's only stationery store, and Valentine bought a package of colored construction paper, a marker, and a box of colored thumbtacks. He had Gaylord drive him to Ricky Smith's place while he made signs. Each one said MEETING INSIDE

HOUSE/LET YOURSELF IN AND TAKE A SEAT. He finished as Gaylord pulled into Ricky's drive.

"Make yourself scarce until a few minutes after eleven," Valentine said, opening his door.

"You want me to come inside?"

"No. Just park out in the street. And have a couple of deputies pull their cars behind yours." He had one foot on the drive and hesitated. "One other thing. Do you have a spare badge I can clip on my shirt? I think it will help."

Gaylord searched his glove compartment, then removed his own from his wallet and tossed it to him. "Make sure you give it back, okay?"

"No problem. I like being retired."

He hopped out and walked toward Ricky's house. At the first tree in the driveway, he stopped and thumbtacked one of his signs. He heard the sergeant call his name and turned to see him parked in the street, his window down.

"No rough stuff, okay?"

"What's your definition of that?"

Gaylord shook his head and drove away. Valentine tacked the rest of the signs around the property, saving the last for the front door to Ricky's house. Then he went around to the back and let himself in through the kitchen. He took the kitchen chairs and put them in the living room, then rearranged the couch and chairs in a semi-circle. Hopefully, anyone who came in would feel at home and take a seat.

He left through the back door and walked across

the backyard to his house. At the back door he found Ricky's cat waiting for him. He bent over, and it jumped into his arms. He'd never been fond of cats, but this one was growing on him. He went inside and fixed it a plate of food.

The rocking chair on the back porch was calling to him. His mind said no, but his body said yes. He fell into it, then checked the time. Nearly ten. He leaned back and shut his eyes. The cat joined him a minute later, and he felt it make kitty biscuits on his chest with its paws. He stroked the top of its head without opening his eyes. Just as he drifted off, he told himself that the sound of the first arriving car would jolt him awake.

He dreamed he was speeding down Las Vegas Boulevard with Lucy Price. The car's tires were bumping the concrete median. In a loud voice he told her to slow down.

"I can't," she said tearfully.

He reached across the seat and grabbed the wheel with both hands. He was not going to let her jump the median and slam into a car filled with tourists. He was going to stop what he knew had already happened. He was going to make the world right, even if it was only in his dream. The car came around a bend and gained speed.

"Slow down," he shouted.

"I can't," she cried.

He brought his foot across the seat and stepped on the brake. It felt like putty beneath his shoe.

The car continued to race ahead. He tried to turn the wheel, but it would not respond. Lucy sat in her seat, crying softly. "You're too late," she said.

The strip's casinos were a blur of harsh neon. He continued to fight with the wheel, then felt the car jump the center median. He shifted his gaze just in time to see the faces of the British tourists in the vehicle they were about to hit. Two men, two women. He wanted to tell them how sorry he was. Only, it was too late.

The sound of his cell phone snapped him awake. He gently pushed the cat off his lap and dug the phone out of his pocket. The caller ID said it was Gerry.

"The cops arrested Huck Dubb a few hours ago," his son said excitedly.

Valentine found himself staring across the backyard at Ricky's house. He could partially see the front of the house; over a dozen SUVs and expensive imports were parked in the front yard. He glanced at his watch. It was a few minutes before eleven.

"Where did they find him?" he asked.

"In northern Florida, about fifty miles west of Tallahassee. The highway patrol set up a road-block, and Huck tried to get away but wrecked the car. His brother somehow managed to escape, but the cops say they should find him in a few hours."

Valentine saw the back door of Ricky's house

open and a man step outside and have a look around. Ricky's gang had assembled and were probably starting to wonder what was going on. He needed to get over there pronto.

"Do the Florida cops think his brother is a threat?"

"No," his son said. "Guy's retarded. Doesn't have a driver's license or any way to get down to Palm Harbor and harm Yolanda and the baby."

"You believe them?" Valentine asked.

There was a long pause. Valentine guessed he'd just put the fear of God into his son. "Cops aren't the smartest people on the planet," he said. "They might have misjudged Huck's brother. We're talking about your family here, Gerry."

"I know, Pop," his son said, his voice measured. "I talked to Lamar about it. He knows the Dubbs pretty well. The retarded brother is named Arlen. Lamar said the greatest harm Arlen poses is to himself."

"Meaning what?"

"Lamar said if Arlen got lost in the woods, he'd probably end up dying."

"Can he use a gun? Did you ask him that?"

"Yes, Pop. Lamar said Arlen would probably shoot himself if you handed him a gun."

Tallahassee was more than two hundred miles from Palm Harbor. If Lamar was right, then Arlen Dubb's chances of finding his way to Palm Harbor and hurting anyone were slim at best. "Okay," Valentine said. "Sorry to alarm you."

"That's okay, Pop. I appreciate you thinking it out so thoroughly. I'm going to head out of here. When are you coming home?"

Valentine looked at his watch and saw the second hand usher in eleven o'clock. It was judgment hour, and he rose from the rocker. "Soon," he told his son.

CHAPTER 47

As Valentine crossed the backyard, he clipped Gaylord's badge to his shirt. It was a strange feeling to be wearing a shield again, but not an unpleasant one. He'd never disliked being a cop like so many guys he'd known. It was something he'd been born to do.

The cat walked beside him, preening around his legs. He scooped the animal into his arms, then entered Ricky's house through the back door. Seven people were standing in the kitchen. Upon seeing him, one of them gasped, while another put her hands over her eyes and moaned.

"We're screwed," someone muttered.

"Let's go," Valentine said.

They didn't understand. He pointed at the swinging door that led to the living room, while rubbing the cat's head. It seemed to calm everyone down.

The seven walked through the door in single file. The rest of the gang was assembled in the living room, the women sitting on chairs and the couch, the men standing. It wasn't a big room, and they were all bunched up and talking in hushed tones. Seeing him, everyone stopped.

"Shit," someone said.

"Cut the profanity," Valentine said, letting the cat slip out of his hands. He did a visual sweep and counted twenty-five heads. Half the faces were ones he'd seen in the past three days; half were strangers. McFarland hadn't bothered to show.

"Thanks for coming," he said. "You're all under arrest."

More gasps. Several people closed their eyes or stared at the floor.

"Hold on a second," a voice declared.

Valentine stared at a guy standing in the back of the room. He was in his late twenties and wore a dark suit and a screaming yellow tie. He had a baby face and a body like Jell-O, and Valentine guessed he'd never done a day of exercising in his life. The guy stepped forward, business card in hand.

"I represent these people," he said.

He stuck his business card beneath Valentine's nose. His name was embossed, the rest of the card plain. LAURENCE MATTHEW BENDER, III. ATTORNEY-AT-LAW, DICKUM & FINE. SPECIALIZING IN MEDICAL MALPRACTICE AND CORPORATE NEGLIGENCE.

"These people have rights," Bender said. "You can't drag them in here like this is a Charlie Chan movie. What you did this morning was entrapment. You broke the law."

Valentine handed the card back. "Did you accept any money from these people?"

"Excuse me?"

"You heard me. Did anyone pay you to be here?"

"Well, no—"

"Then your opinion isn't worth anything. Get out."

"Now wait just a minute—"

Valentine grabbed Bender's arm and gave it a mean twist. He saw the attorney's knees buckle. He loosened his grip and hustled him toward the front door. Throwing it open, he led him outside and down the front steps. Two dozen cars were parked on Ricky's front lawn, and he guessed no one in Slippery Rock had ever heard of carpooling. Up on the road, Gaylord sat behind the wheel of a police cruiser. Five cruisers were parked behind him, with two officers sitting in each. If it wasn't the whole force, it was damn close. Valentine brought Bender to Gaylord's car and threw him in the backseat.

"This guy's gumming up the works. I'd appreciate your babysitting him until I'm done."

"Not a problem," Gaylord said. "Holler if you need anything."

"I'll do that."

As Valentine headed back to the house, he heard the attorney barking like a junkyard dog. Gaylord silenced him with a threat that had something to do with Bender's driving skills when he was intoxicated. Valentine's eyes fell on the gang of people standing on Ricky's front porch. They were staring at the line of police cars, their gums flapping in the breeze. Whatever ideas they'd had about taking their chances in court had collectively vanished from their faces, and they looked scared as hell. It was a good start, and he ushered them inside and shut the door forcefully behind him.

They shuffled into the living room and took their places. Valentine went to the room's center and stood with his back to the swinging door, just in case he needed to make a quick exit. "Here's the deal," he said. "I talk, you listen. This isn't *Jerry Springer*, where people shout out whenever they feel like it. Understand?"

His eyes swept the room, and he saw them nod. Every member of the gang fell between mid-thirties to late forties. They were well dressed and, he assumed, fairly well educated. He also guessed they had never broken a law in their lives, until now. Turning ordinary citizens into criminals was never easy, and he imagined Ricky Smith and Stanley Kessel had appealed to a common denominator among them all. Greed.

"Good. I've seen a lot of sophisticated scams in my day, but none that compares to what you folks did. You practiced in the basement of that house on the outskirts of town and got your roles down perfectly. Then you went out to Las Vegas and did your number on the Mint. Of course, Ricky had a lot to do with how it went, but he needed you folks to sell his streak of luck. And you did your jobs perfectly.

"You also covered your tracks real well. I'm going to guess that Stanley Kessel was the reason, because he seems to be the brains behind this operation. Stanley made sure that nothing was left behind that could be used against you in court. There was a miniature camera in a purse, but that got destroyed this morning. Stanley also picked scams that beat the eye in the sky, so there's no videotape evidence either. The truth be known, there's nothing to tie you to the Mint getting ripped off that will hold up in court."

He saw several people in the gang exchange nervous glances. A man standing behind the couch raised his hand. He was short and wore a tie wrapped around his neck like a noose.

"You have to go to the bathroom?"

"I have a question," he said. "If there's no evidence, then why are we under arrest?"

"You another lawyer?"

"I'm an accountant."

"Well, Mr. Accountant, it's like this: Ricky and Stanley didn't just scam the Mint. They also scammed a horse race." Valentine removed the OTB racing slip from his pocket and held it in the air. "You aware of this?"

The accountant shook his head.

"How about the rest of you?"

The roomful of people shook their heads.

"No," a woman on the couch added for emphasis.

"That's too bad," Valentine said, sticking the slip into his pocket while eyeing the group. It was his only evidence, and he was going to fly out the back door if anyone made a move to jump him. When he sensed no one had that in mind, he continued. "You see, even though I can't prove you scammed the Mint, I can connect you to Ricky and Stanley in all sorts of ways. And I can prove that they scammed the horse race. That makes you their accomplices."

"Would you mind telling us what they did?" the accountant asked.

"Sure. They stuck a satellite dish on the roof of an OTB parlor and used the feed from the dish to show the races from Belmont, instead of using the normal TV signal. The satellite feed had a seven-second delay on it because the satellite is up there in space. Those seven seconds allowed an employee in the OTB parlor to see which three horses came out of the gate first. Most people don't know it, but the three horses that come out of the gate first usually finish in the money. Guys at the track have been using this information for years to place late bets. It's called past-posting.

"The guy at the OTB parlor wrote the numbers of the horses down on a racing slip and passed it through the bars to Ricky. Ricky pretended to write on the slip, then slapped his money down and passed the slip back. Ricky told me he wasn't always accurate when it came to picking the ponies, which should have been a tip-off.

401

"With this race, Ricky *was* lucky. All three horses were winners. He won eight hundred thirty-six dollars and eighty-seven cents for his three-hundred-dollar bet. If he'd been smart, he'd have torn the slip up. But he had to wag it in my face and gloat about it."

"Let me guess," the accountant said. "The slip had the time on it."

Valentine nodded. No one else seemed to understand. He said, "The slip showed the time the bet was recorded, which was seven seconds after the race actually started. Stanley and Ricky couldn't figure out a way to change that, so they didn't."

"How many laws did they break?" the accountant asked.

He was a pleasant enough guy, with a trusting face and caring eyes, and Valentine found himself feeling sorry for him. He wiped away the emotion and counted off the crimes on the fingers of his hand. "Racketeering, wire fraud, and conspiracy. The Belmont track is in the state of New York. The attorney general of New York doesn't take kindly to this kind of stuff. He'll come down hard on Ricky and Stanley, and all of you."

"But we didn't know about this," a woman on the couch said.

"It doesn't matter. You're still part of the gang."

"What are we looking at in terms of prison sentences?" the accountant asked.

The question silenced the room.

"About ten years in prison, with time off for good behavior," Valentine said.

"Unless we cooperate with you."

Valentine started to answer him, then saw a vehicle pull down the driveway and park directly in front of the house. The doors opened, and two people emerged. As they climbed onto the porch, their faces became recognizable. It was Polly Parker and Ricky.

CHAPTER 48

Polly and Ricky entered the house, holding hands. Ricky looked like he'd been doing a lot of crying, his face a sickening red, his eyes bloodshot. Polly led him into the center of the living room and stepped aside. Her ex-husband stared at Valentine with a look of anguish distorting his face. "Do you know what happened in Las Vegas this morning?" he asked.

"Yes," Valentine said.

"Helen Ledbetter was my aunt. I . . . loved her dearly."

"I'm sorry."

Ricky pointed behind his back at the twenty-four members of his gang, who he no longer could find the courage to look in the eye. "Will you let them go if I play ball?"

"You ready to do that?"

"Yes. I'll tell you everything."

"Will you help me nail Stanley Kessel?"

Ricky nodded his head vigorously.

"Will you come clean with me?"

"I just said I would."

"I wasn't born yesterday, kid. This wasn't just

about ripping off the Mint. You and Stanley had something bigger in mind. A lot of time and a lot of money went into this. I want to know *everything*, or no deal."

Ricky's answer got caught in his throat. He began to shake, and cried while looking at the floor. He still hadn't looked at the others. Maybe he never would.

"Okay," he finally said. "Just let them go. Too many people have died over this."

Valentine glanced at the rest of the gang. They looked ready to hit the floor running. He'd gotten what he wanted; only, it no longer seemed enough. He wanted his pound of flesh from these people. The cat had returned and was sashaying through his legs. He picked her up and said, "You folks want to get out of here, don't you? You want to go home and get back to your kids and your jobs and forget this ever happened. Am I right?"

The twenty-four people crowded into the living room nodded as one. It was exactly what they wanted.

"Well, it's not going to work that way," he said, "because what happened isn't going to stay in this room. Sergeant Gaylord will know, and so will his deputies. And they're going to tell the rest of the people in this community how you scammed a casino while people in a burning hotel across the street were jumping out of windows. You used that tragedy to your advantage, and you know it. And now your neighbors are going to know it too."

It was like he'd invisibly punched every single one of them in the stomach. He supposed it was the next best thing to throwing them all in jail. He watched them file dejectedly out of the house, then gave Ricky a hard look. "You'd better not be lying to me, kid."

Ricky couldn't answer him. He looked like a man who'd just come home to find his house carried away by a tornado. He was melting down, his life a total loss. Polly stepped forward and put her arms around him. Ricky whispered something in her ear.

"He'll do whatever you want," she said.

Valentine continued to stare at Ricky. He trusted him about as far as he could kick him. "Why the sudden change of heart? You decide you want to go to heaven?"

Polly answered for him. "Stanley called Ricky this morning. He threatened to hurt me if Ricky went to the police."

"You believe him?"

Ricky nodded. Shame affected people in different ways. For Ricky, it was a bucket of cold reality poured over his head. "Stanley's always had a mean streak," he whispered.

"He's the brains behind this, isn't he?" Valentine said.

"Yeah. Always was."

"What do you mean?"

"When I was a kid, I ran away from home to

be with a carnival," Ricky said. "I was their sign painter. It was great. One day Stanley shows up. He'd run away from home too. Only, he didn't want to paint signs or clean up after the elephants. He wanted to learn how to scam people. He talked me into learning with him."

"So he corrupted you."

"Yeah, I guess you could call it that. Stanley liked to say that it isn't stealing if you don't get caught."

"And it's been one big joyride ever since," Valentine said.

Ricky found the strength to look him in the eye. "I tried to back out a bunch of times, but Stanley always pulled me back in. Out in Las Vegas, I told him no, but then the fricking hotel had to burn down."

"What did the fire have to do with it?"

"Stanley ran across the street when the hotel started to burn. He saw me jump from the balcony and pulled me out of the pool. Then he laid a guilt trip on me and said everyone from Slippery Rock was depending on me."

"So you caved in and went through with it."

Ricky nodded, then swallowed hard. "You really despise me, don't you?"

"I killed three people because of you," Valentine said. "You're goddamn right I hate you."

"What can I do to make things right?"

Valentine looked into his face and sensed that Ricky was finally going to come clean with him.

He grabbed three chairs and made Ricky and Polly sit down, then sat backward in one so he was facing them. "For starters, tell me what you and Stanley were up to. Why didn't you stop after you scammed the Mint? Why rig the lottery and the horse race? And why did you hire a public relations firm to broadcast all this crap to the newspapers?"

"Publicity," Ricky said. "Stanley was going to make me into a household name."

"Why? So he could put your face on a box of Wheaties?"

"He wanted to take me public."

Valentine had lost his appetite for stupid jokes and nearly smacked Ricky in the side of the head. He saw Polly nod, and realized Ricky wasn't joking.

"How much money did Stanley think he could raise?"

"A hundred million dollars," Ricky said. "It would go into a hedge fund, which I'd control. I'd pick winners, and the investors would reap the rewards."

"But the winners would actually be stocks that Stanley was feeding you."

Ricky put his hand into Polly's lap. "That's right. Stanley would buy the stocks early, then sell high. The fund would eventually crash, but by then, we'd all be rich."

"The classic pump and dump."

"Yeah."

"The gang that was just here knew about this, didn't they?"

Ricky nodded. "That was their payoff. Each of them was going to be allowed to buy ten thousand shares when the stocks opened, then dump their shares when the stock peaked. There were other people in town that knew about it as well."

Valentine drummed his fingers on the back of his chair. Another piece of the puzzle had slipped into place. "The guys I shot in the bank. They were pushed out, weren't they?"

Ricky nodded again. "They blabbed about it, so they got voted off the island."

Valentine saw the cat enter the room and climb into Ricky's lap. "Do you have evidence of what Stanley was going to do? Did he write up this company he was going to form?"

"Yes. I have everything," Ricky said.

Valentine pushed himself out of the chair. It was the strangest damn thing. He'd never met Stanley Kessel and had no idea what he looked like, yet still wanted to put him in prison for the rest of his life. Perhaps it was because Valentine had run across so many guys just like Stanley. Grand schemers who sucked innocent folks in, then systematically ruined their lives.

"Go pack yourself a suitcase," he told Ricky.

"Where are we going?"

"New York City. We're going to go see the guys who police the stock market."

Ricky and Polly rose from their chairs. They were

still holding hands, and Valentine guessed that Polly had talked Ricky into coming clean. It was too bad they'd gotten divorced. He had a feeling Ricky would have never gone down this road had they been together.

"You can come, too," Valentine told her.

CHAPTER 49

Valentine went out onto the front porch to wait while Ricky packed his clothes. The cat, which had been preening around Ricky, followed him outside and did its little dance. He scooped it up in his arms.

"Traitor," he said, rubbing its head.

The lawn was empty of cars, and the police cruisers were also gone. He would have to call Gaylord and explain what had happened. The sergeant would be happy to hear that he wasn't going to have to arrest the gang. Valentine wasn't sure it was the right thing to do, but he didn't live here. He started to unclip the badge from his shirt, when he heard a voice call his name. He walked around the side of the house and found Mary Alice Stoker sitting on a swing.

"How long have you been here?" he asked.

"The whole time," she said. "I was on the porch. I heard your speech." She patted the spot beside her on the swing. He sat beside her and made the chains sing. "I once lived in this house. I can still walk the grounds without getting lost."

"Who brought you here?"

"A neighbor. She was involved." She pushed the ground with her feet, and the swing went backward. "You were very kind with them, considering what they did."

"I was more than kind," he said.

"How so?"

He took her fingers and placed them on the badge still clipped to his shirt.

"When did that happen?"

"Last night. It's only temporary."

She patted him on the knee. "You are a good man, Tony Valentine. But there is something that's bothering me."

"What's that?"

"Your friend in Las Vegas, Lucy Price. Why did you abandon her?"

He felt like an invisible dagger had been plunged into his heart. His dream from an hour ago was still rumbling around in his head. He'd been in a car with Lucy but still couldn't prevent her from crashing. The moral had been clear: He couldn't alter the course of Lucy's life, or the misfortune she might cause others. No one could do that but Lucy. He started to get up from the swing and saw the blind librarian stiffen.

"Please don't run away from me as well."

He sat back down and waited for her to resume. The swing had stopped moving.

"As a cop, you know how to help people. But as a person, you're misguided."

"You think so?"

"Yes, I do."

"So straighten me out."

A secret smile crossed her face. She placed her hand on his sleeve and left it there. "You told me a story yesterday about two cops who were summoned to a domestic disturbance. Instead of arresting the young man causing the problem, one of the cops tried to talk some sense into him. The young man hit the cop in the face with a hammer, and the cop's partner shot him dead. You told me that the cops had made a mistake. Had they arrested the young man, neither of those terrible things would have happened."

"That's right."

"But you left out an important part," she said. "You didn't factor in all the other times that those two cops were able to talk sense into someone and keep them from venturing down the wrong path. How many times do you think those two cops did that?"

Valentine shrugged. "Hard to say."

"A lot?"

"Sure. It comes with the job. You get to play Solomon all the time."

"Exactly. Cops have to make life-altering decisions every single day. And what I'm telling you is this: That one tragedy you described to me doesn't cancel out all the good things those two cops did. Evil never cancels out good. It only eclipses it and makes us not see it. But the good remains. It's always there. It is the thing that makes the human experience worth having."

The front door of the house opened, and Ricky and Polly stepped outside. Mary Alice heard the sound, and her grip on his sleeve intensified. "The bad deed that Lucy Price committed does not negate the good deed that you did for her. Nor should it stop you from continuing to help her. In the end, you will prevail, just like you did today."

"You think so?"

"I know so," she said.

It was something one of the little kids he'd met in her library might say. Ricky and Polly were standing on the porch, looking for him. Valentine got their attention and pointed at Ricky's Lexus sitting in the carport. Ricky and Polly walked across the yard and climbed into it.

"I need to go. Can I give you a lift home?"

"My neighbor is picking me up at noon and taking me back to school," she said. "May I ask where you're going?"

"New York. I'm going to put Stanley Kessel in jail."

"I'd like to ask you for a favor. I hope you won't be offended."

"What's that?"

"I have a picture in my mind of what you look like. May I touch your face and find out if my picture is anything like the real thing?"

"First tell me what your picture looks like."

"I most certainly will not."

He found himself staring at her. He'd avoided doing that, as if staring at a blind person was somehow cheating. What he saw was a woman of great character and moral courage. Taking her hand from his sleeve, he brought it to his face and allowed her fingers to run across the contours of his life. Done, she lowered her hand.

"Good luck in New York," she said.

The Lexus had a phone in the dashboard that let Ricky make plane reservations from Charlotte to New York for later that night. The drive to the airport was about two and a half hours, and Valentine got settled in for the ride, then called Gerry on his cell phone.

"I'm in the Hattiesburg airport, boarding my flight," his son said. "I said my good-byes and got the hell out of there. Lamar wants to hire us, but I don't know."

"Had enough of Gulfport?"

"That's an understatement. They're calling my section. Got to run."

"Wait a second," Valentine said, having remembered what had been bugging him since that morning. "Did they catch Huck's retarded brother?"

"Not since I last talked to Lamar."

"When was that?"

"About fifteen minutes ago. He asked me to call him from the airport and let him know I'd gotten there safe and sound."

"And the north Florida cops haven't caught him."

"No. Look, Pop, the poor guy's retarded. If he's running around in the woods, he'll probably end up dying from exposure."

"That's a cheery thought," Valentine said.

"You know what I mean. What's bugging you?"

"When I was a cop in Atlantic City, several guys on the psycho ward at the hospital took off one night. They weren't very hard to find."

"Very funny."

"I'm dead serious, Gerry. Think about it."

"I'm going to lose my seat, Pop. I'll call you when I'm back home."

The connection went dead. His son sounded pissed off. Valentine didn't like to scare him, but something wasn't adding up. If Florida cops were good at anything, it was tracking people. They knew how to hunt and used their skill as well as anyone.

He leaned back in his seat and felt his eyes start to droop. The memory of that night in Atlantic City flashed through his head. He and his partner Doyle had gotten one of the psychos in their car, and the guy kept climbing out. He was as slippery as an eel, and every time he got away, he'd laugh hysterically at them. It had been a long night.

The Lexus swerved to avoid something in the highway. Valentine's eyes snapped awake. People with mental conditions were difficult to take out in public. So why had Huck brought his retarded brother along? He flipped open his cell phone and called Gerry back.

"Pop, we're starting to taxi."

"Did it ever occur to you that the Florida cops don't know what Huck Dubb looks like?"

"But they identified him."

"What if the retarded brother was told to say 'I'm Huck'?" Valentine said. "What if he has some credit cards in his pocket with his brother's name on them? What if the retarded brother is a plant? Just because Huck's a redneck doesn't mean he's stupid, Gerry."

"Pop, you're scaring me."

Valentine looked at his watch. Nearly noon. Nine hours had passed since Huck had gotten pulled off the road. Plenty of time to find another set of wheels and make it down to Palm Harbor. He said good-bye to his son, hung up, and punched in Yolanda's number.

"Please be home," he prayed as the call went through.

CHAPTER 50

Huck Dubb sat in a pizza delivery car and stared at Gerry Valentine's house in Palm Harbor a block away. It was noon, the street deserted. He'd commandeered the car a half hour ago from a shopping center where the pizza maker was located. The driver had been sitting in the car, counting his money, when Huck had stuck a gun through his open window. The driver had given Huck the keys and even thrown in his stupid hat for good measure.

Huck had stolen cars every hundred miles during his trip down from the Florida Panhandle. It had made the trip longer, but also safer. Changing cars every couple of hours made it impossible for the law to get a bead on him.

He stared at the address on the card he'd stolen from the registration desk at the Holiday Inn in Gulfport. The address on the card and the one on the mailbox were the same, but something didn't feel right about the place. It was a quaint New England-style clapboard house and not what he'd expect an Eye-talian to be living in. Taking the driver's cell phone off the seat, he called information and got the operator to verify the address for him.

A Palm Harbor sheriff's car materialized in his mirror. Huck felt his heartbeat kick into high gear. It had taken him nine hours to get here after leaving Arlen behind. For every minute of that nine hours, he'd thought about how he was going to punish Gerry Valentine's family. Cut and strangle and shoot was how he'd decided to kill them. Thinking about it had put a fire in his belly as powerful as any he'd ever felt.

Digging into his pocket, Huck removed his cash and pretended to be counting it while the sheriff trolled past. On the backseat of the car were boxes of pizzas in insulated bags. The food made the interior of the car smell real good. Huck lifted his eyes and saw the sheriff idling beside him. He smiled at the man behind the wheel.

"Hey, officer, how's it going?"

"Can't complain," the sheriff replied.

"Nobody listens. Want a free slice? I got a pie that went undelivered."

The sheriff smiled and said no and drove to the next block. Huck watched him park in front of Gerry Valentine's house and climb out of his vehicle. The sheriff walked around the house and then got back in his car and drove away.

Huck smiled to himself as he started up his engine. The police up in the Panhandle must have figured out that Arlen wasn't him and alerted the police down here. In a way, he was happy he'd run into the sheriff. Now he knew to be on his toes—and that Gerry Valentine didn't keep a dog running around his property.

He parked in the spot the sheriff had vacated. As he killed the engine, his stomach growled. He hadn't put anything in his mouth since leaving Gulfport, and the pizza on the backseat was calling him. First things first, he told himself.

Getting out, he removed one of the insulated boxes from the backseat, then opened the trunk and removed the short-barreled shotgun he'd brought from his grandmother's house. He stuck the shotgun beneath the box. It was just small enough to stay hidden.

He walked up the front path, wondering how foolish he looked in his coveralls and the pizza driver's hat tilted rakishly on his head. At the front door he stopped and peered through a wire mesh screen door onto a porch. Baby toys were scattered across the floor. His breath caught in his throat. What did the Old Testament say? An eye for an eye, a tooth for a tooth. With his free hand, he rapped on the screen door.

When no one came out, he tested the knob and got it to turn. He pulled the door open and stepped inside the porch. It was small and cozy, with newspapers scattered on the furniture. He glanced behind him on the street. Still quiet as a church.

"Anyone home? Pizza delivery."

He could hear music inside the house. It had a

Latin rhythm that made Huck instinctively tap his foot. He tested the front door and found it unlocked. He opened it and slipped inside the house of the man who'd killed his three sons.

Huck had been a criminal since he was eight. He'd learned from his daddy, who'd made ruckus juice out of a still in the back of his house and sold it for a buck a gallon to the blacks and farmhands. If he'd learned one lesson from his daddy, it was that you had to move fast. Whatever the crime, speed was key. Everything else was secondary.

He put the pizza box on the floor. The music was coming from a room off to his right. Gloria Estefan and Miami Sound Machine. He drew a hunting knife from the sheath hanging beneath his shirt, then walked down a short hallway and entered the room. More baby toys scattered on the floor, a crib in the corner. Gerry Valentine was a proud new daddy. It made Huck that much more enraged. Then it hit him what he'd do. He'd kill the wife and take the kid. That would put a knot in Gerry's colon for the rest of his life.

He walked into the center of the room and looked for a picture. He didn't want to end up killing the goddamn cleaning lady. In the corner of the room was a small desk with a computer in its center. On its ledge was a family photo. He got close enough to make out Gerry and the woman in his arms. She was a real beauty.

Gloria Estefan's singing was getting to him. He liked Latin music, especially to dance to. What people back home called cutting the rug. He found the stereo and turned the music up. He was about to ruin another man's life. It made him feel incredibly powerful. He went into the hallway and walked to the foot of the stairway. He listened hard for a few moments, thought he heard a noise. He put a foot on the stairs, then halted. He needed to be sure she wasn't downstairs, or risk letting her get away.

He went to the end of the hallway. It cut to his right, and he stuck his head around the corner. The hallway led to the kitchen in the rear of the house, and he squinted at Gerry Valentine's wife standing at a sink in the kitchen with her back to him. She wore jeans and a T-shirt and stood motionless at the sink. He guessed she was cleaning dishes.

He pulled his head back around the corner. Knife or gun? He decided on the gun. It was quicker. He'd rush into the room, shoot her, and be done with it.

Payback time.

Mabel Struck was serving homemade eggplant lasagna to Brownie and Little Pete when the telephone in the kitchen rang. She'd invited them to lunch after they'd agreed to help her, then learned from Brownie that neither man ate meat. So she'd found a vegetarian recipe online that looked easy to make.

"Will you excuse me?" she asked.

"Of course," the two retired carnival men said.

"Please start without me. I don't want your food to get cold." She went into the kitchen and picked up the phone. After all the work they'd done—and so quickly!—having them for lunch was the least she could do. "Hello?"

Her caller was the chief of the Palm Harbor police department. He told her the news, and Mabel leaned against the wall and brought her hand to her mouth.

"Oh my God," she said. "I'll be right over."

The chief didn't think that was a good idea. There was a lot blood in the house.

"I'm coming anyway," Mabel said.

She put the phone in its cradle before the chief could reply. Her head felt light, and she stared out the window at the gloriously sunny afternoon. It seemed unfathomable that something so horrible could happen on such a beautiful day. She found herself wishing Tony was here, so they could go across the street together. Only, she couldn't lean on Tony for the rest of her life. Sucking in her breath, she went to the back door and pulled it open.

Yolanda sat on the back stoop, rocking the sleeping baby in her arms. Lois had started wailing a few minutes ago, and Yolanda had brought her outside so Brownie and Little Pete wouldn't have their eardrums ruined. The younger woman looked up at her.

"Is everything all right?"

"Our trap worked," Mabel said.

Yolanda rose from the stoop. "Are the police there now?"

Mabel nodded. "Your neighbor heard a shotgun blast and dialed 911."

"Did they catch him?"

"Yes. He shot himself in the foot. The police think . . ."

"What?"

"They think he might die."

Yolanda grabbed Mabel by the wrist and looked her in the eye with a steely gaze. "Don't feel sorry for him. He was going to hurt me and my baby."

"I know. It's just—"

"He got what was coming to him."

It was exactly what Tony would say, and Mabel found herself nodding. Cradling the baby in her arms, Yolanda hurried inside with Mabel right behind her.

Three Palm Harbor sheriff's cars and an ambulance were parked in front of Yolanda's house. Yolanda identified herself to the uniform in charge and asked to be let inside. The sheriff stared at the baby in her arms, then at Mabel.

"She's with me," Yolanda said.

"It ain't pretty," the sheriff warned her.

"Please let us in," Yolanda said.

The sheriff led them inside the house. Everything looked normal until they reached the rear hallway that led to the kitchen. The floor was sheeted with blood, the sight of it so unsettling that Mabel felt her breath go away. If it bothered Yolanda, she didn't show it.

Mabel stared at the door at the end of the hallway. That morning, Brownie and Little Pete had painted a trompe l'oeil on it that showed Yolanda standing at the sink with her back to the door. The painting was poor compared to those at the Showtown, but the bad light in the hallway hid the imperfections. Huck Dubb must have been looking at it when he fell.

"Where is he?" Yolanda asked the sheriff.

"Out in the ambulance," the sheriff replied. "He hit the trip wire your friends ran across the floor, and blew his foot clean off. We're trying to find a hospital that will take him."

"Why bother?" Yolanda said.

Mabel could no longer stomach the blood and left the house. There was a massive oak tree on the front lawn, and she stood beneath its cool shade and tried to regain her composure. The ambulance's back doors were open, and she watched the EMS team work on Huck Dubb. He was a big man and looked like a beached whale lying on his back. No matter how horrible a person he was, she didn't want to see him die.

Then she looked at the gang of sheriffs standing by the curb. They were talking and laughing and enjoying the beautiful day. And they were eating something. Her vision was poor, and she had to stare before she realized what it was. Pizza.

Staring up into the clouds, Mabel thanked God for looking out for them.

CHAPTER 51

One St. Andrews Plaza was the address of the U.S. Attorney's Office in New York City. The building was eight stories of steel and dirty glass and housed some of the most powerful federal prosecutors in the country. Valentine had visited there before and always wondered when the feds were going to clean the place up. So far, no one had bothered.

Next door to the U.S. Attorney's Office was St. Andrew's Church. It was one of the city's great historic Roman Catholic churches and dated back to the late 1700s. At seven thirty the next morning, Ricky Smith climbed the steps of the church to go to confession, while Valentine and Polly waited outside on the sidewalk. From where they stood, they had an excellent view of the Brooklyn Bridge, and the early morning view was spectacular. Polly was wearing her Sunday-best clothes. So was Ricky.

"Will these men be fair with Ricky?" she asked.

"Yes. Ricky's coming forward makes a huge difference," Valentine said.

"Will he have to testify against Stanley in court?"

"Probably."

She chewed on a fingernail. "Will Ricky go to jail?"

Valentine stared at the line of traffic coming off the bridge. He had a feeling that the AUSA—the Assistant United States Attorney—would be more interested in prosecuting Stanley Kessel. That was what his gut said. But, the AUSA might put the screws to Ricky, as well. It was one of the chances you took turning in state's evidence.

"He might."

"How long will Stanley go to jail?"

"Ten to twelve if he's lucky."

"Do you think that's long enough?"

Valentine shrugged. Stanley Kessel had corrupted an entire town; Valentine didn't know what the proper punishment was for a crime like that. At ten minutes before eight Ricky came outside. Confessing to a man of the cloth affected people differently. Ricky stared at the sidewalk as if it were about to open up and swallow him whole. Polly took his hand and gave it a squeeze. "You okay?" she asked him.

"Not really," he replied.

"Sure you want to go through with this?"

He looked at her, then at Valentine. "Positive," he said.

The lobby in the U.S. Attorney's Office resembled a police station, with surveillance cameras perched on the walls and a metal detector that everyone entering the building was required to pass through. They gave their names and photo IDs to a stern-faced receptionist, then stood by a wall with a gang of others waiting to go upstairs.

Valentine assumed the people they waited with were crooks and their attorneys. He killed a few minutes trying to discern which were which. It was impossible to tell the difference, and he finally gave up.

At eight fifteen the AUSA's assistant came downstairs and got them. They passed through the metal detector and were wanded by a guard. When Valentine tried to get his ID back, he was told it would be returned when he left. Riding up in the elevator, the assistant said, "Everyone gets the same treatment. It's the new world order."

They got off on the seventh floor and were escorted to a conference room consisting of a long table, six chairs, a flickering overhead light, and ceiling tiles that looked ready to fall on their heads. Two men rose from chairs as they entered. They identified themselves as Robert Knuts, AUSA, and Special Agent Stephen Thomas Roberts of the FBI. Knuts had a shock of blond hair and a ruddy complexion; Roberts was a tough-looking Irishman with dark eyes that looked capable of drilling a hole in your head.

"Have a seat," Knuts said, pointing at the chairs opposite him and Roberts. "Would you like something to drink?"

They declined and sat down. Ricky had started

breathing heavily, and Valentine wondered if he was going to bolt. The only thing that seemed to be holding him down was Polly. She was as solid as a rock.

Ricky pointed at the tape recorder sitting on the table. "You going to record this?"

Knuts nodded. "Do you have a problem with that?"

Ricky started to say something. Valentine sensed that he was going to tell Knuts off and blow it. Instead Ricky snapped his mouth shut.

Knuts put his finger on the record button, and the machine started to whir. He identified himself into the machine, gave the date and time, then glanced Ricky's way.

"The floor is yours," he said.

Ricky started at the beginning and explained how he and Stanley had learned to cheat while apprenticing with the Schlitzie carnival in Florida. Then he talked about returning to Slippery Rock, and the scams he and Stanley had pulled while growing up. To hear him tell it, virtually every promotion and sweepstakes that had run in Slippery Rock during that time was corrupted, and more than once Valentine saw Polly close her eyes and sadly shake her head.

Stanley moved away from Slippery Rock after getting caught stealing test answers, and Ricky didn't see him for many years. During that time, Stanley was in New York becoming a stockbroker and making his fortune, while Ricky stayed in Slippery Rock and bounced around between jobs. Then, one day three years ago, Stanley appeared on Ricky's doorstep. "He took me out drinking and told me about this scam he'd been thinking about," Ricky said into the tape recorder. "Stanley's speciality was helping small companies go public. He knew that most of the companies were dogs. But every once in a while, there was a good one. Stanley was convinced that if he fed me the good ones, and I bought them when they were low, I could establish a track record of picking winners. Then, he could promote me to investors as the world's greatest stock picker.

"We kicked it around for a while. I told Stanley it wouldn't work, because I didn't know anything about the markets. Stanley said that most stock pickers didn't know anything about the markets, either.

"Stanley said the key was making investors believe that you had the golden touch. He was convinced we could do this by making people think I was the world's luckiest man. He thought the best way to do this was by scamming a casino. He said the publicity would give me instant credibility. The other scams that came after that were my idea."

"How much money did Stanley think you could raise from private investors?" Knuts asked.

"A hundred million at the start."

"At the start?"

"Stanley wanted to use the initial capital to establish who I was, then establish a hedge fund that I would manage. Stanley said the sky was the limit once we got going."

"You must have discussed a figure."

"Half a billion dollars," Ricky said.

The sound of Polly's sharp intake of breath made everyone's heads snap. She covered her mouth with her hands and stared at her ex in disbelief. Valentine saw Knuts's hand reach over to the tape recorder and turn it off. Then the AUSA looked at the FBI agent sitting to his right.

"Your turn," Knuts said.

Valentine had dealt with scores of FBI agents over the years. They ranged between good guys to world-class jerks with an occasional wacko thrown in the mix. It was hard to tell into which category Roberts fell. He was Irish, which was usually a good sign, and looked like a normal guy, except for his eyes. They had the intensity of someone who'd been to hell and back and hadn't enjoyed the experience. Valentine saw him reach into his jacket and remove a party-size bag of M&M's. Tearing them open, Roberts poured a handful into his cupped palm, then slid the bag across the table in Ricky's direction.

"Help yourself," the FBI agent said.

Ricky fished a couple of candies out and popped them into his mouth.

"I run the FBI's office in Lower Manhattan,"

Roberts said. "Mostly I deal with white-collar crime and brokers gone bad. I spent yesterday afternoon with a friend of yours."

"Stanley?" Ricky said.

"That's right. He came to my office and told me the same story you just did."

"Did you arrest him?"

Roberts shook his head. "Nothing to arrest him for. There's no crime in claiming someone's the world's greatest stock picker. Every brokerage house on Wall Street does it. And Stanley claims that he never gave you any inside tips. He says you talked about it, but it never happened. That true?"

Ricky started coughing like he was choking. "Yes," he finally said.

"So the only real crimes here were ripping off the Mint in Las Vegas and past-posting a horse race at an OTB parlor," Roberts said. "Stanley says that his involvement at the Mint was something called visual prediction at roulette and that what he did wasn't illegal." He stared at Valentine. "I'm told cheating at casinos is your speciality. That true?"

"That's right," Valentine said.

"Is visual prediction against the law?"

"No."

"So Stanley didn't break any laws at the Mint."

Valentine felt Roberts's eyes drilling a hole into his soul. "That's correct."

The FBI agent turned his attention to Ricky. "Stanley says that the OTB deal was your doing

433

and that he had nothing to do with it, along with everything else in Slippery Rock."

"That's not true," Ricky said, his face growing red.

"Can you prove Stanley was involved?"

"He funded the whole goddamn operation."

"Stanley says he lent you some money."

Ricky put his elbows on the table. He looked ready to explode, and Polly put her hand on his arm. Through gritted teeth he said, "And you believed him?"

Roberts picked up the bag of M&M's and poured some more into his hand. His demeanor hadn't changed, and he fished a couple of candies out and popped them into his mouth. He chewed and swallowed before speaking again. "It has nothing to do with what I believe or don't believe. I deal in evidence, and right now, you don't have any. Personally, I think Stanley Kessel is pond scum, and I'd enjoy throwing him in jail with a bunch of guys who lost their pensions in the crash and then watching the fireworks. But I can only do that if you'll help me."

Ricky pushed his chair back from the table. It was a classic gesture from a witness who was about to go south. Roberts and Knuts also pushed back. For a long moment, no one cared to speak. Valentine looked into everyone's faces. *Shit*, he thought.

CHAPTER 52

Roberts and Knuts left the shabby conference room without a word. Ricky rose and went to stand by the sooty window. Polly started to follow him, and Valentine touched her sleeve and eyed the door. She hesitated, then reluctantly walked out.

Valentine went to where Ricky stood. Ricky was staring down at the street scene below. It was like watching life through a dirty lens, and he mumbled a harsh profanity under his breath.

"Want me to leave?" Valentine asked.

Ricky shook his head. Removing his wallet, he extracted a photograph from behind the plastic protector and propped it on the windowsill. It was of a woman with silver hair and a thin smile, and Valentine guessed this was Aunt Helen. Ricky said, "When I was a teenager, my aunt moved to Slippery Rock for a year and took care of me while my parents went through their divorce. She protected me from all the fighting. She was a tough old gal, but she was always good to me." He swallowed hard. "I wanted to pay her back. That was why I brought her in."

"You recruited her?"

"Yeah." Ricky picked the picture up and slipped it back into his wallet. Then he stared down at St. Andrew's tiled rooftop. He shook his head at something he could not undo. "Tell them to come back," he said.

"You mean Roberts and Knuts?"

"Yeah."

"They're busy men, Ricky. I can't order them around."

"I'm ready to talk."

"About Stanley?"

"Yeah, about Stanley."

Valentine went to the door. Ricky called to him. "One thing," he said.

"What's that?"

"I don't want Polly in the room this time."

Roberts and Knuts returned to the conference room ten minutes later. They took the same seats, Roberts throwing his bag of candy in the center of the table while Knuts started the tape recorder. Ricky slid the candy back the FBI man's way, then gave them hard looks.

"Either of you gents ever hear of Cascade International?"

Knuts and Roberts both shook their heads.

"It's a company in Aventura, Florida. They make expensive casual clothes for women."

"I think my wife bought some clothes there," Knuts said. "North Miami Beach, right?"

"That's them," Ricky said. "Their flagship store is in the same building as their headquarters. Eight thousand square feet of couture. Dresses, shoes, lingerie, you name it, they sell it."

"What about them?" Roberts said impatiently.

"The company went public last year. Guess who brought them to market."

"You tell us," Roberts said.

"Stanley Kessel. The stock opened at a dollar and is currently trading at nine bucks, which makes Cascade worth a cool seventy million. Which is pretty amazing, when you consider the company only has one store."

Knuts and Roberts leaned forward. "Come again?" Roberts said.

"You heard me. They have one store."

"Explain yourself."

"Cascade is an illusion of Stanley Kessel's creation. It's a paper company. The annual stock report says they have thirty-six stores, and all are doing gangbuster business. The stores are spread across the country. Tuscaloosa, Panama City, Savannah, Fresno, and every other city that you've heard of but can't easily travel to. Get it?"

Both men shook their heads. They didn't get it at all. Ricky looked at Valentine.

"Why don't you explain it to them, doctor?"

The two men glanced at Valentine. It seemed obvious, but he said it anyway. "The Miami store is a front. Stanley put the other stores—which are phantoms—in out-of-the-way cities that people from Wall Street weren't likely to check out." He looked at Ricky. "That about it?"

Ricky nodded.

"That operation in Miami cost a lot of money," Knuts said. "Who fronted Stanley the capital to get it started?"

Ricky stared at the tape recorder. He seemed to be fighting himself, then finally spoke. "Stanley got his funding from a gang of Miami cocaine dealers. Those are his partners."

Roberts rose from his chair. "Cascade is drug money?"

Ricky nodded. "The company has an account with one of the big Miami banks. The drug dealers launder money through the account. That was the trade-off Stanley made with them." Ricky glanced at Valentine. "Those were the guys beating me up at my house."

"So, I did kill a drug dealer," Valentine said.

"That's right. The four principals move with Stanley all the time. He calls them his business associates. They're really part of the cartel."

"How do you know this?" Roberts said.

"The first time Stanley came to see me, he told me about the Cascade deal," Ricky explained. "He sucked me in by selling me ten thousand shares at the opening price. I sold out a month later and made a huge profit. It's what I've been living on."

"You realize I'm going to have to arrest you," Roberts said.

Ricky nodded. Knuts and Roberts went to the other side of the room and took out their cell phones. They began the process that would eventually put Stanley Kessel behind bars. Valentine glanced at Ricky and saw him silently weeping. He put his hand on Ricky's shoulder.

"You did good," he said.

"You think so?"

Valentine nodded, and Ricky found the strength to smile.

"I guess there's a first time for everything," he said.

CHAPTER 53

Valentine was standing in the hallway five minutes later, watching Ricky say good-bye to Polly, when Roberts rushed past and took an elevator downstairs. The FBI agent was moving fast, and Valentine sensed that he had a bead on Stanley Kessel. He'd come too far to miss the grand finale, and started to leave.

"Wait a second," Ricky said as he entered another elevator.

Valentine put his hand on the door to stop it from closing. Ricky stood awkwardly in the doorway, his wrists handcuffed together. Another FBI agent stood nearby, eyeing him.

"Tell me one thing," Ricky said.

"What's that?"

"Do they have art classes in prison?"

"They sure do," he said.

When Valentine reached the lobby, he saw no sign of Roberts. Going outside, he saw the FBI agent jump into a black sedan and the vehicle pull away from the curb. He went into the street and hailed a yellow cab and was soon following Roberts uptown.

The cab driver was Pakistani and drove like he was fighting for the pole at the Indy 500. Valentine told him to keep his distance, then settled back in his seat and watched the city pass by. As a cop, he'd loved the thrill of a chase, but he didn't love it anymore. It meant that something bad was waiting at the other end, and he'd had enough bad things happen to last him a long time.

"They are stopping," the driver said. He pulled the cab up behind the sedan and threw his flag up. "Fourteen dollars and thirty cents, please."

Valentine paid the fare while staring out his window at the street sign. Forty-sixth Street and Third Avenue. The tony east side. Ricky had said that Stanley had a townhouse on the east side and liked to hang out here. Getting out, Valentine saw Roberts standing in front of a fancy restaurant called the Gold Door. Roberts saw him, as well, and hurried over.

"What are you doing here?" the FBI agent said angrily.

"Getting some lunch. How about you?"

"Don't be funny," Roberts snapped. "Stanley Kessel is in there, and we're going to nab him and drag his ass downtown. Don't you dare step inside that door, or I'll throw you in the same cell as Stanley and his drug-dealing buddies. Understand?"

"Yes, sir."

Another sedan pulled up to the curb, and three men jumped out. They had short hair and dark suits and had FBI written all over them. Roberts gave them orders like a drill sergeant, and then they marched into the restaurant.

Valentine went over and leaned against the cab. His driver had double-parked the vehicle and was standing in the street, staring at the Gold Door. "There is going to be fireworks, yes?"

Valentine ignored him, his eyes peeled on the restaurant.

"You are a cop, yes?"

He didn't think the question deserved an answer.

"You look like a cop on that TV show, *NYPD Blue*," the driver said. "Not the fat one, the other one. It is my favorite show on television. I watch it every week."

Oh, brother, Valentine thought.

The driver came over and stood beside him. Dropping his voice, he said, "There is something I think you should know."

Valentine wanted to tell him to take a hike. Except, something in the driver's eyes told him otherwise. "Go ahead."

"There is an exit in the back of this restaurant that is connected to an alley," the driver said. "When celebrities and important people eat here, they use this exit." He pointed to an alleyway a few doors down. "Over there."

Valentine pushed himself off the cab. Stanley Kessel was one of the smartest criminals he'd ever encountered. He'd covered all his bases and then some. There was no reason to believe that he hadn't covered this one, as well. Valentine took out his wallet and extracted five twenty-dollar bills. He handed them to the driver.

"I want you to use your cab to block that exit."

The driver refused the money. "You do not have to pay me. I will do it."

"You sure?"

"Of course. It is the correct thing to do."

Valentine went around to the back of the restaurant with the words ringing in his ears. *The correct thing to do.* When was the last time he'd heard someone say that? His mother, fifty years ago. Coming around the alley, he spied a black limousine sitting outside the restaurant's back door. Two men sat in front. They were the Cubans he'd sucker punched behind Ricky's house. Stanley's drug-dealing pals.

A row of garbage pails lined the alley. Valentine went to one and fished out an empty Jack Daniel's bottle. He thought about the best way to handle this. Pulling his shirt out from his pants, he staggered over to the BMW with the bottle clutched in his hand. The Cuban in the passenger seat got out and pointed at him.

"Get lost, old man," he said.

Valentine watched the Cuban turn his back and start pissing against the alley wall. He staggered up to the driver's side and saw the window come down.

"You heard him," the Cuban behind the wheel said. "Get lost."

Valentine removed the twenties he'd offered the cab driver and let them fall to the ground. Then he pointed. "I think you dropped this, mistah," he said.

The Cuban stared at the money. He started to get out, and Valentine threw his weight against the open door. The Cuban yelped and fell to the ground.

Valentine walked around the car to the guy taking a leak. He could tell that the guy wanted to fight him; only, he couldn't do it without pissing on himself. Valentine hit him in the head with the bottle. The guy went down holding his dick.

Valentine heard shouting inside the restaurant. He went to the back door and listened. Stanley was not going easily. He thought about rushing inside, but then remembered Roberts's warning and decided to stay by the door.

Next to the door was an upturned crate. A half-smoked cigarette lay on it, a whisper of smoke trailing off one end. He couldn't help himself, and put the burning end up to his nose and inhaled. He heard both Cubans groaning. Normally, he didn't like hurting people, but this was different. These guys were drug dealers.

He'd worked narcotics in Atlantic City for a while and discovered how drug dealers operated. They went to parties and handed out free coke or heroin. Someone always got hooked. The dealer would feed their addiction until they ran out of money. Then the dealer would move on.

Inside the restaurant he heard the *pop-pop-pop* of gunfire. He threw the cigarette away and cracked the door open. Down a darkened hallway he could see a man standing with his back to him, shooting an automatic handgun into the brightly lit restaurant. The man was walking backward as he fired.

Valentine shut the door and stepped away from it. He felt his heartbeat quicken. He could run, or he could try to take Stanley down. Running was the smart choice; only, if he did, Stanley might get away, and all this would be for nothing.

Valentine pressed himself against the wall beside the doorway to the restaurant. He reminded himself that he was no longer a cop and the rules were different now. The door banged open, and the man stepped outside waving his automatic.

"Hey, Stanley," Valentine said.

The man turned, startled. He was short and had perfectly tanned skin. He wore a light-gray designer suit that was spotted with someone else's blood. Without hesitation, he aimed the automatic at Valentine's heart. Valentine grabbed Stanley's arm with both hands and pointed the gun's barrel skyward. It went off with a loud retort.

"Drop it," Valentine told him.

Stanley kicked him in the shins. Then he reached up with his other hand to grab the weapon. The faces of Beasley and the scarecrow and Juan all

445

flashed through Valentine's mind. Three dead men, about to be joined by a fourth.

He twisted Stanley's wrist so the automatic was pointing downward into the stockbroker's face. Gave him a second to change his mind. Stanley looked into Valentine's eyes with hatred.

"Fuck you," he said.

Valentine squeezed Stanley's hand, and the gun went off in his face.

CHAPTER 54

That night, Mabel cooked dinner for Gerry and Yolanda in her house. She fixed them her favorite meal—chicken and dumplings with corn bread and collard greens, then strawberry shortcake for dessert. It was food to feed the soul, and her guests ladled more praise on her than she was used to. It was also a lot of work, and afterward she scrubbed the pots in the sink while Gerry helped her dry. In the next room they could hear Yolanda lying on the living-room floor, playing with the baby. Gerry had stepped off the plane that afternoon not knowing if his family was all right, and the look of relief had yet to disappear from his face. He dried the last pot and put it away in the cupboard while Mabel hung up her apron.

"I need to talk to you," he said.

"Of course."

Gerry turned on the back porch light and stepped outside onto the stoop. Mabel joined him and swatted away at the mosquitos that had instantly appeared. Gerry stood with the drying towel stretched between his hands and spoke in a hushed tone. "I need to ask you a huge favor."

Mabel nodded, then saw a look on Gerry's face that said a nod was not enough.

"Certainly," she said.

Gerry put the towel over his shoulder, then reached into the pocket of his shirt and removed a folded square of paper. With the paper came a small metal key. He handed both to Mabel, then cupped his hands around the older woman's.

"A man on his death bed gave me that key. It's for a safe-deposit box. The bank where the safe-deposit box is located is on that piece of paper. The name of the man's sister and her address are also on the paper. I want you to take the key to her."

Mabel unfolded the paper. The man's sister lived in a retirement village in St. Augustine on the other side of the state. It was easily a four-hour drive.

"What's in the box?" Mabel said.

"Money."

"How much money?"

"A million and a half dollars."

Mabel sucked in her breath. "Why . . . can't you do this?"

A sad smile spread across his face. "I was going to. Yolanda and I were going to make the trip together. Go to St. Augustine and see the sights, then track down the sister. Only, the more I thought about it, the more I realized it was a bad idea."

"But St. Augustine is a fun place to visit. You

can see the old fort and the village. Did you know that it's the oldest city in America?"

Gerry shook his head. "That's not what I mean. I'm afraid that sometime during the trip, I'd start thinking about all the things Yolanda and I could do with the money. Like buying a bigger house, or a new car, or prepaid college tuition for the baby. And maybe I'd talk myself into asking the sister to share the money. You know, like a finder's fee. I'd figure out a way to convince myself that it was okay. I'd tell myself that since the sister doesn't know the money existed, she shouldn't object to sharing it."

"What your father calls criminal logic."

"That's right."

"So you're afraid of being tempted," Mabel said.

Gerry looked directly into her eyes. "Yes."

"But you know it's wrong. I can hear it in your voice."

"It doesn't matter."

"It doesn't?"

"Money does that to me."

Mabel folded the paper around the key and slipped it into her pocket. A look of relief spread across Gerry's face, and she took him into her arms and held him like he was one of her own children.

"For you, dear, anything," she said.

EPILOGUE

"The State of Nevada versus Lucille Price," the bailiff announced.

Valentine saw Lucy Price's attorney jump to his feet. He was a short guy, heavyset, and approached the bench while buttoning the middle button of his jacket. The judge was a woman and seemed to appreciate the gesture. Her courtroom was filled with drunks and prostitutes and crackheads. Little things counted here.

Lucy's attorney explained to the judge that his client wanted to change her plea. The judge looked at Lucy sitting in the front row, then at her attorney. It wasn't a kind look. Lucy spun around in her chair and shot Valentine a dagger. He was sitting two rows back, and it felt like a slap in the face.

"It's okay," he whispered.

She made a face like she didn't believe him, then spun back around. He'd flown out from New York and shown up on her doorstep last night. He'd avoided her for so long, she'd slammed the door in his face. But he'd rung the bell again. This time when she answered, he'd begged forgiveness.

450

She let him take her to dinner at Smith & Wollensky on the strip. For his money, it was the best restaurant in town. She ate a Cobb salad, while he ate a New York strip steak. By the time dessert came, she was holding his hand and whispering to him.

During the drive home, she fantasized about them running away together. That was why he'd come, she speculated. He'd rented a private jet, and it was now sitting on the tarmac at McCarran, its final destination someplace exotic, like Acapulco or Cancun. Listening to her ramble on, he'd felt immensely sad.

When they reached her doorstep, she'd tried to kiss him.

"No," he said.

"But—"

"I'm sorry," he said. "I'll be back first thing tomorrow."

"We're not . . . running away?"

He'd put his hands on her shoulders and shaken his head. The look in her eyes had been painful. The death of hope was always wrenching.

At seven o'clock the next morning, Valentine drove Lucy to the Clark County Courthouse on South Third Street, two blocks south of the Fremont Street Experience. He'd been to the courthouse on several occasions to act as an expert witness in a trial. That it was located near several seedy casinos in the worst part of town had always seemed a perfect metaphor for Las Vegas.

Lucy wore a conservative blue dress and little makeup and said nothing during the ride. Parking was not available in front of the courthouse, and he drove to the mammoth county parking structure a block away. As he parked, he told her that he'd called his friend Bill Higgins and gotten the skinny on the judge. "Her name's Redmond. She used to be a public defender and has experience dealing with problem gamblers. That's in your favor."

"Why's that?" Lucy said.

"She understands how casinos seduce people. A person with a gambling problem becomes falsely elevated in a casino. It changes who they are, just like a drug."

"Is that what happens to me?"

"Yes," he said.

"And this judge knows that?"

He nodded, and Lucy stared at the car's dirty windshield. He saw her start to tremble. She had come to that petrifying brink where her fantasies adjoined the real world. Taking a deep breath, she said, "You're saying I should change my plea and throw myself upon the mercy of the court. Aren't you?"

"Yes," he said. "If you go to trial and lose, you'll do hard time."

The idea of jail petrified her, and for good reason: Nevada had some of the worst prisons in the country. They talked it over for a few minutes, and finally she agreed. They walked to the courthouse together and found her attorney in the courthouse lobby. When Lucy told him she'd changed her mind, her attorney had looked relieved.

"Ms. Price, please step forward."

The bailiff motioned for Lucy to stand. She rose on wobbly legs, the bottom of her world about to drop out, and approached the bench with her attorney holding her arm.

"Your attorney has informed me that you wish to change your plea to guilty," Judge Redmond said. "Is that correct?"

Lucy nodded woodenly.

"Do you understand that by changing your plea, you are giving up your right to a trial by a jury of your peers? Do you also understand that I will pass judgment this morning and may send you to prison?"

Again the wooden nod. The judge lowered her eyes and reviewed the facts of her case. It was all there in the file: Lucy's gambling problems, busted marriage, the whole ugly story. Valentine hoped the judge would see the same thing in the file that he'd seen in Lucy the first time he'd met her: a damaged woman desperately in need of help.

After a minute, the judge closed the file and gazed down at her. "I'm ready to pass sentence. Ms. Price, is there anything you wish to say before I do?"

Lucy shook her head.

"Then you're ready for me to make my decision."

Lucy tried to answer, but the words refused to come out. She looked over her shoulder again, and Valentine saw panic in her eyes. *It's the correct thing to do,* he'd said as they'd gotten out of the car. The words had given her strength, so he repeated them. She smiled faintly, then turned back around.

"Yes, Your Honor," she said. "I am ready."